SCORPIO

LAUREN LANDISH

Edited by VALORIE CLIFTON

Edited by STACI ETHERIDGE

Photography by WANDER AGUIAR

To the most important Scorpio in my life. I love you baby girl, forever and always.

SCORPIO

BY LAUREN LANDISH

Join my mailing list (www.laurenlandish.com) and receive 2 FREE ebooks! You'll also be the first to know of new releases, sales, and giveaways. If you're on Facebook, come join my Reader Group!

Your heart shall be his, then will come the sting. You will suffer . . . and then you shall burn.

The words chill me to the bone. That's my fate. At least, that's what the fortune teller says.

Destiny, horoscopes... who believes in that? I sure don't. I make my own future, thank you very much.

But when I meet Scott Danger, the words come back to haunt me. His name even comes with a warning label. Handsome, rich, and sexier than any man should be, he's pursuing me hard and fast. Little ol' me, a bartender with a penchant for makeup and old country music.

He's dominant and seductive, a predator caged in gilded threads, and I want to run just so he'll chase me . . . catch me . . . take me. Shit. I'm in so much trouble, but I think I like it.

Still, those eerie words… do I tempt fate?

PROLOGUE

MADISON

*L*ove. From the dawn of time, it's been with us, our silent companion weaving through the millennia.

It seems strange that such a simple word, four small letters, can play such a role in our lives, our past and our future.

Wars have started over it. Men and women have fought and died for it. We have holidays dedicated to it, and we spend billions of dollars when it blooms . . . and billions more when it dies.

There are some who say that love is fated, that forces beyond our control somehow whisper in our daily lives, guiding us this way and that like the wind propels a sailboat. We can steer against them sometimes, but if you fight the winds long enough, karmic laws of nature pretty much dictate that a hurricane's going to come around and wreck you.

To avoid those storms, to avoid being pummeled against the rocks of life, you have to listen to the whispers and let them guide your future along its predestined path, smoothly, beautifully, and in its own time. They say that the winds of fate can be measured, that you'll have clues before you meet that someone who's supposed to be your soulmate. That somehow, some collection of the stars, planets, and maybe your own handprint can reveal your happily ever after.

Tell that to Romeo and Juliet. Star-crossed lovers? If that were true, maybe those twinkly lights could've foretold their futures a little more clearly and they could have avoided the whole deadly mix-up. That surely would've been a better happily ever after for those poor kids.

Nope. To me, horoscopes, fortunetelling, and predicting the future are baloney. I get it. Life is overwhelming, and it's a comfort to believe there's some magical plan or a greater power controlling things. To hope that even in our darkest days, there's a reason, a lesson, a brighter destiny just around the corner . . . if we could just figure out how to take advantage of the winds of fate to get there.

But you want to know what reality is? Reality is the old saying that if you sow the wind, you reap the whirlwind. You can't control it. You can't predict it. You just hang on and try to ride it out. And when love jumps in your path, it might not be sweet and pleasant. It might attack and smack you in the face. And even in that moment of jaw-dropping shock, you know there's not a damn thing you can do about it.

CHAPTER 1

MADISON

Daily Horoscope, September 19th
Libra - Saturn in retrograde means that caution is necessary. Trouble will
find you, even when you're not looking for it.

"You know what you need to break you out of
your slump?" Tiffany chirps from the passenger seat of the beat-up Toyota Corolla we share to carpool to work. I turn down the loud, vengeful Carrie Underwood song blasting through the radio and look at my best friend and roommate, already dreading her suggestion. "A psychic reading!"

"Oh, hell no!" I say laughingly, shaking my head to reiterate my point. The wind through the open windows ruffles my honey-blonde locks, sending them whipping around my face, further illustrating my 'no'. We already have a tradition of Tiffany reading our daily horoscopes aloud every morning, so her suggestion isn't completely out of left field. I don't know if she's a true believer or not, but the morning readings are usually in good fun, leading to laughter and attempts at straight-faced concern for *'our future'*, as Tiff usually says in a faux-spooky voice.

Except for the ones like this morning, something about trouble finding me. Uh, news flash, stars. Trouble already found me, and I kicked its ass to the curb like a boss. Well, okay, not like a boss, more like a freaked-out kitten scrambling to get away. But I fucking did it, and that's what counts. So thanks for the warning, dear horoscope, but you're a day late and a dollar short this time. Typical. Would've been a great caution notice months ago.

After enduring almost a year of progressively worsening hell at the hands of a prick whose name I refuse to even think, I have my good days more frequently now. Those days where I'm all 'I am woman, hear me roar!' and the idea of kicking ass and taking names is just natural.

Then I have my less frequent bad days, crying over stupid shit like our song on the radio or getting angry and being *this close* to banging on his door to give him a piece of my mind.

Both the good and the bad days are better than the rare dangerous days, though. Those are where I feel so alone that it seems like going back to that asshole, or an asshole *like* him, wouldn't be all that bad. That's when Tiffany usually jumps in to save me from my own bad ideas with pizza, happy hours, or root beer floats.

Luckily for me, today happens to be one of the good days, which is why I don't immediately open a can of whoop ass on Tiffany for her wacky idea.

"You know I've never believed in that shit!"

From the passenger seat, Tiffany stops fiddling with her lipstick long enough to glare at me in exasperation. For the past twenty minutes, she's been incessantly nagging me about getting on with my love life, a ritual she's picked up ever since she thought I was *okay enough* to move on. Her advice to get over the last man is usually to get under another, at least for the night.

I get it. Tiffany's the sort of girl who lets everything roll off her like water down a duck's back, but these things take time.

"Don't let one loser mess up your outlook on men for the rest of your life. Girl, there are plenty of fish in the sea, and you only need to catch one big one who will treat you right to see that they're not all the same. To do that, you gotta keep your hook in the water, reel them in, and give them a look-see to decide if they're a keeper or a toss-back-er." She mimes like she's pulling in a big fish on a line, as if she's ever held a fishing pole in her life.

This coming from a chick whose last boyfriend left her in the pouring rain on the side of a back-country road after a two-minute session of heated passion. Apparently, he'd kicked her out and told her to walk her "stupid ass" home after she complained about his being a two-pump chump and took matters into her own hands to have an orgasm. Some men think that's hot. He apparently didn't. Though that might've been because Tiffany told him to "watch and learn a thing or ten about how to get a woman off." The implication of his lack of prowess was a bit too much for his ego.

Of course, Tiffany's got all the luck, and the fucker was pulled over by the cops a few miles later. He'd gotten mouthy with the wrong cop and got thrown in jail for a cool-down period. Best part? He called Tiffany with his one phone call and she hung up on him.

So she doesn't have the best track record with successful relationships, but that doesn't stop her from doling out sage advice to me. She usually tells me there's no harm in looking for Mr. Right and Mr. Right Now at the same time. But today, it's a different pep talk, so maybe she's got that going for her.

"What harm could a little psychic reading do?" she asks in her country-girl accent that makes my twang look downright cultured, turning her attention back to the makeup mirror in the sun visor. She rubs her finger along her bottom lip, trying to get the look of her bright red lipstick just right. "You could use a good reading in your life right now . . . pun intended."

I toss her a quick 'don't go there' look and get a mischievous ruby red smile in return. Just my opinion, but I think Tiff needs to lay off a bit on the makeup. She's pretty without out it, with her raven-black hair, luminous eyes, and pale porcelain skin, but I don't bother saying so since I'm basically a walking billboard for L'Oréal and Estée Lauder.

Honestly, I wear heavy makeup for two reasons. Okay, I'm lying, maybe three.

One, Dolly Parton is my idol. Growing up with a cantankerous aunt as my only mother figure, I would often steal her Dolly records and listen to them for hours while studying the album covers. Sure, she was a bit old-fashioned even when I was a kid, but it didn't matter. She looked awesome, this weird mix of cheap and classy at the same time. Dolly always pulled it off, no matter what, and owned her backwoods roots with no apologies. And so I modeled my look—hell my attitude—after her. Big hair, big lashes, big . . . well, maybe not her whole look, but I did what I could with what Mother Nature and Victoria's Secret gave me.

Two, I'm a bartender and it kind of comes with the territory. You want to look your best every day for your customers, especially when most of your tipping clientele are men. The dim lighting of a bar requires a heavy hand since it doesn't exactly lend itself to subtle barely-there natural looks. I need the extra volume of lashes to bat, the red lips to pucker, and the powder to look flawless as I work my ass off.

And three, I feel more confident with a layer of foundation on my face. I'm not sure why, but a part of me feels like it puts a barrier between me and whoever I meet . . . especially the men. I'm more comfortable when they see me but don't see the *real* me, if that makes sense. So I never leave the house without my makeup.

It's a habit that's been impossible to break ever since . . .

Angrily, I steer my thoughts away from that mental trip down memory lane and press the gas as we pass a speed limit sign that says seventy, letting the hum of my engine act as a poor substitute for my mood. It's times like these I wish I had something with a little more muscle . . . something that rumbled and screamed when I revved it up.

"Hey!" Tiffany presses. "Stop ignoring me! It could be fun, even if you don't believe in it."

"I'm not hearing you," I reply, pushing the gas just a little more. "Besides, we don't have time. Our shift starts in an hour. Stella will have our asses if we show up late."

A slight smile plays across my lips as I think about Stella, our boss and owner of the restaurant and bar where we both work. A hard-working woman in her mid-fifties, she's been like a mother to me ever since I went out on my own.

Tiff smudges her lips together and then lets them go with an audible pop. "Girl, please. You know those boys want to get their beers and whiskey from *us*. Stella wouldn't know what to do without us. You need to live a little, loosen up, and have a little fun. Seriously, let's do it!"

I grip the steering wheel tightly and feel an old, familiar ache in both of my wrists like a ghost as on the radio, Carrie wails about a cheating bastard who's going to get his just desserts. "I don't know if I consider that fun. I'm just not into being told I'm going to die in seven days like that movie *The Ring*."

Tiff huffs out a laugh and waves my comment away. "You're not dying before me. Unless I kill you, of course. Which I might end up doing . . . sooner rather than later, if you keep being so stubborn."

I tap the brake a little, causing Tiff to jerk forward. Her tube of lipstick falls to the floor and I grin faux-evilly at her.

"You bitch!" she yells, stretching her seatbelt so she can bend forward to retrieve it. She has to grunt as she finally snags it, giving me a death stare.

"That will teach you to threaten me." My smile fades as quickly as it came as I apologize. "Sorry, did that a little harder than I intended." I giggle.

Tiff is still set in her mission, brandishing the tube of lipstick like it's a weapon. The bright red is only inches away from my perfectly contoured cheek. "An hour is more than enough time. Probably won't take but twenty minutes." She gives up on dotting me with the expensive and hard to remove lipstick, but she continues her plea. "And don't be so quick to dismiss it. My Aunt Nelda went to one. And every word turned out to be true."

"Seriously?" I ask incredulously. I can't help but laugh, thinking about Tiffany's aunt and all her crazy antics and quirks. "Your aunt doesn't help your case at all! That lady scares me."

Tiff snorts, laughing right along with me. "I can't argue with that, but still . . . the story is true. They'll probably just tell you that your dreams and aspirations are right around the corner if you keep working hard, which you know, obviously. It's just reaffirming, but you need to hear if from someone other than me." She shakes her head and starts in on her customary rant that I've heard at least a thousand times in the past few months. "You've got to start living again! Besides our shifts at Stella's, you never go out anymore and always have some excuse. Ever since Rich . . ." Her voice trails off and she bites her lower lip as a burning sensation forms in my throat.

I cough, an uncomfortable silence filling the cabin. The only sound is country music pouring from my speakers and the rush of wind past the windows. But even in that din of noise, the silence is palpable. I have to force myself to stare out the front windshield as we head down the highway.

"I'm sorry, Maddie," Tiff says softly, quickly. "I didn't mean—" She stops as she sees my expression.

For a moment, my throat tightens and I can't breathe. I count the white stripes of the road as they whiz by . . . one, two, three, four. Luckily, the panic passes quickly. I'm doing better. This time.

Damn it, and today started off so well.

8

I keep my eyes on the road, my expression neutral even though I'm angry. At Tiff for mentioning him, at myself for giving a fuck, and at him, of course. For everything.

I can't get this worked up every time I hear his name, dammit! "It's okay. Just please . . . don't mention him again, 'kay?"

Out of the corner of my eye, I see Tiffany stare at me for a long moment. "Sorry. I won't . . ." she says and trails off. I see the look in her eyes. She is sorry, but there's more. Hope. She wants better for me and somehow hopes that she can help me find it and my old happy self again. "Maddie, I just think this could be good for you, something exciting and different."

She's still set on doing this reading thing. I open my mouth to refuse one last time, but I relent, thinking to myself, *What's the worst that could happen? It's just a bit of cheesy fun to take my mind off everything.*

"Swear that you'll never ask me to do this again. And that you'll accept that I'll date when I'm good and ready," I say.

Placing her hand over her heart, Tiffany nods. "I, Tiffany Donna Meyers, swear on my sweet little innocent unborn babies that you won't hear another word out of my sexy ass . . . and by the way, if you're wondering, the palm reading shop is on Third Street, directly on the way to *Stella's*."

I laugh and shake my head as I switch into the right lane and make my way to the nearest exit.

Maybe Tiff is right. Maybe I need to do something different . . . something I'd never normally do. Just something to shake my mind up and get me moving in the right direction again.

Never one to give in easily, I tease her. "You're going straight to hell, you know that?"

Tiffany cackles evilly, delighted that she's managed to win me over. "'Course I am. I'm driving the party bus there, but that's why you love me."

After following Tiffany's directions, I pull up to a rough-looking section in downtown, several blocks from *Stella's*. It's the kind of area where you'd be scared to leave your car for more than five minutes out of fear of someone stealing it. Luckily for me, I'm poor, and anyone desperate enough to steal my beat-up piece of shit is probably so bad off that I might actually feel bad reporting them to the cops.

"Remember," Tiffany tells me as we get out of the car and I double-check my locks, "keep an open mind and just have fun with it. She's gonna reveal that you're going to hit the lottery and get a super-hot husband, have beautiful little children, and a gorgeous home with a white picket fence. All that good stuff. Exactly what you need to hear."

"Mmmhmm, sure," I mutter halfheartedly, letting Tiffany lead the way past several run-down shops. Honestly, my expectations are about as low as they can get, which is good since then I won't be disappointed.

"Here we are," Tiffany cheerfully announces a moment later, stopping us in front of a neon sign that reads *Marie Laveau's House of Voodoo*.

"Oh, for fuck's sake!" I exclaim, placing my hands on my wide hips and glaring at the sign and then Tiff. "Seriously, Tiff? *House of Voodoo*? I don't want to put some voodoo hex on Rich. I just want to forget he exists."

"Ooh, I didn't even think about that, but a voodoo hex ain't a bad idea." She puts on an evil smirk before continuing, "But for real, the name's just for attention, I'm guessing."

I glance back at our vehicle, already wanting to leave. If I'm gonna do this, let's at least do it someplace that looks and *sounds* legit.

"Oh, no, Miss Thing, you're going inside," Tiffany tells me as if sensing my thoughts, opening the door and giving me a pointed look. "Kicking or screaming. We have a deal, remember?"

I glower at her for a moment before giving up. It's just a few minutes. Let's just get this over with. Hell, if nothing else, maybe I'll get a good laugh out of it. And if not, at least Tiff will be off my case.

I step past her and into the shop. There's a small dark room with colorful paintings and murals all over the walls. I don't get more than a second to check out details because the smell of strong incense immediately greets us along with a heavy accent. Jamaican, maybe. I'm not sure.

"I've been waiting for you two girls," calls a deep-voiced woman from the back. "Come to me."

I glance at Tiffany, whose eyes have grown as large as saucers, and then roll mine. "Oh, please," I mutter, wanting to laugh. "She probably says that to everyone who comes in."

"Shh!" Tiffany hisses, dragging me along to the back. "I don't want no voodoo curse cast on me!"

It's even darker in back, but my eyes have adjusted now and I can see. There's a large round table in the middle of the room with a deep red cloth draped over it to the floor. A dark-skinned woman with a colorful rag wrapped around the top of her head and long, thick white dreads sits at it, two flickering candles on either side of her.

She gives us a warm smile when she sees us, flashing pearly white teeth and clasping her hands together cheerfully.

"Welcome, my children! My name is Marie," she says, motioning at the two wooden chairs in front of the table. "Please, sit."

We slowly take our seats. Before either of us can say anything, Marie looks pointedly at me.

"This reading is for you," she says matter-of-factly, her smile ebbing away. "You are the one for whom the spirits have been talking to me . . . the forgotten daughter."

Shocked, the hairs on the back of my arms prickle and my mouth drops a little. There's no way she could know that my mom abandoned me at birth and that my aunt raised me.

11

"How did you—" I stop myself.

It was just a lucky guess. Nothing more. This woman is a fraud. She probably heard us outside. Or Tiff told her? Maybe this is a setup?

"You're not a believer," Marie says perceptively. "You think I'm a fraud."

I'm a little taken aback by her forwardness, but she's right. There's no such thing as a psychic power. "Honestly, I don't believe in this type of stuff—"

"No worries, child. This reading will be free," Marie says, cutting me off and gesturing at my hand.

I glance with uncertainty at Tiffany, who gives me a gentle nod of approval. I look back to the woman, whose eyes haven't left me.

"Your hand, child," Marie demands impatiently, holding her hand out. "The spirits might be talking now, but they go silent on their own timetable, and I never know when they'll be back."

Shaking my head in disbelief, I let her take my hand and stare into my palm. After a moment, she takes a finger and traces it across my lines, tickling my flesh while appearing deep in thought.

She looks up at me, a small smile on her face. "You're a Libra, aren't ya, darlin'?" she asks.

I glance over at Tiff, who just grins and shrugs. "What . . . how did you . . ." I once again stop myself.

Another lucky guess. She's got a one in twelve chance, and if she's wrong, she just says that I have 'Libra traits' or something. Hell, the idea that Tiff is setting me up is starting to seem a little more likely right about now.

"Yep . . . yep." She nods, muttering to herself as if she doesn't hear me, her eyes never leaving my palm. "You've been hurt by someone recently . . . stuck in limbo. I see anguish and pain."

I stop myself from looking over at Tiff this time, just taking it in. *It's nothing. Most people have been hurt by someone in their lives. Hell,*

12

you stretch the definition enough, we get hurt by people every day. Just think of tax season.

"Yep . . . yep . . ." Marie frowns, staring hard at my palm. "I see a scorpion . . ."

I grimace and Tiffany makes a face too. "A scorpion? Does that mean something?"

Marie doesn't appear to hear as she whispers unintelligible mumbles to herself. But her next words are clear, ringing out in the room. "Your heart shall be his . . . then will come the sting. You will suffer . . . oh, girl, will you suffer . . . and then you shall burn."

Her words drain the blood from my face and a chill goes down my spine. Her prediction seems to carry the tone of doom, but surprisingly, it's Tiffany who is the first to react, jumping up from her seat.

"What the fuck, lady?" she yells with rage. "You tell my aunt she'll find fifty bucks. You tell her friend that she's going to find a new younger lover, and you tell my friend she's going to suffer and burn? I came here to cheer her up!"

Marie sits back, her face calm. "The spirits—"

Tiff jabs a manicured finger in her face, definitely pissed beyond listening. "I brought her here so you could tell her she has good things on the horizon! Like I've heard you tell everyone else!"

"I do not control the future, merely tell it, my child," Marie tries to explain, but Tiffany gives exactly zero fucks right now, and I'm still too shaken up to say anything.

"Aren't you supposed to tell your clients what they want to hear?" Tiffany shouts. "Not tell them their lives are going to get even more fucked up!"

Marie weaves her hands together, looking to me and ignoring Tiffany's rant. "Child, be safe. Be cautious. The scorpion is crafty."

Tiffany yanks me up from my seat and begins dragging me from the room. "Come on, Maddie. Let's get the hell outta here!"

I glance back once to see Marie, her eyes closed, her palms up on the table, seemingly unaffected by the blast she just blew in my future or by Tiffany's bitchfest. By the time we get to my car, I can walk myself and Tiff lets go. I slide behind the wheel, still not saying anything.

As soon as she closes her door, Tiff begins apologizing to me profusely. "Maddie, I am so sorry," she moans, her voice thick with emotion while she shakes her head. "If I had known she'd say something like that, I never would've—"

"Did you know that woman or tell her anything about me?" I demand, my voice low and dangerous. "Everything she said was right."

Tiff slowly shakes her head, her eyes full of regret. "No. I've passed by this place a few times, and my aunt really has been here before. That's how I knew about it, but I've never seen her in my life. I swear."

I study her for a moment, and I can tell she's being honest.

"You said that she was supposed to tell me what I wanted to hear," I say, feeling shaky inside but not knowing why.

What Marie said has to be bullshit. My heart would be his? Definitely not a chance that's happening. I'm avoiding men and definitely avoiding love.

Being stung by a scorpion? What the hell does that even mean? There are no scorpions around here!

It's all just bullshit. Just like I always thought it was. Nothing has changed except that she said some spooky mumbo-jumbo generic stuff that scared me.

Tiffany pauses, taking in a deep breath and letting it out in a sigh. "Yes! I just thought maybe if you heard someone other than me tell you some positive shit about your future and I could convince you it was true, maybe you would feel better, start living again. Like our morning horoscopes amped up on crack."

I see the hurt in her eyes . . . and the worry. Warmth flows down my sides. In her own crazy, fucked-up way, Tiff's only trying to help. Although, I could think of a hundred other ways to go about doing so than a palm reading by a mad woman.

"You really couldn't think of a better way than *that* to convince me, genius?" I ask jokingly, trying to shake off the bad feeling I have by making light of the situation. Fuck that lady. I'm not gonna let her stupid prediction ruin my week when I've been doing good lately.

Tiffany sniffs and then laughs, shrugging. "It's just basic psychology I learned in college. It's a self-fulfilling prophecy. You believe something good is true and that it's going to happen, so you're more likely to make the decisions that make it happen for real." She shakes her head. "But shit, Maddie . . . I swear I didn't know it would be like that. I really am sorry."

I wave her concern away with a nervous chuckle and start the car, eager to get away from the palm reading shop. "It's okay. You were only trying to help . . . and as crazy as this little idea of yours was, you're the best friend a girl could ask for."

Tiffany looks genuinely relieved. "So you're not mad at me?"

I shake my head. "Of course not. Just stop pushing me toward random guys and nagging me about dating, 'kay? It'll happen when I'm ready for it to happen and not a minute before."

Tiffany nods. "You're right, girl. I really do need to stop. I just want to see you happy again, and while it's always good to be fine on your own, or locked into a happily ever after fairy tale, a single night filled with multiple orgasms wouldn't hurt. I just want you happy, for now and forever." She pauses, peering at me closely. "Uh, so, you're not going to steal one of my bras or put salt in my foundation like you did that time I threw ice on you to wake you up for work, are you?"

I grin, remembering that incident and how pissed Tiffany had gotten at me. "As long as you never ask me to go to a place like that again."

We both look at each other for a moment before bursting into laughter.

And just like that, the mood brightens. I navigate the last few blocks to Stella's and pull into the parking lot, on time for our night shift. Tiff and I are okay, and I can understand where she was coming from to try and cheer me up, but even as I walk inside, there's a wiggle at the back of my head, repeating Marie's prediction.

CHAPTER 2

SCOTT

Daily Horoscope, September 21st
Scorpio
Your lust for power will be your downfall. Humble yourself and you will
see the success you so badly desire.

PERHAPS I'M FATED TO BE THE MISFIT, THE HARD LUCK one, the one who doesn't seem to find his place. After all, when you're born at the stroke of midnight on October 31st at ten pounds, seven ounces, you make one hell of an impression. I was a bitch to birth, as my mom likes to remind me whenever I piss her off. The most painful birth she's experienced, she usually says.

But in my twenty-six years of living, I've learned one valuable lesson. Pain can be the best teacher, no matter the circumstance. It's a lesson that's been driven into me time and time again and one that has made me stronger . . . physically, emotionally, and mentally.

Unfortunately, most folks hit that first twinge of pain and give up, afraid to feel it, to grow from it, to learn from it. So they stay stagnant, unfulfilled and not knowing how to get ahead.

They don't recognize that until they find the courage to push through, the harsh reality is that they're never going to overcome it. They're never going to reach their dreams, their goals, or their potential.

I relish the pain and the obstacles it can bring. I know that with every sting, with every cut, with every bit of pain that the world inflicts on me or I inflict on myself, I'm making myself stronger.

Twenty-six years of pain. By this point, I'm strong enough that when someone hits me with an iron bar, the bar is the one that breaks. When the snake tries to bite me, it's the one that withers up and dies.

No pain, no gain? If that's true, then I've gained the world, and the only thing that can stop me is me.

"AND SO, WE HAVE A WINNER WITH THIS DEAL, FOLKS," I declare confidently, turning away from the floor-to-ceiling windows and the spectacular view of Bane's skyline at sunset to address the men and women of the Board. "At the outset, my deal may look riskier than either Chase's or Olivia's," I say, nodding my head respectfully to my older brother and sister, who are sitting at the opposite end of the fourteen-foot table that fills the conference room. "But nothing could be further from the truth. Yes, the AlphaSystems deal will only net us twenty million up front, and yes, it will take at least five years to recoup our initial investment. But after those five years, the cash flow will surpass that of the other deals, and more importantly, my plan will gain us sizeable leverage, virtually creating an entirely new industry under the Danger Enterprises umbrella."

The room starts to rumble with a chorus of murmurs and whispers, but before anyone can say anything discernable, Chase coughs loudly, drawing my eyes to him.

Like me, he's got dirty-blond hair that he always wears slicked back. And he's got the chiseled jawline that the Danger blood-line is notoriously known for.

"So you say this deal is better than ours, little bro-I mean, Scott," Chase says, quickly correcting himself. But he flashes a mock grin and pointedly straightens the cuff of his Armani suit with the smooth flourish he knows drives me nuts. "Yet you failed to illustrate how. I'm sure I speak for everyone here when I ask how in the world you came to that conclusion? You're not even close to my figures."

He challenges me with his arrogant blue eyes and the conde-scending smirk he always uses to piss me off.

I return my brother's smirk, refusing to let his fraudulent slip of tongue or his attempt to trigger my irritation ruffle me.

Instead, I smoothly make my way to the front of the room, inten-tionally looming over him.

"Well, big brother," I say in false deference before tapping the stack of papers on the table, "If you would read the chart in front of you, it's all right there, spelled out very clearly. I've laid the groundwork, done the math, and had it double-checked by our in-house business analysts. This deal is great for Danger Enter-prises, a way to look forward and take our company to the next level." I motion at the papers in front of every board member. "See for yourselves."

The room fills with whispers and murmurs once again as the gathered executives peer closely at my report filled with graphs and notes. I sit back in my chair, and for the next several minutes, I watch them flip pages, their fingertips following the upward trajectory of profits, their excitement obvious on their faces. My grin grows by the second.

"My word," says Charlie Reynolds, a graybeard executive who's been with Danger Enterprises for as long as I can remember. He sits back in his seat, looking at me with newfound respect and admiration, shaking his head in what is almost awe. "Ladies and gents, this is impressive."

The room stays quiet, but it doesn't matter. I can see it in their eyes. They're coming around, agreeing with me. It's better than wild applause.

I've fantasized about this happening since the moment I took on the daunting task of securing this deal, and now that the moment is here, it's all I can do to keep from shouting in triumph.

Everyone seems happy except for two people, and they're scowling as if I pissed in their morning cereal.

Unsurprisingly, one is Chase. The other is my father, Robert Danger.

At sixty, his once-lustrous blond hair is now streaked with grey. His broad shoulders are hunched together as he leans forward in his chair at the head of the table, his hands steepled under his chin as if he's praying. Not only is he glaring at me, but his cold blue eyes have a hateful look about them, almost as if he detests my very presence in the room.

It's a look I've grown accustomed to. For as long as I can remember, I've been my father's least-favorite child. I've never quite figured out why. Maybe it's simply because Chase is his favorite and I'm a spare son, or perhaps because I'm quick to take command of a situation and father doesn't like to be challenged. Definitely not by me.

Whatever the case, he has made it no secret that he'd prefer Chase to be his successor. The empire has its crown prince and I'm just the backup plan.

It's a mindset I intend to change very soon. "So—"

"Quiet!" Dad snaps irritably, and the board room almost instantly stills.

He looks around the room for a moment, as if daring anyone to speak, before settling his eyes back on me. "Very nice work, Scott," he says, somehow making his words sound more like an insult than a compliment, "but I'm not yet convinced that this is the direction we should be moving in."

It's an effort to keep from gritting my teeth. This should be a slam-dunk for me. "Then let me convince you—"

"The meeting is over," Dad says dismissively, turning his attention to the room at large. "I'm going to take a couple of days to go over these proposals before we call a vote."

The executives look at each other for a moment before gathering up paperwork and rising from their seats. The restrained formality of the meeting is over, but my father's words have put a considerable damper on the excitement, and everyone is quiet, merely giving each other telling looks.

"You three stay," Dad commands. Everyone in the room knows who he means. It rankles me that my father still talks to us like we're servants or something.

I keep my cool as the room quickly empties, pretending not to notice the bastard grin on Chase's face. Liv is the only one who is graceful, as she always is, studying me with a cool but inquisitive expression.

She sits regally in her chair like an ice queen, her platinum blonde hair pulled up into an elegant bun, her startling green eyes a reflection of our mother's.

For some reason, her calm demeanor pisses me off more than Chase trying to fuck with me. At least he's being transparent by being a dick, whereas Liv always hides her true intentions and thoughts behind an impassive mask.

She looks harmless enough, but I've learned to be wary around my dear sister. It's the slow knife that kills . . . and Olivia can be very slow and very deadly.

"You three surprised me today," Dad says, bringing me out of my thoughts. He sits back in his chair, appraising each of us with shrewd eyes. "Very nice work. Well done."

21

I don't miss the slight smile that plays across his lips when he looks between Chase and me. He won't say it, but he enjoyed our little tiff during the meeting. It's become his favorite form of entertainment, watching us go at each other's throat in our quest to impress him.

It's been going on for so long, it's almost second-nature to us. From a young age, he's forced us to compete for his affection, always pitting us boys against one another while basically ignoring Olivia.

First, it was who could excel in school, bring home straight As or get the recommendation for advanced placement classes. Later, it was who was a better athlete. It didn't matter that Chase was older. I was expected to make just as many goals, beat his personal records, and do more all the same. And if I did, Chase made damn sure to beat me again the next time.

Later, in our college years, Dad would have us work in the various subsidiary groups that make up Danger Enterprises. He'd pump the executives for feedback, encouraging them to work us even harder just to see who would break and who would perform best.

In the end, only one of us will hold the reins of power at Danger Enterprises. I intend for that person to be me.

There are a few moments of silence, so I decide to speak up. "I think we all showed good insight . . . but one of the plans was—"

"Scott, your grandstanding is bound to get you into trouble," Dad says, cutting me off. "Bragging about it doesn't help either."

I arch an eyebrow. "Grandstanding?" I ask incredulously. This coming from the man who made himself synonymous with the city of Bane to the point that I swear they're going to rename the whole place 'Danger' when he's dead? "Such as . . . ?"

"The whole bit about your deal being the best. Walking around here as if you're the CEO. It's . . . unseemly," Dad says.

Chase snorts, but I don't pay him any mind. "I was just—"

He charges on, holding up a hand to silence me. "You have talent, you have potential, and you are perhaps more passionate about the business than anyone I know." He pauses, letting that sink in, but then he drops the other shoe. "But you are far too ambitious. Your ego is bigger than your talent. Your deal will get us slaughtered in the long run. When it comes down to it, you are impetuous and impulsive. Your brother is a better business-man, prepared to take things over when I retire with a steady hand, guidance, and a realistic outlook on the future. Not this pie in the sky magic math that only looks good on a chart." He pushes my carefully crafted presentation to the center of the table, dismissing it. "We need real dollars and cents, smarts that will sustain Danger Enterprises, not a boardroom performance."

His words drop on me like hot coals down my shirt. Anger boils up from the pit of my stomach. This arrogant, deluded old man thinks that I'm not prepared to run this company? I'm the one who has a plan to position us for not just the next few years, but the next *generation*.

But I don't show emotion. I can't let him think he's getting under my skin. I don't lose control, at least not with someone watching. I take the pain from his words, twist them and trans-form them, and turn them into fire, into something useful to help me reach my goals.

Dad's full of shit anyway. He hates that I'm passionate about my work, that my aspirations are even bigger than his. And that despite his wanting me to fail, and sometimes even intentionally kicking my footing out from underneath me, I get back up every time, stronger than before. He knows I'm the best fit to take his place, today as evidence, but he wants to put me in my place. Maybe if I sat back and did what he asked, like Chase does, things would be different. That's part of the reason he wants Chase to run the company, because he wants to have some semblance of control in place. Chase will allow that, but I never would. It'd be hard when I have so many ideas to further our brand, more than he ever dreamed, and that pisses him off. That I could be better. Better than Chase, and better than him.

They all look at me, waiting for my explosive reaction to Dad's cutting words.

Instead, I stand up and button my double-breasted suit. "I see. Well, have a good night."

I slowly turn and walk from the room, my rage gurgling in my gut like someone just dropped a whole tube of Mentos in a bottle of Coke. I spent three months busting my ass on this deal, working with my team to ensure it was as good as it could be, and to deliver a picture-perfect masterpiece of a presentation . . . only to have my own father reduce it to no better than a kid fucking around on E-trade with a credit card and a Magic Eight Ball.

Fuck that. I've worked too hard for this shit.

Maybe I should just quit and go somewhere my talents are actually appreciated, I think as I reach the elevator and decide to bypass it for the stairs. *I have to work twice as hard as Liv and four times as hard as Chase, and still, it's never good enough.*

Even as the thought enters my mind, I quickly dismiss it. Danger Enterprises has been my entire life. Just because my dad is closed-minded, I won't let him force me away from something that I fully intend on making mine.

Reaching the floor where my office is, I hear a familiar voice behind me. "Hey, what happened in there?"

I turn to see my best friend and colleague, Robbie Wright, peering at me, his chest heaving as if he's just run up the stairs. I know he didn't. Robbie's just always going like a crazy man. His four-Rockstar-a-day habit probably doesn't help things. He's short and compact, a former college boxer who earned the nickname 'Motorhead' from his team, both for his never-ending energy and his never-ending mouth.

Despite the difficulties in getting him to shut up sometimes, Robbie's my right-hand man. No matter what I need, he's the one I can always depend on, and his brain is as sharp as his suits. He's put a lot into this deal and feels personally invested, just like me.

"It's not being voted on yet," I say flatly, continuing on to my office. Robbie doesn't need an insight into my issues with my father since he's well aware of them already.

Robbie falls in behind me, however, scurrying to keep up. "Fuck, man, I thought you said we'd have your father's backing today."

Not responding, I make it to my office, taking off my suit coat and throwing it over the back of my chair. Despite it being a step down from Chase's office, the floor-to-ceiling windows give a spectacular view of the city.

I take a moment, looking out at the view before me. When Dad was my age, Bane was just another podunk small city, one of those towns where high school football would draw crowds bigger than the entire town's population.

Then my father began what was then Danger LLC. And now, Bane's on the verge of being the next big city of the decade.

There's already a satellite campus of the state university in town, and the Danger name has brought plenty of other industries to town. There have been some growing pains, but overall, Bane's name is on the rise and is being hyped as the next Silicon Valley.

And in the center of it all, standing fifty stories into the air and dominating the skyline, is the Danger Building.

"Hello?"

I turn around and see that Robbie is staring at me. He's standing at the door to my office, his eyes concerned. He's good at reading between the lines and knows this isn't the time to press me.

It's one of the reasons I have him on my team, even if keeping a friend as your subordinate has plenty of its own challenges.

Running my fingers through my hair, I sigh, stressed out. I thought for sure I had this in the bag. "Fuck it . . . I need a drink." I move toward the collection of fine whiskey and crystal glasses on the credenza in the corner but stop when Robbie speaks.

"Hey, how about we hit up a club or a bar instead? Change of scenery might do you some good. I know it's been a while, but a piece of ass might help you clear your mind too."

I should take a pass, go home, and gather my thoughts. I need to stay focused. In time, everyone, including my father, will realize I'm the one suited to lead this company. And I need to be ready when that happens.

But the thought of going home without relieving all this built-up tension is pure torture.

Fuck it.

I've got three months of pent-up energy, and some lucky girl is going to get all of it tonight. Every. Last. Bit.

Grabbing my wallet, I grin. "Let's go."

CHAPTER 3

MADISON

Daily Horoscope, September 21st
Libra – Put your best self forward and watch what happens.

"Woo-hoo, Maddie's got her groove back!" Tiff exclaims, looking me over with jealous eyes. "See? My horoscope readings can be a good kick in the pants to get your shit straight. Get it, girl!"

We're in the break room in back of Stella's getting ready for our shifts, and after that shitty fucking psychic reading, I'm kicking the bad vibes to the curb and grabbing life by the horns.

Starting by going all out with my wardrobe. Okay, maybe Tiff's morning reading was the encouragement I needed to put forth a bit more effort today. But it's hella easier to hear the good stuff than dire warnings, so best self . . . *let's make some magic happen.*

I've turned the sexiness up to eleven tonight, skipping my usual ass-highlighting jeans for a skin-tight blue skirt, black fishnet stockings, and combat boots.

I haven't worn a skirt since a certain bastard told me I looked cheap in them and strongly encouraged me to wear pants.

Even after that fucked-up situation ended, I've kept wearing jeans out of habit.

But tonight, I feel different. Defiant. Fierce.

I'm going to serve up drinks, look damn good doing it, and enjoy my shift.

Tiffany must be feeling my vibe too. "You're gonna need Stella's bat to keep all those pervy bastards off you with all that ass you're serving up," she jokes, looking pointedly at my butt. "Or they might even have to call 9-1-1 for those old geezers who come in here with their pacemakers."

I laugh, shaking my head. "Stop it."

"Just sayin'. You're gonna get extra-good tips tonight, girl."

"Tips would be nice, that's for sure," I say, fussing with my hair. I'm in a good mood, and I'm not going to let anything or anyone change it. Including crazy voodoo ladies.

Turning around, I check myself out in the big mirror attached to the break room door . . . and damn, do I like what I see.

Tiff's right. I look slamming tonight. This outfit is highlighting all my best assets, both T and A, my hair is cooperating, hanging shiny and smooth down my back, and my legs look long from my hem to my boots. I might not be 'hot' according to the skinny bitches' magazines, but what the hell do they know? I'm a fucking knockout . . . a curvy fantasy of a woman most guys wish they could get their hands on.

For the first time in a while, I actually feel sexy. Comfortable in my own skin. Confident.

It's been so long since I've felt this way. I've missed it. Missed . . . being myself.

The thought triggers a twinge of anger in my gut, the memory of my past threatening my flow for a second. But I dismiss the voice in my head that isn't mine, the one with ugly things to say that tear me down, with a pep talk of my own.

He's nothing. A ghost of my past that got me where I am today. Strong, beautiful, ready to live the life I want.

Tiffany is unaware of the range of thoughts, both good and bad and good again, rolling through my mind. Instead, she's focused on posing beside me, our reflections looking back at us from the mirror. She shakes her head, making her big curls bounce around her face. "Shit, if I'd known you were going all out tonight, I'd have dressed up too." She putzes around with her top, trying to make the V-neck into something a bit more plunging.

"I could grab you some scissors if you wanna just slash at that? Really let it all hang out." She glares at me, but I can see the hint of a smile popping out at the corner of her mouth. She knows I'm teasing, so I flip my hair and wait for her to sass back.

But she doesn't crack a joke, instead just shimmies her chest at me. "I think the girls are fine where they are, and no shirt, V-neck or otherwise, could hide this awesomeness." We both burst into laughter, dissolving into hitched breaths and wide smiles.

"What are you two girls giggling about?" asks a stern voice from the doorway before I can respond. I turn my head, seeing Stella standing with her hands on her hips.

I've known Stella for a long time, and I don't think she's changed a bit since day one. Large, meaty arms from a lifetime of hauling drinks, pulling kegs, and raising two stubborn boys stand out from an ample bosom. There's nothing sweet or dainty about Stella. She works twice as hard as anyone I've ever known and has dealt with drunken customers, even really big guys, with a fierce mask that dares them to try her and see what happens.

Still, for all of her no-nonsense solidness, Stella's very prim in her own way. She's wearing a dress that reminds me of an old-fashioned school teacher, her gray-streaked red hair pulled up into a bun on top of her head.

The best thing about her, though, is her heart, stern but infinitely loving.

Tiffany laughs at Stella's unsmiling expression, knowing it's just image . . . for now. "Well hello, Boss Lady. I was just telling Miss Tits here about how she's a knockout tonight. What do you think?"

Stella turns her attention to me, her expression immediately warming and softening as she looks me up and down. "My, my, I ain't seen you dress like this in a while. I almost forgot how much of a beauty you are when you're not moping around. Not quite the lady that I know you are . . . but you will definitely make a man's blood boil."

"Thank you," I reply, feeling a little shy. "I just felt like having a little fun tonight."

Stella nods sagely. "I said it before, but if I knew where that bastard who wronged you lived, I'd go shoot him dead right now. Welcome back to the land of the living, honey."

Loving warmth fills my heart as I take in Stella's words. I'm so indebted to this woman. Besides helping me with a job, she's been a constant source of emotional support.

It's funny how fate brought her into my life. I met her when I first got to town and needed a job on the weekends. Stella had a sign in the window and hired me on the spot.

A year later, when I was at my lowest, Stella was the one who said I didn't need to go back home to Aunt May.

I was determined to stand on my own two feet, and Stella understood that. She never judged me as I was figuring things out.

And if it wasn't for Stella, I'd have never met Tiff, who I ran into my second night on the job. We hit it off, laughing our asses off and meshing immediately. Now we're roommates, two crazy gals making it in an unfair world, in a town that's growing wicked fast, and trying to keep our sanity in the meantime.

"Damn it, is it hot in here to you two?" Stella asks, wiping at the sweat on her brow before fanning herself with the towel at her waist. "I'm sweating like a hooker in a revival meeting."

Tiff shakes her head, already laughing. "I've told you before, if I had titties that big, I wouldn't even be able to stand. It's no wonder you're sweating like a mouse in the lion cage at the zoo carrying those things around."

It's not the best joke. It's not even a very good one. Still, I laugh so hard that both of them look at me like I'm crazy.

I swear, the only reason I got through the dark months was Tiffany. Her making me laugh is like a dose of medicine, and right now, I feel so good that even a cheesy joke like that is enough to make me burst out.

Stella mutters something about a dead waitress and having space to hide the body in the back before shaking her head, giving us a rueful smile. "Maybe I need to get that reduction the doc's been going on about. Let's face it, I don't exactly need these things to nurse babies no more. My baby making days are long over."

"No way!" I protest vehemently. "People pay good money to get those. And yours are real, which makes them even better. Look at Dolly Parton. She loves hers."

Stella scowls. She knows about my Dolly fanhood, but she's more of a Reba McIntyre fan herself. "Honey, Dolly's got way more money than I've got. She can hire some young boy toys over there in Dollywood to carry hers. One for each side." Stella uses her hands to lift her full breasts up a few inches higher, mimicking what the imaginary titty-carrying-guys would do.

We all laugh, giving each other a quick hug. "Here's to every woman having a boy toy, or two, to take care of us."

Stella wipes at her eyes as she calms down. "All right, all right, enough joking around. It's a packed house and there's work to be done. Way things are lookin', you two arrived just in time. Lord knows, Carl is about to burn the whole damn place down if he doesn't get some help. If he wasn't my son, I'd have fired him a long time ago. I don't know what I'ma do with that boy."

"Have him join the Army?" Tiff quips. "They know how to deal with a fuckup or two."

"Tried that . . . Navy wouldn't take him either," Stella gripes, fanning herself some more. "You two hurry out there. I'm gonna go sit under the fan while I do next week's delivery order."

"Right, Boss," we reply, and I give myself a final once-over. We walk out of the room and pass the kitchen when we hear a high, clear laugh.

"Damn, girl, that is some grade-A pussy tonight. Looking *fine*."

If it had been from anyone else, I'd be in their face in a hot second. But this is from Devin James, Stella's cook, culinary wizard, and good luck charm.

Or at least he claims that he's a good luck charm, since he's the 'good luck fairy.' His words, not mine. With green eyes and spiked dark hair, he's a short little ball of energy who can outwork any two regular short-order cooks I know.

"You trying to get hit over the head with one of those pans?" I shoot back, coming into the kitchen.

Devin turns, his grin widening as he looks me up and down. "Oh, stop it, you know I was just playing. You look good. What's the occasion?"

"The occasion is, I'm gonna whoop your ass for talking shit," Tiffany chirps. "And you wish your ass looked this good."

Devin snorts, smacking the ass of his pristine black work jeans. "Honey, do you smell what I'm cooking in this kitchen? It's so good I have these chicken hawks begging for more. As for my ass . . . I could give you some lessons on how to work yours."

Devin turns, dropping his ass and popping it left and right. He nearly smacks into the stove, making me laugh. "Don't hurt yourself. Or burn the place down."

Devin turns back around, grinning, but I hold up a hand. "I'd love to sit here and chat, but we need to hit the floor." I punch my ID into the timeclock. "Heard it's hot tonight."

"You damn right. On that note, watch out for that broad Ms. Crabtree at table nine," Devin warns. "She's downing them tonight. She's just staring at the drinks and then slamming 'em down Viking-style."

"I'll keep a look out," I promise Devin. Ms. Crabtree is flirting the line between being a heavy drinker and being a full-blown alcoholic since her husband passed. We all keep an eye on her, feeling sorry for her situation but not really able to do much about it besides listen when she gets weepy.

Heading through the double doors to the restaurant, I see that Stella was right. The place is packed.

It's hard to really fit Stella's into a simple category. The food's too good to call it a bar, but we're too much of a dance and hangout joint to call it a gastropub. It's just Bane's longest-running authentic night hangout, and the ambiance is just as unique as the rest of the place. There's a lot of wood on the floor, but before anyone starts thinking it looks like a redone Hooters, Stella has some real country and rock shit going on the walls. There's a guitar that's signed by Johnny Cash, along with one of Prince's feathered hats he wore for the *When Doves Cry* video. Both are in protective plexiglass cases so any rough-housing doesn't damage them.

Overall, I'd call Stella's one of a kind, and either you get it or you don't. If you don't . . . well, Stella's got enough customers that she doesn't really give a shit. She's got bankers drinking right next to auto mechanics, and like the old show said, it's where everybody knows your name.

"Thought you'd never get your ass out here," growls Carl Wilson, Stella's son and early-shift bartender. Tall and actually decent-looking when he cleans up and spends a little time grooming, Carl's always been a fuckup, despite Stella's repeated attempts to make something of the man.

The hardest part about dealing with Carl is that he's about as useful as a bikini in Antarctica. He's often an ass, thinking he knows a lot more than he actually does, which is why Stella has me work the taps anytime there are more than twenty people in the place. I roll my eyes at his commentary, not caring enough about his opinion to correct it.

Carl doesn't notice, though, as he cracks his neck like some sort of pro-wrestler and starts cashing out the register. "You know, if I had to serve up one more fruity-ass girly drink, I was going to lose it. Who the fuck in this town wants appletinis?"

"People drink what they drink," I reply, checking the mix station and fixing two mistakes without saying anything. "Our job's to give 'em what they want."

"Speaking of which," Carl says, finally noticing me. "What's the occasion? You're looking hot tonight. Cruising for some dick after your shift?"

I resist a scowl. He's not worth getting mad over. "Just feeling fab," I say, walking over to the other register and logging myself into the POS system. "You should try it sometime."

I don't mean for Carl to overhear me, but he does. Yanking his apron off, Carl stomps to the end of the bar and pulls a stool over, plopping down and stabbing a finger down the bar. "That guy over there wants a Twisted Bliss . . . and three stools down, he wants a blended whiskey, neat, using Evian. And I'll have a Cranberry Stoli Shaner Bill."

I know he's trying to fuck with me by not telling me who 'that guy' is, but I know almost every face at the bar, and I already know who wants the Twisted Bliss.

"Hey, you got two hands, two legs, and something like a brain," I sass, grabbing my ingredients for the paying customers. "Get your Shaner Bill your damn self, since I know you're not paying."

"Hey, I've been busting my ass all day," Carl counters, unable to keep the whine out of his voice. "You're ten minutes late."

I snort, shaking the mixer bottle for the Twisted Bliss. Ten minutes late, my ass. We both know my shift officially starts three minutes from now. I swear, Carl is such a liar.

But I don't worry about his bullshit tonight. I've got work to do.

I get the drinks for the two guys while Carl grumbles about having to get the drink himself.

I tend to avoid conflict with Carl. We usually just shoot the shit back and forth, keeping it superficial and not getting too into it. Besides, no matter how much he pisses me off, it's a show of respect for Stella. She may be like a second adoptive mother to me, but blood is blood. And I owe her for giving me this job when I literally had no way of supporting myself. So I put up with a lot from Carl for her sake.

I quickly forget about him as the drink calls come fast and hard. Tiff shakes her ass around the floor and grins at me every time she picks up an order. I can tell she's thinking of the tips we're banking tonight.

My forearms are literally burning from shaking so many cups, and I'm going through blender pitchers so fast the bar back is running to the kitchen on a nearly nonstop basis.

But tonight, I don't mind the extra work. I'm looking great, making bank, and feeling good for the first time in a long time. I feel like the girl I used to be is back. No more hiding or kowtowing to some man.

Speaking of men, I do a scan of the room, focusing on the customers more than their drinks this time. There are a few cuties here and there, some of whom are even looking back at me. Hell, even Carl is giving me some serious eye, and I'm pretty sure he doesn't even like me.

My eyes flicker to the door as two men walk in, my jaw almost immediately dropping to the floor.

Damn. They're new, or at least I've never served them. And I would definitely remember them. Well, *him*.

The guy in front commands the room without even trying, an almost palpable magnetism surrounding him like an aura. He's built like a machine, tall and wide at the shoulders, but a narrow waist behind the belt holding up his dress slacks.

Hypnotized, I watch him move through the room. I'm openly staring by the time he runs his fingers through his dark blond hair, his arm muscles bulging against the sleeves of his dress shirt.

I can see that I'm not the only one who's noticed. Tiff practically goes ass over teakettle as she catches a glimpse, bumping into the corner of the table she's serving. But the two university girls who are sitting there don't notice at all because their eyes are locked on the guys too.

The two men walk up, claiming the last two seats at the bar. Up close, I can see they're both handsome, but I only have eyes for Mr. Swag . . . nothing against his shorter companion.

I know I should stop, but I can't help staring. He says something to his friend, giving me a glimpse of his nearly perfect, blinding white teeth. And when he smiles . . . oh, my God, those dimples. Not just any dimples either, but deep ones that turn his blue eyes into twin twinkling orbs of sexiness.

This guy is trouble, my mind warns.

My guard has been up so high that I haven't dared look at a man in a sexual way in a long time. But this one . . . Tiff said the best way to get over a guy was to get under another, which is sounding like a fucking genius idea right about now. But whoo, getting under a man like that might be more than I can handle. Even if I am feeling myself tonight.

The dimple-faced hottie looks at me, and I swear I'm about to burst into flames.

He opens his lips as if to say something, but my eyes are drawn away by a sudden commotion.

It's Tiffany, and she's trying to calm Ms. Crabtree down. "Now Ms. Crabtree, there's no need for that," Tiff says, while behind her back, I see her patting her left hip in our signal that means *cover my ass*. "I'm just saying that Maddie's busy and might be a few minutes getting your beer, so I'll bring it with your food. That way, we can get something in your belly, 'kay?"

"Fuck that!" Ms. Crabtree slurs, slamming her empty glass to the table. "I want another round now. And tell Devin to make me a cheeseburger worthy of my Budweiser!"

Glancing over at Carl, I hook a thumb to the back, silently telling him to go get Stella. If shit does escalate, Stella is our best bet to handle Ms. Crabtree without bouncing her like a drunken frat boy.

"Ma'am," Tiffany says evenly, "there's no reason for you to talk like that—"

"Girl, get me a fucking beer. If Maddie's busy, pour it yourself. Lazy bitch . . ." The last part is under her breath, but everyone hears Ms. Crabtree call Tiffany a bitch, including Stella, who's speed-stomping across the floor.

"Roberta, I've told you before to watch your language," Stella says in her no-nonsense way. It helps that the two women have history and were friends back when Ms. Crabtree was a sweet woman, before she lost her way.

"Ah, fuck off, Stella. Just leave me be . . . and bring me a beer, will ya?" Ms. Crabtree goes back to watching the television over the bar, mistakenly assuming Stella has gone off to do her bidding.

She'd be wrong. Stella slams a fist that's been work-hardened by three decades of running this place into the pine of the table, not even flinching as she does it. "Roberta, you're drunk and belligerent, but you're also a good friend, so I'm going to ignore the trash you're talking. But you listen and listen good. You've got thirty seconds to clear out of here and head home, or I'm calling the cops to take you to the drunk tank for the night."

For a moment, I wonder if Ms. Crabtree is going to push back, but her shoulders slump and she looks down, nearly crying. "I'm sorry, Stella. I just miss him . . ." and the tone of the whole room changes just like that.

Stella wraps an arm around the woman's shoulders, helping her stand. "I know you do. Come on, Roberta. No need to do that out here. Let's go to my office, and I'll call you a cab." Stella's voice is softer now, the mothering caretaker in her out in force.

IT REMINDS ME WHY I LOVE STELLA SO DAMN MUCH. She's tough and strong, but she's not a bitch. She never lets someone go uncared for. She loves us all, sometimes with tough love, but each of us is thankful for Stella . . . me, Tiff, Devin, even Ms. Crabtree.

"Miss?" calls a deep voice.

The sound startles me, and my heart skips a beat as I turn back to the hottie at the bar. In the commotion, I'd forgotten about him for a moment. But when I look at him now, all those same heated thoughts bloom again.

My skin pricks as his eyes rove over my outfit and I fight the urge to pose for him. But I can't stop the tremble in my knees.

I have a half-second of panic and almost flee, but since I'm the only bartender tonight, that's not gonna solve anything. I take a breath, attempting to settle my belly. I don't know what's wrong with me. Hot guys come in here all the time, granted, maybe not as hot as him, but he's not that special.

But my racing heart seems to think otherwise.

Get yourself together, girl. He's just a customer. Walk over and do your job, just like usual. No big deal.

Pep talk complete, I put on a confident smile and straighten my shoulders.

But as I make my way over to him, I can't help but think I'm walking straight into trouble.

CHAPTER 4

SCOTT

$\mathcal{F}$rom the moment I stepped into the bar, my eyes have been glued on one thing only.

Her.

There's some commotion behind me that draws her attention, and I take advantage of the distraction to look her up and down fully.

Her breasts are fantastic, deep cleavage visible in the daring V-cut of her T-shirt. The combo of the sexy hosiery, tough-girl boots, and tight outfit, along with her wild mane of blonde hair and porcelain doll face make her look almost like a badass rock goddess.

It's not even been a full minute since I laid eyes on her and my brain is already burning with images of my lips brushing against the soft skin of her neck, down to the hollow between her breasts. I'd flip her skirt up, rip the fishnets to get at her sweet pussy, and make her leave those boots on as I fuck her.

If I wasn't so damn turned on, I'd be embarrassed at the lust raging through my blood.

Shit, maybe it has been too long.

LAUREN LANDISH

Needing her eyes on me the way mine are on her, I call out and she turns to look my way. I let my eyes trace her body, making my approval obvious. I can see her steadying intake of breath, but I keep my smile of delight to myself.

I watch as she moves closer, her hips swaying naturally from side to side. Her full red lips spread in a wide smile.

"How can I help you boys this evening?" she asks when she finally comes over, her voice filled with a natural country twang that tells me she's grown up in the South.

I've never particularly cared for country accents, even though Bane is a Southern city. The people in my usual circles are mostly private school-educated, and the first thing they teach you in speech class is enunciation and a cleaner, crisper sound. It's a sign of education, breeding, and class. But in one simple sentence, I'm suddenly rethinking decades of teaching because I can imagine that sweet twang as she drawls my name and begs me to fuck her. I can feel the blood rushing to my cock.

You can help me by wrapping those ruby-red lips around my shaft and humming Dixie, a naughty voice at the back of my head whispers.

"What can I get you?" the bartender asks again. I swear, she doesn't even look at Robbie, just me.

"I'll have a Glenfiddich double, neat," Robbie says. From the corner of my eye, I can see he's leaning forward, taking in the bartender's lush curves. "And a Suicide Burger."

"Brave man," the bartender says without even glancing at him.

Instead, her whiskey eyes are locked with my baby blues. "And you?"

"What's the best vodka you have?" I ask, not trusting myself to look away from her.

"I have a bottle of Snow Queen," she says, biting her lip a little. "That good enough?"

"It'll do. Snow Queen dry martini, dirty, with double olives."

"Coming right up," she says as she gives a wink, which is innocent enough, and I'm sure she tosses them around all the time, but it succeeds in stirring my desire more.

She walks toward the back wall, eyeing the upper shelf for the distinctive bottle of vodka, and then I watch, mesmerized as she lifts up to her toes and reaches overhead, her ass popping out. I can feel my cock hardening by the second as I stare at her ass, imagining her whole body arching like that as I plunge my cock deep inside her.

"Fuck, she's hot," I whisper, startled when I realize I've said it out loud.

Robbie raises an eyebrow at me, grinning at my hushed admission. "Enjoying the scenery?"

I tear my eyes away from the bartender's assets and give Robbie an even look. "Just an observation," I lie through my teeth smoothly.

Robbie chuckles. "Sure, sure."

I ignore him and look around the place. It has a honkytonk meets biker bar meets dance club sort of vibe to it . . . but maybe it's that strange mix that lends it a unique charm.

"So, have you been here before?" I ask casually, and Robbie shakes his head. "Then how'd you know about the food?"

"Logan comes here a lot," Robbie says, shrugging as the bartender comes back quickly with our drinks and sets them down in front of us.

"We'll have your burger up in about five minutes, handsome," she says as Robbie tosses a couple of dollars on the counter for a tip. I dig in my pocket, tossing out two twenties.

The bartender looks at me a second, then blushes slightly as she pockets the money in her apron. She gives me a little smile, and that tiny gift feels like a big win.

"Thank you," she finally whispers, so softly I almost read the words on her lips instead of hearing them. But I can imagine her sweet twang rolling over the syllables, and it's sexy as hell.

I barely hold back my groan. Fuck, I'm already ready to nut in my slacks. It'd be pretty fucking pathetic if it weren't for the fact that I haven't been laid in centuries.

"You're welcome," I finally reply, letting my voice rumble as I get a look at the name tag pinned to her apron. I take a sip of my martini, enjoying it. "Madison."

I even love her name. She smiles fully when I say it, and I feel myself return the grin. "And you are, stranger? Ain't seen you around here before."

"Scott," I reply, wanting to offer my hand but knowing this isn't quite the time. "And this is my friend, Robbie."

"Pleased to meet you both." She flashes a brief smile at Robbie, but her eyes almost immediately come back to mine.

Right where I want them.

"Does that happen often here?" I ask, knowing she has customers waiting, but I need more of her time, her attention.

"Hmm?" she asks, immediately turning her attention away from the other customers and back to me.

I nod over to where the where the yelling woman had been sitting. "People getting . . . sloppy."

Emotions race across Madison's face so fast I can't place them all, but she seems to settle with sadness and it makes my heart ache to see her upset. "Sometimes. We occasionally have guys who get a little rowdy, but Ms. Crabtree is different. She's not usually that over the top." Madison's eyes tick-tock from me to Robbie and back. "It's really y'all's first time here?"

"It is. It's our first night out in a long time, actually," I reply. "Just wanted a few drinks after work to unwind, and Robbie heard good things about the grill here."

"Well I'm glad you chose Stella's," she says. It looks like she wants to say more, but some bastard at the end of the bar signals her. "Enjoy your drinks. Holler if you need anything."

My eyes follow her ass as she walks off, and Robbie turns to gawk at me. "Forty-dollar tip?"

"What?" I deadpan. "It was a good vodka recommendation. Just tipping for a job well done." Even I can hear the lie in my voice.

"Why not make it a hundred next time?" he asks incredulously. "Now I *know* you have the hots for her."

I ignore his jest, my eyes on Madison as she serves customers along the bar. As I watch, I see other guys flirting with her, and my hand grips my drink a little harder each time. But while she talks back, there's something guarded about the way she handles it. It's like how she talked with Robbie, calling him handsome. It's a practiced routine and there's a line she's drawn.

It's intriguing to see how she dances out of that flirtation and skates past leering looks, all the while maintaining an air of unawareness. She's not playing dumb—in fact, she's pretty skilled at manipulating the customers—but it's subtle.

Even so, I've never been one to share, and I want her flirtations, her smiles, her laughs for myself. She may not be mine, but I want to lay claim on her. Hell, I'd love to punch a couple of the guys down on the other side of the bar who are looking at her like a piece of meat.

I'm shocked at the possessiveness I feel. I've known her for all of five minutes.

Robbie interrupts my thoughts right before I can call Madison over again. "So what was your dad's deal, anyway?" he asks. Someone from the kitchen puts Robbie's plate down, and he gives the guy a big thanks. Turning to his burger, he picks it up and gets to work demolishing it.

I'd avoided his questions on the way over, but I give in now, a little more loose-lipped from the vodka. We chat about work and

43

my asshole of a dad for a few minutes, but my eyes track Madison's every move. She looks at home here, completely in her element, which strikes me as odd for such a doll of a woman.

Still, I can't ignore the little voice in my head that's telling me that a girl like her shouldn't be working in a place like this. Not with all these drunk assholes gawking at her and thinking they're worth her time. Newsflash, fellas . . . you're not, but I sure as fuck am.

Robbie's story about some asshat in accounting has caught my attention for a moment, and when I turn my eyes back, Madison is leaning on the bar in front of me, her tits practically in my face as she smiles at the punchline of Robbie's story. I really don't know if she's doing it on purpose or just doesn't notice it, but damn if I'm not enjoying it.

"Eavesdropping, huh?" I ask teasingly.

"Not really," she replies, "but your glass is empty. Should I set you up another?"

I grin. "Why the hell not? Gotta be careful with the vodka though. It could get me in trouble."

Madison smiles, taking my glass from me. "You look like a man who can handle trouble."

It's flirty, and I fucking love her boldness. "I usually try to avoid trouble if I can help it, but I can handle myself when the situation warrants it."

Her eyes track across my body . . . from my hair to my face, along the width of my shoulders, down to my forearms where I've rolled up my sleeves, to my hands clutching the new drink she just sat down. "Yeah, I bet you could handle yourself." Her voice is quiet, and it honestly sounds like she meant to think it, not say it. Louder, she says, "So, what do y'all do?"

I open my mouth to tell her, mindful that I normally don't open up to random women in bars. Or anyone, for that matter. Better to be safe. But before I can impress her with my fancy title, she interrupts.

"Wait, let me guess. Luxury car salesman?"

I give her a hard look. "Do I really look like I sell cars for a living?"

She laughs. "No, not at all. I did at least say 'luxury', though, so don't be offended." She smirks, and I know she was only teasing me. "Obviously, some sort of businessman . . . banker, hedge fund manager, alphabet soup type? Am I getting close?"

I grin back. "Closer than you'd think, although I have to ask . . . alphabet soup?"

She smacks and holds up a finger as she runs down the lists, "You know, CEO, VP, R&D . . . stuff where your title is all letters. You're that type, for sure."

Curious now, I ask, "And what makes me look like *that* type?"

Her grin is full of devilment. "Well, other than the custom-made shirt and huge ass watch, you've got this whole air of 'I'm important'. I bet you're hell in the office . . . demanding, power-ful, bossy." Her list sounds like some of my best traits, and it sounds like she thinks so too.

I'm about to continue our flirty back and forth when a voice from down the bar interrupts us. "Ay, bitch! Quit flirting with your next sugar daddy over there and bring that fine ass over here. I need that Jack 'n Coke I ordered five minutes ago! Or if you ain't gonna make my drink, at least come closer so I can look at those pretty titties and imagine—"

I'm out of my seat before the jackass even has a chance to finish his full sentence. Grabbing him by the collar, I yank him off his stool, ignoring Robbie's attempts to get me to stop. "Yo, Scott, relax. The last thing you need is a lawsuit—"

"Apologize to the lady," I growl, ignoring Robbie and jacking the guy against the bar. "Now."

Madison's quick to jump to the man's defense, her eyes going wide as she pleads with me. "It's okay. You can let him go. There's no need for that. He's just drunk. I've heard it before, and this won't be the last time either."

"No," I reply quickly, increasing my pressure on the man's neck. "Apologize!"

At first, he resists, and I think he might actually try to fight me. Shit, part of me even wants him to so I can take out the frustration I've been dealing with on him.

Luckily for both of us, the man sags after resisting for a moment. "I'm sorry."

His apology isn't at all sincere, and I'm ready to take it further before I look into Madison's eyes, which are pleading with me to let it drop.

In disgust, I yank the guy away from the bar and give him a push toward the door, hoping he'll take the hint and leave. I stalk back to my stool and sit back down.

A guy at the end of the bar raises his glass to me. "Thanks, man," he slurs, obviously pretty damn drunk himself right now. "But next time, please try to keep your hands to yourself. He wasn't hurting anyone, and Maddie sh-should've been making his drink but she was too busy talking to do her job pro . . . proply . . . properly." Every other word has some lisp or odd emphasis on it, making him sound even more drunk.

Yeah, and if you weren't a drunken fool, you'd have done the same thing, I think, dismissing him immediately but noting that he called her 'Maddie'.

Getting to my seat, I see Madison walk over, appearing frazzled rather than relieved. She leans on the bar, but it's not quite as close as before, and I recognize that she's got her shield up again.

"Hey, I really appreciate your doing that, but I'm fine, really. I'm used to that kind of talk," she says while Robbie still gawks at me, shocked that I lost my trademark cool. "Thought you said you avoided trouble? You don't need to add a bar fight to your night."

"You shouldn't be *used* to that kind of talk. I don't care how drunk these people get. No man should talk like that to a lady," I reply evenly, looking her in her eyes. "There's no excuse."

"Yes, I agree, but—" Madison begins to say, but I'm rolling and interrupt her.

"Hell, you shouldn't even be working here. You're better than . . ." I seethe before stopping, shocked at the vehemence in my voice and how possessive and judgmental I sound once again.

Damn, I haven't had that much to drink, have I?

This night is definitely a night of firsts. It's the first time I've been this attracted to a random chick at first sight, and the first time I've lost control of my temper since I was a teenager.

Madison's eyes become flinty, and she looks even more guarded now. "Can't argue with that. Most of these guys wouldn't know how to treat a woman if an instruction manual fell into their laps," she says, her voice becoming harder, louder with every word. "But I don't need you or anyone to take up for me. I can handle myself. And I most certainly don't need anyone telling me where I should be working." She goes stiff and pushes away from the bar. "I hope you boys have a good night."

She walks off, leaving me stunned. I was just trying to help and to tell her that she shouldn't have to put up with drunken assholes harassing her. Hell, in just the few minutes I've spent with her, I can tell she deserves a whole fucking lot better than that. It was supposed to be a compliment. Maybe I didn't say it right . . . maybe because all my blood is in my cock instead of my brain right now?

Robbie picks up the last bite of his burger to stuff it in his mouth before narrowing his eyes at me. "Damn, man, what was all that about? Was it really worth possibly getting your face rearranged?"

I laugh, checking to see if Robbie's serious or just being sarcastic. "Shit. I was about to introduce that guy to a couple of buddies of mine, Curb and Stomp."

Robbie chuckles. "Dude . . . this is so unlike you. Don't get me wrong. I like seeing you a little loose for a change. But I'm telling you now . . . if some girl here makes eyes at me, I'm ditching your ass."

"Sounds like I'm stuck with you then," I joke back.

For the next half hour, we sit back and bullshit, intentionally avoiding both work and the incident with the drunk guy. I think Robbie is sticking to topics that won't piss me off on purpose. He orders a couple more drinks, but I've been taking it slow, not because I'm worried about driving, since I'm not, but because I just don't like losing control to something as stupid as alcohol. And I've done enough of that for tonight.

I try to make eye contact when Madison comes by, but she ignores me, staying professional and nowhere near as engaging as before.

Eventually, Robbie finds a couple of girls to flirt with, taking turns spinning them around the dance floor and keeping himself entertained. But I stay at the bar, sipping at one last martini with my eyes fixed on just one person.

I know why I'm staying, and I'm glad Robbie's found something, or *someone*, to take up his time. I'm determined to get in the last word with Maddie. A red-haired woman hollers out last call, and people start to empty out, although a few people try to get that one last drink in before they have to go.

The woman seems exhausted, though, and I don't think she's got a lot of patience for the customers nursing their last beers. "Lord, I can't stand on my feet a minute more," she puffs, leaning against the bar as she talks to Madison. "Where's Carl? I need him to drive me home."

"Don't think that's happening," Madison says, pointing to *Carl* slumped over at the bar.

"What will I ever do with this damn boy? How the hell am I gonna get home, especially when I need him to drive?" she complains.

I'm about to offer an uber when the other waitress walks up, taking off her apron. Robbie's eyes roam over her body again, and I'd say he'd have a shot if he hadn't been grinding away on some other chick twenty minutes ago. Checking her shirt, I see a nametag . . . Tiffany.

"Stella, I'll take you two home," she offers. "I already prepped for tomorrow, so there's not much left to do. Maddie can close up tonight, right, babe?"

Madison gives Tiffany a *gee, thanks* look and Tiffany winks back. I can tell these two are close friends.

Stella raises her hands, wiping her forehead. "You're so sweet, Tiffany. I really don't know what I'd do without you girls."

Madison smiles at Stella, and I can sense her genuine care for the woman. "Okay, y'all go on and I'll handle cleanup. Stella, you've had a lot to deal with tonight. Get on home and get your feet up."

"All right, let's go, Big Momma," Tiffany says to Stella before moving over to grab Carl under his left arm.

"Okay, don't forget to set the alarm and lock up," Stella reminds Madison, then she looks our way. "We're closed, boys. Like the man said, you don't have to go home, but you can't stay here."

I toss back the last of my drink and look at Madison, waiting for her to say something. It's like a contest of wills, who will speak first. Finally, she breaks, not looking happy about it. "Have a good night, gentlemen."

"You too, Maddie," I reply, her name rolling off my tongue. I give her a small smile, hoping she'll see the apology on my face.

Madison gives me a soft look, and I think for a moment that she's going to ask me to stay, but she waves goodbye instead. I go outside with Robbie, who looks like he's got energy to burn, as usual. "It's not too late to hit up some of the bars by the university," he says. "You know those girls don't start class until noon, so they're up late."

"And you've got work at nine," I remind him. "Maybe another night."

Robbie and I are just about to get in the back of an Uber when I see Stella and Tiffany come stumbling out of the bar, Carl's feet dragging heavily on the blacktop between them. They pile into an older red car, Tiffany driving, Stella riding shotgun, and Carl laid out across the back seat.

A thought hits me, and I give Robbie a tap on the shoulder. "See you tomorrow."

"Huh? What the fuck are you doing?" Robbie asks.

"You're going home. I'm going back inside."

Robbie blinks, stunned. "What the hell, man? It seems like I should be talking you out of this, but I'm too drunk to think about why it's a bad idea."

"No worries. Take the Uber, and I'll catch another later," I tell him, turning to head back toward the bar. "See you tomorrow . . . no later than ten."

CHAPTER 5

SCOTT

*M*y footsteps are determined as I walk back into the bar. My mind screams at me . . . *Stop! Don't do this. Just go home, jerk off, and forget about her.*

But I don't listen. I refuse to leave, wondering . . . *what if?*

The door swooshes open, almost silently, and I see Madison bent over one of the tables as she cleans it with a rag, her ass pushed out toward me. God damn, she's so fucking sexy.

Her skirt rides up as she reaches to the far side of the table, giving me a teasing glance at the cleft of her pussy, covered by black panties and fishnets. My cock jumps to full attention. I almost think she's teasing me on purpose, but I realize she hasn't heard me come in.

I'm tempted to perv out and watch the hypnotic sway of her ass, see how long it takes her to realize she has an audience. But I'm gentlemanly enough to not want to scare her, considering I'm already treading on thin ice with her. I clear my throat, startling her. She jumps, her shoulders pulling up to her ears as she lets out a little squeaking noise, and she jerks around in surprise.

Her eyes go wide with shock to see me standing there. "How did you . . ." she starts before drawing herself up. "The door should've been locked. You need to leave. We're closed."

"I know," I say, staying back to put her at ease. "I just didn't think it was a good idea for you to be here alone. I couldn't go . . ."

Despite my friendly tone, she moves over behind the bar. Smart girl. Even with a friendly face like mine, you can't assume shit about people nowadays. She needn't worry, though. I might be a bastard in the boardroom, but here, I just want to smooth things over with her. Get back to how we were at the start of the evening before everything went to hell in a handbasket.

I shouldn't care what some random bartender at a bar I've never been to, and probably won't return to, thinks of me. But there's something about Madison, and I do care. And it does make me nervous for her to be here alone. She's right, the door should've been locked, and anyone could've come in here. She's lucky it was me.

She gapes at my audacity. "Excuse me?"

I smile, approaching the bar and sitting down slowly, several stools away from where she's standing. "Look, do whatever it is you need to do . . ." I say, gesturing around the bar. "I'll just hang out and make sure you're safe, if that's okay. Please."

I think it's the 'please' that does it because after I plead my case, so simply and honestly, she lets out a disbelieving laugh but doesn't kick me out. "You don't quite strike me as the knight in shining armor type, and I'm sure as fuck not a damsel in distress. I'm fine."

I lean on the bar, keeping my distance and letting her set the pace. "You are fine. And I'm sure you've done this a hundred times before, but it'll help me sleep better if I know you closed up with no more problems tonight."

Madison scowls at me but leans on the bar herself. "It was a weird night. Must be a full moon or something. Ahh-wooo." She smiles a little, laughing at her own poor imitation of a wolf howl, and I smile too because she still hasn't kicked me out.

"Good. It's settled then." I knock on the bar top once, like a judge closing session, and hope that will be enough to appease her because I can sense she still wants to argue.

Madison looks speechless for a moment, then laughs, picking up a cloth from the bar and sliding it my direction. "If you're going to stay here under the guise of 'keeping me safe', at least make yourself useful."

Cleaning might not be my strong suit. In fact, I'm pretty sure I have never wiped down a dirty table in my life. We have staff for that. But if that's what it takes to stay with Madison, I'm game. And the fact that she's giving in so easily makes me think she actually wants my company too. "Of course, I'm happy to help. With anything you need." I let the double entendre of my words add gravel to my voice, and I see the hitch of Madison's breath. She's teasing, keeping things light and being cautious, but she's not unaffected by me. Thank fuck.

"I don't need your help with anything," she's quick to respond, but she's wiping the surface of the bar with focused concentration. "But I don't want to be here all night either, so get started with the tables by the window and work your way around the floor." She motions at the mish-mash of tables and booths around the room as if she's my boss.

I hold my tongue but smirk as I grab the towel and start wiping the tables down as she instructed. As we work, Madison looks over. "What happened to your friend? Should I expect him to waltz in the door any minute too?"

"No, I locked the door. Can't be too careful, you know. Any old riffraff could come in," I say, winking at her. "But I sent Robbie home in an Uber. I'll grab another one when we're done."

Madison pauses, then keeps cleaning. "What a knightly thing to do."

I laugh, shaking my head. "That's all you. I never said I was a knight. But if I were, I'd be your knight. Not his."

Madison lowers her head, but I don't miss the blush of pink that rushes across her cheeks. Fuck, how does she do it? She's so sexy in every mood. I was just as rock hard when she was smiling and sweet as I was when she was yelling and raging. And the blushing bashfulness is a temptation all its own. It's an odd realization, and it makes me want to test my response to her every whim. Or maybe test her responses to me.

"So, about my getting pissed off . . ." she starts.

"Yes?" I ask, encouraging her to continue.

"You do realize that I have a reputation to maintain, right? This is my job, my bar, my customers when I'm on shift. And I can't get white-knighted or they'll never respect me. I can handle whatever needs to be done."

I sigh, knowing she's right and that maybe I overstepped more than I'd like to admit. "I understand. I don't like it, but I do understand. And while you most definitely can handle it, you shouldn't have to."

She laughs, a full belly riot. "You know, for a complete stranger, you sure do have a lot of opinions on what I should be doing with my life."

I grin at her. "What can I say? I've always been intrigued by beautiful creatures . . . and you certainly are beautiful."

She smirks at me. "Ohh, and you were doing so well. But now the cheesy one-liners are coming out. How many times have you used that one? Ten? Twenty? You do remember that I'm a bartender and hear basically every line in the book and then some."

I shrug. "Might be a line, but it doesn't make it any less true. You are beautiful," I say honestly.

Madison blinks, then nods. "Thank you. And thanks for earlier too. He did deserve it."

Her admission feels like the best victory I've gotten in a long time. I knew she was glad I'd helped, even if she didn't want to admit it. "You're welcome. You're a tough girl, but you deserve better than that."

Madison avoids my eyes, looking around the room and checking my work. I follow her eyes, admitting, "Damn, I didn't realize we were moving so fast. I should've slowed down." I tease her, giving her an obvious wink.

"So . . ." she says as she uses the big broom to sweep up one side of the floor while I mop the other. "Guess I should tell you, I figured out who you are. You're beyond alphabet soup."

"Oh, really?" I ask, maneuvering around a table leg.

Madison pauses, leaning on the broom. "Why are you doing this?" She tilts her chin up, gesturing toward my swishing mop.

I shrug, hoping to avoid the question but deciding honesty might be the better course of action. "You told me to help if I wanted to stay, so I'm helping." The implication that I want to stay with her, and what that could mean, hangs heavily between us.

She smiles, and I can see that she's pleased with my answer.

"How long have you been working here?" I ask.

"A few years now," she answers vaguely. "Came to the city, needed a job, and Stella was hiring. Things have worked out well. Okay, get this half, then we'll get the glasses from the dishwasher."

"Okay," I agree, a little surprised at how bossy Madison can be. "And what brought you to the city?"

"Careful with the water," she says, cutting me off. I set the bucket down, and she comes over, sighing. "This is hardwood floor, not tile."

She's close, looking up at me after cleaning up my spilled mop water. From this angle, I can practically see down her shirt, and I smile, taking in her eyes and her cleavage at the same time.

She stares at me like she wants to say something but isn't quite sure how. Her chest is heaving and her eyes are darkening, the pupils so big I could get lost in them. "You really are a Danger."

"Scott Danger. Danger is my . . . family name."

Madison chuckles at the joke I've been doing since Austin Powers was still quotable. "I'm gonna be honest. I thought you were nothing but trouble when I first laid eyes on you. And that was before you went all alpha-male on my customer."

"That might not be far from the truth," I reply, stepping a little closer. We're close enough now that I can feel the warmth radiating from Madison's body, and I can see her breathing quicken, even as she raises an eyebrow.

"Oh?"

I reach out, letting my instincts take over. She doesn't resist when I grab her hip, pulling her against me, her breasts pressing heavily against my body and my cock pulsing in my slacks. "But I think you might be more trouble than I am. Look what you're doing to me."

I mean that she's had me cleaning the bar, but the hitch in her breathing says she took it another way.

I growl lightly, pressing my body closer against hers until I feel my cock touch her belly. "*Feel* what you're doing to me."

She gasps as she realizes what the warm, heavy bulge pressing against her stomach is. Her open mouth is tempting. I want to kiss her, make her gasp again and swallow her breath. I start to lower my mouth toward hers, but she pushes against my chest lightly. "I think . . . I think you should go. I've got to close up," she protests weakly.

Her eyes betray the lie coming out of her pink lips, and her hands are tightening on my chest, no longer pushing me away but pulling me closer.

"Are you sure about that?" I rasp.

Madison doesn't reply, her breathing almost ragged, but whether she knows it or not, she presses more of her body against me, her eyes searching my face for something.

I reach up, brushing a lock of hair out of her face. "Let me show you what you deserve . . . at least for tonight. Let me treat you right." I murmur, gazing into her whiskey eyes, which are sparking with need.

She bites her lip, and I can see the battle waging between her body and her brain. She wants this, wants me . . . but she isn't sure.

I don't rush her, letting her decide for herself, but while I wait for her to make the call, I run my fingers up and down her back, caressing every inch. "Fuck, you feel good."

Her lips part and a soft sigh escapes her lips as I trace up to the back of her neck. "Scott."

I hear the need in her voice, her decision made. I lower my mouth to hers, and the first touch is just as electric as I imagined it would be. She gasps, and I press the advantage, sliding my tongue to meet hers as we start to move. We bump into the brass rail at the bar and grind against each other, her fingers grabbing handfuls of my shirt then my hair.

"Oh, fuck," Madison moans as I bring my right hand up to cup her breast, pressing into me. "You're going to get me in so much trouble."

"No trouble . . . just Danger," I tease, kissing down her neck. My knee presses between Madison's legs, her thighs parting until her pussy is pushed against my thigh. I lift my leg, grinding against her as she shifts her hips, searching for more. "Damn, girl . . . that's it. It's not my cock, but ride me."

Madison whimpers, reaching down and clutching my ass for leverage. "Don't stop . . . oh, my God . . ." she begs as her body takes over. The soft plea strikes me to my core, and I push harder, the roll of her hips in time with her whimpers. "Yes, yes, yes."

"That's it, come for me," I demand, my cock pulsing as I grind against her. I haven't dry humped in years, not since high school, probably, and even then, it wasn't remotely this hot.

Her breathy moans, her using me to get off, the soft weight of

LAUREN LANDISH

her breast in my hand, the warmth of her skin, the clenches of her thighs around mine . . . I'm about to come in my slacks like a fucking teenager. I force myself off the brink, wanting to watch her as she edges closer to her orgasm.

Madison throws her head back, her nails digging into my arms to hold me in place as she cries out, "Oh, fuck! Yes!" Her hips buck, and I can feel the pulses of her orgasm against my leg, the heat from her pussy burning through the fabric of her panties and my slacks.

She trembles, coming off the high, and pushes me back. I'm stunned for a second, but she spins in place and bends over one of the bar's padded leather stools. She looks back at me over her shoulder. "Scott . . . fuck me. Please."

I don't have to be told twice. My eyes are fixed on her denim-covered ass, and I remember my earlier fantasy to fuck her in this outfit, her fishnets ripped open at the crotch. A groan escapes, rumbling from deep in my throat, and I have to palm my cock to keep from spilling right then.

Knowing this is going to be fast and hard, and hoping she can handle that, I rip my shirt open. I hear a button pop and maybe even a seam let go, but all I can think about is giving this beautiful woman the powerful fuck she deserves. Never in my life have I wanted something—no, *someone*—so badly.

As I drop my shirt, I rub my hands down my abs, putting on a bit of a show for her. But I'm shocked at her reaction. Instead of a look of lusty need, she goes pale like she's seen a ghost.

"Scorpion," she whispers, staring at the tattoo on my chest.

I chuckle, looking down at the result of a drunken night out. "Yeah? I got it when I was in college."

"Why?" she asks, still frozen in place.

"I thought it fitting to put a scorpion since it's my Zodiac," I tell her, not mentioning that in my wasted stupor, it had seemed logical to brand myself with a symbol of the man I

58

wanted to be . . . strong, intimidating, the threat you don't see coming. In the sober light of day, I realized it probably had something to do with being the underestimated youngest in my family and wanting to sting back for all the years of pain. But that's all way too deep right now, so I keep it simple. "I'm a Scorpio. Born October 31st, actually, a Halloween baby."

Instead of saying anything, Madison stands up, pulling her skirt back into place and adjusting her shirt, putting herself back together. Suddenly, she's not begging to be fucked, but scared, frightened for some reason. "Get out."

"What?" I ask, stunned. I'm literally about to nut on myself here, and she's telling me to leave. "Why? What's wrong?"

She shakes her head, tears in her eyes. "I made a mistake. We shouldn't have done that. I shouldn't have let you stay. Please leave."

I stiffen, seeing that she's not joking, and feel a stab to my gut, or maybe that's my heart? I know I just met her, and I'm a pretty fucking confident guy, but taking my shirt off and having her freak out isn't exactly doing good things for my ego. "If that's what you want?"

Her eyes are locked on my tattoo, so I grab my shirt and slip it back on, trying to button it. As the tattoo disappears from sight, she looks away. "It is. I'm sorry, Scott."

"Can I at least stay until you close up and leave? We don't have to do anything. I'll just wait and make sure you're okay," I promise, not wanting to give up so easily.

"No, I can handle myself," she whispers, resolute. "Thank you."

She offers a weak smile but is obviously still scared for some reason. Scared of . . . me? Of my tattoo? Of scorpions?

Every nerve in my body is screaming at me to challenge her. Demand why she's changing her mood on a dime. But I've taken too many liberties already, and I don't want to push my luck.

"I guess I'll see you around sometime," I finally say. Reaching into my back pocket, I find my wallet and retrieve a business card. Seeing a pen, I scribble down my number and leave it on the bar. "You have my number if you want it. Just call. If it means anything . . . I do want to see you again." I begin to turn away but then add, "I'll have the Uber driver wait outside to make sure you close up and leave safely before I go."

She doesn't answer, and the knife in my gut twists again.

As I walk out the door, I'm shaken. I'm mad at myself for getting into that situation, disappointed that it didn't end the way I thought it would, and hurt that Madison could just dismiss me without explanation.

That's what really gets me the most, I think. If she'd just explained, maybe I could've talked her through whatever spooked her? But this is one of those times where I may never know what bothered her so much.

"And I hate not knowing," I mutter as I reach for my phone to call an Uber.

CHAPTER 6

MADISON

"*A* scorpion tattoo?" Tiff asks from her perch on my bed, her voice on edge. She's been following me around our postage-stamp sized apartment ever since I popped out to search for coffee. She took one look at my fucked-up hair and disheveled clothes and squealed, thinking the best. And she was sorely disappointed when I told her that my appearance wasn't from a happy ending to my night.

With my schedule today, I had to rush it, grabbing four hours of sleep before dragging my spent ass out of bed for this morning. I know I must look like hell because she'd barely skimmed our horoscopes before beginning the inquisition of question after question.

"You for real?"

I nod, kicking my clothes across my tiny bedroom. It's not much, four walls and a ceiling, but the rent's still fucking ridiculous.

Unfortunately, the growth of Bane has meant lots of 'real estate investors' gouging people like Tiff and me on rent. Which is why we share this place and damn-near waltz to get around each other when we use the kitchen.

"Yes, an elaborate one with a stinger, claws, the whole nine yards," I say as I slip on my pink T-shirt for the day that says

Volunteer: May's Animal Rescue. Reaching up, I poke myself in my boob. "Right here on his chest."

My skin pricks as I remember his hard chest and washboard abs in front of me. I wanted him to take me so badly in that moment. I didn't care that I'd just met him. The way I felt in his arms felt so right. He was rough and gentle at the same time, not rushing and not forcing me but driving me wild with his lips and the feeling of his body pressed against mine.

But when I saw the tattoo, that voodoo woman's words pierced my arousal like a speeding bullet.

Your heart shall be his . . . then will come the sting . . . you will suffer . . . oh, girl, will you suffer . . . and then you shall burn.

A shiver courses down my spine at the memory. I know her mumbo-jumbo is a bunch of bullshit, but I couldn't help being chilled by the coincidence of meeting a man with a scorpion tattoo who also happened to be a Scorpio mere days after her dire prediction. And the way he made me feel, he damn-near could've had my heart if he'd asked. Hell, he could've had my soul.

But none of that matters now, and I shake my head once, almost violently. "I kicked him out as soon as I saw it."

Tiff makes a face, like she doesn't believe what she's hearing. "So let me get this straight . . . you haven't had any dick since you left that worthless sack of shit, and just as Mr. Sex-on-a-stick was about to make your year, you kicked him out of the bar because of a mad woman's prediction? Damn me and my stupid voodoo ideas!"

I hold in a groan as I turn away from the mirror and fix a scowl on Tiff. "Yes, I did *exactly* that. And who cares why? Why is that so hard to believe when I just met the guy?"

Tiffany gives me a look and drops her voice into a deadpan of Whoopie Goldberg from *Ghost*. "Molly, you in danger, girl!" she intones dramatically, shaking her head before continuing in her natural drawl, "of suffocating because your head is so far up your ass. Girl, get over yourself."

"Oh, shut up," I growl, yanking my hairbrush through my hair and wincing as I snag a tangle. "You'd have been scared shitless and would've done the same thing if you were in my shoes. Besides, Stella would've had my ass if she ever found out." I'm reaching for straws now, and even I can hear the weakness of my excuses.

Tiff shakes her head. "Wouldn't hear it from me. So unless you couldn't keep your big mouth shut, why not get a few strokes in yourself?"

"It doesn't matter now. And I did the right thing sending him on his way, although maybe I shouldn't have done it so . . . harshly," I reply, setting my hairbrush down and trying not to cringe at the memory of the confusion written on his face and how he'd waited in the Uber outside even after I'd been a bitch to him. When I walked out and saw him wave, I almost caved and invited him back in, thinking we could fuck and then part ways. But I held fast, sure I was doing the right thing. But now . . . I don't know.

I keep talking, trying to convince myself as much as Tiffany. "He was a total stranger. I should've kicked him out the second he came back in. And I don't have time to play what if. *What if I'd let him fuck me at work? What if the psychic was a loon? What if I overreacted?* The point is, I was frazzled by the prediction and it's over and done with now."

Tiff looks as if she wants to argue then smiles. "Okay. I suppose I should be happy. You're showing *some* progress, at least. Shit, getting an orgasm with a hot stranger, you're a step up from me, girl. I smell some T-R-O-U-B-L-E in your future, so getcha some."

"Not trouble, danger," I growl, wishing I wasn't so blabbermouthed. I'm usually only this way before my morning coffee, but today, I needed to share my whirling thoughts and Tiff caught me at a talkative time.

"Huh?"

"His name was Scott Danger," I explain. "You didn't recognize him?"

"No shit?" Tiffany asks, surprised. "You mean like the big ass building in the middle of the city, right?"

"Uh-huh."

Tiffany whistles. "With a name like that, maybe you were right to kick him out. It's gotta be a bad sign if his name is an actual warning label."

I ignore her joke and tug on my shorts. "Do you feel like volunteering today? Aunt May hasn't seen you in a while. She'd love to see you."

Tiff shakes her head, flopping back on my bed and grabbing my pillow in a tight hug. "Nope, nope, and nope. You know I love animals, but I can't take being around cats. I turn into a ball of snot and misery. Send Aunt May my love though. I'm gonna sit back and chill, psych myself up to go to work tonight. Driving home Limp Dick and Momma Stella was a nightmare."

Laughing, I leave my bedroom and grab an OJ and a small snack from the kitchen. I contemplate grabbing another cup of coffee but decide I might be better off spacing the caffeine rush out instead of gulping my daily allotment at once. I'll pump myself up with sugar on the twenty-minute drive to the animal shelter instead.

Crossing Bane is really weird, mainly because I can see how much the city's grown since I first got here. When Aunt May first opened up her place seven years ago, it was out in the boonies, on a tract of land inconveniently located at the end of a two-mile deserted dirt road.

Now, as Dolly sings to me about how it's all wrong but it's all right, I pass two Starbucks, a McDonald's, a Piggly Wiggly, three housing subdivisions, and an elementary school before pulling into May's shelter. Even if Bane has gotten fancier, the shelter still looks rundown. Its history as an outbuilding for the farm that used to take up this section of land is readily apparent.

Still, it's got spirit, and if May only makes ends meet by depending on volunteers like me . . . well, that's just some extra money she can spend on the precious fur babies.

I'm surprised, though, when I see a van and camera crew from a local TV station parked out front. The shelter normally gets zero attention, and we have to beg for donations. But May's out front now, talking excitedly to someone with a WISV-TV jacket on, but she looks up as I approach.

"Hey, Maddie, my darling niece!" May says, coming forward with her arms outstretched to give me a big hug. May's still got most of the figure that turned heads when she was a young woman, but her face is heavily lined. May used to be a heavy smoker before a heart scare caused her to stop when I was in high school, but the damage had been done. Still, her smile lights up her face, and I'm glad to see her, the sense of coming home filling me with warmth.

"Hey, Auntie, how're you doing?"

May hugs me as tight as she can, which isn't nearly as tight as I can take, but it still feels good. "So good to see you. Haven't heard from you in a good week. Maple and Syrup missed you," she says in her deep accent. I know it's where I got mine from. "You need to call me, girl!"

"I'm so sorry, Auntie. I've been so busy at work that I haven't had a time." I nod over at the camera crew and the guy in the jacket. "What's all this about?"

May turns, the excitement making her eyes sparkle. "Oh, that's just the morning wakeup news" she says with a false air of 'no big deal', even though I know she's bursting with happiness. "They came out to interview me for their Sunshine Story of the Week. It's a segment they run to highlight a local Good Samaritan and showcase their cause. I'm hoping to spread a little animal joy to the folks of Bane."

"Oh, my gosh, Aunt May, that's awesome!" I exclaim honestly as I give her a hug. "I can't think of a better person to be recognized for what she's doing to give back than you."

It's true. Aunt May is the type that'd give the clothes off her back if she saw someone who needed them. She always wants to help, especially with the most downtrodden in her mind, our dogs and cats.

It hasn't always been that way though. She's told me stories, warning tales, really, about her younger days. She'd been quite a party girl, and the wrong crowd was her crowd. She'd even been arrested once after a bar brawl broke out and the cops had cuffed everyone, country boys, bikers, and women alike, before sorting it all out at the precinct. She jokingly told me that was when she knew handcuffs weren't her kink and then laughed her ass off when I'd yelled 'TMI' and covered my ears.

But all her wicked ways changed when her younger sister, my mom, had shown up late one night with me in tow. Aunt May said she'd tried to get my mom to come in, tell her what was going on, but she refused. Instead, she handed me over, carefully wrapped in a baby blanket, and ran away to hop in a waiting car. That was the last time we'd ever seen or heard from my mom. But Aunt May changed that very night, suddenly responsible for someone other than herself.

She quit drinking, partying, and hanging out with the wrong folks and got a steady job to support me. Now, over two decades later, I have her to thank for the woman I am today.

So I'm truly happy for her as I smile warmly. "Congratulations, Auntie!"

"Thank you, honey," Aunt May says, blushing but obviously pleased with the attention for her beloved animals. Before she can say anything else, the TV station guy taps her on the shoulder, asking if she's ready, and May nods. "Sure, just one sec."

She turns to me and grins wide. "Okay, they want to start their filming inside. Can you go on in and ride herd on the other volunteers? I've got them washing down the pens right now."

"Sure, that's easy . . . and stinky, so better them than me," I joke, although I've cleaned the kennels more times than I can count. I head inside, finding two girls and a guy in back, hosing down the pens while half the dogs are outside. I barely have a chance to say hello before I hear familiar barks coming my way. I turn to see Maple and Syrup, two basset hounds May rescued and decided to keep as mascots, coming around the corner. They're waddling as fast as their little legs will go, excited to see me.

"Hey, babies!" I say as Maple, the slightly darker brown one, tries to jump up. I bend down and hug her, letting her give my face a bit of a tongue bath before Syrup gives me the same treatment. "Yes, yes, I love you too."

I hear the volunteers laughing as the two stout dogs almost knock me over from my kneeling position, trying to love on me the same way I'm loving on them.

In the background, I hear the camera crew come in and start filming. I try to keep Maple and Syrup with me so their barks don't interrupt. Rubbing their bellies and hearing their grunts of happiness make me smile. I really do wish I could do something like this full-time. These poor babies are just like me, abandoned and just needing a bit of love to shine. Thankfully, I've got Aunt May, and so do Maple and Syrup, but there are millions of animals not so fortunate. "If I could save you all, I would," I whisper into Syrup's doe brown eyes.

Maple thumps her tail, and I pet her side as Aunt May comes over. "How'd I do?"

"Sorry, was trying to keep Maple and Syrup occupied so they didn't disturb, but from the little I saw, you did amazing."

May nods and starts scratching Maple behind her ear. "They want me to maybe come in and do a live interview."

"Really?" I ask, giving her a smile. "That's great!"

Aunt May beams, looking around. "They'll probably only air a minute of it, but yeah, we could use the attention. Donations are starting to run thin, so it's coming at a good time. We'll get by, though. We always do, so don't worry. How's Tiff doing?"

"Crazy as ever," I reply, standing up and watching as Maple and Syrup wander off to find more folks willing to rub their bellies. "She told me to send you her love."

"Hmmph . . . she could've come in and said hi, you know."

I laugh and point across the room to the dozen or so cats May's currently taking care of. "No way you'll get Tiff in the door back here. Unless you want her high from all the Sudafed."

May grumbles. "And Stella? How's she doing?"

I shrug, keeping my hands busy by putting away the supplies cluttering a tabletop. "She's okay, but to be honest . . . I think she's going through . . . well, let's just say she's been complaining about being hot and sweating hard the past few weeks. Last night, she looked like she was taking a shower half the night."

May shakes her head. "Bless that woman's soul. I'm glad that time of life is past me. Lord, my flashes were so bad I thought I'd been dipped in gasoline and set on fire. And my hoo-hah itched like I had fire ants in there."

"Aunt May!" I gasp, shocked. "TMI!"

May shrugs, grinning. "Just being honest. Give Stella my regards when you see her."

"I will. So, where do you need me today?"

"We've got a new puppy I'd like you to work with. He's a bit rowdy, needs some TLC to calm down before he can socialize with the other critters or be eligible for adoption." Her voice trails off, and I can see her to-do list rolling through her head.

A little TLC. *Something I was lucky to have*, I think to myself.

May peers closer at me, seeing me lost in my thoughts. "Is everything all right with you? I know things are different now with you having a place with Tiff and all, but I worry about you sometimes."

"I'm fine," I say, shrugging. "Really."

"You're lying to me, girl. Or you're lying to yourself," May says, but her tone is kind. "You know, Dolly says not to live a lie, so tell me what's going on." I smile at the way she throws Dolly-isms and lyrics into regular conversation, knowing I'll get the reference.

May leads me to the door to the outside, where we find the other half of the dogs playing in the big open half-acre space that makes up the exercise area. Carefully avoiding the 'dog presents,' I find enough guts to talk. "Tiff has been hounding me . . . telling me I need to date, or at least find a guy to hang out with." I'm close to Aunt May and she's definitely cool, but I'm not crass enough to tell her that Tiff told me to get laid.

May chuckles, and I'm almost certain she caught my meaning, but she continues on as if we're talking about actual dating. "That fool girl, bless her heart. Honey, you find a man when you're good and ready, for whatever you're ready for."

I giggle at the look on May's face as she wiggles her eyebrows at me. "Can you believe she took me to a palm reader?"

"A palm reader?" May asks as the dogs bark and play in the background. "Let me guess, she told you that you'd meet Prince Charming and make whoopee pies?"

"I think that's what Tiff intended, but things definitely did not go according to plan." I give the quick version of what happened with Marie and her creepy prediction as May hangs on every word. "So we hightailed it out of there as Tiff gave her a piece of her mind."

"Good, so many charlatans out there. Don't believe a word of it."

I hug myself, shivering despite the warm weather, and look over at her. "I know . . . but Auntie, I met a guy last night."

"Ooh, did you now?" she asks, sounding interested. "Tell me."

I nod and tell her all about my night at the bar, Scott and his tattoo, and how I kicked him out. I leave out the part about him making me cream myself on his thigh. "I just can't believe that she said I would get stung by a scorpion, and then I met him."

May laughs. "Well, did he *sting* you?"

"Pardon me?" I reply, shocked.

"Did the guy sting you?" May asks, using her fingers to show me exactly what she means. "With the stinger all men got between their legs?"

I laugh. That's Aunt May, demure and crass all in the same conversation. "Of course not!"

"Then what she said was a bunch of this," she says, kicking a petrified dog turd with her boot. "Damn, gonna need those three out here after they're done inside."

"I don't know. It scared me," I admit. "You know I don't believe in that stuff. But I don't—"

"You like him."

I stop, turning to May to make sure I didn't just hear a hallucination. "What?"

May gives me a measuring look, and since she's not one to bull-shit, I brace myself as she speaks. "I can tell by the way you're talking and I can see it in your eyes. You were interested and that scares the bejesus outta you."

I want to argue, but it's the truth. Scott was interesting and challenging, not to mention hot as hell. And he worked my body like a master. I can only imagine what he could do with our clothes off. And though it pissed me off that he jumped in to save me, there's a part of me that appreciated the gentlemanly gesture. I can't believe that even after my freak-out, he waited to make sure I was safe. That was truly above and beyond, and it made me feel . . . worthwhile. I haven't felt that way in a long time from a man, and Scott had barely even met me, but he was respectful enough to take care of me like I was precious.

But by now, he's probably forgotten all about the bartender who ran hot and cold and left him with a serious case of blue balls. I'm embarrassed about how I acted and would rather avoid the situation than face it. "Well, it doesn't matter now. I'll probably never see him again. He probably thinks I'm crazy and have some serious mental issues. A rich guy like that doesn't need a bartender adding drama to his perfect life."

"We all got issues, honey," May says, putting an arm around my shoulders. "You, me . . . even our little buddies here got issues. But you know what makes a good life? Admitting those issues, finding ways to work around them with the people who can add something to your life, and giving them a chance. And giving yourself a chance too."

One of the new arrivals comes up and nuzzles against my leg for a scratch. I bend down to pet him, cooing, "Who's a good boy?"

May chuckles as the dog's tail wags so hard his butt wiggles. "And honey, you never know. Maybe the old coot was right and we're just interpreting what she said wrong. It don't have to be a bad thing . . . maybe she did mean 'stinging' the old-fashioned way." She winks and points at her nether regions again, a big grin on her face. "Girl, some things in life are just meant to be, and you gotta enjoy them while you can."

CHAPTER 7

SCOTT

Daily Horoscope, September 25th
Scorpio - Do not resist that which you desire. Deprivation only leads to
greater lust in the end.

FUCK ME . . . PLEASE!

Those words play over and over in my mind. Maddie's soft begging cries still ring in my ears. It's been days, and she's all I've been able to think about.

It's unsettling. I'm not one to let my mind wander aimlessly. I put my mental efforts to good use . . . focusing on work, strategies to increase my power, and ways to become the businessman I want to be. But Madison has managed to penetrate my armor, and my thoughts have been a never-ending loop of replaying what happened and fantasies about what *should* have happened. She's consuming me from the inside out, leaving me fascinated and curious . . . and hungry for more.

I've wanted to go back to the bar. Twice, I've even gotten as far as picking up my keys and heading to the door, only to stop myself. I forced myself back to my desk, trying to concentrate on work.

I'll admit that pride has been part of what has kept me from chasing Madison. I don't normally go out on a limb like that, handing out my personal cell number. Usually, I take women's numbers so that I'm the one in control. But I knew she wouldn't give it to me, so I veered from my norm and gave her mine.

And not only did she refuse me and kick me out, but she hasn't called me. It's infuriating.

Sitting in my office, I settle back into my leather-tufted chair and try to calm my raging thoughts. I turn my eyes and look out the floor-to-ceiling windows, taking in the city skyline.

The windows allow me to look out, day or night, without fighting the blinding sun. And from the exterior, the yellow metallic coating makes the whole tower sparkle like a tall, flaming sun . . . hinting at the danger and Dangers inside.

Still, it's not the best office in the building, but I'm determined to move up. Soon enough, I'll lay claim to Dad's office and then I'll finally have the penthouse office in the Danger Tower.

But now, there's something else I want to claim . . . Madison's sweet body. My brain immediately jumps back to its rolling loop, happy for the momentary permission to indulge. I think about the way she felt grinding against my thigh, the heavy softness of her breast in my hand, and her breathy sighs and moans echoing in my ears. My cock hardens in my slacks and I have to grip the armrests of my chair to stop from taking matters into my own hands. With a deep breath, I shudder, making an effort to gain control of my thoughts. It's harder than it should be.

Let it go, Scott, I tell myself. *She hasn't called. She's not interested.*

Besides, I can't afford any distractions right now. With this deal looming, I need to get my head on straight and make sure my dad and the board see the opportunity I've laid out as the best option, the *only* option. To do that, I can't waste time thinking about pussy. I've probably just built it up in my head anyway. I was half-gone on horniness, and the martinis didn't help. Because of my skewed memory, I've built her up to pedestal proportions because she didn't play according to my usual rules. Madison was a simple mistake, that's all it was.

A mistake that you would make again if given the chance.

Maybe, except for the way she looked at me when she saw my tattoo. The expression on her face in that instant haunts my dreams. I know my tattoo isn't that bad. It's pretty fucking awesome, actually. So what went wrong?

With a mental shake, I chastise myself. Whatever her issue was, it doesn't matter. Right now, I need to work. There's too much at stake, and I can't let Dad choose Chase once again. Chase's plan is smart, I'll give him that, but it's safe, predictable, and low-risk. Considering the irony of our family name and the odds Dad had to tackle to make the company what it is today, I'm surprised Chase is so close to getting the nod.

Maybe Dad is getting soft in his old age? Not that he's old, really, but venture capital can be a young man's game, needing quick and decisive action and a willingness to go big for the financial rewards. Maybe that's the angle I should play? Pander to Dad's desire to be the alpha big dog, setting the tone of the business, because that's what my plan offers.

That's good . . . potentially, even a great way to sell my idea.

Refocusing, I pull up my laptop screen. Ignoring the fresh coffee that my secretary, Delores, set out for me and the curl of steam rising from the ebony surface, I get down to business. First thing, check emails.

Many of them are from the executives, all lauding my deal in couched language, the code words there but the message clear. *Good job, but I won't stick my neck out to back you if the old man says boo.* Fucking cowards. Useful cowards, but cowards nonetheless.

I answer each one, thanking them for their time and highlighting the benefits of my plan. I add a hint of language suggesting that my plan is more befitting the goals of Danger Enterprises. It's

75

not explicit enough for my taste, but I need to play this carefully. After the last email, I open my master spreadsheet to go over the numbers once again, needing to find as many angles as possible to make the vote go my way.

My door opens suddenly, with no warning knock, but before I can yell at the intrusion, I see the look on Robbie's face. He's already talking fast as he falls into the chair across from me. "Dude, check it out. The office is abuzz with gossip right now, and you're holed up in here, clueless to the mother fucking tornado whizzing by."

I look up from my laptop with an arched eyebrow and glance over his shoulder through my open door to the cubicle room. I can't see much. I don't like being disturbed, and I think looking over people's shoulders doesn't help productivity . . . but it does look busier than normal.

"Apparently, Chase got your father to agree to a meet and greet with Lightspeed Venture to review the proposal. Lightspeed has wanted an influx of cash from Danger Enterprises before to help expedite their design-to-market timeline. They've requested meetings with your father several times with no luck, most likely because he didn't see them as a good investment option. But now, when Chase decides to deem their latest project worthy and does a whole proposal on investing in them in front of the board . . . magically, your dad's schedule opens up and he's willing to consider them? It's suspect, and I don't like it, not one bit." Robbie looks at me, measuring his next words. "Look, Scott, your brother is wily and smart, and I hear the brainchild behind Lightspeed is fucking brilliant. With the two of them in a room selling the profit margins and making techno babble sound like abracadabra, your dad's sign-off might be as good as done. And you know the board is going to lean wherever he throws his weight, even if it's not the right thing to do." Robbie shakes his head a bit.

I sit back in my chair, thinking out loud. "Chase is definitely up to something. He's no fool, so if he's backing Lightspeed, especially considering they've been turned down before, there's a reason. I need to know more about their latest tech, everything we can find, especially the stuff not in Chase's reports. Any bugs, delays, or issues that he might be underselling."

We're both quiet for a moment, all the ramblings sinking in as we analyze. "I feel like it's a big chess game, and Chase is already positioning his pieces and planning three steps ahead, while I'm the pawn sacrificed on the first play."

Robbie nods. "Yeah, and what about Liv? Do we know anything about her proposal at all? What was the company name?"

I cringe. "Never even heard of them. Something called. Honestly, after the presentations, I'm not too worried about her proposal even though it's really good. She's gutsy and willing to make some inroads into new areas of investment that no one else would consider for Danger Enterprises. But we both know Dad's not going to follow her lead even if it would make him bank. That's not how he works, how he manipulates us."

I let my eyes roll up, staring at the ceiling and focusing on all the different ways this Lightspeed meeting could play out. Robbie quiets, letting me work it out and knowing I need a minute of quiet without distractions.

Distraction. The piece of my brain where Madison is already residing jumps to life . . .

Fuck me, Scott!

Maddie's words and eyes flaring with passion flash in front of my eyes. I shake my head, willing the image to dislodge and let me think, but all I can think of is her creamy skin under my hand and her moans as she came against my thigh.

"Earth to Scotty . . . beam your ass back here with the rest of us," Robbie says, drawing my attention back to him. "What'd you come up with?"

"What?" I reply, my eyebrows knitting together.

Robbie rolls his eyes. "You said 'yes' while you were mentally off on a trip . . . thought that meant you came up with something."

I shrug. "Didn't realize I said anything. Was just thinking. Not about this, though," I say, touching the stack of papers on my desk that we both recognize as our team's proposal.

Robbie's eyes open wide, incredulous. "You're thinking, but not about this? What the hell, man? This could be catastrophic."

"I know," I growl at him. "I'm just distracted. But we've got this. I'll figure it out."

Robbie laughs. "Distracted? You? That's funny, man. You're like the most focused guy I know. Hyper-focused . . . to the point of it being a clinical condition. What's got you daydreaming if it's not business?"

I don't say a word, not willing to share how fucked up my brain is. First rule of business, don't show your hand . . . not even to friends. But Robbie is a friend, a good one who can read my poker face like a pro because he's had years of experience doing it.

"The girl! The fucking bartender!" he says gleefully.

"Shut the fuck up, man," I order, more his boss than his friend. But he ignores the warning tone.

"So, did you fuck her? I just assumed you'd gotten your pipes cleaned and it was back to business as usual. You do it on the bar or bent over one of the tables? Please tell me you didn't hit it on the floor. The cleanliness of that wood was sketchy," he says irreverently.

"You looking for details?" I ask, my voice harsh. At his grin, I relent. "Nothing happened. I helped her clean up the bar and made sure she left safely . . . alone."

As I say it, my fingers dig into my thighs under the desk, not letting Robbie see my frustration with how things had played out. I'd come so close to giving her what she wanted so badly. Fuck, who am I kidding? What *I* wanted. But she pushed me away over a tattoo? It still doesn't make a damn bit of sense. I'm tempted for a split second to spill the truth and get Robbie's take on it, but I refuse to let him see me as some pussy that's pining over a girl after a passing encounter, so I bite back the words.

"*Right*. Man, I've known you too long for you to run that line of lies by me without bullshit flags waving left and right," Robbie insists. "You expect me to believe that you, Scott Danger, cleaned tables in a bar and let her go without sealing the deal?"

"Believe whatever the fuck you want. It's the truth." My words come out cold and crueler than I intended. Robbie shifts in his seat at the change in my demeanor, suddenly uncomfortable. He's pushing against the line, one I don't want to cross.

He retreats, back to safer verbal territory. "Fine, whatever you say. But magic pussy aside, we do need to address this Light-speed situation head on. You got a plan? Because Chase sure as fuck does, probably one that's going to upstage both you and Liv. And you know Ice Queen has one to upstage both her brothers, just to spite you for having penises while she's stuck with a man-eating vagina." Robbie shudders, knowing my sister's repu-tation for being a cold-blooded killer when it comes to sex . . . leaving a puddle of besotted men in her wake after she's done with them. I don't want to know why or how. She's my sister, and most of the time, I don't even really like her, so I definitely don't need to know her sex life secrets.

I nod, knowing he's right. But this is uncharted territory, and one wrong turn could leave us adrift in these choppy waters. Or worse . . . crashed and stranded, left with no option but to follow Chase into the doldrums of his plan. "No shit, Sherlock. They're both just as manipulative as I am, so they're going to be on their A-game. The level of competition has never been this high. The stakes have never been this important. My brother's hold on the company is going to be solidified or not with this deal. This is my chance. My one chance."

Robbie nods. "What do you need from me?"

"I'm going to put in a few calls to some friends I have in Light-speed's arena . . . see what they've heard. I need you to be my eyes and ears. Listen to our team and have them listen to Chase and Liv's teams. Let me know anything that seems pertinent. And I need everyone brainstorming for a new angle, a new brick to put in the wall that proves our idea is the best."

Robbie rises from his seat, looking relieved that we're working the problem, even if it's early stages and we're easily the underdogs. "All right, man. I'll keep my ear to the ground and be in touch."

When he leaves, I let out a frustrated sigh. There's still so much tension coursing through my body that I feel like a giant wound-up spring. And it's only getting worse. I'd like to think that if I'd gotten my chance with Madison, she'd be a forgotten memory by now.

But deep down, I know that's a lie. There's a high chance I'd be even more enthralled. And that's fucking scary.

I turn back to my laptop and send off a quick email to a business friend of mine who knows a lot about Lightspeed before checking the 'dirt sheets' for business news. I'm in the middle of an article when a thumbnail of a video on the sidebar catches my eye. "Bane humanitarian recognized for rescuing animals." It's a local story, so I click to keep up with what's happening in town.

I click, and the video starts playing in my sidebar, so tiny I can barely see it, but something about the figures in it seem familiar. I blow up the video to full-screen and my heart catches in my throat.

An older woman with a happy smile on her face is being interviewed in the foreground, while in the back, three pink-shirted people work with a couple of dogs. But what captivates my attention is the girl in the pink shirt and cutoff shorts off to the side. I'd recognize that honey hair and figure anywhere. It's Madison. Almost as if I'd conjured her from my mind.

A stifled moan barely escapes my lips as I see her bend over to pick up a brown pup. It's just like that night at the bar. Not really, of course. She's more covered up in this video. But my body responds all the same, my cock so hard it's pressing against the restriction of my slacks.

Sweat starts to form under my collar as I watch her handle the small dog. Her every touch is soothing and loving, calmly caring for him. She seems so at peace and into what she's doing that I feel a bit guilty for being rock hard. But her passion for the animals is apparent, and as selfish as it may be, I want those touches for myself. Her attention, her hands, her time . . . mine.

The footage only goes on for a minute or so before an ad starts. I'm tempted to start the video over, watch her again and again. Instead, I push my chair away from desk and spin around, palming my throbbing cock in a useless bid for relief.

I've never jacked off in my office, but fuck, for the first time in my life, I'm sorely tempted. By her.

She needs to be the one getting me off, I think. *On her knees with her lips wrapped around my cock while she rubs her sweet little pussy. Fuck, I'd love to bend her over my desk right now.*

There's a swift rap on the door and it opens less than a second later. I almost jump guiltily, like I'd actually had my cock out to do a little 'self care.' Swiveling in my chair, I see it's my secretary, Delores. She's smart, knows more about business than a lot of MBAs I've met, and works like a fiend. She and I are a well-oiled machine most of the time, and she anticipates my needs before I even think them quite often. Right now, I just hope she can't read my mind.

"Mr. Danger."

I clear my throat, trying to look nonchalant. "Yes, Delores?"

She comes in and sets down a mug of light green liquid. "Your morning green tea. And Robert Danger wishes to see you."

Of course, I always try to have some green tea at ten fifteen instead of coffee. The caffeine buzz lasts longer, and I personally think the benefits to my breath are worth it. "Tell my father I'll be right there."

"Of course, sir. And . . . I cooled down your tea for you, so you can finish it quickly." She smiles and leaves, letting me have a moment of privacy to curse and prep myself for my father's summoning.

Of course he'd want to see me while I have a raging hard-on and a distracted mind. But I know this won't wait. I need to see what his thoughts are about the Lightspeed development, maybe even pump him for info about what Chase has up his sleeve.

Gulping my tea down like it's a shot, I wipe my lips on the napkin Delores included on the saucer. I grab my suit coat from the hook and slip it on. Buttoning it, I wait until my blood stops pounding.

This can't go on. I need to focus on work, but to do that, I need to deal with this fantasy I've built up about Madison. One way or another.

Fuck pride. I'm going back to that damn bar.

CHAPTER 8

MADISON

Daily Horoscope, September 25th
Libra
Be bold and brave. Confront your fears and reap the rewards.

"So, how were the puppies?" Tiff asks as I come in the door, tired but happy. She looks like she's had an easy day, stretched out on the couch in a pair of cotton short shorts and a tank top that would get her arrested if she left the house, considering the boobage she's flashing. "And May?"

"It was awesome! You missed out on a great day. The news was there to interview May," I say smugly, knowing Tiffany would love to have a quick fifteen minutes of fame on the nightly news. I nudge her feet out of the way and flop down on the other end of the couch.

Tiffany squeals. "What? The news? Why were they there?" And before I can answer, she kicks my thigh with her foot. "And why didn't you call me? I would've medicated to handle being around the cats if it meant being on TV."

I laugh because she's not kidding. She would've popped an allergy pill and held those snuggly kittens up to her face for kisses if they were filming it for the news. "Wasn't about the volunteers. It was about May. She got the *Sunshine Story of the*

Week for running the rescue. Although me and a few of the folks who were there are probably in the background as they interviewed May."

I say the last part as a dig, teasing Tiffany, and she huffs. "Ugh. Can't believe I missed that. But this is cause for celebration for May and comforting for me. Sounds like it's chocolate root beer float time. One scoop or two?" she says, swinging her legs off the couch and heading into the kitchen.

Root beer floats. Tiff's answer to everything that happens. Good news, you need a float. Bad news, you guessed it. Happy, sad, stressed . . . you get a float, and you get a float. She's like Oprah handing out her favorite things, if all her favorite things were creamy, bubbly goodness. "Two," I answer, knowing if I say one, she'll likely give me three. "And you'll never guess what May said."

"What?" Tiff asks. "That I never have to be 'volun-told' again? Oh, I mean 'volunteer', of course," she says, sarcasm dripping from every word. But she doesn't mean it. She really is happy to help when we need her, but it's not her pet cause like it is mine and May's.

I laugh, shaking my head. "Nope, actually, on that front, she said she'll see you next weekend. For some indoor work with the books . . . no kittens." Tiffany gives me two thumbs up then licks a running drip from her hand. "I told her about Scott and the whole prediction thing. She was kinda all over the place, telling me the voodoo lady was full of shit but then saying maybe she had a point and we'd just interpreted it wrong. But either way, she thinks I should give Scott a call. I was like, no fucking way! I mean, I didn't go into all the details," I say, lifting my eyebrows pointedly.

"You haven't with me either, you greedy bitch," Tiff mutters in amusement.

"But still . . . go out with a guy like Scott Danger? Besides the fact that we live in completely different worlds and this isn't some made-for-TV movie where the rich executive rescues the down-on-her-luck street urchin, there's the fact that he has a temper. He went all Hulk-smash alpha-male on that drunk guy. Isn't that what I'm supposed to be getting away from? I should just find a nice, sweet, sweater-vest type and fall in love with him." I sigh, not happy with that scenario either.

Tiff walks out of the kitchen with two big plastic cups filled to the brim with foamed up root beer and offers me one. "Maddie, you'd be bored to tears with Mister Rogers. That's not you, not your type, and that's okay, girl. You like powerful guys, and as long as Scott's using all that testosterone in your defense or to fuck you good and hard, it's fine." She takes a big breath, and I'm honestly scared about what she's about to say if she's prepping herself to say it.

She continues. "The lesson from your experience with Rich isn't to play it so safe that you're bored. The lesson is to choose your alpha guy more carefully. Granted, you just met Scott, but so far, so good. I'm with May on this one. Call him."

Shit. When both Tiff and May agree, they might be on to something. I'd hoped at least one of them would be on my side and agree that hiding like a scared little turtle, safe from danger and from Danger, was a good idea.

I sigh, taking a big suck of root beer float. Man, that's good. And just what I needed to fortify myself for another shift at the bar.

THANKFULLY, TIFFANY DRIVES TONIGHT, AND I CATCH a snooze in the passenger seat. I know that running with just a few hours of rest is a stupid idea, but rest is a luxury I can't afford. There simply aren't enough hours in the day to do the things I want to do, like work with the animals at May's, along with the things I *need* to do, like work the bar and get some money for rent. Tiffany jostles me awake as she puts the car in park, and we head inside to do our last-minute freshening up. It's a tradition for us, two minutes to look our best before facing the crowds.

"Hey, girls, what's shaking?" Stella asks when she sticks her head in the break room. Before we can answer, she continues, "Saw you on TV, Maddie. You looked good, and May did a great job talking up the shelter."

"Thanks! Hopefully, it'll get her some more donations," I reply, adjusting my lipstick. I look at Stella in the mirror, realizing her cheeks are a soft tawny color, not her usual pink flush. "Stella, you look better today. What's up with you?"

"Oh, I went to the doctor," Stella admits. "Got me on something to help with these damn sweats. Not too bad, just a single pill a day, and my doctor says that I'll be able to stop them in a little while, so I'm not on my first OPP."

"OPP?" Tiff asks, fluffing her hair. "You're down with OPP? There's a song about that," she says, laughing.

"Very funny. Not like that, you dirty girl. It means *old people pills*," Stella grumbles. "You know, the type that once you go on, you don't come off 'till you die? Old age doesn't start until you need a daily dose of something just to haul your ass outta bed in the morning, and I'm fighting with all I got to stay young." Stella preens a bit, running her hands over her ample curves, which are encased in a modestly slim dress that flounces down around her calves.

Stella leaves, and two minutes later, Tiff and I are behind her, stopping in the kitchen where Devin's already slinging some hashbrowns and what looks like one of his creations, 'pork chop fries.'

"See you're serving up heart attacks already."

Devin laughs, pulling the basket of thinly cut pork out of the fryer to drain. "Honey, you know I serve up heart attacks every time I walk down the street. I got better buns than Cinnabon."

"Yeah, well, you'd better cook better buns than them too," a large, countrified voice says from the screen door to the alley out back. The door opens, and Daryl, Stella's older son, comes in with a loading dolly stacked high with boxes of food. "So, where do you want them? Let me guess—in the back?"

That's Daryl, always making cracks and jokes. If it were with anyone else, they'd probably think it's in bad taste, but he and Devin just have this kind of jokester relationship. They both take it in stride.

"Same place as always. And be careful when you put the dry goods in the pantry. You wouldn't want the door to close on you."

"Why's that?" Daryl asks, his eyebrows pinching together in confusion. "It's not like it's the freezer."

"Nope . . . but you'd die before coming out of the closet," Devin cracks, making Tiff and me laugh. Daryl grumbles something under his breath and starts pushing the food toward the back.

"That was a good one. He didn't even see it coming!" I remark, and Devin shrugs.

"Probably a little distracted. When he was unloading the beer earlier, I heard him tying into Carl's ass real good about manning the fuck up," Devin confides. "So far tonight, Carl's been acting like he knows he's in the shit. Dunno how long it'll last, but I'll take what I can get, especially since Daryl can get onto Carl in a way none of us can."

Tiff and I head out to the front of the house, and I can see that Devin's right. Carl looks like he's actually working, and when I clock in, he doesn't have a single bitch or gripe as we swap out. The bar's even in decent shape. I'm checking the bottles when a familiar, sexy-as-sin voice pierces my concentration.

"A dry Snow Queen martini, dirty with two olives, please."

I turn around and it's him. He looks just as handsome as before, although he's dressed more casually this time. Instead of a 'straight from work' business look, he's wearing a short-sleeved button up. It probably still cost more than my last paycheck, but the checkered pattern feels less stuffy and formal. Even better, the short sleeves let me see his arms. God, those corded fore-arms. He must see me staring because I realize he's clenching his fists. Is he flexing for me or trying not to reach out and touch me? I find either idea enticing.

My mind flashes back as heat fills my stomach, remember-ing what it felt like as he held me close, the way his muscles felt under my fingers as I came, and the size of the bulge I felt pressed against my belly. I turned that down, for no better reason than some psychic bullshit and my own fears.

Well, fuck that.

Even though I've already decided where I'd like this evening to go, my first instinct is to run. Maybe see if he'd chase me. Instead, I hold steady, mixing his drink without a word and setting it on the table in front of him.

"It's on me this time. Seems I owe you an apology of sorts." He dips his head and takes a small sip of the drink, licking his lips. My eyes zero in on the movement, and I want to jump across the bar, kiss him, and taste the martini from his lips. "What are you doing here?"

"Figured it was time for us to see each other again . . . since you seem to have lost my card," Scott says with a little smirk. "Thought I'd offer a challenge."

"A challenge?" I ask, smirking at his cockiness. "You come into my bar, after what . . . after what happened last time, and you want to throw down a challenge?"

"Yep," Scott says, reaching into his pocket and peeling off two hundred-dollar bills. He lays them down side by side on the bar. "Drink for drink, your choice of liquor, although I'm partial to Cuervo Especial." He gestures to my left.

I glance over to Stella, who's sitting at the far end of the bar. She shrugs and gives me a grin. "Win or lose, I'm keeping the two hundred. Your call, honey."

He's bold, I'll give him that for damn sure. "All right, you're on.

Let me set us up." I grab a bowlful of limes, his preferred Cuervo Especial, and a stack of shot glasses before walking around the bar to a table. I line the glasses up, pouring the first shot as I sit down across from Scott.

It's a slow night, but the prospect of a drinking challenge, especially one with me, sends a buzz through the group and they crowd around the table. I can hear murmurs of people making bets, some on me and some on Scott. I know who the smart bet is. Me.

Scott smirks, listening to the mouthy crowd. "I have to ask—do you accept drinking challenges regularly? Some of them seem to be under the misguided notion that you're going to win."

"You might be twice my size . . . or more, but I work in a bar. I can hold my liquor better than you'd think," I brag. "You're going down."

Scott lifts one eyebrow, and I realize what I said a moment too late. "Perhaps those are the stakes? Considering you accepted without knowing what's at risk here?"

I give him a hard look. "I'm gonna throw you a bone, Danger. I win, favor of my choice. You win, favor of yours. Deal?"

He smiles widely, saying nothing as Tiffany blows on a silver whistle, quieting the crowd. "Okay, folks, same rules as usual. Every minute on the minute, you take a shot. You have one minute to drain the glass completely. Miss one, you lose. Ready?"

I lick the back of my hand, sprinkling a little salt on my skin. With a smirk, I tell Scott, "May the best woman win."

Tiffany blows the whistle again. "GO!"

I lick the salt, slam the shot, and bite into a lime. I hold the lime in my teeth, giving Scott a green smile before setting the sucked fruit on the table.

The crowd is watchful for a couple of rounds, no one expecting a drinking contest to end that quickly. As we match drink for drink, though, there's a buzz building in the assembled group.

"Goddamn, I hope someone called a taxi for these two," someone says, causing a few laughs.

"Yeah, right. Call an ambulance instead. Unless those torpedo tits are hollow, she's going to need her stomach pumped." There's another round of laughter at that.

Scott growls, turning around in his chair to stare a hole through the guy. "Shut your fucking mouth. Don't talk about her tits. Don't even *look* at her tits. Or I'll put you in the ground," he slurs.

I'm vaguely aware that now everyone is looking at my tits, and I sit up extra tall, pressing them out to look their best. Hah. Take that, bossy growly man. I look at Scott, in my drunken stupor wanting him to see my perky assets, but his attention is still on the jerk in the audience.

"Yeah, right. You couldn't even stand up on your own right now. You'd be the one in the ground," the douchebag replies.

"Forty-five seconds," Tiffany says, and Scott blinks slowly, realizing he's got a shot in front of him.

"But—" he gestures wildly at the mouthy guy.

"Forty seconds."

Growling, Scott tosses the shot back too fast, sputtering a little as it burns its way down. His eyes start watering, and his face turns pink as he tries to catch his breath. "Fuck . . . you put chili pepper in that fucking thing?"

"Nope, same bottle as before," Tiffany replies, refilling his glass. "Twenty seconds."

Scott swallows roughly. "Fine. Let's go."

At the minute call, Scott picks up his drink, but at the first sip, he starts coughing, his shot glass falling to the table to spill all over the surface. I drink my glass and slam it down on the table in victory.

There's a whoop of cheers, along with some grumbles as folks start to settle up their bets. The room is a bit spinny and that last shot is still hitting me, so I don't say anything as Stella brings us both a glass of ice water.

"Here, sip it slow," she says. She has to help Scott because he can't even hold the glass steady. "Good try, boy. But ain't nobody ever beat Maddie."

He squints at Stella. "Might've been nice to know that before we started."

She laughs. "Well, boy, you're the one who challenged her. I reckon it was your job to know what you were getting yourself into. Don't write checks your body ain't prepared to cash." Scott nods, and Stella must feel he's been suitably chastised because she continues. "I got two double-bacon fries coming for each of you, on the house. And a free lie-down in the back until you can hold vertical on your own."

Tiff helps me up, the cumulative effect of the multiple shots hitting me as I try to move. "Wait," I mutter, looking back at Scott, who's trying to stand on his own. "Didn't learn your lesson the first time, did you?"

"What?" he asks, staring at the table and digging his fingernails into the wooden surface for leverage to stand. He slowly makes his way to his feet, although if it's by sobriety or pure force of will, I can't honestly tell.

"Threatening the douchebag. I told you I can take care of myself." And with that, I blink my eyes over to the jerk who'd been this close to getting punched tonight. "You. Don't look at my tits, don't talk about my tits, don't even think about my tits. These tits are not for you." My declaration is met with good-natured laughter, probably because I just said tits like four times, and I've got said tits grabbed in my hands to reiterate my point. The jerk nods a sort of apology and moves back toward his seat.

I turn to Scott. "See? I got this."

Scott nods, then chuckles. "Would you believe me if I told you I'm not a total asshole? I meant it to be gentlemanly." 'Gentlemanly' takes him three tries to say, but the gesture is appreciated either way.

I laugh softly, the world swimming before me. Where are those fries? They sound like heaven right now. "Well then, I know my prize. You're taking me on a date, Gentleman Danger. Hey . . . I think that's a paradox."

Tiffany laughs, still helping me shuffle walk toward the back.

Scott trails behind, laughing. "Well, fuck. If I'd known that was your prize, I would've let you win a few shots ago and saved us the trouble and the hangover. All I wanted was to take you to dinner."

"Well, clear your schedule then. Because it's a date," I say loudly. My stomach lurches, and I look at Tiffany. "Hey, we need to hit the bathroom before I lie down. Tequila must go down, but tequila is coming back up."

She turns the other way, directing me to the bathroom. Vaguely, I hear Stella yell out behind me. "Carl, looks like you're working a double."

I giggle a bit. Serves him right. I'm always covering for him, so tonight, he can cover for me. Because I just won myself a date . . . with Danger.

CHAPTER 9

MADISON

Daily Horoscope, September 30th
Libra - New adventures can be a good thing.

"*O*kay, keep it calm, girl. Enjoy the adventure. It's just a date," I remind myself of Tiff's horoscope reading this morning, even if my heart clenches at the prospect of going on a first date for the first time in ages. I button my shorts. They're not my shortest ones, but they still show off about a mile and a half of my legs. I take a deep breath, composing the butterflies in my stomach.

It's been almost a week since Scott and I had our impromptu drinking contest. At first, I was worried he wouldn't even remember his drunken promise to take me out and I'd get stood up for our date after radio silence.

The reality has been anything but. After I sent him a text the next morning, telling him my skull felt like someone had taken a sledgehammer to my temples, Scott sent me a funny GIF from an old cartoon of just that. The seal had been broken, and since then, we've swapped several texts a day, but it hasn't helped my nervousness.

Looking at myself in the mirror, I think I've nailed the fun and flirty look, a chiffon tank that floats against my body, shorty shorts, and lace-up heeled sandals.

And when I pair my outfit with big curls and my full face of makeup, I feel comfortable. My usual 'mask' for the world provides just enough distance to put me at ease.

Heading into the living room, I twirl on a toe, spreading my arms out wide. "How do I look?" I ask Tiffany, who's sprawled out on the couch. "Do I look worthy of a Danger?"

Tiff looks up, her iPhone in one hand and a donut in the other, to eye me critically. "Girl, I don't care what his name is. He's gonna be eating out of the palm of your hand. Especially since he's already on the hunt," she says with a wink.

Tiffany originally thought that Scott had shown up at the bar for the drinking contest because I called him after May and she encouraged it. But she was doubly excited when I told her that he came in before I had a chance to call, teasing that he was solidly on my hook and all I had to do was reel him in nice and slow and hop on his dick. I faked being offended, but she and I both knew that was pretty much what tonight was.

Tiff bites into her donut, talking with her mouth full. "You ready for this? Need a refresher course in what goes where or anything?" She smirks at me, crumbs of glaze dropping from the corner of her mouth to her chest.

I roll my eyes. "No, I've got this. It hasn't been that long." At her narrowed eyes, I admit, "Okay, maybe it has been a while, but it's like riding a bicycle. You don't forget how."

She takes the last bite of her donut, licking her fingers for the last few crumbs. "You get everything all clean and fresh below? Shaved or trimmed is standard protocol these days. No bush allowed."

I laugh at her serious tone, like she's educating me on something I don't know. "Yeah, Tiff. Legs, pits, girly bits clean and smooth. Lotioned and perfumed and ready for whatever the night might bring. What are you planning?" I ask, looking at her sweats and messy bun and the box of donuts sitting on the table.

"A muck bang. Not mine, but online . . ."

"Do I want to know what a muck bang is?" I ask, confusion on my face. "Never mind. Knowing you, I know I don't."

Tiffany sits up, turning her screen toward me anyway. All I see is a guy sitting at a table looking like he's about to die. "It's a broadcast where people eat a ton of food and interact with their audience. This idiot just put down three bags of tortilla chips in four minutes."

"People actually watch that?" I ask, confused.

"Uh, yeah, it's a popular thing," Tiff says as if I'm that far behind the times. "It makes me feel better about polishing off my third donut. If I ever get tired of working at Stella's, I might do it. Get residuals from the videos online and everything."

"You're full of shit."

Tiff laughs. "Okay, maybe I am. Seriously, though, this dude eats all this stuff and is skinny as a rail. I'm so damn jealous. It's addicting to watch. Don't knock it until you try it. And it's hella better than watching pimple popping videos." Her body shudders at the disgusting thought, or maybe at the overload of sugar, I'm not sure which.

"No thanks, I'll pass. You can watch for the both of us."

"Okay, you're off the hook. For now. But I'm making you watch some with me one day," she says, pointing at me like she means business while grinning. "But back to the business of the night. Ooh, that sounds sordid." She fakes a vampire-ish accent, repeating, "Business . . . of the night . . . I vant to suck your caaahhck." I giggle and she goes back to her real voice. "I'm so excited for you, honey! You're finally doing it!"

Tiff leans over, wrapping her arms around me in a big hug. I lean in, a little relief filling me. "Thank you. I've gotta admit, I'm really nervous."

Tiffany laughs. "Don't be. That man wants you so damn bad. You're the one in control, honey!"

Yeah, I'm in control all right. Up until I see him face to face, then I'll melt into a puddle.

She's on a roll and continues. "And don't you ever forget it again. Just because Rich treated you like shit doesn't mean another man won't treasure you the way you deserve. Not saying Mr. Danger is Mr. Right, but don't start the date with doubts and baggage. Just enjoy the moment for what it is, whether that's crazy-hot sex or a lovely dinner. Or if you play your cards right, maybe both."

I realize that Tiff said Rich's name and I didn't even flinch. I really am getting better, stronger every day. It's about damn time. Enjoy the moment. It's been a long time since I've done that, and honestly, I'm not sure I really remember how. It seems like I lived in a world full of perpetual worry, stress, and anxiety for so long, and then when I left Rich, I stayed in that place emotionally. But recently, I have felt brighter, less stagnant, and ready to move on and be happy. It's a good feeling.

I smile at Tiff. "You're the best. I'm hoping for option three, playing my cards right for dinner and a hot night." Even saying it makes it feel real, possible . . . exciting.

There's a knock on the door, and Tiff jumps up, giving me a little happy dance wiggle. "Show time, babe. Do what feels right, and getcha some."

She looks through the peephole, then turns back to me, smiling goofily and fanning herself. "Girl, you'd better get some of that, or I'm gonna." I laugh, knowing she's solidly in the chicks-before-dicks camp with me. But when she opens the door, I can see her point. Scott looks fantastic, dark jeans hugging his thighs and a slim-fit T-shirt that shows off his biceps, topped with his All-American blond and blue-eyed goodness.

Tiffany adopts yet another accent, this one more appropriate for a James Bond movie. "Come on in, Mister Danger." She empha-sizes the *Mister* to mess with him.

"Ugh," Scott says with a chuckle. "My dad is Mr. Danger. Please, call me Scott. Tiffany, right? Where's—"

Scott's words stop as he comes further into the apartment and sees me. He looks even sexier than before somehow, his freshly shaven jaw dropping as he stares at me.

"I see you took my advice to heart," I finally say as Scott gathers his wits. "You look great."

"Yeah, well I wanted to show you that I can do as I'm told . . . on occasion," Scott says jokingly, sticking a hand in his pocket and making the veins on his biceps swell by the simple gesture. "Fig-ured the tux would be too much."

In this moment, I wouldn't care if he were wearing a tux because it doesn't matter. I feel like Cinderella standing in front of Prince Charming, but not the scene with the glam fairy godmother dress. I feel like I'm wearing rags, even if this is one of my best casual looks. Scott just wears everything with this confident ease that I would kill to have. But as he looks me over, slowly absorbing every detail from my pink-painted toes to my honey-blonde curls, I suddenly don't feel so schlumpy. I can see the effect I'm having on him . . . the way his eyes darken, the pace of his breathing picking up, and the tension thickening between us. I feel sexy, powerful. *Seen*. It's a heady combination.

"You look beautiful," he murmurs, his voice deeper than usual. "Just . . . beautiful."

"Thank you," I tell him, realizing a moment too late that my voice is breathy too.

I clear my throat, and Tiffany saves me, jumping into the conver-sation. "So, on that note, beautiful people, I'm out. Excuse me while I spend my evening buried in donuts and weird internet videos. Maddie, I won't wait up." She grabs her box of treats and her phone and disappears down the hall with a holler, "Have fun tonight. Don't do anything I wouldn't do!"

I keep my groan inside. Oh, my God. I swear I'm going to kill this girl.

But her antics seem to break the ice as we both chuckle. "Yeah, so that's Tiff, my roommate and co-worker. And this is our place."

Scott looks around the apartment, politely nodding. I feel embarrassed. I know he's probably got a closet bigger than my living room, and I bite my lip as I look around, trying to see it through his eyes. "Not what you're used to, I'm sure."

Scott looks back at me and shrugs. "I had a similar place in college. Small and cozy. This place suits you, though. It looks warm and inviting."

His words are sweet, more congenial than I'd expected from someone as privileged as he is, and I realize with a flinch that as much as I feared him judging me harshly, perhaps I'm doing the same thing to him. Wanting to let any preconceived notions go, I laugh good-naturedly. "I think your opinion of me might be a bit biased, but I like it."

He shrugs and I grab my purse. "Ready?"

Scott leads me down the stairs and outside. I blink, too shocked to even gasp as I see his car. It's . . . "What the fuck is that thing? It looks like it should be moonlighting in *Star Trek*."

Scott grins and leads me over. "It's a Lamborghini. Don't worry, I won't push the limits. I'm a safe driver. Promise." He winks.

Scott opens the door, his hand taking mine as he helps me inside. It's a nice gesture and reminds me that despite some of my misgivings, none of my old boyfriends ever held the door for me, whether it was our first date or our fiftieth. This is a sweet change of pace. "Thanks."

I take the few seconds to admire the interior as Scott closes the door and goes around to the driver side. It's just as Sci-Fi futuristic as the outer shell of the car.

With leather seats that feel buttery smooth, both firm but

somehow molded to my body, and a nearly silent interior, I feel like an idiot as I caress the dash in front of me.

Scott pushes a button, turning over the ignition. The engine settles into a sexy purr that rumbles through the entire vehicle. I'm dumbstruck, not only by the fact that Scott has a car like this and that I'm riding in it . . . but that he'd bring it to my neighborhood. People are probably watching out of their windows from every direction. I remind myself that I'm not focusing on what he has that I don't or how we live completely different lives. I'm enjoying the moment, taking the night as it comes.

"So, where are we going?" Scott asks as he pulls out and turns right, toward the main road. "You said casual."

"Right. You know where Ice Land is?"

"Ice Land?" he asks, shaking his head. "Nope. Where is it?"

"Head over to the Interstate, and then get off at Highway 42," I tell him, grinning. "You'll see it as soon as we get there."

Scott nods, and we cruise, his car seeming to float along the road as it handles like a dream. I feel even more like a princess, although maybe one who got dropped into a Fast & Furious movie instead of a horse-drawn carriage.

"Can I ask you something?" I comment as we reach the Interstate. Scott nods, not taking his eyes off the road as we hit the onramp. He barely taps the gas pedal from what I can see, but we're somehow zooming along in the fast lane. "Well, were you serious that you stayed in a place like mine in college? I just . . . can't picture that."

Scott nods, his eyes cutting over to me for a moment. "Despite my name and the expectations that go along with it, I didn't have everything handed to me. My father believes in fostering competition between the siblings, making us work for rewards. So each semester, one of us got their education paid for depending on who'd done best with grades, internships, letters of recommendation, and whatever other factors Dad wanted to consider. Let's just say I'm not the favorite child, so I learned how to survive on microwave ramen and canned chicken."

I grimace, not at the crappy food, but that a dad could treat his own kids so poorly. "Wow, that sounds . . . shitty. I'm sorry. I always wanted a brother or sister, but in my head, it was so we could be a team against the world, not battle each other for the last piece of cake."

Scott grins. "Oh, I didn't even tell you about the fights for the best cookies. Those were epic."

He says it jokingly, lightening the conversation, but it somehow reaffirms my thoughts about his dad's treatment of the Danger children.

We get to Ice Land, and as we park, Scott looks on approvingly. "I hope you know . . . I do know how to skate."

I chuckle and take his offered elbow. "I have a suspicion there are a lot of things you can do."

"How'd you find this place?" Scott asks as we approach. "It's pretty far from your apartment."

"After-school job in high school," I supply. "And here we are."

The first time for anyone in Ice Land is a little unique. Part ice arena, part restaurant, part . . . well, lots of different things. Ice Land was opened fifteen years ago by a former NHL referee who just loved the game. It's got its own character.

We sit down, and Scott looks around. "You find unique places to work."

"You're telling me. But then again, I don't work in the tallest building in town. So, which floor do they have you on? The top?"

Scott shakes his head, a tight smile on his face. "Not yet, but soon. Real soon."

There's obviously a story there, and I remember how stressed he was that first night at the bar. "So . . . how're things with work? You seemed caught up with something that first night."

Scott waves it away, seemingly not wanting to open up. "Oh, I was blowing off steam. Robbie had a few drinks, and I was talking out of my ass because I was frustrated about a deal not going through the way I expected. Well, I *was* frustrated until I got distracted by something much more interesting."

Scott looks me up and down, his gaze burning my skin everywhere it touches, and I can feel the flush rushing to spread across the expanse of my chest and up to my cheeks.

The attention feels good, making my brain scramble, and I forget the line of questions about his family and his work. The waitress comes over and we order dinner.

As she leaves, Scott refocuses on me. "So, that was a lot about my family, more than I'd usually share on a first date, for damn sure. How about you? Any juicy family secrets you want to spill?" he says teasingly.

But he has shared a lot, and I think he's telling the truth about not usually doing that . . . with anyone, much less on a first date. I feel like I need to give him a bit too, even the playing field. I take a deep breath. "Not too juicy, but I was raised by my aunt. My mom abandoned me when I was a baby, so Aunt May is the only mother I've ever known."

"Oh," Scott says, his voice dropping as he grabs my hand, holding it gently in his. He seems to be searching for the right words. "I'm sorry. I had no idea."

I smile, feeling the heartache behind his words. He really is sad for me. Before tonight, I probably would've thought he'd had a perfect life, with perfect parents and a perfect future. But even with just the little tidbits he's given me, I think maybe I'm the lucky one here. He has both parents and loads of money, both things I've never had, but I had Aunt May's unconditional love.

"It's okay," I say quietly. "I'm sure it's shaped me in some ways, but I got lucky."

"How's that?" he asks curiously.

"Well, I had Aunt May and she had me. Back when I was little, she wasn't on the best path, and she says I saved her from that lifestyle. She was a great role model for me, raised me up right and helped me become the woman I am today. She was the best stand-in mother I could've ever wished for, and now I have Stella. She's my boss, but she's like a second mother to me too. And of course I have Tiffany. . . she's my rock and always brightens my days. I might not have grown up with much, might not even have much now in terms of tangible things, but I do have three women who love me and have helped me through some shitty days. And that makes everything else less important somehow."

"You might be right. You do sound lucky. Everyone should have someone who loves them like that," Scott says, but the way he says it, I wonder if he's got anyone like that. I don't want to push anymore though. I can tell he's sensitive about his family situation, and we just dropped some pretty major bombs considering we've barely started our first date.

I decide to redirect us to safer ground, something almost every man can talk about forever. "Okay, stupid question," I say, grinning. "Your car . . . what's the deal?"

Scott laughs. "It's a limited edition and I loved it, so I bought it. I don't drive it too often, but it seemed warranted tonight."

I whistle. I don't know a lot about cars, but I know it's a big deal that he wanted to show off a bit for me. I would've been just as happy if he'd picked me up in an Uber, but I'll admit, there's something extra sexy about seeing him control all that car. "Well, it is gorgeous. Insurance must be a pain though."

Scott laughs. "Yeah, I guess." He gives me an odd look, and I'm wondering what he's about to say, thinking it'll be about his Lambo . . . because guys, cars, and hours of chatter are a sure thing. But he surprises me. "So, are you going to tell me? Why'd you freak out about my tattoo? I mean, things were going great, at least from my perspective, and you just flipped on a dime."

I blush furiously, surprised he went there, but I do need to explain, so I guess sooner is better than later. Although never would've been the best choice. I shake my head, looking skyward for strength to say this with a straight face. "You're not going to believe me."

Scott leans back, giving me a sardonic look. "Try me."

"Well, I had a pretty bad breakup a while back, and since then, I've been a bit gun-shy. So Tiff took me to a psychic . . ."

It doesn't take long to tell him the story about Marie's cryptic prediction, even with pauses to sip at the soda the waitress brings. Still, Scott listens intently through the whole story. "So, in the end, we left with Tiff yelling and me confused and maybe a little scared that she'd put a voodoo curse on us. And then just a few nights later, there you are . . . with a big ass scorpion on your chest."

I taper off, shrugging. "So yeah, it scared the shit out of me and I freaked. I'm sorry."

Scott nods his head, pursing his lips. "That's a helluva coincidence, so I can see why you'd freak. Hell, I'm a little weirded out myself hearing that story. Can I just promise not to burn you or something? Cold pizza and cereal from here on out. Deal?" he says with a smirk.

"You think I'm batshit crazy, don't you?" I say with a laugh. "And don't even pretend like you had plans to cook me dinner or breakfast." Nope, I didn't miss that little nugget of information. If he's thinking dinner and breakfast, I'm thinking we're gonna be up all night. Especially since he's not running after my explanation.

Scott sips his own soda, shaking his head. "I can't blame you, and I don't think you're crazy. I probably would've reacted crazily too. I think I'd be more worried if you actually believed in it. I mean, everyone's got little habits and quirks, even some full-out superstitions, but living your life by someone else's words . . . no, thank you. I'm in charge of my destiny, thank you very much, and I'll direct it with hard work and focused concentration."

I smile. "That sounds like you. Making fate your bitch and telling her what you want and how soon to make it happen."

Scott does a little snap of his fingers, looking at the air beside him. "Yes, Fate . . . make it snappy, please. I do hate to be kept waiting." His voice is full of entitlement and disdain, sounding nothing like his usual crisp self.

I giggle and he laughs with me. Fuck, I'm glad to address the elephant in the room, and that went way better than I'd ever hoped. Now, we can leave my freak-out in the past and see what happens with the rest of our night.

Our food comes, and as we're digging into our burgers, Dolly comes on over the speaker system. Sure, Whitney Houston may have made *I Will Always Love You* more famous, but I still know it as a Dolly song.

It makes me want to slow dance, and I sigh, looking out at the rink. "What is it?" Scott asks, setting his food down. "The song?"

I nod, chuckling. "I told you I used to work here, but before that, I was pretty much a rink kid. Aunt May would drop me off at the old ice arena downtown in the summer because she worked near there. I'd skate and hang out with my friends. I thought I was going to be a professional figure skater. At the time, I had no idea about the costs involved or that I was . . . well, let's face it, name one Olympic ice skater over five foot five or with bigger than B-cup boobs."

Scott pretends to think for a moment. "Nope, never been done. But you could've been the first."

"Yeah, right. Anyway, I did one competition, when I was eight, to this song. I didn't even have a proper costume, just a dance leotard and tights that Aunt May bedazzled for me. But I felt like a princess out there, everyone cheering for me as I skated my heart out. I even hit the one jump I had."

"Show me."

"What?" I ask, taken aback. "You mean on the ice? I haven't put on skates since I quit working here."

"Well, no time like the present. Besides, what have you got to lose?"

I've got a lot to lose. I feel like I'm just starting to find my footing again, with myself and maybe even with Scott. I know I've got some baggage, some damage, but literally falling on my ass sounds like it might be more than my fragile ego can take. Still, skating is one thing I know I'm good at, and if I don't take some calculated risks, I won't get any rewards. And something tells me I'd like Scott's rewards a lot. Finally, I nod, letting a smile sneak across my face.

"All right, I am the Queen of Blades. But if I'm going out there, you are too."

Scott grins. "Just give me ten minutes and I'll be the King," he says with a confidence that is just so sexy. "Remember, I said I knew how to skate? Hockey, not figure, but I guess I'll *figure* it out."

I groan at the bad pun but still grin. "Just don't bust your ass when you have to deal with a toe pick."

It takes us a few minutes to get our skates, and even though they're crap rentals, Scott doesn't seem to mind as I lead him out on the ice. Dolly is done by the time we step out, but the next song isn't too bad.

I start him off with basic strokes, teaching him the little I remember on how to ice dance. I guide his hands to my hips, and it feels good as he holds me with a sure, firm grip. He's confident in everything he does, even when he's not a hundred percent sure about it . . . but I'm starting to like that about him. It makes me feel more confident too, willing to go out on a limb and even fly a bit.

As we circle the ice, leaning this way and that and making basic strokes, I can feel myself starting to relax. The way Scott looks at me . . . I haven't felt a man look at me like this in a very long time, and it makes the butterflies in my belly come to life and start fluttering again.

We move closer, and I can feel the warmth from his body as he lowers his lips toward mine. I feel a bump at my back as we hit the wall, but my eyes are still locked on Scott, and I see the tilt of a smile on his lips as he takes in our new position, with me pinned against the wall by his body. He reaches for the wall beside me, caging me in his arms, but his skates swoosh out from underneath him and he's suddenly flailing for purchase. I grab his arm, helping him stabilize, and I realize we have an audience when I hear laughter as a teenager whizzes by and yells at him, "Smooth moves, buddy."

Scott laughs, inching over to stand beside me and holding onto the wall. "Guess I still need a few more lessons."

A new song starts, and Scott offers me his hand. "Let's try again."

The song's old. I remember this Wyclef song from way back when I worked here, but the remix of Stayin' Alive still gets people skating and having fun. We join in, just flowing around the rink, not doing anything too complex, just some swizzles and other basic moves until Scott pivots and starts skating backward, holding my hands. "See? Told you I can skate."

I watch as he shifts his hips left and right. It's not much, and not even that graceful, if I'm honest, but he might as well be performing a full-out Magic Mike show as far as I'm concerned. I'm mesmerized by the movement for a moment, and when I look up, Scott has a shit-eating look on his face. *Busted!* I push at his chest, gently so I don't knock him off balance. "Okay, so you can skate and you can wiggle your ass to move backward like a hockey player."

"And you like it," he growls, teasing me.

I raise my eyebrows, liking that tone almost as much as the way he moves. "Well, I'm not complaining!"

"Good," Scott says, deftly taking the curve with me.

Wyclef stops, and I hold my breath, hoping for another good song. Fate must be intervening because Fifth Harmony comes on. "Ooh, okay . . . last one."

"Well come on, one last dance and then we'll get some dessert," he says, taking my hand and leading me back around. This time, he takes charge, even as the then five-member group goes on about girl power. But it's okay. I'm having a great time, the two of us really dancing on the ice and moving our bodies.

As the song ends, we sit down and Scott grunts, taking off his skates and showing me toes that look like they've been squished. "Ouch. What happened?"

"Had to grab a pair two sizes too small," Scott says with a chuckle. "It's okay. I'll feel all ten of them in a few minutes."

He gets up, limping with me to the return counter. I reach over and take his hand. "Tell me, Mr. Danger—was it worth it?"

He grins. "For you? Of course, it was."

Scott motions toward the door. "Come on, I saw the desserts here. Didn't look fresh at all."

"Okay," I agree. We head out, and the car is still in the lot by some miracle I don't understand.

"Where to?"

He's giving me a chance to call it a date and go home. But going back to my apartment alone is the last thing I want to do right now. Reaching across the space between us, I put my hand over his.

"Show me more of you," I say. "I feel like you've seen me at work, came to my apartment, and I picked skating because I was comfortable with it. I want to see you too . . . the real you. Take me wherever that is, whatever feels right."

He pauses, looking out ahead. "You sure?"

My heart hammers in my chest. I don't know where he's going to take me, but somehow, I know exactly how it's going to end. And I don't know if I should be overflowing with excitement or fucking terrified.

Despite the emotions I feel bubbling inside, I flash a radiant smile. "Absolutely."

Scott grins and starts the car, and again I'm serenaded with the purr of the engine. This time, it turns me on.

"Buckle up."

CHAPTER 10

SCOTT

Daily Horoscope, September 30th
Scorpio - Opening yourself to the slings and arrows of others also opens you to new opportunities.

Turning down Bane Boulevard, I glance at Madison, who's looking around agog. "Ever been in this neighborhood before?"

She nods, then shakes her head. "Does catching the bus to go to the DMV count? I mean, I've ridden *through* here, but that's about it."

I nod and point ahead of us. Danger Tower dominates the downtown skyline. It's like a fortress rising up in the middle of the city. Sure, maybe by the time I retire, there'll be bigger buildings. Bane is growing by leaps and bounds, after all . . . or maybe I'll be the one to build something bigger and better than Danger Enterprises.

Either way, as we pull up, Madison's neck is twisted as she tries to crane to see the whole building. She looks to me as we enter the parking structure underneath. "All of this is Danger Enterprises?"

"No, just the top five floors," I reply. "We rent out the rest. Makes the company a tidy profit."

I lead Madison over to the executive elevator, which allows me to bypass normal night security with the swipe of an ID card and a PIN code. "I'll take you up to my floor first."

Our stomachs drop as we go up, the express elevator creating a type of whoosh effect. Madison squeals, "Whoo, oh my gosh!" as she stumbles a bit.

I reach out to steady her, my hand on her hip. I can feel the dip in her waist beneath my palm, and I'm tempted to squeeze her, pull her closer to me, but she's just getting her footing. I look down at her. "Should've warned you about that. I'm just used to it, I guess."

"Not sure I'd want to get used to that. It felt like a roller coaster." Madison laughs, and I'm delighted that when she's surrounded by all this fancy steel and chrome inside a building most folks would love a chance to visit, she's impressed with a fast elevator ride. Something so simple, and yet . . . new, with her by my side.

I watch her reactions closely, knowing she'll love what comes next. As we get higher, the back wall becomes transparent, giving a tinted view of the city before and below us. I see her eyes light up and her jaw drop as she gasps . . . but she's more beautiful than the view outside.

"Oh, my God, it's a glass elevator! I feel like Willy Wonka!"

"Yep, best views in the whole building from here," I admit. We're silent, watching Bane reveal itself as we climb into the sky, stopping three floors from the top. "Here we are."

I feel a familiar change as the doors open, and as I step out, I'm not just Scott Danger, guy on a date with a really sexy woman anymore. I'm also Scott Danger, Executive Vice President of Danger Enterprises. The weight of the change is a heavy mantle on my shoulders, but it feels right. Or at least it feels . . . normal.

"This is the bullpen," I say, referring to the short cubicle area that dominates the center of the room. "All of my junior analysts work here, arranged into sub-teams that allow them to talk over the cubicle walls if needed."

Madison nods as she looks around. "And the doors?"

"Offices for team leaders and senior executives. I've tried to place them close to their teams as best I can . . . and this is my office."

I open the oak doors to my office, and I can see Madison's breath catch, her hand coming to her mouth as she looks it all over. "My God. Are you serious?"

I smile, walking in comfortably and sitting behind the desk. Madison's steps are tentative as she comes in, her eyes roving around the room. I wonder what she thinks. Does she like the furniture, the view, me sitting in the middle of my world? "The windows are my favorite part. That chair over there is where I do my best thinking."

Madison moves to the armchair near the bank of windows and runs her hand along the soft leather. I'm jealous of the chair, wishing her touch was chasing along my skin. She sits in my chair, her smile wide and teasing. "How do I look, sir?"

I lean forward. "You look fucking perfect in my office and in my chair." I see the blush rush across her cheeks and can't help the whisper that escapes. "Beautiful."

I rise and move to sit in front of Madison on the big block that serves as a table. "You said to show you more of me. That's why I brought you here. This is me. Where I spend my days and nights, my time and energy, my everything. I saw your work. I wanted to show you mine."

Madison looks around the room once again, and I can see her assessment. I hope she doesn't find it lacking, the room or me. She takes my hand, her eyes meeting mine. "It's stunning, truly gorgeous, Scott."

"But?" I ask, because it's obvious that's going to be the next phrase out of her mouth. She's not impressed and it cuts my heart. It's never enough, not for my dad, and not even for Madison, apparently.

Madison winces, hearing the harshness of my leading question. "But . . . are you happy? It's pretty, of course, but it's just a building. An office. Are you happy here? That's what matters, Scott."

I can't answer that, not for her and not for myself. I grip her hand tighter, pulling her to her feet as I stand. "Come on. There's something else I want to show you."

Madison's looking a little unsure of herself as we take the elevator all the way to the top floor, and I can almost read her mind as she quietly watches the elevator come to a stop. She thinks this is a ploy to impress her and get in her pants. That I'm doing this for a quick one-night stand and have probably done this a million times before.

She'd never believe me if I told her otherwise, so I say nothing as the doors open. But I don't let go of her hand as I lead her out to my dad's floor of Danger Tower.

"Are we supposed to be up here, Scott?" Madison looks nervous, biting her lip as she looks around. The decor on this floor is more inline with my dad's taste . . . shiny and minimalist, much like the man. It feels cold, austere.

She looks cute, flustered, and wide-eyed. I'm tempted to take her right here, but this isn't the place. Not in some hallway.

"Come on, the boardroom's just ahead," I say, pulling her along with me.

I don't say anything as I open the doors to the boardroom. The room is striking in its own way, with white walls covered in hand-selected contemporary art and white leather chairs surrounding a dark wood and metal table.

"So, what happens here?"

"Not as much as you might think," I admit, looking around. "But this . . . this is sort of the altar of the company. Here's where final decisions are made, where you sink or swim. So far, I've swum better than I've sunk, but I'm going to stand at the other end of this table one day. This company is going to be mine. Despite what my father or brother says, I'll be the one who takes over and leads Danger Enterprises into the future."

Madison nods and places a hand on my shoulder. "Show me."

I look over and smile, nodding before going to the front of the table and spreading my hands, placing them on the edge as I look over the empty seats, imagining them filled with board members who are looking to me for that final nod . . . that I'm the king at the top of Danger Enterprises. It feels good, and I look up at Madison, who's giving me an odd expression. "How do I look?"

"Powerful," she says, coming around the table and approaching me. "Like you're at home. Like you have everything you want."

"I don't have *everything* I want," I reply as she gets closer, looking into her whiskey eyes with fierce intensity, feeling drunk on the fantasy of leading this empire and drunk on her looking at me like I can be that man.

Madison licks her lips and looks up at me. "What is it that you still want?"

"You," I growl, pulling her close. She doesn't resist as I sit her on the edge of the table in front of me, caging her in with my arms on either side. She's panting, and I can see the pulse in her neck quickening.

The first touch of her lips on mine is like an explosion going off. I'm ravenous, devouring her mouth as I taste her tongue, my hands roaming over her back to cup her ass and squeeze. Madison moans, adding fuel to my fire.

Kissing down her neck, I bury my face in the valley between her breasts, inhaling deeply and relishing in her intoxicating scent.

I'm lifting her top to find her bra when she pushes me away a little, gasping for breath. "Wait. We shouldn't do this here."

I groan, my cock so fucking hard it's pressing against my zipper "Why not?"

"This is the board room. What if someone found out?"

I shake my head, running my hand up and underneath Madison's top, underneath her bra and rubbing one stiff nipple, making her gasp. "No one is going to find out."

"Still . . ." She groans, objecting even as she arches her back to press her tit into my grasp more.

"Yeah . . . makes me want to do it even more. Fuck you right here on this table, and then every boring meeting I have to sit through, I'll be fantasizing about tonight. Thinking of how good you looked spread out for me, taking my cock right here on the boardroom table."

Before Madison can reply, my lips find her neck again, sucking and tasting her warm skin, and she presses against me, her need just as intense as mine. I pull her top off, then her bra before laying her back on the polished wood of the table. I kiss down lower, finding the soft cushion of her breast capped with a hard nipple that fits perfectly between my lips and teeth as I suck. "Fuck, yes, Scott . . . just like that."

I'm careful at first, walking that line of giving her enough to tantalize, but not so much that she shatters too soon. She's sensitive, and her every response tells me just how much she wants this.

It seems like I've wanted her forever. Since that first night, she's been in my mind, in my dreams, and in my fantasies. Time is oddly disproportionate to my need.

I kiss down Madison's body to the waistband of her shorts and pause, looking at the silkiness of her stomach and wanting to ravage her, to pound her mercilessly and unleash all my desire . . . but holding back, savoring the moment. I lay a line of sweet kisses along her belly, giving myself a moment to calm, my breath shuddering as I try to wrangle my fraying control.

"Scott."

I look up and see the desire flaring in her eyes as she lifts her hips. "You're vibrating. I can feel you holding back. Don't. Give me all of you. I can handle it. Please."

My intake of air hisses between us, the permission to not be a gentleman releasing a pressure in my mind I didn't know I had. I stand up, nearly tearing her shorts and panties down her legs and tossing them to the floor.

I collapse into the chair, my dad's chair, at the head of the table. There's something about taking that throne of power while I take control of Madison that's doing strange things to my mind.

Her bare pussy glistens with moisture right in front of me, and I lick my lips before kissing her inner thigh and dragging my tongue to the bottom of her pussy. In one long lick, I taste her honey from bottom to the hooded button of her clit, nibbling on it before licking lower.

"I need you on my mouth," I growl as I bury my tongue deep inside her walls, feasting on her juices and sucking hard on her sweet folds. Madison arches her back, her heeled sandals pressing kinkily into my back as I take the only dessert I've been interested in all night. I slide my hands under her hips, holding her immobile as I flutter my tongue until she's gasping, her breath coming in tortured hitches.

"Fuck, Scott . . . oh, fuck, I'm gonna—"

"Come," I tell her, flicking the tip of my tongue over her clit. Madison cries out, and her back arches even more as she starts coming, her thighs clamping around my ears as I suck hard on her button. Even as she's still pulsing, I stand up, unbuttoning my jeans and shoving them down my thighs along with my boxer briefs. I'm lining up with her sweet pussy when she stops me.

"Wait," Madison gasps, her hand pressing against my chest. "I want to see before you fuck me."

I take my shaft in my hand and squeeze as Madison lifts up to her elbows to look at my cock. "Is this what you want?" A drop of precum leaks from my tip and she moans.

"Can I taste?" she asks, her mouth open as if she's waiting for me to fuck her face.

I jack myself again, more gathering at the tip. "If you suck me, I won't be able to stop, and I want inside your pussy. It's all I've been dreaming of." I swipe my thumb across my head, coating it with my precum and then offering it to her. Madison's pink tongue swirls around my pad, getting every drop and sucking it the way she would my cock. I groan at the thought. "Madison . . ." There's a hint of warning in the gravel of my tone.

"Mmm, you already on the edge? Imagining me sucking you like this?" She nips at my thumb and I can't take any more.

I pull my thumb from her mouth, gathering her hair in my fist. "More. Now."

Madison agrees, spreading her legs wider for me. "Fuck me, Scott."

Her words are dirty, but they're soft. She'd said she didn't want me to hold back, but I can hear the unspoken plea for me to not hurt her. Not physically, but emotionally.

We stare into each other's eyes as I rub my cock through her folds, and I tease at her clit with my head, taking my time even though I want to bury myself inside her hard and fast. I press inside her slowly, groaning as her pussy takes me in.

The feeling of being accepted by Madison's body is like coming home, a tight squeeze offering comfort and joy. I press her thighs down, pinning her to the table with my hands as I pause, pulling back before stroking half of my cock in and out of her, both of us moaning as her pussy grips my aching shaft. "That's not all of you."

"Not yet. Patience," I tease her. "You're so fucking tight. Tell me I'm not hurting you."

Madison's head thrashes against the table. "Not hurting . . . need more."

I stroke my hips in and out, burying more and more of my cock deep inside her until I feel my thighs bump up against the lip of the table. I grab her hips, pulling her deeper onto my cock and making Madison grunt sexily. I growl, my eyes squinting because it feels so good. "Fuck!"

I pull back and start pounding Madison harder, watching her face for any sign of pain, but she wants more, reaching down and grabbing the edge of the table to pull herself onto my cock as I stroke in and out. I give her what she asked for. I give her everything.

Our hips slap together as I speed up, fucking her mercilessly as I abandon myself to my desires. Madison's eyes leave my face to look at my tattoo, but she's not scared. This time, she's fascinated, tracing the lines and shapes with soft fingers before digging her nails into my skin as I bottom out deep inside her.

"Look at me," I command, staring into her eyes as we climb higher. Her pussy clenches around me as she obeys, and I ride her hard, claiming her as my cock swells even more before exploding. The feeling pushes Madison over, and our cries mix into deep moans of satisfaction as our tongues swirl. Her pussy milks every drop from me before we freeze, and I hold myself inside her as long as I can.

"Amazing," Madison whispers when she can speak again, stroking my tattoo again. "It's not scary. It's . . . beautiful."

"What is?" I ask.

"Your sting," Madison says, smiling as my cock slips out and she gets off the table to slide her legs in her shorts and panties. "Didn't hurt at all. It felt so. Fucking. Good."

CHAPTER 11

SCOTT

Daily Horoscope, October 1ˢᵗ
Scorpio
'It's complicated' is a pessimist's way of admitting he is too weak for the
hard work the situation requires.

"AND SO, WITH THE NEW TARIFFS THE GOVERNMENT IS imposing on imports, there is a short-term profit opportunity for us."

I tune out the guy at the front of the boardroom, one of the higher-level execs who isn't a member of a 'family team.' He's useful from time to time, but there's a reason he's found himself stuck in short-term, low-risk projects.

I'm just about to scan the room to see what Chase and Olivia are thinking when my phone buzzes. Glancing around to make sure nobody's watching, I take it out, keeping it in my lap.

I can't believe what we did last night. Please tell me you're in a boring meeting right now, imagining me on the table like you said. ;)

Madison. I got her home about one in the morning before going back to my place and crashing for a few hours. Still, my lack of sleep hasn't hurt me. If anything, I feel energized and renewed. And yeah, sitting down at the board table today, I had a few hot flashbacks.

I tap out a response quickly. *You like that I'm getting hard in the middle of a meeting because of you, don't you?*

There's a delay in response, which makes me smirk as I look up and pretend to pay attention to the presentation going on up front.

I have a feeling she wants to play coy and act like she's the good girl and that I made her bad. But I know she loved every last fucking minute of it. I know I damn sure did. Even after getting home, I had to quickly stroke off, wishing she was there for round two to cure my aching balls.

Finally, her response comes back.

I love it. Loved last night too.

Underneath the table, my cock hardens and my balls ache for release. I hold back a groan, knowing I can't let a sound out. I have to delay this until after the meeting when I can take care of things in my office. Maybe I can call Madison and listen to her rub her sweet pussy for me while I jack off.

A few seconds later, I get another text. *I've never done something so bad before.*

Fuck. I almost type out a reply that I can show her bad, that I want to fuck her against those windows in my office, that I want to feel her soft lips wrapped around my cock while I sit at my desk, that I want to bend her over the bar at Stella's and claim her so no one will ever disrespect her again.

In a meeting. Can't talk.

Aww, I get with a frowny face. *Well, I'm off to the rescue.*

I should tell her to have a good time and put my phone away, but I can't help myself.

Are you wearing those shorts I saw you in on TV?

Yeah, why? Like them?

My cock hardens even more, and I know I have to end this quick.

Fuck, yes. I can't wait to see you tonight.

I shove the phone back into my pocket, hoping she doesn't text me back. The vibration might be enough to send me over the edge.

"So that's the deal," he says at the front of the room, pulling my attention back to the meeting. I catch Olivia giving me a glance, but her face reveals nothing, which I guess is the best I can hope for.

There's a polite buzz as the speaker sits down and Dad gets to his feet. "An interesting proposal. I'd like you to develop it more and send me the full package. Now, I have an announcement to make."

I cut my eyes over to Chase and Olivia, but they both look as clueless as I do, which worries me. At least when my father's stabbing only one of us in the back, I can predict what the fallout is going to be. Now, we're all just waiting for his decree.

"I've decided that, before the company moves forward with the final decision on the major deals that Chase, Olivia, and Scott presented last week," he says, making me bite my tongue for being announced third again, "I'm going to invite the heads of the various companies involved."

"How so, sir?" Julian, one of the other executive vice presidents who is basically my father's lapdog, asks. Dad gives him a small smile, a Milk Bone to his puppy.

"Glad you asked. I'm arranging a meet-and-greet dinner party downstairs in the ballroom. It'll facilitate our learning more about them and their learning more about us, although I'm sure they're thrilled to even be considered by Danger Enterprises. Kids . . . you can work with reps from your pet projects and each do a presentation of your plan once again. Let's see if anything new shakes out."

Dad looks pleased as punch at his idea, and I sneak another look at Chase and Olivia. To most folks, they probably look agreeable, but I can see the tension in Olivia's eyes as she holds back the eyeroll, and Chase's lips are almost lemon-pucker pursed. Guess his big move of coordinating a meeting between Lightspeed and Dad just blew up in his face. Now, we all get that opportunity. Way to level the playing field, Dad . . . while still controlling the plays like a dictator coach.

There's a general murmur, most of it going along with Julian's ass kissing. I hear lots of 'great idea, sir,' and 'fine plan, Robert,' and a 'that sounds like fun, sir.'

Meanwhile, one person down at the end of the table, Marv Reinhold, clears his throat. "Mr. Danger, while that sounds like fun . . . it might end up having the opposite effect."

Marv's words are like ice in the room, and Dad turns, his face going from pleasantly absorbing the adulation of his sycophants to cloudy. "Excuse me, Marv?"

"I said that it might not be the best way forward, sir," Marv says, his face going slightly pale as he realizes what he's just stepped into. "I'm just saying . . . if the shoe was on the other foot, and Danger Enterprises was being invited to a partnership with another company, and we found ourselves being wined and dined while our potential partner trotted out the other companies they're considering like a dog and pony show . . . well, we'd be grossly insulted and bail on the opportunity. I'd hate for that to happen with these proposals. These companies want the influx of our cash, and perhaps the competitive nature would make them want to win in the short term, but whomever we select will likely never trust us as a business partner in the long term. I'm afraid it's a bit too 'game show' for such a serious matter."

"Game show? You think this is a game, Marv?" Dad snarls, his face showing his fury. I've seen that look before. I've been on the receiving end of it multiple times, and you need to be made of titanium to withstand it. Marv is not titanium. He's not even stainless steel.

"Of course not, sir. That's what I'm saying." Marv starts backpedaling, but Dad cuts him off with an outstretched hand.

"I want to know these companies inside and out before investing millions in their little start-ups. This is happening, so get on board with the *game* plan," Dad tells the table of executives, cold menace in his words as he sneers 'game' with a pointed look at Marv. The whole room is silent as Dad looks around, his eyes a katana ready to behead whoever wants to go against him next.

Nobody, not even me, is willing to say anything, not even to correct him that none of these companies are exactly fly-by-night operations from some guy's basement. All three proposed companies are medium-sized empires poised to launch into something much bigger. With our funds, of course.

Dad nods. "Meeting adjourned. Kids, stay behind."

Marv looks pale but stands with as much dignity as he can muster and leaves with the rest of the board. When it's just the four of us, Dad looks us over. "You three will not disappoint me."

Hell of a pep talk. But that's him, deliver or bust.

"Of course, Father," Olivia says. "I'm sure the guests will enjoy a more festive gathering to present their potential to you and the board." Her tone is even, flattering. But it's a front. It always is with her, especially in her dealings with Dad. I wonder for a split second how she feels knowing that he always dismisses her, even when she does have a great idea. Consequence of having a vagina, according to Dad. A kernel of pity gnaws at my gut for her. She is brilliant and works her ass off to chase down new directions for Danger Enterprises, but she never gets any credit. My lips are this close to tilting up, offering her a brotherly smile, when I see her lean over to whisper to a smiling Chase.

Fuck it. Let Chase smirk and Olivia scheme.

Dad demands my attention from the sibling battle taking shape in my head. "Scott, what do you think?"

"I'm not worried. I know my proposal is good."

He raises an eyebrow, but I'm not bullshitting. I'm confident.

I can see Chase giving me an eye like he wants to needle me, but he stays silent.

Dad gives us both a look and smirks a little. He always has gotten off on Chase and me butting heads. "For appearance's sake, I also expect you all to have dates."

I blink, surprised as his announcement makes me realize . . . none of us have been involved in a relationship to speak of in a while. Sure, Chase plays the field, but I can't see him settling down anytime soon. Liv, who knows? You can never tell with her.

Chase grumbles, sighing. "Really?" If either Liv or I had questioned him, we'd be flayed open. But Dad just gives Chase a sharp look.

"Yes, really. Dates," Dad says, his raised eyebrow communicating that Chase has pushed enough. "Now back to work."

We leave, and I'm surprised when Olivia gets on the elevator with me, because she normally takes the stairs, claiming it's good for her calves. "Can we talk?"

"Sure, why?" I ask as the doors close.

"About the date. You mind if I borrow your friend, Robbie?"

I'm surprised and give her a look before bursting out laughing. "If I told you no, would that stop you?"

She sighs. "I'm not dating anyone, and if I ask someone from my team, it'll lead to issues of favoritism. And we all know how well that *doesn't* work. I'd rather not cause tension in my group."

"But you will in mine? How's it look that you're taking one of my team members, my best friend at that?"

Her face looks pained for a moment, and I flash back to my earlier thoughts about the stranglehold my dad has on her, different from the one he tightens on Chase and me, but no less uncomfortable. I acquiesce, giving her a nod. "Fine."

"Thanks," Olivia says as the doors open and she walks off. Always short, at least with me. Given that Dad has always pitted us against one another, I understand.

On the next elevator stop, I get off and head into my office, where Robbie is already waiting for me. "So, how'd it go?"

"Olivia's going to ask you to escort her to a work event," I tell him before filling him in on Dad's plan. "So I need you to start putting together a presentation. Start with the one I gave the board and polish it up to the point that every bit of it shines."

"Okay . . . and for Liv?"

"It's just business," I reply, unconcerned. "I don't think she'll try to seduce you over to her team, if that's what you're thinking."

He smirks, a light in his eyes. "Or maybe I'm hoping for a bit of seduction to her bedroom? See if I can melt the Ice Queen's cave with my hot sword?"

"That's my sister, asshole." I doubt Liv needs me to protect her. She can protect herself damn fine on her own. But she's my fucking sister, and I know what a perv Robbie can be. So no, just no.

His smile widens. "Speaking of girls, though. You owe me, man, after that whole honky-tonk night. Seriously, I've been working so hard that I've started to go down the porn rabbit hole." He gestures like he's jacking off, then wipes the imaginary sweat from his brow with a pained look.

I roll my eyes, laughing at Robbie's faux-desperation. "You don't need me. Do your thing."

"Hell no, man! Let's go out, make it rain like the old days," Robbie says, grinning.

I think about it but shake my head. "Sorry, I'm going home tonight."

Robbie snorts. "You lying sack of shit. You're going back to that bar, aren't you?"

"Fuck you. That place is a dive," I lie.

I'M SHOCKED WHEN I PULL IN AT STELLA'S, MY BODY driving there on autopilot even as my mind hadn't decided whether to go. The parking lot is packed, and when I get inside, I see it's just as crowded. Stella is at the register talking animatedly with a guy who legitimately has an honest-to-God mullet. Tiff is nearly being fondled by a dusty ass old man, and Carl is slumped over drunk at a table in the corner. It all seems familiar somehow.

The next instant, I see Madison, and all other thoughts flee my mind. She's sexy as always, setting down a Moscow Mule in front of a hipster-looking couple. Desire courses through me as I find an empty foot of wood at the bar and shoulder my way in.

Madison is at the other end of the bar, her back turned, giving me a great view of her ass . . . but also giving the other guys around me the same view. They're looking at her like a side of meat and it pisses me off.

She's mine. And she deserves better than this . . . these assholes. This place. This job. Madison said Stella has bent over backward to help her, but there's only so much Stella can do. And that's a hell of a lot less than I can.

I could give her more, so much more.

Wait. What the fuck am I thinking? She's not mine, and I'm not giving her the world on some fucking silver platter. I barely know her. Just one date, some texts, and an admittedly epic fuck.

126

But something inside me knows that's not true. Something about her is different. It's the way she challenges me, the way she asks me questions and the way she looked at me while I was standing at the head of the boardroom table. She wasn't impressed by the potential power I will have as the head of Danger Enterprises. She was only interested in the power I had over her. She doesn't give a rat's ass about my last name. She just likes me. And that feels . . . strange and exciting.

I saw something in her eyes that night, something that's inside me too.

And it's growing.

I keep thinking she needs me to save her from her hard life. But maybe it's the other way around. Maybe I need her to save me from a life filled with cold indifference. All my worries fade away when she smiles at me or when she's in my arms. I could get addicted to that feeling. Addicted to *her*. Fuck.

Madison plops a beer mug on the bar and turns. Her face lights up when she sees me, and something tight in my chest loosens. She walks my way, and I hold her gaze, not letting it go, even as I catch the head swivels from the guys as they watch her pass in my peripheral vision.

"Hey!" she greets me as she leans against the bar in front of me.

Needing to stake my claim, I lean across the bar, planting a greeting kiss on her lips as I wrap my hand around her neck. It's not as long as I'd like, but the taste of her settles my ire. "How's it going, baby?"

I can see in her eyes how exhausted she is, but whether it's from slinging drinks or from the way she's treated by her customers, I'm not sure. Hopefully, my being a possessive fucker helps settle that matter, at least.

She licks her lips, tasting me too, and I collect her heated flush like a prize. "Better now that you're there. How was work?"

Her country accent seems even thicker than before. But I love it.

"Not too bad. I'd say I've got as many wolves to deal with as you do." I say, giving her a wink.

"Yeah, but you get to wear a suit," Madison points out. "So, Snow Queen?"

"Nah . . . surprise me with something you think I'll like," I reply. I watch as she turns and picks a bottle of cognac off the top shelf. She adds a few more ingredients and then sets the drink in front of me with a flirty smile.

"Here you go. Something high-class and classic. A Remy Sidecar."

"Never had one, but if you suggest it, I'm sure I'll love it. Much like your other suggestions," I say, letting my voice drop low. Every guy around us thinks I'm talking about something sexual, not realizing Madison's suggestions equated to a sweet ice skating date, but I'm damn sure not going to explain. Fuckers shouldn't be eavesdropping anyway.

I take a sip and hum my enjoyment. Her lips part in a knowing smile. "You off tomorrow night? I'd like to take you out . . . my choice this time."

She bites her lip, testing my control and knowing it. "Nah, scheduled to work all evening."

Fuck that. I break her gaze, looking over to the register and yelling out, "Hey, Stella! Madison can't work tomorrow. I think she's coming down with something. Gonna have to get Carl to cover the bar."

Stella laughs and looks at Madison for her reaction. I hold my breath, waiting too. It's a power move, a rather public one, and if she shuts me down, it's gonna fucking hurt. Probably worse than the hangover I got from my last big move.

Madison schools her face as she looks at Stella and fake coughs. "Yeah . . . *cough-cough* . . . not feeling too well. Might have to take the night off tomorrow."

Stella laughs, and I release the breath I was holding. "Sure thing, honey. Carl can cover for you. Lord knows, you cover for his lazy ass enough. You two have fun. I mean, take good care of my girl, Suit. Make sure she's feeling better."

Fuck. Yes.

CHAPTER 12

MADISON

Daily Horoscope, October 2nd
Libra – Roses are fragile, requiring care to flourish, much like Libra's
spirit.

TIFF READS MY HOROSCOPE ALOUD AND I SCOWL. "I don't think there's a single thing about me that says dainty and rosy. Definitely not my cold, dark soul," I joke.

Tiffany looks at me. "You're probably right. You're more like a wildflower. A daisy that just pops up in the middle of the concrete jungle and says, 'Fuck you for saying I shouldn't be here. Look at my awesomeness!' and then makes wishes come true. And for real, girl . . . your soul is cold and dark like cake is bitter. Not. At. All." She snaps to emphasize the declaration.

I look at myself in the mirror, running my hands over the black satin dress I'm wearing, shocked at the girl looking back at me. The package came via courier this afternoon, along with a note from Scott asking me to wear it for our date.

"Uh . . . how do I look?" I ask, glancing back at Tiffany, who's decided to camp out on my bed while I change. It's becoming her favorite perch. "I feel like I'm playing dress-up."

"You might be, but damn if you don't play really well," Tiff says. "Fuck Julia Roberts. You have the whole *Pretty Woman* schtick down pat."

"So you're saying I dress like a hooker?" I ask saucily, earning a raspberry. I turn back, looking in the mirror, and take a deep breath. The fact is, I do look amazing in this dress. Somehow, Scott knew my size perfectly, and even the cups on the dress are close enough to the right size that I'm not falling out all over the place. "It's beautiful . . . but holy fuck, Tiff, how much do you think this thing cost?"

"More than your car," Tiff says as she takes a sip of tea and sets it down. "I Googled the label."

It's the only worry I've had about Scott. He's rich and along with that, powerful. And I am neither of those things, which scares me. I want to be independent, able to have my own opinions and thoughts, to run my own life. But he's just so . . . overwhelming. And I like it when he's bossy and assertive, taking charge and making big plays for me like I'm worth it. I'm not sure what that says about me, but I'm sure it's not flattering.

"Well, regardless, I need to strap these on," I finally say, putting on the heels that came with the dress. I stand up, turning to my right and left and smiling at my reflection.

There's a knock at our door, and Tiffany grins. "Lover boy is here. Hope your thong is ready."

I blush, and Tiffany gawks before laughing. "You really are wearing a thong, aren't you, you slut?" she teases.

"Hey!" I protest, but it's weak because I know that while the fancy dress is for whatever Scott has planned, I chose the lingerie underneath with *my* plans in mind.

Tiff gets up and goes to the door, peeping. "Fuck me!" she says in a whisper loud enough for Scott to hear through the thin door.

Tiffany gulps and steps back, opening the door. As soon as I see Scott, I see what she meant. His suit is perfect, complimenting my dress.

He looks dominant and sexy, a predator caged in gilded threads as he looks me up and down. I feel like prey, and I want to run . . . just so he'll chase me . . . catch me . . . *take* me. Shit. I'm in so much trouble, but I think I like it.

I shake my head, rattling those thoughts loose. He grins, and I know my dirty thoughts are written clearly on my face and he's read every word. "You look stunning, Madison. Shall we?" he says respectfully, even though my naughty thoughts are reflecting back in his eyes, making promises I hope to hold him to later. He offers his hand, and I feel a spark zing from his fingers through me when we touch.

He escorts me to his car, helping me in and then climbing in the driver's seat. "Where are we going?"

"Toast," he says, dropping the name of the best restaurant in town like it's IHOP. "We have reservations in forty-five minutes."

I don't really know what to say, my stomach feeling like it's tearing itself in half as we drive to the restaurant. Even the valet gives Scott's car a long look as we pull up, and going inside, I'm stunned again at all the finery. I feel . . . inadequate, even though I have my hair all done up, my makeup fixed just right, and this gorgeous dress swooshing as I walk. For a moment, in Scott's gaze, I'd felt like it all worked . . . looked right and real on me. But now, I'm just a girl playing dress-up again.

But Scott seems at home, strolling through the restaurant, radiating power and confidence. It's like a shield that protects me from the other patrons' looks because they focus on him, whether they want to be him or be *with* him. But it's his lack of care about what anyone else in the room thinks that's immensely attractive. He's unaffected. Hell, he might be unaware of the attention. Which just shows how much Scott was born to be in charge.

"May I take your wine order, sir?" a snooty-looking man with what sounds like a French accent but is probably from New Jersey asks after we're seated.

"We'll start off with the Casa Blanca Merlot, 1996," Scott says, and the man just gives a slow nod and scurries off.

"So I guess they don't serve fried chicken and biscuits here?"

He laughs, shaking his head. "Actually, they do have panko-crusted chicken, but I don't think it comes with biscuits." He winks playfully but then sobers. I can see him considering his words. "Madison, I want you to explore tonight. Pick something on the menu you've never had before . . . something that you you've wanted to try but never had the reason or opportunity to have."

"Okay. But . . . why?"

He gives me a little smile and looks down at his menu. "Because a little while ago, I let a friend drag me into some honky-tonk where I ordered a Snow Queen martini, something I'd never had before that night. And it changed things for me. Perhaps a change in flavors might be just as impactful for you."

His words warm my chest, and I look over the menu, pointedly ignoring the prices after I sneak a look at the wine list and see that the bottle he ordered simply says *Reserve . . . ask the manager*.

Still, as I take in the muted conversation at the tables around us, the quiet tinkles of sound from the piano in the background, and the soft candlelight, I realize that there is a charm to this life Scott is showing me. Nobody's leering at me, the music isn't so loud I can barely think . . . and the chair I'm sitting in feels softer than even my own couch.

"Ready?" Scott asks as the sommelier and another person, a girl in a simple black blouse and skirt who I guess is our waitress, approach. I nod, closing my menu. "Ladies first."

I order lamb, while Scott goes with something called a scotch fillet, which I see is a cut of beef. Apparently, both go well with our wine selection as the sommelier gives an agreeable nod. As they take their leave, Scott raises a glass to me. "A toast, in Toast, to new opportunities."

We clink glasses, and as I sip the amazing wine, I think . . . Scott obviously enjoys this lifestyle, and it is appealing. But it feels so foreign to anything I've ever experienced. I vaguely wonder if I'll make a fool of myself by using the wrong fork.

I finger the silverware delicately, and Scott interrupts my worries. "Tell me what you're thinking." It's not a question but an order, but his voice is soft, more curious than forceful.

"I don't want to embarrass you with all of this." My eyes cut around the room. "Thank you for sending the dress. The best thing I own would've looked like a rag in this place." I run my hands down the satin again, smoothing invisible wrinkles.

"You are the most beautiful woman here, dress or no dress. It's not the clothing that makes the woman, but I did want you to feel at ease. Keep it and wear it for me again. If it survives the night."

I hear the promise in his voice and secretly wish for him to tear this fancy dress that costs more than my car from my body. I wish for him to need me that desperately. Feeling foolish and knowing that I will lovingly hang this dress in my closet as a souvenir of the night, I try to regroup.

"Really?" I ask, taking a sip of my wine. "You don't mind that this place is so far out of my league, that *you* are out of my league?"

Scott smirks. "Madison, if anyone is out of their depths here, it's me. You don't hold to the rules of polite society, don't give a fuck about how I want things to happen, and you couldn't care less about the things I'm used to folks talking to me about."

I cringe a bit, hearing only bad things in his laundry list of my faults. But he continues, "And that is why I'm here with you tonight. I brought you here because you make me try things, and I wanted to give you the chance to try new things too. At the same time, I'm not trying to change you. I want to know who you are, right now, because I suspect I'll like that woman very much."

I beam under his words, feeling much more at ease, even if I still don't know which fork to use. Fuck it. As long as I don't eat with my hands, I'm calling it good. "What do you want to know?"

"Everything," he breathes. "Tell me all about Madison, day one to present."

"Well, I grew up with my aunt . . . sheesh, that could be a whole novel," I say, shaking my head. "I mean, I told you that Aunt May was a bit of a party girl when I was dropped on her doorstep, but she stepped right up and got herself straightened out for me."

"Right, but I don't quite know what that means," Scott says. "What did she do?"

"A little of this and a bit of that. She's not exactly corporate ladder material, you know? I mean, she runs her animal rescue now, but that was later. When I was a kid . . . well, it's a little embarrassing."

"It's okay. Tell me," Scott asks, and seeing the honest interest in his eyes, I'm driven to respond.

"Well, here you go. Her longest-running job was at 7-Eleven. I learned to read in the stockroom," I confide. "May took a job there because it was close enough to the house that we didn't need to fill up on gas . . . and because at the end of the shift when they had to clean out the hot dog machine, she was allowed to take all of the dogs that were past prime time home with her. We basically lived on those free hotdogs and expired packages of donuts destined for the dumpster."

"You . . . but how?" Scott asks, shocked. "I mean, isn't that against the law?"

"Not if no one told," I say with a shrug. "I learned to read from the boxes and expired newspapers. I learned math counting back change when she let me help at the register for a change of scenery."

Scott swallows, shaking his head. "I . . . well, let's just say it was a little easier. I had a nanny who read Dr. Seuss with me."

"Oh, I had Seuss too . . . and *People*, tabloids, and more. I got to read and color lots of the daily comics. I'd eat old chili dogs and play with a ball that May bought me until we went home. We lived in an old single-wide that May was able to rent cheap at the time. She's worked hard for a lot of years and gotten herself out of there, but things were tight for a long time."

Scott nods and looks down at his plate, contemplating. "I guess I thought I had it rough in college with Dad refusing to pay for school and always shitting on me. It could've been a lot harder."

"Now, Scott, don't you dare feel sorry for me," I heatedly comment, my twang popping out fiercely. "Yeah, my childhood might not have been easy. But May and I stuck together and worked our way up out of that level of poverty. Things aren't bad now, and I'm who I am because of those days." I offer a smile to soften the words, and Scott takes my hand across the table.

"And the animal shelter?" he asks, refocusing my thoughts on my story.

"It just kind of happened. We took in a box of puppies that someone abandoned on the street next to the garbage cans. We lived off generic Beanie Weenies for a month to pay for those pups' dog food, but in the end, we were able to give each of them a good home. It was such a good feeling, so we just kept on."

"Your turn," I tell him, needing a break from share time. "Tell me about you . . . little Scotty with a nanny reading Dr. Seuss.

Where were your parents? Although I think we've established your dad seems like a son of a bitch."

Scott blinks, then laughs. "You're not the first person to call Robert Danger a son of a bitch. For Dad, life is all about what you can do for him."

"What do you mean?"

Scott shrugs. "He doesn't like to talk about it, but he didn't earn our family money himself. The seed of it was my grandfather, who got lucky when some family land turned out to have a very rich copper vein underneath it. Until then, it'd been unincorporated wasteland. He couldn't even rent out the grazing rights as it was too far from any farms. But that mine gave my grandfather about ten million dollars. A lot now, even a lot more then, and my grandfather invested it wisely."

"I don't get it. Why would your father be upset about that?"

Scott sighs. "The short of it? My dad's a prideful man and wants everyone to know he's the powerhouse behind the Danger Enterprises name, not that he's the lucky punk who just inherited the golden goose. Or at least that's my theory on why he's an unhappy, as you called him, son of a bitch."

"So he's competitive? And he wants to make sure his children are the same?" I ask, and Scott nods.

"Yeah, but it's more than that. He's leaving this legacy behind in the company and wants us to be fierce and fight for it to prove that only the strongest can hold the crown because it reflects on his strength. He thinks we're some nascent royal dynasty and he's the first king. It's just the way it's always been, and I guess I never really questioned it."

Scott looks at me for a moment, his eyes probing. "What?"

"Just . . . your Aunt May sounds like a remarkable person. You had it rough, but I think I'd have switched places with you," Scott says. If anyone else had said it, especially someone as wealthy as him, I'd have thought they were being condescending, but I can hear the truth to his words, and my heart breaks for the little boy who wanted his dad's attention, affection, and approval. Honestly, I think that little boy is still alive and hungry inside adult Scott.

Our dinners arrive, and conversation pauses as we enjoy the first few bites of our food. The lamb is amazing, and my eyes nearly water as the rich flavors overwhelm my taste buds. This is the taste of wealth . . . complex and multi-faceted, with a perfect balance that makes each bite an experience. But the realization makes me understand something else.

Scott, for all his attempts at understanding me, has never experienced the pleasure of a macaroni and cheese with hamburger casserole dinner with someone you love who loves you back. He's never had a simple relationship where no one was scheming, merely enjoying a meal together.

People might think that I, the abandoned little girl, would be the inspiration behind May's rescue. But I think Scott would be the better metaphor for that original box of puppies . . . lost in a hard world from the start and wanting a soft place to lay his head but too afraid to risk putting his neck out for fear of getting beaten down.

It makes me angry at his dad. Hell, my mom was nearly a total loss as a human being, but she at least put me somewhere she knew I'd be okay. Scott's dad actively tries to destroy him. He's a monster, but what does that say for his children, his creations?

Scott savors his steak and sets his fork down after two bites. "You're right. My siblings and I are very competitive . . . but I don't hate them. I love them in some weird way, but after all these years, my father has succeeded. He's pitted us against each other, especially Chase and me, for so long and in so many ways that we don't know how to be different. We just butt heads and bare our teeth at one another. And Olivia just watches and does her own thing. They're my competition as well as my blood. And blood isn't going to stop me from taking what I know should be mine."

His words, so passionately delivered, both turn me on and worry me. He craves power, virtually vibrates with it already, and it's an aphrodisiac. My body yearns to feel it, to feel the intensity of his thrall when he focuses it on me. But I know the dark side of power. And as much as I want to submit and see where Scott leads, I'm scared of the consequences. He's a lost boy in a man's body. But I'm sure as fuck no fairy destined to show him the way out of Neverland.

"You know, not everything in life is a competition," I say, already knowing his answer.

"Not so sure about that," Scott admits with a small laugh. "Maybe the rules change or a different game is played, but it's still a competition."

"What about a couple?" I ask. His answer is important, and I can already feel the weight of it in my chest. It's a test, an important one.

Scott sets his fork down, looking at me carefully. "Then it's a partnership. Two against the world, working together as one. But still a competition."

I hold my posture, even though my spirit sags. "But a competition means there's a winner and a loser. Why set yourself up that way? To possibly lose?"

"I don't lose," Scott insists, his voice hard.

I try again. "Can you at least concede that your way of thinking is warped, shaped by your experiences? Just like everyone's, mine included. And that maybe, just maybe, life doesn't have to be 'you versus them,' an adversarial match for a win or loss? That there might be a balance where it's simply good for everyone?"

Scott smiles at me, fire in his eyes, and I can feel that he disagrees. I'm shocked when he finally replies, "And that, my dear, is one of the things that makes you so fucking irresistible. You are . . . good. Down to your core, good. And the mere fact that you can see anything redeeming in me is, quite honestly, a miracle. I want to bask in you, let your light into my soul. But be warned, it's a dark and dirty place inside me, and as much as you try to make me good, I'll more likely turn you bad. *So bad*."

His words had started sweet, complimentary, and had made me smile. But as his words heat, the smile slips from my lips and I gasp. "I want that. To brighten your days, your spirit, and to be dirty with you. Maybe that's the balance where it's good for everyone."

Scott smiles at me. "Madison, make no mistake. The only winner in that scenario is me."

CHAPTER 13

SCOTT

Daily Horoscope, October 2ⁿᵈ
Scorpio - Passion can inspire. Passion can create. Passion can destroy.
Yours could do all three.

I lead Madison off the elevator and into my penthouse. She's spent most of the evening alternating between relaxing and looking shocked as she takes in the experience. And admittedly, some of the conversation has been eye-opening for me too. Both about her past and about my family. Things I've never thought, much less said, seem to click together into a perfectly obvious picture with her.

But now, it's me who's a little unsure. I'm not trying to impress her with my money per se, but I am trying to show her that there's more to life than what she's had.

And this space . . . I rarely bring people up here. This penthouse is my inner sanctum, and even my own family members are rarely up here.

"Wow," Madison says when I flip on the lights, looking around the large open-concept room. "Looks like a mansion in itself."

I chuckle, shrugging off my suit jacket and looking over at Madison. From the first moment I saw her this evening, I've had a hard time keeping my eyes off her. The dress may not be her typical style, but she wears it well and looks absolutely stunning. Her breasts press together and up, the line of cleavage tempting me to lick her, to see if her skin is as satiny as the dress fabric. "It does give me a good place to crash," I say carelessly.

"Crash?" Madison asks, looking at the television on my wall. "I've seen movie theaters with smaller screens than this."

She goes around the main space of the penthouse, oohing and ahhing over things.

"What's this?" she asks as she toes a box near my exercise corner. "Looks like something you'd trip over."

"Attachment for my workouts," I explain. "It just sort of works like a big rubber band. Come on, let me show you the best view."

I lead Madison over to my western wall, which goes straight up for two stories in nothing but glass. "Above us is the floor where I have my bedroom and bath, but . . . Alexa, blinds."

I don't actually have blinds in my windows, but instead, there's an electronically controlled layer in the window that can act like sunshades, going from totally clear to opaque at my command.

The windows clear, and Madison gasps as she sees Bane before her. "You can see most of the city from here!"

"Well, the western half," I agree, looking out. In the middle of my view is, of course, the Danger Building, spearing the heavens. But the rest of the city spreads out around it on all sides.

"It's gorgeous," Madison whispers, her breath catching as the moon comes out from behind some clouds and illuminates the city even more. "I never thought this city could be so beautiful."

"Amazing, isn't it?" I ask, my eyes on Madison.

Madison looks at me, a blush pinkening her cheeks as she realizes I'm talking about her, not the cityscape.

"What else would you like to see?" My voice is husky, need deepening it.

"You said your bedroom is upstairs?" she asks, and I nod.

I reach out, wrapping my arms around her waist and pulling her tight against my body. Madison arches her back as my lips find the silky curve of her neck, and I suck, nibbling and tasting her skin as she reaches back, running a hand through my hair and holding me in place against her. I reach up, finding the zipper on her dress and tugging it down, letting it fall to the floor. "I'm going to make you scream my name as you come."

"Fuck, yes," Madison gasps as her softly tanned skin is exposed to the soft moonlight and my exploring hands. Her dress had a built-in bra, so there's nothing to remove as I cup the soft weight of her tits, rolling her nipples between my fingers as I nibble on her ear. Pressing her against the glass, I let her feel the hard length of my cock against her ass.

"You're a naughty girl. A T-back? It's like you were hoping to get fucked tonight."

"I *am*," Madison groans, planting her hands on the glass and pressing her ass against me. "I've been thinking of this moment for days."

"Me too," I growl, stepping back. "Which is why I need that sassy, smart mouth wrapped around my cock, tasting me like you wanted to last time."

Madison obeys, turning and dropping to her knees in the puddled satin of her dress as I undo my pants and take out my cock. She licks her lips as I come into view and looks up at me.

I growl, reaching down and grabbing a handful of her beautiful hair, its softness spilling over my fist. "Now open up and get me wet while you rub that sweet little pussy for me."

Before Madison can reply, I slide my cock deep into her mouth before holding it there, letting her have a moment to adjust before pumping in and out slowly. She swallows eagerly, slurping and sucking as her eyes flutter closed, her breasts shaking with each stroke.

"That's it," I moan, watching her take me. "You look so fucking sexy with my dick in your mouth."

Madison hums around my cock, the sensation shooting to my balls, and I fuck her mouth faster, watching as she slips a hand inside her panties to rub her pussy in time with my thrusts. It's sexy as fuck, and I look down at her, trembling with need. "Are you wet, Madison? Is your pussy dripping with your cream for me? Tell me . . . no, *show* me."

"Mmm-hmm," Madison groans desperately, slipping her fingers out to show me her glistening juices along her fingers. I bend down, sucking her fingers into my mouth, coating my tongue with her taste.

I let her fingers go with a pop, "Back they go. Rub that pussy. But don't come, not yet. Edge yourself while you suck me."

Her fingers disappear into her panties again, her pace speeding up as she gets closer to her orgasm. I keep going, watching her red lips rise and fall on my cock while her tongue does amazing things inside her mouth, setting my nerves on fire until I can't take any more. I pull Madison to her feet, pushing her against the window to look out on the city.

"Scott, I—" she says, but before she can finish, I tug her thong to the side and bury my cock balls-deep in her pussy from behind. My hips smack into her ass, making her cry out as I bottom out on the first stroke. "Fuck!" Her curse is more breath than sound.

"Fuck, Maddie. I love the way it feels deep inside your pussy."

She moans, her body pressed against the glass so that her tits are squished flat while I hammer into her. The glass is clear, but I don't care. I just want to feel her come around my cock, and the idea that someone might actually see me fucking this amazing vixen fills me with even more energy. "Oh, fuck, I'm gonna—"

"Not yet," I order, smacking her ass hard. I speed up, using my grip on her hips as leverage. My cock throbs as she squeezes me, making each retreat feel like her pussy is trying to hold me hostage, choking me into staying deep inside her.

Madison moans, pushing back against my window to meet my thrusts, fucking herself on my cock. She's close. I can feel the quivers of her pussy walls as she rides the edge, waiting for me. "I . . . fuck, Scott. I can't . . ."

"That's a good girl," I growl, grinding my cock deep inside her. "Wait. With me, Madison. Come now."

I don't hold back. There's no need as I give her everything I have. My cock is on fire, my entire body vibrating. With a powerful roar, I pull back and thrust one more time, coming hard inside her tight pussy, filling her with rope after rope of my seed. Dimly, I can hear her wail, clamping tight around my cock as she orgasms too, and the tightness triggers another gush from my cock.

My legs are trembling, and I lean against her, letting the cold glass and the moonlight hold up our sweaty, glistening bodies. I run my fingers up and down her curves, tracing the lines of her waist, grabbing a handful of her hip.

I pull out slowly, turning her around to kiss her deeply. "Let's go upstairs and *maybe* get some sleep."

"I think I need a rest before round two," Madison admits with a shy smile and sleepy eyes. "Just a quick recharge."

I pull her tight, grinning at how she can turn from sex goddess getting fucked against the window to bashful sex kitten in a wink. And I realize once again that I like this sometimes mouthy, often fascinating creature. She keeps me on my toes with her unpredictability, and that's not something I usually experience.

I lead her upstairs to my bed and then scoop her up, laying her down on my black silk sheets before climbing in beside her. She looks good in my space, in my bed where no woman has ever been before. It feels big, like maybe she waltzed right in through a crack in my heart I didn't even know existed. We can still see out the window, and if I sit up, I can even see the little smear we left from our bodies pressed up against it a few minutes ago. She lays her head on my chest, and it feels good having her warm body against me. "Will you stay?" I feel vulnerable even asking, and I hate the hint of begging in my voice.

Madison lifts up, looking at me. "For how long? Round two or 'till morning?"

I chuckle. "Maybe forever?" The words are light, but fuck if I don't mean them.

"Scott . . ." Madison's eyes flash fire as her eyebrows pinch together a bit. "Don't say things you don't mean."

She doesn't believe me. Of course, she doesn't. Hell, I don't believe me even if it is what I want in this moment. And that's scary as fuck. I don't do shit like this, only casual things that serve me for work, for reputation, for some strategic reason. Madison doesn't give a fuck about my work or any of that. She just likes me for some odd reason, and somehow, that feels like the biggest risk of all. But I don't know if she's the one gambling on me . . . or if I'm gambling on her. Maybe both?

"Just stay . . . and we'll see what happens." I press a kiss to her collarbone to sweeten the deal, and a smile curls the corner of her mouth.

Madison swings a leg over my hips and straddles me, her pussy pressing against my rapidly recovering cock. "Deal."

CHAPTER 14

MADISON

Daily Horoscope, October 6th
Libra – Exposing your hidden treasure means risking it to a thief. Hiding it forever means no one enjoys the bounty, not even you.

I READ TIFF'S TEXTED VERSION OF MY DAILY horoscope, along with her encouragement to *Share that hidden treasure, bitch, and getcha some!* I laugh out loud. That girl cracks me up every time. So I text her back a GIF of an opening treasure chest with a pirate proclaiming he's going to 'take my booty'. I barely have time to hit *Send* before Scott opens the door to my car and climbs in.

"Thanks for letting me pick you up."

Scott chuckles, looking over from the passenger seat of my car and carefully adjusting his feet. Unfortunately, the lever to move the seat isn't working, so it's stuck at Tiff size, and Tiffany is about six inches shorter than Scott. "Well, you said I'd end up with dog hair on me and that it'd be hard on my car. Besides, it lets me get chauffeured around by a hot chick instead of the old-timer who sometimes drives me around."

His humor makes me laugh, and I feel a little relieved. I was surprised at first when he said he was willing to take a day off in the middle of the week to go with me to Aunt May's shelter, but it's the best option, considering my schedule. And yeah, the irony that my shitty bartending job, not his high-powered corporate job, is dictating our dates is not lost on me.

"So, here we are," I say as I pull up in front. "What do you think?"

"Looks . . . industrial," Scott says, opening his door. "I'm guessing the dogs don't get bottled water?"

It takes a double-take for me to get that he's joking, and I chuckle. "Okay, quickly before we go in. Try not to raise your voice or make any sudden movements. Some of the animals here come from abusive homes, and it could undo a lot of work we've done to rehabilitate them."

"Gotcha. Be extra-nice to the pups."

I nod, grinning. "Good. Also, you're going to have to get your hands dirty. Anyone who's afraid to get a little dirt under their fingernails or some dog poop on their shoe won't make it here. Think you can handle that?"

Scott laughs. "Pretty sure I'm washable, and new experiences, remember? Anything else?"

I love that when we'd agreed to 'new experiences' together, it wasn't one-sided where he's whisking me away like some fairy tale, even though I know he'd truly like to. He's making an effort to try my favorite things too, even if they're low-brow and simple. He even watched *Friends* with Tiff and me a couple of nights ago through FaceTime because he was still at work. He'd genuinely laughed at the show and claimed he was going to have to watch from Season One to catch up. I'd just been delighted at his laugh. The way it rumbled made my belly flip-flop in the best way. When he'd had to get back to work, I was *this close* to surprising him for a repeat of our first date. Maybe help him take the edge off with a desktop fucking, but he was working against a deadline and I wanted to respect his need to work, so I'd stayed home.

"Yeah . . . watch out for Aunt May. She's feisty."

Scott raises an eyebrow. "And you aren't?"

I chuckle and open the gate. "You'll see."

Inside, the fusillade of barks that greets us tells us everyone's feeling good, and May comes out of the dog wash station, her hands wet and her t-shirt plastered to her. "Well, now, this must be that man you were promising to show me!"

I blush and handle the introductions. "Aunt May, this is Scott Danger. Scott, this is my Aunt May."

"So nice to meet Maddie's new boyfriend," May gushes, offering her slightly pruney hand.

"Aunt May."

"It's okay," Scott says, shaking the offered hand firmly. "If Madison wants to call me her boyfriend, I consider it an honor. She says lovely things about you too, and I can see why."

May blushes a little. I've *never* seen May blush before. She's pretty battle-hardened and doesn't tolerate bullshit easily. "I see why Maddie likes you. You're smooth. Before you get to thinking I'm an easy sell, though, what are your intentions with my niece?"

I feel like I'm about to die of embarrassment, but Scott chuckles. "If I told you the truth, you'd slap me. If I lied, you'd know I'm lying. I think I'll just not answer and ask where the pooper scooper is."

May laughs, winking at me and whispering out of the side of her mouth. "Yep, this one is smooth as silk." She turns back to Scott. "Good answer, young man. Now, as for work, the poop scooping comes later. For now, let's get you on food distribution duty while I deal with poor Furby over here."

"What's wrong with him?" I ask, looking at the sad-looking Shih-Tzu. "Oh, dear."

"He looks . . . matted," Scott says, squatting down slowly and offering Furby his hand for a sniff. His voice is soft, soothing as he talks to the dog. "Where have you been, little fella?"

"Kept outside on a chain collar," May says grimly, picking up a pair of scissors. "He's real sensitive around his neck, and I think he's got some of that chain twisted up in his fur. I need to get the rest of these knots out and get him dipped. He's a one dog walking flea infestation right now."

"Can we lend a hand?" I ask, but May shakes her head. "Food?"

"The babies are hungry," May says. "You two are my only volunteers today, so we need to scoot to get everything done."

May trims carefully at a knot that's about the same diameter as a tennis ball before lifting it away from Furby, who licks her hand plaintively as she tosses it into the trash. "Come on," I quietly tell Scott, who looks concerned.

We head through to the bigger kennel area, and I show him around. "Okay, there are four color tags on the doors. They match the four colors of food container."

"Why four kinds?" Scott asks, and I point out why as I explain.

"Puppies . . . smaller kibble pieces for small mouths. Regular adult food, just your regular dog food. Then there's the basic ingredient food for the dogs with sensitive stomachs, and finally, our seniors and dental-challenged ones. They get a scoop and then their food is soaked with water to soften it so they can chew it easily."

"Dental-challenged?" Scott asks, and I nod, leading him down to Duchess, a beautiful Dalmatian that's been with us for about four weeks. Going inside, I pet her carefully before having her lie down, and I lift her outer lip. "She's got no teeth."

Scott comes in, giving me a supportive look as he rubs Duchess's tummy. "She's a sweet little baby. Looks like she's had puppies too."

"She didn't come in with any, but it does look that way," I reply, standing up. "But Duchess is a sweetheart, and once she's fixed and all her shots are up to date, we're going to get her a good home."

We get started, and it's heartwarming to watch Scott interact with the dogs. Some volunteers only pay attention to the *cute* dogs. But Scott has a kind word for all of them, rubbing heads when they let him and even kneeling down to get a few belly scratches in.

More than once, I see him looking over at me as I talk with the dogs, a strange look on his face. "What is it?"

"Just . . . someday, you're going to make a great mother," he says, smiling gently.

I turn away with a smile, unable to contain my blush as we keep feeding the pups.

"So, now what?" he asks as he looks over the kennel. "They look like they'll be busy for a while."

"Now we get to take care of the other end of things," I joke, handing him a plastic bucket and a small shovel. "This is the fun part."

Scott doesn't complain and takes the poop kit with firm hands. "Where do I start?"

"I'll show you," I answer, picking up my own kit. "Don't worry, it's not too bad."

We're about ten minutes into the job when May comes out and waves me over. "Hey, Aunt May. How's Furby?"

May nods her head. "Good, good. The chain was in a tangle and not embedded in the skin, thank goodness. He'll be all right soon enough." As she talks, her eyes watch Scott. "How's he doing?"

I glance over at him, admitting, "Working hard. He's doing everything exactly like I ask, and I swear the grass looks spotless where he's scooped."

May looks at me. "He seems like something else. How serious are you two? This isn't exactly a first-date kind of thing."

She isn't saying anything that I haven't asked myself a million times since all this started. I don't know if Scott is playing a game, but he's damned good at it if he is.

"I don't know, Aunt May. He's pursuing me pretty hard, pretty fast. I keep pinching myself and warning my heart that I'm going to wake up any moment and find out all this is a dream. Because this isn't like me, and he admits that it sure as hell isn't like him either. Not sure what that means."

May pats me on the back, smiling. "I think it means that it's something different and exciting for both of you. So don't get in your own way. Just enjoy it . . . whatever it is, for however long it lasts. If he's just after your body, give it willingly and often. If he's after your heart, give it cautiously and slowly."

My eyebrows shoot up when she basically tells me to have sex with him, but her advice about being careful with my heart is spot-on. And timely, because I suspect he's taking big chunks of it without my even realizing it.

She pats me on the shoulder. "Anyway, when you two are done out here, I need your help with some paperwork and Scott can give the puppies some attention. We'll introduce him to Maple and Syrup too, see if he passes their exam."

I nod, leaving and going back to Scott, who's scooping up another happy package. "So . . . you two done talking about me?"

"What?" I ask, heat creeping up my neck. "We weren't—"

"Liar."

I glare at him open-mouthed. "Did you just call me a liar?" I mean, he's right, but damn . . .

"Yep," he says, popping the *P* sound. He grins and crowds into me, taking my mouth in a quick smack before talking quietly into my ear. "This isn't a dream. And I like May's advice about giving yourself to me willingly and often."

I lean back, gobsmacked again. "You heard?"

"Every word," he says, laughing. "You think it took me that long to scoop this big pile of shit? I was staying close by to hear you two gossiping about me. Insider information can be quite valuable," he says sagely.

I can't help but burst out laughing. "Well played, Mr. Danger. As for that big pile, it's probably from Biggie, the Newfie you saw inside. Big dog, bigger poops."

"Yeah, well, I think I've had enough of this side of the job," Scott says, holding up his full bucket. "So where do we dump?"

I show him the main barrel, explaining when he lifts an eyebrow, "May helps make ends meet by selling the barrel to a local organic farm. You know, fertilizer and all. It's sort of a virtuous cycle."

"A stinky ass cycle," Scott grumbles, emptying his bucket. "Okay, so now what?"

"Now, I've got some paperwork to help May with, and you get puppy play duty," I reply.

"I like playing with puppies." Scott leers, reaching for my chest and making me laugh, backing up.

"Not those! Down, boy, before I have to put you on a leash."

Scott stops, shaking his head. "Not likely. Listen, after that, how about we go somewhere?"

"Where?" I ask, intrigued and excited. This day isn't over yet, it seems.

"It's a surprise. But trust me . . . you'll like it."

155

WE SPEND THE AFTERNOON HANGING OUT . . . chatting while walking along the sidewalks of Bane. Later, I easily sweet talk Scott into visiting my favorite food truck, where he jokingly whined about the long line, telling me the food had better be worth it. I'd laughed, knowing it definitely was, but when Scott proclaimed to have fallen in love with the smoky brisket bar-b-que sandwich, I was absurdly jealous of the sandwich . . . for being in his hands, on his mouth, and apparently in his heart. Stupid, but true, even if I'd shaken my head at my own weirdness, concerned I might be jumping in a bit deeper than I'd thought but somehow wanting to swim out even further.

It's getting late when Scott finally says it's time for his promised surprise. I follow his directions carefully, climbing higher and higher above Bane on a deserted road I've never been on. "So, is this the part where the charmer reveals his true psychopathic nature and takes me out to the boonies for nefarious reasons?" I tease.

Scott looks at me, his eyes twinkling as he holds back a laugh, but he plays along. "Perhaps it is, but what sort of bad guy would I be if I told you all my evil plans?" He scans up and down my body, and I think I might like whatever evil plans he's got judging by the goosebumps that break out along my flesh from the caress of just his eyes.

He holds the straight face for a beat longer and then we both laugh, the joke broken, along with the heated spell. "It's just up here. Turn right, and . . ."

"Oh my god, it's gorgeous!" I squeal, slamming on the brakes. Through the maze of turns, Scott has taken me to an overlook point, and the night sky stretches out far and wide before us, the stars and moon lighting up Bane in a way that makes it look special and twinkly.

"Come on . . ." Scott tells me, opening his door to get out. I follow his lead, getting out too but I reach into the back seat and grab a blanket. Sure, there's dog hair on it, but there's dog hair on us too, so it'll do. When Scott sees the blanket, he gives an approving nod so I spread it out on the ground in front of us and we sit down.

"There's the Danger building . . . kinda hard to miss that. I think I can see my apartment too though. See that little flicker? That's the streetlight outside our place that never works right." I grin as Scott leans in, resting his chin on my shoulder to follow the line of sight to where I'm pointing.

We spend the next several minutes deciphering landmarks here and there before finally giving up and laying back to do the same thing to stars in the sky above us.

"So, let's start easy," Scott says. "Dippers . . . big and little?" I point to the Big Dipper, then the Little Dipper.

"Too easy. Orion?" I ask. Scott searches for a moment, then points out the three stars of Orion's Belt and traces the shape of The Hunter in the sky. "Right next to Orion is Scorpius . . . the scorpion. Do you know that story?"

I shake my head, interested even though the scorpion thing still gives me a bit of the willies. Damn Marie planting that nugget of fear about something that hadn't even been a blip on my radar.

"Mythology says that Orion was a boastful, bragger type that claimed to be able to kill any animal. Mother Earth didn't care for that and sent a giant scorpion to kill him. Zeus put Orion in the sky as a reminder, and the scorpion next to him to chase him for all eternity." Scott tells the story well, and a small part of me can see him as the scorpion sent to punish the arrogant Orion. It makes Marie's prediction both more and less scary . . . as long as Scott is hunting me for some fun punishment, I could be in to that.

"I'm a Libra, no fun animal in the night sky for me. Tiff told me that Libras are the only Zodiac in the sky represented by an inanimate object. I get scales . . . borrrring." I say, my hands motioning like weighing scales going up and down.

Scott grins and takes my hand, stopping the movement, "Not boring . . . balance. A little bit this way . . ." he says, pressing towards me and planting a chaste kiss to the corner of my mouth. "A little bit that way . . ." he continues, pulling back and I instinctively chase after him, kissing him but he pulls away. Finally, he leans forward and meets me in the middle, perfectly balanced between us so that neither of us are tilted too far. His words are soft, breathy. "But never overdoing it either direction." And he covers my mouth in a kiss, the kiss I've been wanting all night.

His kiss is hot, fire invading my mouth with his tongue and I burn willingly and beautifully, the flames reaching higher and higher as he stokes my desire expertly. I may be the Zodiac of balance, but he's the one that knows how to keep me right on the edge . . . loving right where we are, never wanting it to stop, but desperately wanting more, so much more of him.

I feel like my scale may be tilting dangerously his direction. Way too soon, way too fast. And I don't know how to stop the shift, don't know if I want to. But a tiny voice in the back of my head echoes . . . *suffer and then you shall burn.*

CHAPTER 15

SCOTT

Daily Horoscope, October 7th
Scorpio – Shine bright like a diamond, or wear them. Either way, show
your sparkle.

MADISON LOOKS AROUND, TRYING TO STRETCH AND hitting the roof of my car. "How do you even go shopping in this thing? It's got what, two square feet of trunk space?"

"About that," I joke, downshifting as we approach a red light. "But that's what delivery is for."

Madison laughs, shaking her head, and I watch as the tendrils that have fallen loose from her messy bun float around her neck. I want to chase them, suck her neck as her hair tickles my face. "Anyway, how'd you like the shelter?"

"I liked it," I admit. "The dogs were fun. You think May would be upset if I donated?"

"Of course not. Why would she? May's never upset about donations. She'll take everything she can get."

I chuckle. "Aunt May seems like a really cool person."

Madison smiles, nodding. "She is. She's not perfect, but she's an inspiration. She's why I don't mind working so hard, bartending and volunteering, because I know she's done worse, and she did it for me. It's a hard life, but it's mine, and I know May's proud of me."

I hum and glance over at her, keeping my voice even so as not to betray how important my next words are. "What if you came to work for me?"

It's been running around my head for days now, trying to figure out a way out for Madison in a way that she'd actually let me help her. But she's looking at me like I'm crazy, so I jump right back in before she can say no.

"I mean, you'll still have to work your ass off." The light turns green and we take off again. "But I think you'd like it better than slinging beer to drunk assholes who leer at your ass all night." I know it's the wrong thing to say even as the words leave my mouth, but the truth is that I hate her being at the mercy of the jerks at Stella's. I don't want to share her at all, but definitely not with losers unworthy of her.

She growls, and it's both adorable and terrifying. Her voice is cold, professional, and distant. "Thank you for the offer, but I'm fine where I am now."

The fact that she won't even consider it pisses me off. "You are fine, but damn it, I just want to help! And I can . . . easily. So let me, Madison." My voice has gotten louder, and I make a conscious effort to lower it, admitting, "Why won't you let me help? I just want you close to me, where I can see you, be with you, protect you. Take care of you."

She looks at me, her eyes shiny with tears. Is she sad? Mad? Both? I don't know. I've never cared to decipher a woman's moods before, but with her, I do. "That's why. I'm fine standing on my own two feet. I don't need a protector or a caretaker, don't need to get used to that and then have the rug pulled out from underneath me when you decide you're done rescuing me. I'm fine at Stella's."

It feels like our first real fight, and I think we both showed our cards a bit more than we'd intended. I have this need to be involved in her daily life, but not in the controlling way she thinks. I just want, for once in my life, for someone to fucking pick me first. I want it to be her, and I'm willing to use everything at my disposal to get her to do so, even offering her a job most folks would kill for. But she still thinks I'm in it for the short term, and that's fair. I haven't done anything to make her think otherwise since a few dates, even as spectacular as our connection has been, do not exactly make a forever-type relationship. I have to show her, not tell her, but I'm getting impatient and desperate to claim her as mine.

I hold in a frustrated breath. "Stella is lucky to have you. You're loyal to her, and that's rare." She nods, looking at her hands in her lap.

Silence falls over the car for a couple of blocks as I steer us toward the downtown shopping district, and Madison finally speaks again. "Where are you taking me?"

I glance over and see that she's not upset, she's not sad. Good, I didn't fuck up too badly. But she does look like she's doing a lot of thinking. Join the club, sweetheart. "You'll see. I think you'll like it."

We arrive at our destination five minutes later, parking in one of the protected parking lots of the shopping district before walking down the treed sidewalk, giving zero fucks that we're in casual jeans and t-shirts. I stop in front of Meinstein's Jewelers. "Here we are."

Maddie stares at the window for a moment then shakes her head. "Oh, hell no. There's no way I'm going in a shop like that."

"Oh, but you are. New experiences, remember?" I reply, smiling, taking her hand, and guiding her into the store.

I glance around at the shop, which is perhaps the most high-end jeweler in the tri-state area. Gold and glass dominate everywhere, with eggshell-white walls that only add to the lightness of the room. Inside the glass cases are diamonds, emeralds, rubies . . . anything your heart desires if you're looking for gemstones.

The security guard gives us a rather hard look, but before he can approach us, the manager greets us warmly.

"Mr. Danger!" he says in a British accent. I've never cared to learn whether he's really British or just fakes it for the clientele he serves. "How may I help you?"

"We're just looking," I say. "But I'll let you know if we see something."

"Certainly, sir. Stefania will be happy to assist you with anything you need." He gestures to a blonde woman who stands back, hands crossed in front of her demurely like she's at attention, waiting for us to ask something of her.

Madison turns to me, her eyes wide. "Scott . . . I don't even want to know what something in this store costs. Why did you bring me here? I thought I've made it clear . . ." Madison hisses, uneasiness in her voice as her eyes take in all the beauty around her.

"You deserve it," I reply. "But what makes you think we're here for *you*?" I smile, giving her a wink. "Been thinking about getting a dick piercing. What do you think?"

Madison gives me a raised eyebrow, as if she's trying to figure out whether I'm serious or not. Of course I'm not. That would hurt like fuck, I bet.

Stefania clears her throat discretely, letting us know that our exchange is being heard and asking if she can be of service, all with one *ahem*.

"Yes. I'm looking for some jewelry for my . . ." I pause, looking at Madison, who looks about three seconds short of a heart attack. What is she to me? Forget it. If Madison can say it, I can too. "My girlfriend."

There. I said it. It felt good too. Madison gives me a shocked look, surprised that I would lay claim to her in public. But I smile back, letting her know that I meant exactly what I said. Hell, if she'd let, me I'd tattoo my name on her ass or hers on mine, if that was what she wanted. But she wouldn't allow that, so a bauble will have to do.

Stefania smiles. "But of course, sir. What might the lady be interested in today?"

She looks to Madison for guidance, but she's still staring at me, a total deer in the headlights look on her face, and I reach out, taking her hand. "Maddie, this is for fun, okay? Tell the lady what you'd like."

Her mouth opens and closes, her large eyes flitting to the sparkling jewelry, to me, then back to the jewelry again. "I wouldn't even know where to start."

Stefania, seeing Madison's uncertainty, gives her a reassuring smile. "How about these earrings? They'd complement your lovely eyes."

Madison gasps, taking the offered gold and topaz earrings carefully, like she's holding precious antiques. "Oh, my God, they're so beautiful! But I'd be scared to wear them."

We keep going, Madison trying to go with something simple and unassuming. I know that in her mind, those are the least expensive items, and she's trying to find some semblance of compromise with my wild desire to spoil her.

"What about this?" Madison asks, pointing out a plain platinum braided bracelet. "It looks sturdy."

I give the saleswoman a little jerk of my head and she steps away. Leaning in, I take Madison's hand and lower my voice to a rumble, the same rumble that I know turns her on when we're alone. "If I wanted you to get a plain band, I'd have taken you to the mall. I want you to get something that's as beautiful as you, that makes you feel bubbly inside when you look at it and know it's from me. I want you to get something that makes me feel like you're mine when I look at it."

Madison swallows and nods.

I cup her cheek, running a thumb across one flawless cheekbone. I turn to Stefania and point out a necklace I noticed Madison fawning over and that would look fantastic on her. "How about this?"

Stefania smiles, both at my taste and probably at the sales commission that she's going to earn for this, and takes it out. It's beautiful, a chocolate diamond pendant the same color as Madison's eyes hanging from a delicate gold chain. I lift it off the velvet and hold it up before reaching around Madison's graceful neck to attach it myself.

"Stunning," Stefania remarks, her work accent dropping in awe. "I mean . . . it's flawless."

Madison blushes and turns toward the mirror on the back wall. Her breath catches as she sees herself, the necklace around her neck, and me holding her hair up. "That's . . . that's not me."

"It's you," I reassure her. "One hundred percent you." Her body melts into mine, her back pressing to my front, and I can feel the want in her. She wants me, but she wants this necklace too, wants to be spoiled. She just doesn't think she *should* want that. But I can show her, make her see that she deserves all this and more. Show her that I'm serious . . . about her and about us.

"How much is this?" she asks.

I'm about to tell her it doesn't matter when the saleswoman speaks up. "It's five thousand plus tax, or we do offer payment plans—"

"I can't accept this," Madison interrupts, shaking her head. "I can't. I wouldn't feel comfortable. That's more than I make in two months!"

She reaches up to undo the clasp, and I stop her, holding her fingers still as I lean in. I meet her eyes in the mirror again and speak directly into her ear, my tone not allowing any argument. "You can. And you will. This necklace was made for you, and there's nobody else in the world who will make this look as good as you do."

Her eyes search mine for a moment before letting her hands fall away from her neck.

I lower my voice so that Stefania can't hear and murmur in Madison's ear, "You look amazing, princess. You're going to look even more amazing when we're in bed and that necklace is swinging back and forth as you ride me until you come all over my cock."

Madison's breathing quickens, and she turns her head to give me a smile. "Is that all you wanted? You didn't need a necklace for that."

"Hell, I know that, Princess," I tease, kissing her cheek. "Now, let's get that wrapped up."

As the saleswoman rings up the purchase, I stay back, letting her and Madison gush a little over the necklace. It's ironic, really, likening her to a diamond. But it's fitting. I walked inside that honky-tonk, and she was shining so brightly, a diamond in the rough just waiting to be discovered.

After I pay, instead of turning left to go back to the parking lot, I lead Madison to the right, down another block. "Where are we going now?" she asks, laughing.

I stop in front of a shop, pulling her close, my voice serious. "I'm about to do something I've never done with a woman before in my life. Let's go inside."

"Why are we here?" Madison asks, looking through the window of the dress shop. "You already bought me a dress, Scott. I don't even have room in my closet for another."

"We're here to let you try on evening gowns," I explain, watching the shock drop over her face. "As for space in your closet, well, if you insist, I'll keep it in my mine, and you can come visit it anytime. Fuck, you can live in my closet with the dress if you want to. You'll just have to put up with my swinging dick every morning when I come in to get dressed," I say, my grin growing larger. The thought of her being in my place, not my closet but in my bed, every morning sounds pretty fucking stellar to me.

My joke makes Madison smile enough to let me lead her inside, where we're immediately approached by a saleswoman. She's about to protest, and considering our attire, I don't blame her, but when she sees the bag I'm carrying, her scowl turns into a smile. "Well, now, what a lovely couple. Welcome. How can I help you today?"

Madison is beside herself and doesn't know where to start. "We're looking for an evening gown, classic but youthful," I reply, running down my mental checklist. "Something that will go well with a chocolate diamond."

Madison whispers to herself as the manager leads us toward the gown section. I can't understand what she's saying, but by the look on her face, she likes what she sees. "I feel like this is the part where I argue? And you make me forget how crazy this is by growling in my ear with your sexy voice until I agree to go along with whatever mad trip you're on? I'm wasting my time protesting, aren't I?"

She's smiling now. That's my girl. I lean in closer. "I can still growl for you if you'd like, but you're a quick learner. You're gonna thank me when you see how you look in a few minutes," I reply. "You'll fit right in."

"Right in with who? What's that supposed to mean?"

I smile, holding my secret for a little longer. "Nothing. Look around, see what you like."

Madison walks with the saleswoman and starts picking out gowns, each one more beautiful than the last. Quickly overwhelmed, I take a seat by the dressing room and watch as they carry in about a half-dozen gowns.

The first three look amazing on her, and I know Madison would turn heads anywhere we went . . . but there's nothing in her expression that quite says, 'I love this!'

"Okay, what about this?" Madison asks as she steps out in a Valentino dress. It's . . . perfect. The pale coffee-colored velvet with black lace accents hugs her body like a glove and is just different enough from her new necklace that it'll stand out. The train isn't long, but it makes her look like she's floating as she approaches me in the borrowed high heels.

"I fucking love that one." Between the coffee coloring of the dress, her warm skin tone, whiskey eyes, and honey-blonde hair, she's like a smorgasbord of caramel waiting for me to devour every inch of her. I can't help but lick my lips, wanting a taste.

Madison grins, and I know it's her favorite too. "It's so beautiful."

She walks toward me, my eyes fixed on her, mesmerized by each step. "Okay, honesty time," she says. "There's a reason you're taking me to all these fancy-schmancy places and playing dress-up with me like I'm a paper doll. Time to fess up."

Damn . . . just another reason I can't get enough of her. She could just roll with the indulgences, but not Madison. She knows something's up, knows I've always got a method to my madness. "Because I want you to wear that gown for me in a few days, be my date, and spend the night on my arm, making an evening full of work-related douchebaggery bearable."

Her pretty face twists in confusion, making me want to burst out laughing. "Huh?"

I laugh, getting up and approaching her. "I want you to meet my family. I can assure you they're not nearly as lovely as Aunt May, but it seems only fair. There's a dinner coming up for Danger Enterprises, and they'll all be there."

I fill in a few details, at least those I know, as Madison's face goes slack in shock. "You want me rubbing elbows with billion-aires? When it could affect your work?"

I smile. "I guess that's one way to put it. I have no doubt you'll charm them the same way you've charmed me." I kiss her gently, but there's fire in our every touch, from our lips to my fingertips along her waist. "On second thought, perhaps you shouldn't charm them quite as much as you have me. I'm a bit of a possessive fucker." I flash her a cocky smile, hoping she sees the charm.

"Really? I hadn't noticed that," she offers back with a wink, but her face sobers. "Scott, are you sure? I'm not asking for more here, and I know that a work event is major for you, like inviting me into your inner circle. It's okay if that's not what you want." She bites her lip, and I know it cost her to say that, to give me a way out.

"Let me be clear, Madison. I think we can both agree that neither of us does things we don't want to, right?" I wait for her to nod uncertainly. "I wouldn't have asked if I didn't want to take you. Actually, I didn't ask, and I'm not going to. You're my girlfriend, and I want you there by my side, at this work function and every fucking where else. And I'll be by your side, at the animal rescue, at Stella's, and anywhere else you'll let me go. I want this. I want you."

Madison's eyes are glossy again as she hugs me, but this time I'm ninety-nine percent sure those are tears of joy. At least I fucking hope so. I need a manual.

From far away, I hear the saleswoman's crisp voice. "Will that be cash or charge, sir?"

CHAPTER 16

SCOTT

"*I* still can't believe just how much . . . *stuff* you bought!" Madison says as we come through the door of my penthouse. "Seriously, George Carlin was right. We're on a pursuit of stuff."

"Yeah, well, for now, let's put it here," I grunt, putting the dress down on the quartz countertop in my kitchen. So sleek on the body, but damn if that thing doesn't take up a huge garment bag like nobody's business.

"That works. Like I said, I've got no space for any of this at home. And if I drag all this in the door, Tiff is going to be all over me like white on rice. I could do without her questions until I figure out how to explain this." She sets down the bag that holds her new shoes to match her dress. "If you're sure you don't mind keeping it here?"

I can hear the doubt in her voice. Back and forth, back and forth. She's like one of the scared puppies she cares for, wanting the love and attention but so scared it's going to be jerked away. Using that analogy, I verbally approach slowly so as not to scare her jittery nerves.

"It's no problem," I reply before jumping in the deep end with the thoughts that have been on my mind all day. "Maybe . . . you could even bring a few more things over?"

Madison freezes and turns to me with her eyes clouding. "Are you saying what I *think* you're saying?"

"Yeah," I reply, feeling a little anxious, not sure if she's going to say yes with a whoop of delight or stomp off and slam the door behind her. I never know with her, although that's part of the appeal.

"I like having you here. You make this cold penthouse feel full and lively. You make me feel like that too. I just want more of that, of you."

Instead of looking happy, Madison shakes her head, looking sad and maybe a little scared. "I just . . . I–I don't know if I can live with a man right now."

"Huh?" I ask, a little perplexed. She had no problem staying the night, and we've been great most of the day, other than when I overstepped with the job thing. Am I overstepping again? Maybe, but her reaction feels . . . different from that. The job offer made her mad, angry. She seems spooked right now, curling into herself in a small way.

I brush a wisp of hair behind her ear and place my hands on her hips. "Madison, are you still scared of me? Are you still spooked about that voodoo prediction shit about my scorpion tattoo? Because if so, I can—"

"It's not the tattoo," she interrupts me before taking a deep breath. "It's . . . you."

"Me?" I ask incredulously. "What have I done to frighten you?"

Madison takes a step away from me and turns around, her arms outstretched. "It's all of it. You, your status. Your wealth. Your lust for power. It scares me. That tattoo, the Scorpio stuff . . . I don't really believe in it, if I'm honest, but you are a force of nature, Scott, just like a scorpion, and I don't know if I'll survive your sting. You really could burn me to ash so easily, and that is what terrifies me."

I don't really know what to say to that. I know my confidence and drive can be intimidating, but they're the qualities I take the most pride in. "I've always been proud of striving to be my best."

"There's nothing wrong with it," she adds quickly when she sees the look on my face. "It's just . . ."

Her eyes grow distant, and I know it's something behind her mask, in the corners of her life that she hasn't shared with me yet, but I feel like I need to know. This could be an obstacle to our future. "What is it?"

"Nothing," she says, dabbing at her eyes and trying to put on a smile. "We're just so different, and I'm a bit of a commitment phobe, that's all."

"If that were it, you wouldn't have told May I'm your boyfriend," I reply, moving closer. "Tell me, please. You don't care about my money, obviously don't want it, which is unusual for me. But that means it's something else . . . something about the combination of us that worries you. Why does my being a go-getter and being confident bother you?"

"I can't," Madison replies, taking a step back. I take another step forward, and she doesn't move, which encourages me.

Placing a hand gently on her cheek, I look into her frightened eyes. "Madison, I've never hurt you. I never will. But please don't shy away from me on this. Whatever it is, share it with me. Let me fix it." I realize my mistake and instantly correct myself. "Let me carry the burden with you."

"Scott," she whispers, her voice faltering when I lift an eyebrow.

I stroke her cheek, reassuring her. "Tell me, why don't you think you're worth it? What made you think you don't deserve to be happy? Your mother?" I prompt.

Madison's eyes fill with tears, and she steps back, sobbing as she shakes her head. "No . . . yes . . . no. God, don't you get it?" she asks, gesturing around again. "Nobody, no man, for damn sure, has ever treated me this way! You hand out thousand-dollar gifts like they're Tootsie Rolls. It's just too much, and I don't know how to handle it! I sure as fuck know not to get used to it because it'll only be worse when I'm back to Ramen dinners in a cold apartment because I can't pay the heat bill again. And I'm alone, so alone."

My sweet Princess. I'd give her the world if she'd let me. I'd have bought her a necklace ten times as much if I thought she'd have worn it. "Madison, you don't ever have to be alone. I treat you this way because you deserve it. You are worth more than whatever baubles I can buy you at some store. You're everything, can't you see that?"

"I wasn't worth shit to him, especially when he was putting his hands on me," Madison blubbers, and it all comes together. Not her mother. A man.

My blood boils and I see red. "That son of a bitch. Give me a name."

Madison sniffs and looks up. "Really?"

"If that's what you want," I affirm for her. She shakes her head like I knew she would. My girl, she's too kind to want to hurt someone. Even if the motherfucker deserves it.

I go over to the fridge and get out two bottles of Perrier, handing her one. "Or if it would help, just tell me about it?"

Madison's silent as she opens the sparkling water, taking a sip as we sit down on the barstools at the counter. "His name . . . his name was Rich," she says softly, her head hanging low. I hate him already for making her feel like this. "He and I met at work."

"Stella's?" I ask, and she shakes her head.

"No. I was doing couple of nights a week at Stella's, but at the time, I was also working an office job. Rich came in. He was an executive for a company and had an appointment with my boss.

He was persistent and kind, brought me flowers and coffee when he came in every time after that first meeting. I was flattered, so I figured what the hell and gave him my number. We started dating not long after. Everything was peaches and cream . . . for the first couple of months or so."

"And then?"

"It started with words. How I needed him, how he'd take care of me because without him, I couldn't make it on my own. Then, eventually, a smack on the ass became . . . more. And each time, he'd remind me that I'd be nothing without him."

I sit on my stool, my hand clenching around the green glass bottle of Perrier as I imagine this asshole treating Madison that way.

"It came to a head one night. He grabbed me, held my wrists really tight, and dragged me to the bedroom saying he was going to teach me a lesson I'd never forget. He pinned me down, held my wrists, and laid on top of me." She rubs at her wrists mindlessly as she talks. "I cried out, loudly, I guess, and a neighbor knocked on the door, threatening to call the cops. Rich was worried about his image, so he stopped, but I'd already seen the truth. He crossed a line that night, and neither of us came back unchanged. So when he went to sleep, I packed a bag as quietly as I could and left."

"Where'd you go? May's?" I ask, horrified at her story.

Madison shakes her head. "No. Aunt May had done so much for me, I didn't want to ask for even more unless I had no other choice. I had a key to Stella's from when I closed up, so I went there and slept on the couch in her office. Stella came in the next morning and asked what happened. I cried as I told her the whole story and she held me. I had to hold her too because she wanted to go after Rich. But finally, I convinced her that I just wanted to live my life . . . free of him and on my own two feet. She offered me a place to stay and bumped me to full-time so I could quit my office job and I wouldn't have to see him again."

I nod. "Have you seen him or has he tried to contact you since?"

"No! Thank God," Madison says, her bottle rattling a little. "He never even came to Stella's, just wrote me off like I was nothing. I don't know what I'd do if I did see him. Some days, I think I'd beat the shit out of him for all the times he hurt me. Others," I admit to myself, "I'd probably just hide and avoid him."

I growl and down the rest of my water to calm myself a little before replying. "He'd better pray to God he never comes around when you're with me." I see her stiffen, and I lower my voice as much as I can. "Do I really remind you of him?"

"No," Madison admits and looks up for a minute before she continues. "It's just those qualities you possess . . . strong, powerful, dominant, confident. Like Tiff says, it's definitely my *type.* But it also makes me wonder what will happen when *you* don't get what you want."

Her words jolt me a little. I'm not going to lie. I feel very possessive of her right now. But only to protect her, not to control her. I'd never hurt her, definitely not physically, and not emotionally. But I worry I am already, just by being myself. And while I'd pluck the moon from the sky for this woman, I don't know if I can change who I fundamentally am for her. I don't think she'd like me if I did either.

She stares at me, noticing the turmoil on my face. She reaches up, placing a hand on my chest, and starts tracing a finger over my tattoo through my shirt, already having the lines memorized. "But I realize that those qualities don't mean you're like Rich. It's just my self-doubt and insecurities. You're a good man, Scott, and you have everything the world has to offer at your fingertips. Which makes me wonder why you're wasting your time with someone like me."

I place my hand over hers, lifting her hand to my lips and kissing her fingertips. "Listen to me. Your value is not determined by that asshole's inability to see your worth. You're not a waste of my time, and you're more than what you realize. You're . . . everything to me."

I almost see her crack a smile. Almost. I stand and move behind her, drawing her close into my arms. "Thank you for sharing that with me. I know it was hard. I think I get it better now, why you let me in, then run away. It's scary on many levels. I'll admit that not knowing what you'll do, how you'll respond, or what you'll think is part of the mysterious intrigue about you that I love. It drives me crazy, but I fucking love it. I hope that the reverse is also true, that my ambition, possessiveness, and confidence can be the flame that draws you to me too."

I turn her and my lips finds hers. Our kiss deepens, and I cup her soft breast through her T-shirt, causing her to whimper.

"I've got you," I say, stepping back and taking her hand. She stands, and I let her lead the way, surprised when she doesn't head upstairs but instead to my couch, where she has me sit down before straddling my lap and kissing me even more deeply.

We explore each other, taking it slow and soft even though my desire to conquer her urges me to go faster. But this is Madison's time, the time to let her see that I don't have to control everything every time.

Instead, I hold back, letting her place my arms behind my head. "Stay," she whispers. I watch as she reaches down and pulls her shirt up and off, dropping it to living room floor. Wordlessly, she presses her breasts against my face, and I nuzzle them, covering the tops of them with butterfly kisses until she undoes her bra and releases them for my worship.

"Even as you worried me, you drew me in," Madison moans as my lips find her left nipple and I suck, tugging at it lightly with my teeth. "Because you make me feel alive."

She grinds on my lap, my cock pulsing and surging inside my jeans as she rides me. My hands clench the back of the couch with the desire to touch her skin, to feel her body with my fingertips. But I control myself, giving her what she most needs in this moment . . . reassurance that she holds all the power. Any power I ever take in our coupling is only from what she gives, and right now, she wants it all and she can have it. She can have anything, everything.

"That's so good," Madison murmurs as I kiss over to her other nipple. She lets me suck and nuzzle for several long moments of heaven before standing up.

Madison unsnaps her jeans and pushes them down, kicking off her untied sneakers before looking up and grinning at my still body and heated eyes. "You can take your jeans off, you know. I didn't tie your hands."

I grin, pulling my T-shirt over my head even though she didn't say so and shucking my jeans and tennis shoes. My cock springs straight up, nearly arcing over to slap me in the stomach before bobbing back and forth to my heartbeat for Madison's approval. I place my hands back over the edge of the couch behind me, giving her a raised eyebrow. "Maybe I like your being in control. Doing all the work."

Madison grins at my challenge and saunters the short distance, straddling my hips again and taking my cock in hand. "Do all the work, huh? And if I decide the only work that'll be done is by your right hand? What then?"

I return her grin, holding up my right hand. "On myself or your sweet little clit? Your choice."

Madison pants softly and pumps my cock with her hand. "You say just the right things," she says, sinking down. The head of my cock spreads her open, and she sighs, smiling at me as her hands rest on my chest, one covering the scorpion tattoo that started this whole wild ride. "Grab my ass while I fuck you."

I obey, happy to have permission to touch her, and reach around to cup Madison's perfect ass as she starts to rise and fall. Her pussy grips my cock as she rides, her eyes rolling back as she bounces on my cock. I let her go at her own pace, my hands supporting her as she takes what she needs.

"That's it, beautiful," I murmur, encouraging her. "Use me. Take what you need. I'm here for you."

Madison's hips speed up, rising and falling in time with our heartbeats. Her breasts sway and bounce in front of me, and I take one into my mouth as she leans back, her pussy squeezing and milking my cock while I add to the sensation.

"Scott . . . oh, fuck . . . I'm gonna . . ." she moans, riding faster and faster, leaning forward and planting her hands on the back of the sofa.

Her back arches fiercely as she takes me balls-deep, and I grab a handful of her ass, encouraging her. She cries out, overwhelmed by the feeling as her body goes over, her climax rolling through her in shuddering waves that set me off too. I'm close behind, kissing her tenderly as my cock swells, the sweetest orgasm I've ever felt rolling from the tips of my toes all the way through the end of my cock, both of us gasping and shaking.

"I . . . I've never felt that before," I gasp as Madison lays her head on my shoulder, her body still trembling. "Never."

"Me either," she says softly, running a hand through her hair and sitting up, my cock still inside her.

I nod, stroking her back tenderly. "I don't want it to stop."

She nods and leans forward, kissing my lips tenderly.

We stay there, looking into each other's eyes until my cock finally softens and slips out before getting up and heading upstairs. There's no need for a round two. This time was something . . . different. Instead, I set my alarm and slide into bed, Madison joining me. After turning the lights out, she murmurs in the dark. "Scott . . . maybe I could bring a couple of things over. Nothing major, just a few T-shirts for work?"

It feels like a win, a small victory, but one nonetheless with this woman. An olive branch, one she hopes I'll take gently and not leave her with more scars. I grin against her hair, pulling her tight against me. "A few T-shirts or your whole wardrobe, Maddie. I'm good with whatever you're ready for. Oh, except one request."

She looks back at me, and in the moonlight, I can see the question in her eyes. "What's that?"

I give her a smacking kiss. "A toothbrush. I'll get you one to keep here." And then I wink at her cockily.

She grins and snuggles back in as my little spoon. Yep, definitely a winner, and Madison is the best prize I can imagine. That fucker Rich didn't know what he had, but I'm fucking glad because now she's mine, even if she doesn't fully realize it. She's mine, and I'm fucking hers.

CHAPTER 17

MADISON

Daily Horoscope, October 8th
*Libra – Your mask hides the real you from the world, but also from
yourself. Is the sacrifice of not living as your true self worth it?*

*T*he morning sunlight diffuses through the room,
waking me up early. Part of it, of course, is that I went
to bed early. Stella's stays open until midnight every day but
Sunday, so going to bed before two in the morning is early
for me.

I stretch and realize that Scott is still sleeping peacefully beside
me. Glancing over at the bedside clock, I see that it's not even
seven in the morning yet, and the only reason we're getting any
light at all is because of how high up in the sky we are compared
to the rest of the city.

I get out of bed, nature calling me to take care of my morning
needs. I take my phone to the bathroom with me, checking my
notifications. Tiff's morning horoscope is boring, just the cut-
paste from whatever website she uses with no notes. Vaguely, I
wonder if she's mad at me or something, but I try to dismiss it
as just a busy day and a ho-hum prediction.

I'm stunned as I come back out. The sun's risen a little more,
and now the whole city is bathed in a pink-orange glow. It's so

beautiful that my heart catches in my chest, and I think about how removed this place is from my usual life. I normally wake up at noon to the sound of the garbage trucks emptying the dumpsters at the gas station next door.

How did I get here?

I'm still a little in shock at yesterday's whole turn of events. The whole shopping spree of a day was completely out of my comprehension. But the better part was after, when he'd listened to me talk about Rich without making me feel less than because of what I'd put up with. And the way he'd kept his hands behind the couch for me said more than a whole speech's worth of words.

He's possessive and domineering, but he's just as much mine as I am his. I feel like he wants me to revel in my own power as much as he wants power over me. That balance is exciting and the antithesis of what happened with Rich, who was threatened by my spirit and tried to squash it, squash me into the cartoon version of a girlfriend he wanted. I'd told Scott last night that he reminded me of Rich, and yeah, they share some traits, but the truth is . . . Scott is nothing like Rich. Scott makes me feel like what I am, who I am, is just right. Enough. Worthy.

As I stare out over the city through the huge windows, snippets of memory play across my mind . . . Scott at the bar, ice skating, the fancy dinner, the sex. As a smile steals across my face, a disembodied voice echoes through my head.

Your heart shall be his . . . and then will come the sting . . . you will suffer . . . and then burn.

Damn it. I still don't think that fucking prediction is real, but considering I was just contemplating that Scott has my heart, the fact that my mind dialed it up is chill-inducing. May had joked about Scott's dick being 'the sting', but now that I have real feelings for Scott, have given him my heart, or at least a growing chunk of it, Marie's prediction seems more dire. I'm floating on a high right now, and a sting seems like a haunting threat to what we're building.

I try to shake the pall of doom from my mind, not wanting to create a self-fulfilling prophecy of my own by worrying about Marie's dark words. No. I've got something good here, and I'm going to appreciate it, nurture it, and enjoy it, not stress about maybes and mights.

I head into the kitchen, checking out what Scott stocks in his fridge. It smacks of the essence of bachelorhood, but he's got more than takeout leftovers and microwave meals at least. There's eggs, real cream . . . and bacon. All I need. I might not be able to spoil him with shopping sprees, but I've got my own special skills and I can treat him the best way I know how.

Finding some mixing bowls and a fry pan, I get to work, singing some Dolly to myself while I whip up some breakfast. Too bad this man doesn't know the benefits of good old-fashioned cast iron, but I guess the copper-bottomed pan does an okay job of crisping up the bacon. As I take the last piece of bacon out and get ready to fry up an omelet in the grease, I hear a grunt and a sniff behind me.

I spin, luckily only having a fork in my hand, which clatters to the marble flooring. It's Scott, standing there in just a pair of boxer shorts and nothing else and looking tastier than the best-crisped bacon on the plate beside me.

He's staring at me in surprise and worry floods me. Did I over-step? Should I have been rooting around in his kitchen? "Something wrong? I thought I'd make you some breakfast."

"Your face," he says.

"My face?" I worriedly ask, wondering if maybe I've got a bad pillow line or something. "What's wrong with my face?"

Scott recovers and steps closer. "Nothing. Your makeup is just worn off. You look beautiful."

I turn, staring at my reflection in the black polished surface of the fridge in horror. I feel so vulnerable, so naked without my makeup, something that I've used as my protection for so long, a layer between me and everyone else.

Scott wraps an arm around me, turning me toward him as his eyes scan my face. I instinctively dip my chin, trying to block his view, but he lifts my face with a gentle hand on my jaw. "Don't hide from me, Madison. Let me see you . . . all of you. You're gorgeous." He runs a soft finger along my cheek and then down the bridge of my nose. "You have freckles. Why would you hide them? I want to kiss each one, memorize them in every light."

I look at him like he's crazy, but there's only honesty in his eyes. My voice is quiet. "Are you saying you don't like my makeup?"

His eyes meet mine. "I'm saying that I already knew you were stunning, but you have never been more so than right now . . . barefaced, half-dressed in my shirt, with your hair a mess from my hands."

And in his arms, his words washing over me, I have never felt more beautiful. I believe him because I feel the same way about his appearance this morning . . . mussed hair, scruffy shadow of a beard, his chest on display, even that damn tattoo. It feels like a secret view, not the suited executive everyone else gets. This Scott is just for me.

He pulls me close, and what starts as a soft, tentative good morning kiss quickly turns into a full-on tongue wrangling, Scott's cock hardening to press against my hip as he cups my ass. "Mmm . . . you didn't put your panties back on. I might want some dessert after breakfast, but coffee first," he teases with a groan, letting me go and heading to the coffee maker.

"Okay, you can get the coffee started. But after that, sit your cute butt over there while I finish things up."

It doesn't take long to make the omelet, and I slide each half onto a plate and divvy up the bacon. "Breakfast is served, sir."

Scott chuckles, but we're soon both too busy eating to say much, the sound of forks scraping on plates dominating the space for the next few minutes. "Damn, you're good," Scott says as he chews the last bit of his bacon. "And why are you slinging beers instead of food?"

"Better pay," I quip, making him nod. "You liked it, I take it?"

"Best omelet I've ever had," Scott says honestly. He takes my hand across the table and pulls me toward him with a wink. Thinking it's time for that dessert, I get up and move to him, sitting down in his lap to face him. He settles his hands on my thighs, and I lace my arms around his neck. "What's your plan for today?" he asks, his thumbs tracing circles along my skin.

"Not much, some errands and I work tonight. You?" I say, distracted by the sparks he's creating along my legs.

"Currently, I'm wishing I could stay here all day, buried inside you. But I have to go into the office today."

"When?" my voice is breathy.

Scott chuckles low in his throat and peeks at the clock behind me as he squeezes my ass. "I have to be in the team room in less than hour. I'd say I could skip the meeting, but since I called it, I kinda need to be there. It's about our presentation for the dinner gala."

"I understand," I reply, trying not to sound disappointed. I know he's got to work, but I'm all riled up with no time on the clock. Instead, I try to focus on the rest of what he said. "I'm still nervous about going," I admit. "I know you got me the gown and all, but I still don't know how to act around all those important people."

"You don't *act* like anything. Just be yourself. They'll be as charmed by you as I am. I'm going to have the most beautiful woman there on my arm, give a presentation that impresses the board and maybe even my father, seal the deal, and then fuck you in the car on the way home to celebrate." His words are gravel, and I can hear that each piece of his plan is just as important as the rest.

"Well, I can help with some of that, at least. I do hear orgasms can clear the mind, help you focus and do better work," I say sagely with a nod. "How important is your meeting this morning?"

Scott plays along, nodding as he grinds his thick cock against my core. "I have heard that, in fact. Think it was on the news and everything. My meeting is essential. Without it, we'll be *pounding* away, and making the deadline will be *so hard*."

I grin, slinking out of his lap and dropping to my knees before him. "Well, I want your meeting to be *short and sweet*, get right to the *climax* so you can get your work done." I slip the waistband of his boxers down and his cock pops free, bobbing toward my face.

I slide my hands along his shaft, stroking him for a moment before taking him in my mouth. There's no time for teasing, so I get right to it, moving up and down and sucking him hard as I swirl my tongue along the underside of his cock.

Scott groans, grabbing a handful of my hair and directing my pace. "Fuck, Madison. It's gotta be fast, but fuck if I don't want to do this all damn day."

I still, looking up at him, and a beat later, he unclenches his eyes and looks down at me. "Fuck my face, Scott. You let me use you last night and it was amazing. It's your turn. You're in charge."

He searches my face for a moment, even as I wait with my mouth wide-open and ready for him. He must see what he wants because he adjusts in the chair and slips his cock back into my mouth, slow and easy at first, which surprises me. I guess I'd expected him to just deep-throat me on the first pass. I think I kinda wanted him to do that. He presses further into my mouth, his tip touching the back of my throat, and I swallow, encouraging him.

"Fuck," he groans and then unleashes his control. He strokes in and out of my mouth, holding my head on either side to keep me still. His thrusts get more forceful, slipping into my throat with every pass, and I moan my enjoyment, giving him permission to keep doing it. To go harder. Rougher.

Tears are streaming down my face, and vaguely, I'm glad my makeup is gone or else it'd be mascara running down, leaving tracks in my foundation. But I fucking love it, love Scott dominating me, taking me, seeing me bare-faced and full of his cock.

I watch him from below, watch the way he measures how much of his cock he's pounding into me, taking care even as he lets loose and enjoys the feeling, the visual of his cock in my mouth.

"Maddie, I'm coming . . . fuck . . . swallow me." He holds himself deep in my throat, shallow thrusts matching the pulses of cum I taste as he roars above me. I swallow, over and over, loving the reward as much as the act.

Scott sags, and I swipe at the corners of my mouth, wiping away the saliva along my lips.

Scott smiles down at me, his hands gentle in my hair once again as he twirls a lock around his finger. "You said you've done a little office work."

I'm a little confused by the turn of topic but answer anyway, "Yeah . . . why?"

"That job offer's still on the table because fuck if I want to leave you now." He looks satisfied, happy, relaxed, and I did that for him. "I think I'd like ordering you around. See if we can christen my office, my desk, the elevator, and every-fucking-where else in the building."

I laugh. "You don't give up, do you?"

Scott grins. "Never."

PULLING UP IN FRONT OF STELLA'S, I FEEL A LITTLE strange. Tiffany wasn't at home when I caught a cab home to get my car, and well . . . it's been days since I've really seen her. We've texted, including her daily horoscope reading via text instead of over breakfast, but with my dates with Scott, our work schedules, and a few hours sleep here and there, I haven't actually laid eyes on my best friend in too long.

Now I'm going back to work, and I feel strange. Good, but strange.

"Probably the lack of makeup," I mutter, touching my face. Not that I'm barefaced, but not my usual full-face layer of foundation, concealer, contour, highlight, and bronzer. I look good without it though, I'm surprised to realize as I give myself once last glance in the visor mirror before going inside.

"Girl, where have you . . . I haven't seen you in forever!" Tiffany says when I come in. "I thought you got kidnapped by bikers or was gettin' anal probed by aliens! Or maybe it was Scott Danger? I—"

Tiffany stops when she sees me take off my necklace and put it in my handbag. I've been wearing it since he gave it to me, not only to lend a sense of reality to this time, but also to get used to the weight. That . . . and hell, it was sexy as fuck to watch it swing as Scott fucked me from behind after that stellar blow job. The quickie on the breakfast table had only taken a few strokes to make me come, the diamond sparkling in time to his cock setting my pussy on fire.

But that was around Scott's apartment, not Stella's. She doesn't necessarily have to put chicken wire up around the stage when bands come to play, but I'm not gonna risk it. It's too beautiful and means too much.

"Holy fuck," Tiff exclaims. "A gift from Mr. Danger?"

There's a piece of me that wants to hide it from Tiff, worried about what she'll think of the extravagance, about what that might say about me. The other part of me wants to stand up on the bar and show it off to all of Stella's, yelling, "Look what Scott Danger gave me! Me! Little ol' Madison Parker!"

Knowing she won't let this go, I slowly pull the necklace back out of its special storage bag and hold it up for her inspection.

"Well gawt-*damn*, honey, that is one helluva 'thank you' from a fine-ass man!" Seeing the uncertain look on my face, she adds steel to her voice. "Girl, have fun and let him buy you what he wants," Tiff says, pointing at me. "Ain't no harm in that unless there's something else you need to share with the class?" One of the many reasons I love this girl. She's all onboard with me getting ridiculous gifts if they're offered, but if there's a catch that makes me uncomfortable, she'd throw that necklace right back at Scott or use it to garrote him. All for me.

Then she stops and stares at me, horror-stricken. "You're not going to bail, are you? Leave us peons down here in the beer drippings?"

"Of course not!" I reply, surrounding Tiff in a big hug. "You and Stella are family."

Tiff pulls back, her face still close to mine. "Girl, I was kidding. You do you. And if you get a chance to get out, get up, you'd better fucking take it if it's what you want. I'll be here for you, just like always . . . happy or sad, rich or poor, good or bad. Although let's be honest, if we're picking, go for happy, rich, and bad."

"Don't you mean happy, rich, and good?" I say with a smile.

Tiff smirks. "What's the fun in that?"

"Tiffany Donna Myers—"

Her voice picks up and she gives me a smile. "Besides, we can't be roomies forever. The first time you walk in while I'm having a muck bang and getting screwed at the same time, you'll be out of there."

"Will you stop it?" I ask, and Tiffany chuckles.

"What? All that Cheez Whiz spread all over his body that I lick off and then—"

Luckily, before I can puke, Stella pokes her head in the door, looking like she's been through a washing machine, she's sweating so damn much. "So glad you're here. Carl is already drunk and barely standing on his feet. Need you out there, and don't worry about his drawer."

"You look hot," I comment, putting my bag in my locker. Some women would take it as a compliment, but Stella knows what I mean.

"Ugh, the blasted medicine isn't working a lick. These hot flashes are killing me," Stella moans.

Daryl walks in, a heavy crate over his shoulder like he's carrying an old-fashioned eighties boombox. "What's killing you, Momma?"

"Oh, nothing. I'll be fine, Son," Stella replies, wiping at her forehead. "But Carl out there getting shitfaced doesn't help things."

"Want me to take him out back and knock some sense into him? I'm sure I could set him straight," Daryl offers.

Always perfectly on-time, Devin pokes his head out of the kitchen. "Not sure your fine ass is gonna set anybody *straight*. Rawwr," he teases, grabbing the air in front of him like he's grabbing ass.

Daryl laughs, flipping Devin the bird. "You wish, motherfucker."

Devin smirks. "I'm literally not a mother fucker. Daddies maybe, but no MILFs in my history fo' shur."

Stella fans herself, looking embarrassed. "Boys, stop. You're making my hot flash even worse."

Devin busts out in one quick laugh, preening even though he's wearing a grease-spotted apron and a bandana around his head. "I do have that effect. But I came in for a reason. Someone needs to get back to the front of the house. Carl just gave away a round to the whole bar on the house."

Stella growls, "That boy . . . it's coming outta his paycheck." She stomps off, heading toward the front with steam virtually pouring off her, from the hot flash and the anger both. Daryl follows close behind, although I'm not sure if it's to hold Stella back or to beat the shit out of his brother.

I turn back to Tiff as Devin heads back to the kitchen, the silence deafening after the revelry of having almost the whole crew in the small room. She hands me back the necklace, and I carefully store it away safely once again.

Tiff watches, smiling warmly. "You know, babe. You look great, happier than I've seen you in a long time. Welcome back to the land of the living." She moves a strand of hair into place and pats my cheek, letting me know she's noticed the difference in my makeup because normally, she'd never touch my done-up face.

"Thanks, Tiff. I feel great."

As I head out to the bar, that seed in my center takes hold, putting down big, thick roots and letting me stand tall, proud.

The glowing warmth lasts all of two seconds because as I tie my apron on, Carl approaches. "What took you so damn long, Maddie? Where the hell have you been?"

The warmth turns to hot anger. "I'm here on time. Stella said to leave your drawer. Guessing she told you the same thing when she and Daryl just had a little family meeting with ya." The dig hits home, and I see his cheeks flush to match his red nose. Normally, I don't push Carl and definitely try to stay out of any family drama. But tonight, I feel fierce, invincible.

I push past him, ready to tackle my shift. From behind me, I hear Carl. "You have a really nice ass for such a bitch. That's the only reason you work here . . . as an ornament for the drinkers. Well, that and because Mama feels sorry for you." I turn to face him, seeing the hateful sneer on his face.

His words hurt, even as I know they're crap. I'm a damn good bartender, and while Stella has helped me a lot, she doesn't pity me.

A tiny voice in my head whispers, *You don't need this. Stella could find another bartender and be fine. Walk right out of here, tell Scott you'll take the job at his office, work your ass off, and learn. Hell, live in that fancy penthouse with him and have amazing sex morning, noon, and night. A girl could do worse for herself. It'd be so easy, better.*

No. That's not me. I haven't known Scott that long . . . not really, even if it feels like a whirlwind of getting to know each other and he's deeper in my heart than anyone has been before. But I'm not gonna let Creepy Carl run me off just because I now have someplace to run to. I can handle him, deal with his shit the best way I know how . . . by shutting him down. Hard.

"Damn, Carl, if your mama feels sorry for me, what pity she must feel for you. Her useless son who can't get through the day without being drunk. And you go ahead and take a peek at my fine ass as I walk away, because it's the only action you're getting besides your right hand."

It's harsh, it's mean. It's bar room rules at their finest. Don't dish it if you can't take it. But one of those big, strong roots of happiness inside me shrivels at the ugliness. I sigh, promising myself to avoid Carl at all costs and not let him, or me, destroy my joyful buzz.

CHAPTER 18

SCOTT

Daily Horoscope, October 8ᵗʰ
Scorpio - Today, learning to let go and let others contribute is your best path forward.

*T*he team meeting room is nothing like the sleek modern boardroom upstairs, but that's okay, I sort of like it. Around this long, plain wooden table sit about a half-dozen of the best business minds, and I know when I take over, the sycophants upstairs are going to find themselves replaced with this younger, hungrier, smarter generation. Maybe we'll crash and burn, but I believe otherwise. These people are the ones I want beside me as I lead Danger Enterprises into the future.

"So I think the big thing we need to hammer home is the long-term market positioning," Robbie says from his end of the table, sitting next to my speech writer, Teresa. "It's the biggest advantage we have over Olivia and Chase."

"That's true, but not the most important point," says Teresa, who I hired because in addition to an MBA, she's got a way with words. I'd lured her away from a lucrative political speechwriting career and felt fortunate she deigned to put her business mind to work for me instead of some slick politician.

Robbie's jaw drops a bit and Teresa continues. "We need to show how the market is going to pay off *faster*. The key is speed."

"What do you mean?" I ask, and Teresa grins, adjusting her glasses.

"Sir, your father isn't focused on a twenty-year market capitalization, even if it's good for the company. He's flashy and wants a big payout that will pump up the stock price right now. So that when he gives up control, he can lay claim to being in the *Forbes* top 50."

Money and pride. For my father, that's what it always comes down to. "Where's he at now?" I ask, not having a clue because that list isn't something I remotely care about.

"Right now?" Robbie asks, tapping at his tablet. "Estimates put him at about one hundred and seven, give or take a couple of spots."

Teresa presses. "If we can show how your deal will vault him up that list faster than our competitors . . . or even better—"

"Show how those deals will send him down the list," I finish for her. "Of course, we can't say they'll lose money. That's not true and everyone knows it . . . but if we can show how relative to the other Top-100, he won't keep pace, we'll have an angle."

Teresa nods. "It has to be subtle. We can't just attack Chase and Olivia directly, or we'll risk turning off the whole board, including your father. But it can be done, with precision."

"Good," I reply, tapping the table. "Teresa, I want you to take Keith and start working on that angle. Do a cursory check on who the biggest movers on that list are and what they're investing in so we can use that in our play. Get me a draft by the end of the day."

Keith isn't much for speaking up in these meetings, but I can always trust him to be listening and do what needs to be done. "On it, sir."

"Okay then, everyone has their jobs. Get to it."

The team breaks up, and I gesture to Teresa as she walks by. "Yes, Scott?"

"Teresa, regardless of how we pitch this to my father, I want it to be clear that this plan will position the company for total domination, now and later," I comment, making Teresa smirk.

"You mean position *you* for total domination?"

"Isn't that one and the same?" I ask, and she rolls her eyes, nodding before leaving. I spy Robbie, who's hanging back, and lift my chin. "What's up?"

"You got a minute?" he asks, waiting until the room's cleared and the door closes before continuing. "Anything else you need? On the downlow, for the party?"

My head tilts, taking him in. "What do you mean? I think we're solid. Or is there something you want to add?"

Robbie straightens his spine, seeming to brace himself for what he's about to say. "Do you need a date, or are you bringing the bar girl?"

I narrow my eyes at him. "Yes. I'm bringing Madison," I say, emphasizing her name and taking offense at the dismissal of her as simply a 'bar girl'. "Although that's not really your business."

He sighs. "Scott, look, man. This deal is important, a fucking pivotal moment in your career and we all know it. Are you sure you want some random chick of the week from a bar on your arm? That's all I'm saying."

My blood boils as I seethe, angrier at my best friend than I've ever been. "She's not a random chick of the week. I fucking care about her—*a lot*. And you will never speak of her like that again."

Robbie cringes at my harsh tone but doesn't back down. "Fine, so she's important. Hell, maybe she's *The One*, but is this the time to test that? You're not the only one with everything riding on this. The whole team needs this win, and its my job, the job you hired me for, I might add, to foresee any issues and handle them. That's all I'm trying to do . . . protect you, protect the team, protect the company."

I let the big inhale and exhale of breath I force into my lungs fill the room, silent as I stare Robbie down. "I get it, man. You're coming from a good place, and I appreciate it. Truly, I do. And any other time, any other girl, you'd probably be right. But not this time, not this girl. She makes me feel . . ." I search for the word to describe how Madison makes my heart swell, my body hum, and my mind fire on all pistons. "She just makes me . . . *feel*. Does that make sense?"

Robbie grins, big and wide for a moment before a laugh bursts past his lips. "Son of a bitch. You're fucking falling in love with her! Never thought I'd see the day. Well, shit. That does change things, doesn't it?"

He nods, and I can see his mind at work. I can't care what he's thinking about, though, because his words are resonating through my mind. Love Madison? Do I? Is that what this is? I know she's constantly on my mind, even as I work, which has always been my one true focus in life. And my body fucking burns hot with the need to claim her again and again. Being with her, inside her, feels like home. And I'm homesick every moment I'm away from her.

While I'm having an existential crisis of revelation, Robbie's mind has been turning more productive circles. "All right, we can sell this. Settling down definitely makes you look more mature to the board, a plus considering you're the baby of the family. They'll take you more seriously, and by default, that'll translate into taking your plan more seriously."

I stop him. "Robbie, she's not a ploy, not a pawn. She's just . . . mine. And I want her there by my side."

Robbie nods. "Of course, yeah, man. But whatever it means to you, to her, it also means something to the board. You handle your relationship. That's all you, so don't fuck it up. My job is to set the frame for the business side. Deal?"

I grin. "Deal. Thanks for looking out, Robbie. Really."

He nods. "Holy fuck. Scott Danger in love. Will miracles never cease." He pauses to laugh. "Actually, no, let's keep those miracles rolling . . . at least until the board signs off on our proposal."

He struts out, a man on a new mission, and I smile. The truth of the last few moments sinks in, filling me with unexpected happiness. Holy shit, I love Madison. I really do.

I'm still sitting at the head of table, smiling like a loon when a knock disturbs me. I look over, surprised to see Chase standing in the doorway.

"Hey, little brother. How's the prep going?" he asks, coming over to sit down beside me at the table. The fact that I'm at the head of the table and he's sitting to my right doesn't escape me. In fact, it gives me a little jolt of victory even if it's premature.

"Going well here. And you?" Our words are stilted, cautious as we don't trust each other, never have and likely never will.

"Fine." He looks out the window of the room, seeing Teresa talking animatedly as her assistant types along with her dictated words. Luckily, we can't hear her. "You think your silver-tongued she-devil will deliver for your speech?"

He's showing that he knows my team, knows their roles in my strategy, and likely the strengths and weaknesses in each of us, our proposal included. But I know his too.

"Chase, the numbers don't lie. Your plan is good, no doubt about that." He looks surprised at my admission, and quite honestly, I am too. But I continue, "But we can do better, be better. And trading on the fact that you're the golden son only gets you so far and doesn't serve the company. It makes you lazy, makes you take the easy, safe way. The board will see that. Their loyalty to Dad has limits."

Chase nods. "I guess we'll see about that, won't we?" He's quiet for a moment and then continues, barbs in his every word letting

195

me know that maybe I hit a little too close to home for his comfort. "You think you're this wunderkind, somehow above, or outside, all of Dad's shit. But you're not. None of us are. It's his game, his boards, and his fucking rules, and if you don't play by them, no amount of genius from your team of crackpots out there is going to put you at the head of that table upstairs."

"And you think you should sit there instead?" I sneer.

"It doesn't matter what I think, only what Dad thinks. And for that reason alone, I will sit there. I will lead this company. No matter what you do. You're simply no threat because you don't play his game. I do. You might think it's weak, but I call it smart," he says evenly.

CHAPTER 19

MADISON

Daily Horoscope, October 17th
Libra - New stages and new opportunities abound. Be open to the possibilities.

"Dude, how spot-on is that? New opportunities abound and you're going to this big, fancy dinner gala? Girl, your 'scope is right. You'd better be open . . . for fucking *business* . . . in the bathroom, in the boardroom, in Scott's office, and anywhere he's down to get down. You feel me?" Tiff jokes as she reads my daily horoscope to me. She's actually got a point this time. About the opportunity, not about the sex everywhere. Well, mostly not about the sex.

"You sure this is okay?" Tiffany asks as we pull up to Scott's building. "I mean, he knows that I'm coming over to help you get ready, right?"

"Considering I refused his generous offer to schedule a spa day for me today, yeah . . . he knows you're coming over," I say with a smile.

Tiff looks at me, grinning widely. "I still say you should've taken him up on that. We can do makeup any ol' time, but a spa day? Rare treat. Bet he would've let me go along too, stingy bitch."

She's teasing, but I know she probably would've loved a day of relaxation like that. It just didn't feel right to take advantage of Scott that way though. I can get myself ready. Lord knows, I've got the makeup skills.

"Hey, talk to me," Tiff says as we take the elevator up to the penthouse. "I at least need to know where his red room is."

I appreciate that she can sense my nerves and is trying to keep things light. "Why, so you can try and steal something for your own use?" I joke, trying to let go of my tension, but it falls flat even to my own ears. "Sorry, I'm just . . . God, the thought of all those high-society types, all of them thinking I shouldn't be there. It's got me shittin' bricks. Even worse, some of them are part of Scott's family."

"And?" Tiff asks, like this isn't a super-important thing for Scott. To her, it's just a night to get dressed up and see how the other half live, maybe make a few jokes about the high-falutin' folks.

But it's more to me. "Tiff, I'm just a simple girl who's not used to these kinds of things. What if I end up embarrassing Scott?"

"Girl, you've got more common sense than most people," Tiff says. "Scott wouldn't be bringing you if he wasn't confident you could handle it."

"He tells me to just be myself, and everything will be fine," I admit, and Tiff smirks knowingly.

"I'm sure they'll find you refreshing and endearing," she reassures me in a faux-hoity toity voice.

"Or depressing and offensive," I say, still not sure but needing to let the nerves go in favor of getting ready. Maybe being all gussied up will make the swarm of bees in my belly settle into graceful butterflies?

The elevator dings, and the doors open to the small alcove that leads to Scott's front door, a security measure only since his is the only door on this floor.

I open the door, and I wonder if I was this dumbstruck when I came the first time. Probably . . . maybe even more since he brought me here when the lights were perfect and right now, we're just getting plain old mid-morning Bane from the big windows.

But Tiffany's impressed. "Holy shit! Girl, I can see why you've practically dumped my ass! If I had this to sleep in every night, I wouldn't come back to our raggedy ass apartment either. I'd have just sent you a text to box up all my shit and stick it by the door for the moving guy."

"Oh, come on, I haven't dumped you," I whine, and Tiff raises a disbelieving eyebrow at me. "I haven't."

"I know . . . but shit, I wouldn't blame you if you did. Imagine the muck bang I could have in that kitchen!" She giggles as she looks it over. "I'd have a million YouTube hits in a day!"

"Please don't . . . and don't say *anything* about that to Scott. He already thinks you're weird."

Tiff laughs. "He's right. Now how much time do I have to poke around before we need to get started?"

I check my phone and see we've got a little bit of time. "Fifteen minutes, maybe?"

"Whoo-hoo!" Tiff cheers, scampering off. "Seriously, you've got like the best boyfriend ever, babe," I hear her as her voice gets further away. "All he needs is a big Icelandic masseur named Magnus with a propensity for foot massages and I'd be set for-evah!"

Tiff runs around, oohing and ahhing over this and that. Her delight is contagious, and we're giggling like school girls by the time we settle down for some serious beauty pampering.

We get masks on our faces, paraffin wax dips on our feet, and deep conditioner in our hair before plopping down on the cushy rug in Scott's master bathroom to wait for the magic to happen.

Tiff looks around the room, her face more serious than her previous giddiness. "So, babe, this is all wildly impressive. But really . . . are you happy with Scott? Or is this just about the amenities?" Before I can answer, she holds up a staying palm toward me. "No judging either way. It's just that he gave you a key to his penthouse, Madison. That sounds serious, and as your friend, I want to know where your head is so I can advise appropriately."

"Well, things are admittedly moving pretty fast, but it's been amazing. He's . . . he's great, and I feel better with him, more 'me', if that makes sense. For a while, I was waiting for the other shoe to drop because fairy tale shit like this can't be real," I say, looking around the bathroom at the jetted tub, huge shower, sparkling mirrors, and chandelier. Yeah, there's a chandelier . . . in the bathroom. I shake my head at the craziness. "But the longer we go, the more I trust it, trust him. I'm still scared sometimes, but it's a tiny sliver of fear. The rest of my heart is full, doing a happy dance of hallelujah!" I say, smiling and certain my eyes are dopey with little hearts surrounding them like a picture filter.

"Fuck, Madison. I'm so glad! Truly, nobody deserves happiness more than you, and double snaps that you found it with a guy like Scott. I would've felt horrible if you hadn't given him a chance because of that stupid tattoo shit and had missed out on this," she says, gesturing around the room but including me in the encompassing circle of *this*.

"No worries, Tiff. That seems like a lifetime ago. I'm not going to let that fake mumbo-jumbo affect Scott and me. Not anymore," I tell her honestly.

"But I can still read your horoscope to you every morning, right? Even if you move in with Scott? It's tradition, you know."

"You'd better! I need your daily guidance to go about my day," I tell her with a wink, both of us knowing that our daily ritual is more about our friendship than astrology.

"GOD, YOU'RE SO FUCKING BEAUTIFUL."

Maybe it's not the most elegant or gentlemanly thing that Scott's ever said to me, but right now, standing by myself in the bedroom as he comes out from his walk-in closet in his tuxedo, it's powerful and makes me want to cry.

I sent Tiff home early, mainly because I needed some time to get my head right. Tiff was an amazing help today, but her constant chirpiness was starting to frazzle my nerves as much as my own concerns, and I needed the time to make sure I'm ready for tonight.

Scott's simple, honest words help me. "Thank you," I reply with a blush. "I'm still scared to death, though."

Scott sweeps me into his arms, turning me around in the sunset light before kissing me softly but deeply as he cups my neck and caresses my tongue with his own. "Don't worry," he says, giving me a cocky smirk, knowing he just knocked me off my equilibrium with just a kiss. His voice is calm, confident as he reassures me. "Everything will be fine."

"Promise?"

Scott nods. "Princess, you'll be noticed. You're too beautiful not to be . . . but you're going to charm and captivate everyone." His compliments bolster me, at least enough to get out the door. "Now, let's go. The car looks great after it's detailed."

I can't really notice too much of a difference. I think Scott's ride always looks amazing, but the inside does smell great, and as we drive over, it almost feels like I'm riding a horse, the rich smell of saddle oil giving me good vibes. "We use this same oil at the shelter."

"Really?" Scott asks, surprised. "What for?"

"The leashes and collars. May got them for free but then had to pay the money on the oil to keep them in good condition."

Scott keeps up his questions, and I know what he's doing. He's trying to keep my mind busy, and his distractions mostly work, but as I see the Danger Tower approaching, I start trembling. When I see the twin search lights stabbing the sky and the traffic starts to back up as we circle the block in a line of limos and other cars, Scott reaches over, patting my hand. "Relax. It'll all be okay."

"Tell me again who's going to be here," I say, needing the names fresh in my head even though I've already memorized them.

Scott indulges me again. "My dad and my mom, my brother and sister, but you've got all of them pegged. The business folks to know are Neil Johnson from Lightspeed—that's Chase's proposal company. Kenny Mackleroy from AlphaSystems—that's mine. And Winnifred Smith from—that's Olivia's company. All the rest of the people there will be executives and staff of Danger Enterprises, one of the three proposed companies, or a date, maybe a few city bigwigs. That's it, my family and three company head honchos are all you have to remember. The rest is just regular mingling like you do on a Saturday night at Stella's."

I nod, feeling like the names are solid in the forefront of my brain, and give him a tight smile as we're waved to the front of the line, pulling even with the red carpet. Scott jumps out, leaving the valet to handle the driver's side and quickly coming around to my door. The flashes startle me as he opens the door to help me out, but I do my best to grasp his offered hand and then take his elbow. "See? Nothing to it," Scott remarks quietly, just for me, as he gives another nod to a photographer. "Listen to them. They think you're amazing. They don't know the half of it. If they only knew that your pussy is the most delicious thing I've ever tasted, they'd be amazed. But I'm not sharing. Your pussy is mine."

The shock of Scott's words hits my brain, and for a split second,

I'm sure I look like a deer in the headlights, but then I laugh, which I'm sure was his goal all along. I hear a mad rush of clicks as photographers catch our interaction, my laughing smile and his cocky smirk.

His obscene humor calms me and turns me on, making all this seem less important than the two of us. At least for a moment, which is all I need to get myself in check.

I start to look around as we walk toward the grand entrance, taking in the scene surrounding me. Everyone looks like *somebody*, and the fact that Scott is proud to have me on his arm is doing wonders for my self-esteem. He's showing me off to the cameras and giving waves and nods to some of the other people he knows. And each time, I see . . . do I see approval?

Oh, my God, I do. It calms my nerves bit by bit, but as we enter the atrium of the Tower, my heart jumps again when Scott's steps tighten and he leans over. "My family is just ahead. See my father?"

I've never seen Robert Danger in person before, but I've studied his photograph over the past week as I've tried to prepare for this. I give Scott a nod, but my feet feel like they're weighed down with concrete.

He smiles at me, guiding me to his family. He raises his voice, greeting them. "Glad to see everyone. Mother, it's been too long." There's a formality to his voice that I'm not used to, and I realize this is Executive Scott Danger. He sounds detached, professional, and while his baritone is sexy no matter what, I prefer his more casual, teasing tone or his rumbly growls.

Scott's mother is easy to pick out of the assembled group, as she's the only woman old enough to be such. Reading her face, I think she'd rather be anywhere *but* here, but it's better than Robert, who gives me an icy look. I do my best to keep my chin up as Scott turns to me. "Everyone, this is my girlfriend, Madison Parker. Maddie, this is my father," he says, continuing around the circle.

Everyone except for Olivia is coldly hostile, especially Robert's date. Or maybe it's his girlfriend, I'm not sure. Either way, she's younger than me, and while I hate to be judgmental, she probably doesn't know a thing about business except how to spend Robert's money.

Olivia, though, gives me a polite handshake. "It's good to finally meet you. I've heard you were pretty, but I think the rumors don't do you justice."

Before I can thank her, Chase speaks up. "Yep, seems my little brother did something right . . . for once."

For some reason, I feel a need to defend Scott, but before I can, he responds to his brother himself. "Chase, jealousy is not becoming. By the way, where is your date?" Scott says, looking around like Chase's date might be hiding somewhere in the atrium.

The sting seems to hit its target as I notice a slight flush to Chase's neck, but his expression doesn't change. "My date is here. She simply ran to powder her nose."

Robbie approaches, offering a handshake of greeting to each male Danger before thrusting his elbow out to Olivia and they excuse themselves to mingle.

A redheaded stunner strides toward our group, her tiny frame incongruous with her large presence. Chase watches her approach with a predatory smile, "Oh, here's my date now." The pixie smiles coyly and Chase introduces her. "This is Gabrielle Williams. Gabby, this is my mother, Patricia Brookhurst." He continues around the group, and I catch Gabby's subtle glance up and down Scott's body as she shakes his hand. Her handshake with me is limp, so I make sure to squeeze back extra-hard, communicating without words that he's mine.

Scott's mom breaks the small talk suddenly. "Well, enough chitter chatter. Shall we head upstairs and get this show on the road? I'm sure we'd all like to get the presentations over with."

I look at Scott. Is his mother always this rude? He'd told me that his parents' divorce wasn't exactly amicable, but that his mom made her dutiful appearances at business functions because she retained a voting share in the business as part of the divorce settlement. But for something Scott has told me is a pivotal moment in the company, she seems shockingly blasé about tonight.

"I agree, Mother. I think Madison and I will head upstairs." He dips his chin politely and leads me toward the bank of elevators. One dings, and we step inside, blessedly alone for a moment.

"Brrr . . ." I say with a smile.

"Oh, come on now. That wasn't so bad, was it?" Scott asks. "I think Olivia actually likes you."

"Are you kidding? She was polite . . . but the rest of your family hates me."

Scott laughs lightly, taking my hand. "They hate everyone. I think they even hate themselves sometimes . . . except Chase. He thinks the whole world revolves around him."

"Is he always so . . . I don't know, an ass?"

Scott laughs again. "No, unfortunately, that's usually reserved just for me. Keep your eyes open and you'll see what I mean. For now, it's time to mingle."

Mingling turns out to be a nearly exhausting half hour of Scott and me moving around the room, shaking hands and being introduced to more people than I can remember. Most of them are men, although there are a few women. I don't include the dates because it seems a lot of them are merely accessories.

Scott, though, always makes sure I'm introduced, and while I can't add a lot to the conversations, I do what I can, and Scott never lets me be ignored. Still, by the time we sit down to the dinner portion of the evening, I'm glad to have only one table of people to deal with. We make our introductions, and I make it a point to memorize these people's names since I'll be with them for the next couple of hours.

Scott leans over and whispers in my ear, "You're doing great, a total natural. You've got everyone in the palm of your hand. Me included." Before I even say thank you, he whispers again, "By the way, if you want to see Chase in action, now's your chance."

Robert gets up first, looking out on the crowd as waiters quickly bring around appetizers. Scott told me tonight's meal will be served in between each of the presentations, giving people time to discuss each one at length over the next course. "Ladies and gentlemen, honored guests, thank you for coming to Danger Enterprises's gala, A Night for the Future."

"What a load," Scott murmurs as Robert goes on for about ten minutes. I see what he means. According to Robert, everything tonight is about showing Bane what could happen in the next twenty years and getting the city excited . . . oh, and all of it, of course, is due to Danger Enterprises, and more specifically, *him*.

"We're going to build the greatest city of the twenty-first century. The greatest," Robert continues, smiling broadly. "When our children and grandchildren look back on this evening, they're going to say that this was the night Bane made the leap from a growing potential to absolute greatness." He pauses for the expected round of applause, basking in the worship from the audience, but I can see little signs that not everyone is as zealous as Robert would like to think. There are sighs here and subtle eye rolls there. It seems Scott may not be the only one with an issue with Robert Danger.

"With that, let me introduce my son Chase, a great visionary with a business plan I think you'll find exciting. He'll be outlining the first of the potential projects that we could bring to this great, great city's future."

"Thank you, Father," Chase says, and even I have to do a double-take. Gone is the sniping asshole who sneered at me, and instead, standing up in the spotlight, is a suave, commanding man with an electric presence. "I'd like to talk to you about opportunity this evening, about a future brighter than we've ever dreamed possible. But one that we can make a reality by working together, Danger Enterprises and Lightspeed, changing our city, our state, our country . . ."

Chase's words are hypnotizing, and even I'm buying into what he's saying as he uses his video screens to maximum effect. "He's good," I tell Scott as Chase continues, "but you're still going to kick his ass."

Scott chuckles, but I can see his fist clench around his napkin as Chase finishes up.

Robert retakes the podium, clapping his son on the back in a fatherly embrace, the approval apparent to everyone in the room. "An amazing vision for the future," Robert says as Chase sits down, and I see him shake hands around his table, celebrating his win already.

"Folks, while the staff clears the plates and brings out the main course, I'd like to tell you about one of the current projects Danger Enterprises is doing to create the foundation for the future. This great project, with some of the best people in the world, all of whom work for me, of course, is going . . ." The audience laughs at his joke and Robert drones on.

When he finally sits, our table is abuzz with talk about Chase's plan. While the general consensus is positive, I look to Scott for the catch. "So, I'm no business genius, but that sounded good. I'm on your side, obviously but . . ."

Scott smiles at me. "No, you're right. And honestly, it's something we should do. But my plan is better, pure and simple."

I smile before planting a soft kiss to the corner of his mouth. "Good enough for me, Mr. Danger. You ready?"

Scott nods and stands as his father finishes a much less glowing introduction of Scott and his proposal. He buttons his jacket, squaring his shoulders, and I see a transformation in him too. Gone is the man who's let me see inside his life, behind his mask. Now he is Scott Danger, the future of Danger Enterprises . . . and I'm glad to get to see this side of him too.

"Kick some ass, baby," I whisper as he walks away.

By the time he takes the microphone, my heart's hammering, but it's all in support of him.

CHAPTER 20

MADISON

*S*cott looks out at the crowd, and I can feel the tension building in the room. He's just waiting, standing at the podium, commanding attention by simply being there. It's like he's waiting for a specific moment or some kind of sign, but I have no idea what it is, and neither does anyone else, it seems. But every eye is on Scott, unable to tear themselves away from his presence.

With a sudden *bong!* that reverberates through the entire room, the display behind Scott flashes to life.

"Mankind is sustained by the dreamers. Those who, in the midst of mediocrity and comfort, choose a path riddled with scorn and disbelief," Scott intones, his voice ringing out over the audience.

The screen behind him flashes through images of great inventors . . . Leonardo da Vinci, Thomas Edison, Nikola Tesla, Tim Berners-Lee, and Steve Jobs.

"These greats each had a vision, one they could foresee that no one else believed possible. But you know what?" Scott asks, allowing for a dramatic pause. "The naysayers were wrong. Just because they couldn't conceive of such a thing, didn't make it impossible." Scott nods once, and the screen changes to images of the lightbulb, a tesla coil, flying machines, and a plethora of computer-related images.

"What we are presented with today is an opportunity . . . a chance to be a believer, not a small-minded naysayer." Scott smirks, giving a pointed, albeit respectful, look to his father.

"When you hear the term 'artificial intelligence', what do you think of?" The screen flashes a picture of Arnold Schwarzenegger as *The Terminator* and the crowd laughs. Scott grins along with them, sharing in on the joke. "I know, great movie, but ultimately, fiction. But in the real world, we already have AI. How many of you talk to Siri or Alexa every day? Or have you gotten some rather eerily accurate suggested items on Amazon or Pandora? These are all algorithm-based forms of AI, right here in our daily lives, happening now. There are others you might not know . . ." Scott talks about a bunch of companies I don't know anything about, but I see several nods in the audience, so the tech folks are still following along with him, thank goodness.

"What I'm asking is that you suspend your inherent need to say no just because it might be impossible to you or me." The audience is mostly quiet, but I hear murmurs of agreement. I glance at Robert Danger just in time to see him roll his eyes, obviously annoyed with the dramatics, but Scott has the audience eating out of his hand, me included.

"Then let me introduce you to someone. Xena, can you say hello to the people?" I see people lean forward, excited to see who Scott is bringing out.

Instead, a new voice comes over the speakers, obviously artificial but still managing to sound like a friendly female voice. "Hello to the people?" It's a parroting of Scott's words and questioning tone.

Scott grins. "Xena, no offense, but you sound like a robot." His joke earns a laugh from the crowd.

"My apologies, Mr. Danger. Hello, my name is Xena. I'm a Genone artificial intelligence developed by AlphaSystems. My primary function is to analyze existing networks and webs, design efficiencies, and recommend growth opportunities. My most recent task was to monitor traffic flows within the city limits of Bane. I have a recommendation for changing light patterns at 27 intersections to decrease the average commute time by twelve minutes for the average driver. Also, a stop sign is needed."

There's a moment of hushed amazement, and then murmurs break out all over the room as people talk to the others at their tables. Scott smiles, waiting a moment before clearing his throat to continue. "Now, I'll admit that I'm not a tech genius. But Kenny Mackleroy of AlphaSystems is, so I'll let him explain." The screen flashes to a video of a grey-haired man who talks excitedly about the possibilities. Admittedly, Mackleroy comes across as a bit of a mad scientist, but the video tour of his facility and the things he has actually created and what they can do is quite compelling.

The video ends, and Scott continues. "As I said, I'm not a tech guy, but I am a business man. I see what other companies are investing in, what their growth projections are." Scott looks at Chase and Olivia. "And while that's fine, safe, and even smart, we have the opportunity to get in on the ground floor of something Earth-changing here. To bring this to Bane as an extension of Danger Enterprises.

"This partnership brings with it a five-million-dollar trust at the local university for STEM student scholarships from a grant already in place, thousands of jobs for residents, and tens of thousands of new people in Bane over the next decade. This is the future . . . of Danger Enterprises, of Bane, of our world. If you find the courage to be open to the possibilities. Do not be a naysayer simply because it is beyond your capabilities. Let the dreamers dream and take the rest of us along for the ride."

It's powerful, it's bombastic, and it casts him as some sort of leader of more than a company but of an entire city . . . and I'm on my feet along with everyone else as Scott leaves the stage, the light following him as he approaches me.

"You were wonderful!" I exclaim as Scott approaches, his cocky grin softening into the smile I've come to see more often.

"Was I?" he asks, stepping closer. "I kept looking for you, but the light was too bright."

"Well, I could see just fine. I couldn't take my eyes off you."

Scott nods and pulls me tight, kissing me even with the spotlight still on us. I'm taken aback, thrilled. A full-blown kiss, right here in front of everyone, during one of the most important moments of his life. He doesn't care what anyone thinks of me or of our relationship. He cares about me, and he'll let the whole damn world know it. It makes me feel heady and important.

After we settle back in, there are still ten minutes before dishes are cleared and the dinner course is over. But Scott doesn't even get a chance to eat because people keep coming over to shake his hand and congratulate him for a job well done. Noticeably absent from the appreciation is Scott's entire family. Although I hadn't expected his dad or brother to say anything, I'd hoped that maybe his mom or sister would see reason and at least tell him 'good job'.

Olivia presented her plan after Scott, and while it was presented well, it didn't have the same 'oomph' behind it. I almost feel bad for her because I would've hated going after Scott. Nothing would've stood up against what he laid out.

Once all the presentations are made, the lights change, and Scott reaches over, taking my hand. "Shall we dance?"

I nod, taking his hand and heading out to the dance floor. A band has taken the stage where the presentations were given, and a singer takes the microphone.

The saxophone and guitar start up, and Scott takes me in his arms. "I don't know this one."

Scott smiles, turning with me. "*Expose*. Just listen. I heard this a lot growing up. My mom liked this group."

Seasons change . . . people change . . .

I've heard this part, and as the singer adds her sultry voice to the sensuous instrumentals, I lean my head on Scott's chest. It feels good, but at the same time, I feel sad. The lyrics hit me deep. People change, and too often, we're sacrificing tomorrow to hang onto today's pleasures.

"It's so horrible."

"What is?" Scott asks, looking down at me.

"The way your family is," I reply sadly. "It's like you hate each other. Especially you and Chase."

Scott nods, glancing over to where Chase is dancing with his date. "I don't *hate* him. But it's all we've ever known."

"That's horrible," I murmur absently. "It's hard to fathom how it could get this way. I don't have a lot of family, but what I do have, we're very close."

Scott hums, but my mind goes back to what he said on stage. "They're all your naysayers and you're the dreamer."

He smirks. "Not sure about the dreamer part, but they definitely underestimate me."

"You are a dreamer, maybe not in a wild way like those inventors. You're more of a bespoke suit type, filled with power and ambition, but you see possibilities where others don't or are unwilling to. You see a possibility in me . . . broken, moody, aimless. You make me dream too."

Scott stops dancing, looking down at me. "What do you dream? Tell me, Madison, and I'll fucking make it happen. Anything."

"I dream about you, wish that this fantasy were real, but I'm so scared I'm going to wake up and it'll have all been pretend, my heart hoping for things I'm not destined to have." My voice is soft, sad.

Scott cups my face. "You deserve everything. You're not broken or aimless. You got knocked down, licked your wounds, and got right back up to fight another day. When I found you, you were standing tall on your own two feet, telling me to fuck off by kicking me out and not calling. And it was glorious and tempting, but I'm here now and you don't have to be scared. You and me, Madison. I am your heart's destiny and you're fucking mine. *Mine*."

I feel his cock stiffen against my hip as he rumbles deep in his chest. Grabbing me by the arm, he leads me from the room.

"Where are we going?" I ask, surprised at his turn, going from sweetly poetic words I'll always cherish to growly sexy in a single word.

My heart is pounding, and we don't even make it to the elevator before he's kissing me and pulling me into a darkened service corridor. We stumble a little, but Scott finds and pushes me into a small alcove where we're not visible from down the hallway.

"Scott what are you do—" I start to ask before he cuts me off with a passionate kiss.

"I have to have you. Now," he growls. "I need you to feel that you are mine . . . inside and out, heart and fucking soul, Madison. That this is our destiny."

My protests are lost in the rain of kisses on my neck, my desire warring with my sense of decorum. "We can't do this here."

"We can. We are," he grunts out, his eyes frantic. "I promise I'll be gentle tonight, but right now . . . I can't." He presses on my hips, guiding me.

I moan, nodding as I turn around the way he wants and start to hike up my dress. Scott's hands help me, a whimper slipping from my lips as the cool air touches my ass. Scott kisses the back of my neck, pulling me tight against his body, and I can feel his cock straining inside his tuxedo pants. This is so bad, so dirty, but I want it . . . I want *him* as much as I want to breathe.

"Hold right there," Scott rasps, and I hear the sound of a zipper being pulled, a shiver going down my spine as I anticipate feeling him slide his perfect cock inside me.

"Please, Scott. Make me yours."

Suddenly, there's a harsh laugh and a golf clap. "Ooh, yes, Scott, take me," a laughing falsetto says in a porn imitation, and I gasp, spinning around as Scott takes a stumbling step back. Chase stands there with an amused expression on his face. "You really do know how to pick them."

Scott growls, adjusting my dress so my ass isn't showing before zipping himself back up. "Chase, get the fuck out of here."

"Why should I?" Chase asks, his attention on Scott. "I see she isn't a bartender after all. Just a whore who sees a paycheck in your last name."

I flinch, my eyes blurring with tears as Chase's words pierce me to the heart.

Chase looks at me, an ugly smirk on his pretty face. "How much is Scott paying you?"

Before I can say anything, Scott's fist lashes out, catching Chase by surprise and sending him stumbling into the wall. "Fucker!"

"Scott, no!" I cry, but Chase pushes away from the wall, punching Scott back, and the fight is on. There are no rules, no real intent here other than to vent years of rage built up by their competitiveness. There's a flurry of fists . . . to Scott's gut, to Chase's nose, some so fast I don't even see where they land.

"Stop it, you two!" I yell as their feet get tangled up with each other and they fall to the floor, turning it into a grappling match. I should be able to do something, considering I've broken up plenty of barroom brawls, but these guys are huge and going at it full-throttle, not drunk and sloppy, so I'm reduced to hollering and standing out of range of their fists and feet. "Stop!"

"What the fuck are you two doing?" A voice says, coming out of nowhere.

The sharp hiss pierces through the red haze of fury the two are feeling, and I look to see Olivia hurrying down the hallway, her gown swishing on the carpet.

The brothers roll off each other. Scott has a busted lip and Chase's nose is bleeding, but it could have been worse. So much worse.

Scott wipes at his lips with the back of his hand and gets up, while Chase is sneering at him, looking pleased even though he's battered and still on the ground.

"Gotcha," Chase says, and the realization hits me. Chase didn't care about me and Scott having sex in an empty corner hallway, or even about me, really. But all of it, his taunting, his words . . . it was to get inside Scott's armor. To needle him into making a mistake, exposing a weakness.

With a single punch, Scott exposed that weakness and showed that I'm a liability. I feel used, a pawn in the war between the two brothers, and somehow, that hurts more than the actual taunts themselves.

"Chase, shut the fuck up," Olivia says. "Use your handkerchief to mop that up before something shows on your shirt. Can't do anything about the rumpling, but the lights are low."

"You're a fucking dead man, Chase," Scott seethes, but Olivia holds up a hand.

"What the hell are you two thinking, fighting like you did when you were eight? You're both damn lucky nobody saw you."

"Olivia—" I start, but a single glance from her cuts me off. Scott said she's been dubbed the Ice Queen, and from the coldness in her eyes, I can see why.

"You two, get out of here," she says to Scott and me. "Chase, you're coming with me and leaving in five minutes after we get the blood stopped and cleaned up. Both of you had better hope I don't tell Father."

"You'd blab just to win?" Scott asks, and Olivia sighs in frustration.

"Not to win . . . but because you two insist on acting like this company is nothing more than pieces on a board. The people in your pitches, in your presentations tonight, they're not marbles to fight over. They're real people with real feelings. That you two are still acting like this means I don't know if I can trust you not to destroy their lives in your little sibling rivalry. I won't have that. Now get the fuck outta here."

CHAPTER 21

SCOTT

Daily Horoscope, October 17th
Scorpio – Conflict can destroy your future. Do not allow hard feelings to prevent progress.

The elevator dings, and Maddie unlocks the door for me. I'm limping a little, probably from the way Chase and I tumbled to the ground during our fight, but I haven't complained. Nor will I, because no good comes from whining. Once inside, she helps me take off my tuxedo jacket before hanging it up. I slump to the couch, suddenly exhausted. Looking down, I see the blood spotting my shirt. I hear Maddie's disapproving *tsk* before she turns to leave.

"Where are you going?" I ask, and Madison stops, turning back to me.

"To get something to help you clean up. Just give me a moment."

Thank God. I had a quick flash that she might be ditching me at home and bailing after that fiasco. But apparently not. She disappears, and I lean my head back, a headache threatening to pound apart my skull. Part of it, I'm sure, are the punches Chase landed. He got a good one in to my temple that will likely leave an ugly bruise. Just as much of it, though, is from being pissed at myself.

How'd I let that happen? His catching me with my cock out and the two of us about to go at it shouldn't have led to all that. Hell, his words were damning, but normally, I'd have been able to brush them off with returned barbs of my own. But that was the first time his arrogant snark had been directed at her . . . my Madison. That was the straw that broke the camel's back.

The object of my obsession walks back into the living room, having changed out of her fancy gown and into one of my undershirts. My necklace still hangs around her neck, though, the perfect mix of casual and fancy, both in us and in her wardrobe. A tiny smirk hints at the corner of my mouth, but I school my face as the movement cracks open my lip a bit more. "Ouch," I grumble, snapping back to the present as Madison presses a rubbing alcohol-soaked cotton ball to my lip. "I don't need that."

"Shut up and let me take care of those. You two were rolling on the carpet," Maddie says, scolding me like a school child but straddling my lap. "I'd use peroxide but you don't have any."

I grit my teeth as she dabs at the cuts. "You sure you're not trying to just get some pain in?"

"If I wanted to hurt you, I'd have let you go to bed with the carpet fuzz still embedded in these," she replies.

I do my best to hold still until she gets done, hissing when she's finally finished with a cut on my cheek. "Fuck. Think you got it all?"

She sighs, looking a little worried. "Are you angry with me?" she asks.

I let out a sigh. I made her doubt her place here, with me. And I know that's a shitty thing to do when her heart is so damn fragile and just starting to trust me. "No, Maddie. I'm not mad at you. I'm mad at Chase for saying those awful things. But mostly, I'm mad at myself for letting him get to me. He fucking deserved it, but he's probably going to use that against me. Against us."

"I'm so sorry," she says softly as she looks down at her hands.

"You have nothing to be sorry for," I say, putting my hands on her thighs. "I'm the one who lost control. I swear it won't happen again. I'm not . . ." I can't say her ex's name, but it lingers in the air like an evil spirit.

Madison grabs my hands. "I know, Scott. God, I know you're nothing like Rich. You were defending me, and there's this whole weird mix of sibling rivalry. But your fighting your brother didn't remind me of . . . that, not at all." I feel a whoosh of air leave my lungs in relief.

"Maybe I shouldn't have gone? Then he wouldn't have that ammunition against you. Things could've just been the same as always, even though that's still pretty fucked up with you two." Madison shakes her head.

"Listen to me. I wanted you there, by my side. And I'm damn glad you were. I'm sorry it turned ugly and you got stuck in the middle of it. But it's not about you, I swear. Chase and I have always fought, sometimes with words and sometimes with fists. The presentation setup was just too much pressure and we both boiled over. I hate that you were collateral damage. I'm sorry for losing it and not protecting you." I wince, expecting her to give me a tongue lashing about not needing me to protect her, but she's distracted and it slips past her.

"You two . . . it seems like everything you do is just another way to throw punches—literal or figurative."

Her words make me think. Has there ever been any genuine love between us? Chase or Liv? It's always been competition. It hasn't been violent between me and Liv . . . but Chase and I have fought for two decades.

"Dad has put us against each other since we were old enough to walk. We couldn't even share a swing set. Dad intentionally had it installed with one seat. I couldn't even share that with him."

Madison shakes her head. "Your father sounds like a monster. What sort of man could do that to his children?"

I nod and tell Madison about the things I haven't told her, the parts I haven't told *anyone* before. "Dad just always felt superior to others, usually people with less money, but sometimes people he just deemed weaker for some reason or another. I think he's got this constant need to see which of us is the 'better son' and at the same time, ensure that neither of us surpasses him. If he's not winning, if people aren't looking up to him with respect and fear and admiration, then what's the point?"

"It's sad. He could do so much good," Madison murmurs. "He's so arrogant, though. It twists him, makes him just . . . destructive. But you can change it."

I arch an eyebrow. "You think so?"

Madison nods. "It doesn't have to be this way. Don't you see? It's his chess board, his rules. And while he's busy competing with the whole world for dominance, he's shrunk your focus to only competing with Chase, keeping you small. Or smaller than him, at least. Stop competing with Chase, with your dad, and just be you. Make your own board, your own rules, and play your own damn game."

Her words make me think, but I admit, "It might be too late for that. Even if Chase hadn't said what he said about you, this proposal setup is do-or-die for us all."

Madison strokes my hair, almost petting me, and it calms me, clears my head to hear her words in my heart, not just my head. "He may have meant what he said. But I think it's more likely that he was poking around to find a weak spot to exploit, just like y'all have always done. I was just a new pawn on the board."

She sits back, her whiskey eyes sparking with fire as they meet mine. "You're a smart man, Scott. Even if you win this proposal, if you take over the company, *you still lose*. Your father is the real winner. In my eyes, the only way this works is to come together with your siblings. Something your father obviously never wanted. Beat him at his own game. The three of you. Together. You told me you felt like everything is a competition. A winner and a loser." She pauses, and I nod, knowing I still think that's largely true. "Well, why in the fuck do you three let him win and y'all lose every time? If it's a competition, use what you have, each other, and be winners together and make him the loser for once in his monstrous life."

Her words start to hit home. Can I do that? Just completely change the power structure and dynamics of this game we've played our entire lives? I don't know if I can or how to go about it, but I know if I have a snowball's chance in hell, it'll be because of Madison. "You know what? I'm glad to have you in my life," I say, wrapping my hands around her waist and pulling her close, pressing my forehead to hers intimately. "I'm realizing more every day that you're the best thing that's ever happened to me."

"Those are strong words, Scott." It's a statement, but the question is in her tone, and I nod, tracing her up and down her back with my fingertips.

"I mean them." I pull Madison closer, kissing over the curve of her chin and down her throat, marveling at the feeling of her soft skin. I can feel the pull of the small abrasions on my face, especially my lip as I move against her, but I don't care, needing her skin against mine too much.

"Mr. Danger . . . are you trying to seduce me?" Madison murmurs teasingly. "Because it's working."

"Good. Because I need you tonight," I reply, pushing her shirt up and exposing her breasts. I push both of her nipples together and nibble on them, loving the way they pearl up under my attentions. Madison moans and grinds down on my lap as she arches her back for more. My cock bulges in my trousers, pressing against her panty-covered pussy and sending heat rising in my groin.

"Mmm . . . you have me . . . you have me!" Madison gasps, looking down at my hungry mouth. I suck hard, and her eyes widen before she shudders, pushing herself down on my bulge and groaning in frustration, wanting more. "Goddammit."

"Shh, that'll be round two," I promise her. "For now, just ride me like you did the first time. Let yourself feel good."

Madison nods, abandoning herself to rolling her hips on my rock-hard bulge, rubbing back and forth until I can feel myself rubbing between her lips and over her clit. I reach down, smacking her ass and squeezing her cheeks, easing them apart and sliding a finger deeper until I feel the silk of her thong and the puckered tightness of her asshole. "Mmm . . . is this mine too?"

Madison's eyes are wide, nerves and need warring in their depths, but she rolls her hips faster, trembling on the edge. "Yes. Anything . . . all yours."

I smile, biting on her nipples as I slip into her panties, coating my fingers in her honey. I press against her tight ass, whispering soothing words to help her relax as I slide one finger slowly into her ass. I hold still, letting her adjust as she rides me through my slacks. As she begins to buck, I press in and out, adding a second finger, and she's pushed over, moaning my name as she comes, pulling my head tighter and smothering me with her soft tits. I moan, drawing it out for her as she freezes, then sags against me as her body dissolves. "Mmm, so fucking beautiful," I murmur, kissing up to nuzzle her ear. "Are you ready for more?"

Madison, still panting, nods. "Anything. Everything."

I smile in victory, easing her off my lap. "Bend over the couch." My voice is hard, gravelly with need, but she does as I say.

Madison grabs the back of the couch, looking behind and easing her thong to the side to expose herself to me. She's so damn perfect . . . dripping with her arousal and her tight little ass right there for me to claim for the first time. I'm tempted, so fucking tempted . . . but she's got me so wound up I'm not in control. I'd hurt her, and I can't allow that. Instead, I open my pants and push them down, taking my cock in hand and slapping her ass cheeks with it before tracing it over her wet pussy. "Mmm . . . I need you hard, rough, so I'm gonna fuck your sweet pussy this time. But this ass is *mine*." I emphasize the promise by grabbing a handful of her ass in each of my hands and squeezing hard, loving the way my fingers create little divots in her lush curves.

"Oh, my G—" Madison says, but her words turn into a long gasp as I drive my cock all the way in, grabbing the T-shirt like a handle before thrusting hard over and over, knowing that she can take it.

Her perfect body takes it all as only Madison can, pushing back into me and challenging me, moving with me and turning my frustration and anger into something better. She makes it pure, sweet bliss as her pussy clenches around my cock and her moans fill my ears with her primal music. I pull on her shirt harder, and she squeezes around my cock, taking all of me in and sending tremors through my body.

"That's it. Give it to me," she moans, somehow knowing exactly what I need. "Oh, fuck, Scott. You're gonna make me come again. Fill me up . . . just like that."

Her dirty words add to the pleasure, and I smack Madison's ass. She yelps, squeezing my cock and fucking me back just as hard.

I can't last long, but I don't need to. Madison's wild underneath me, the two of us bucking and twisting, my cock grinding deep inside her. With a roar, I come, filling her body deep and hard. My balls ache, but the last of my pain and anger is pouring out of me, transformed into hope as Madison clenches her pussy around me and cries out my name, her body convulsing as she shatters too. I wonder if she feels as reborn as I do, like my whole world-view just fragmented and reformed into a new picture. One where it's us as a couple, and my siblings and me are no longer competitors, but dare I say, friends. And my dad no longer has any control over any of it. But I don't ask her, letting the possibility take seed in my mind.

CHAPTER 22

SCOTT

Daily Horoscope, October 30th

Scorpio - A good captain understands the truth: they are only in control of themselves. The ship is at the mercy of the wind and waves.

know I should be analyzing the results from the European division because the new tax laws coming out of Brussels are driving a lot of people nuts. Danger Enterprises and me included.

But I can't.

Ever since the gala, I've been on a roller coaster of emotions. True to her word, Olivia seems to have kept quiet about the fight because Dad hasn't said a thing. So at least that's a relief. Chase is basically ignoring my existence, which would usually be welcome, but Maddie's words keep ringing in my head, and I wonder if there's any way to repair so many years of damage between us. And the board hasn't voted yet, which makes me antsy, ready to begin the real work of partnering with Alpha-Systems.

All that work turmoil is settled when I'm with Maddie, though. She's been spending more and more time at my place, and she even made a passing comment that made me think she's considering moving in with me. Halle-fucking--lujah! Because the nights when I come home to an empty place are hell, a reminder of how much she means to me and that I need her with me, by my side, as much as possible.

I'm staring at the same line of text I've been reading for the last ten minutes when there's a knock on my door, and I look up to see Robbie giving me a thumbs-up. "Good news, Boss Man."

"What's that?" I ask, pushing my keyboard aside and waving Robbie in. Fuck it, this is why we have accountants. They're paid to know this tax law shit better than me, anyway.

Robbie helps himself to a seat. "AlphaSystems is upping the ante."

I lift an eyebrow, saying nothing. I've already heard. Much to my surprise, Dad's idea for the gala may have actually started an odd type of 'bidding war'. It seems the proposed companies are starting to offer incentives in an attempt to secure their partnership with Danger Enterprises. They don't have money—that's why they want ours—but they have ownership percentages, profit sharing, and whatever other methods they think will sway the money their way.

"In addition to doubling our stock options, they agreed to name the scholarship fund at the university after your dad . . . the Robert Danger Advanced Technology Fund."

I whistle, smirking a bit. "Like he'd know advanced technology if it bit him in the ass, but talk about playing to Dad's ego. He'll love the immortality of having his name attached to something like that."

"That's what I'm thinking too," Robbie says. "I don't care what money Chase's boys might be offering because we know the money is there in every option in different amounts. But Robert Danger's name in the paper every year as he hand-selects a recipient and personally delivers the scholarship? That sort of shit sticks."

"You heard any gossip about what's going on upstairs?" I ask.

"Decision is going to be soon," Robbie says. "The whole board is involved now, and you know they're playing it close to the vest. Closed-door chats and all."

"The more they think about it, talk to each other, the better our odds. Shows that they have doubts about blindly following Dad's order. I've had a couple of them call my home line to ask questions, and hell, Charlie caught me in the parking garage last week. I think that's a good sign. I'm hopeful, at least."

Robbie nods. "Makes sense. By the way, heard something else," Robbie mentions. "You and Chase still aren't talking to each other?"

"Yeah, we haven't dealt with the shit show after the gala. Maddie said some things that have really made me think about my relationship with Chase and Liv, but I just don't know how to go about changing a lifetime of rivalry, especially with this axe hanging over our heads," I tell him dejectedly.

Before he can comment on my confession, my intercom buzzes. "Sir? Your father wants to see you."

"Of course. Tell him I'll be up right away," I reply, looking at Robbie.

"First thing to do with your brother and sister . . . apologize. All three of you have been absolute shits to each other forever. Start with 'I'm sorry' and go from there," he says like it's that easy.

Easier said than done, but I know he's right. "Thanks, man," I say, getting up to head upstairs. In the minute it takes me to get to the board room, I see that Chase and Liv have already beaten me there. *No surprise. Dad probably called me last*, I think bitterly.

Still, I have room for hope. Chase doesn't have his normal arrogant smirk on his face, and Liv has her usual detached façade. They're not confident either. So whatever's going on . . . I've still got a shot.

Dad's back is to me as I enter the room, looking out over the skyline, his hands stuffed in the pockets of his suit and his shoulders squared.

He turns as I take my seat, and I see that his eyes are fiery as he stares daggers at all three of us. "You think I didn't hear about the little incident at the gala? Scott, starting a fight with your brother like a child? Grow up, son. This is business, not playground roughhousing. Just another example of your inadequacy and infantilism."

"I'm sure you know that's not what happened," I growl, glancing at Chase, who for once looks as surprised as I feel. He didn't know this was coming either. "I—"

"If it were up to me, you'd be out on your ass! Your actions could've cost us dearly. God, imagine if one of the board members or one of the CEOs of the guest companies had walked in on that display of juvenile delinquency. Although I guess I shouldn't expect better from you. By now, I know you're always such a disappointment," Dad yells. "Unfortunately, the verdict's coming down, and it's not solely my decision on which route we go. I can't fire you because it'll lead to too many questions, and I guess there's the off chance they'll pick your deal." He says the last part with a snide grin, like it's a complete impossibility.

"Hasn't stopped you from doing what you've wanted before," I growl, glancing at Liv and Chase. Both of them look a bit shell-shocked at Dad's display, and I realize he usually saves his harshest criticisms of my character flaws for when it's just the two of us. They've never heard him talk to me like this. I do what I always do . . . take the pain, transform it, and turn it into something useful.

Dad huffs at my outburst, turning to face the window again, rudely dismissing me the same way he always does.

Usually this is the point where I walk away, but today, I can't. "You're wrong," I say flatly.

Dad turns around from his window view, eyeing me incredulously. "Excuse me?"

"I said you're wrong. The board is considering my plan. Hell, they're considering them all, but we all know my plan is the one that's intriguing them. That's why they're having closed-door discussions without you. You can't control this and it's driving you crazy. You're such a narcissist that you don't realize you've already lost," I say, stepping forward. "The fact is, the whole gala was just an excuse to stroke your own ego. You're behind the times and out of touch."

My father is fuming, literal beads of sweat popping on his forehead as the heat of his anger enflames him from the inside. "No matter which way the board goes on this, it's still not a clear-cut decision on who will take the reins when I retire. That's a separate vote and one I will be heard on again before ballots are cast. So watch yourself, Son. This old dog still has bark, but more importantly, he still has bite."

He gets up, passing me as he walks to the door, and I hold my breath, literally unsure what he's going to do. But he simply bypasses me without incident before stopping in the doorway. He looks back, making eye contact with each of us before settling his eyes on mine. "Scott, of all my children, you are the most like me. A chip off the old block." He says it with a smile, like it's a compliment. It's the worst thing he's ever said to me and my stomach rolls as he strides off down the hall.

I collapse into the white leather chair nearest me, stunned and questioning whether I'm really like him. He's been the villain in my story all along . . . the absentee father, the harshest critic, the self-important narcissist. Could he be right about me?

Liv comes over, sitting daintily in the chair nearest me like the lady she mostly is. "Scott, he's wrong." My eyes click to hers, and I know I'm silently begging her for more. "Dad is an asshole, always has been and always will be, with issues we can't begin to decipher or cure. You're ambitious and driven, with a hard outer shell. But you're not him. None of us are. We're affected by him, but we're not broken like he is."

I lay my hand over hers and realize it's the first time in years that I've touched my own sister other than handshakes and poses for pictures at events. "Thanks, Liv."

There's a beat of silence, then Chase speaks but never looks away from the view out the windows. "Is he always that cruelly critical with you?"

I huff a humorless laugh. "That? Other than telling me I'm like him, that was a fucking rah-rah pep talk compared to our usual rehash of my faults."

Chase's eyes cut to mine, and I can see the disgust. "I had no idea. His talks with me are usually about how I'm destined for greatness but have to fight and earn every accolade lest you steal them from me."

Ours eyes lock on each other, flashes of our past playing out between us in the tense air. The competitions, the fights, the hatred, but also the hard work, the accomplishments, and the empire we've helped sustain. It hasn't been pretty, but it's gotten us pretty damn far. Although I'm not sure the benefit has been worth the cost.

Chase's eyes drop first and he takes a breath, but I don't let him say anything else, don't want to dwell on what has been. Maddie is in my ear, telling me that there's another way, or there *could* be. "Chase, I'm sorry. About the fight, about the . . . well, about a lot of things. I'm sorry." Maddie was right. Saying it does feel good, releases a knot in my core I didn't know was there.

I turn to Liv, apologizing to her as well. "Liv, I'm sorry for so much too."

She smiles, a genuine full smile that is so rare I can't remember the last time I saw it. "Apology accepted, brother." She leans back in her chair, pointing first at Chase and then at me. "And not that either of you fuckers asked, but my conversations with Dad? Nonexistent. Never happen. I get the pleasure of dealing with his weaselly PA, which is hell all its own. Guess I used to think I was missing out on some father-son bonding thing, but now I'm thinking I'm the lucky one who missed out on all that damage."

It's inappropriate, irreverent, and downright cheeky, all things Olivia Danger is not. But it's exactly the right thing to say, and we all suddenly burst into laughter. I don't think we've ever laughed together. Ever.

CHAPTER 23

MADISON

Daily Horoscope, October 30th
Libra - Beware outside evils, as well as internal demons.

iff groans as she reads my horoscope. "I think the outside evils are the ones we have to worry about most tonight! I hate working holidays like this. Everyone's sloppy drunk and forgets to tip. And Mama needs the moolah so I can buy my own candy. Trick or treat myself!" She snaps like that's already a done deal. It probably is, considering I've seen no fewer than three empty bags of candy already littered around the apartment like dead soldiers, PMS-edition.

"I'm not sure Devil's Night qualifies as an actual holiday. The holiday is Halloween." Sure, Devil's Night is total fiction, but some folks do use it as an excuse to get rowdy.

"Pshaw . . . is Christmas Eve a holiday? Yes. It's the pre-party for Christmas. Devil's Night is the Halloween pre-party. Ergo, a de facto holiday." She laughs, a smug look on her face like she actually won that argument.

"Whatever, bitch. You tell yourself what you need to so that you make peace with eating another Snickers bar. Better yet, get a king-size and we'll split it. We're gonna need the chocolate to get through the night without getting hangry."

"Oh, speaking of . . . did I tell you about the video I saw?" Tiff starts, but I put up a staying hand.

"Please, don't. No overeating videos. No pimple popping, shopping haul, or prank videos either," I say solemnly before grinning at Tiff's pout. "Actually, I wanted to talk to you about something."

Tiff sets her curling iron down on the counter and turns. "All right, shoot. Or do I need to sit down?" Without waiting for an answer, she sits down on the closed toilet in the tiny bathroom we share to get ready.

I give her a nervous smile. "Well. It's just . . . I've been thinking."

"About what?" Tiff asks.

My stomach tightens. I'm sure she'll be happy for me, but still . . . "I've been giving some serious thought into moving in with Scott."

Tiffany doesn't look upset, but instead screams and kicks her feet in the air as she pumps her fists. "I knew it! You two-timing whore you!"

I laugh. Tiff's never short on a loving insult. "He's mentioned it to me a few times. I know he's serious, and at first, I just didn't think I was ready. But I'm starting to feel more comfortable. I didn't give him an answer yet, but I brought it up this morning and he was buzzing. Like literally, a peacock walking around like my moving in was a win for him!" I say, looking around at our apartment through the open door and mentally comparing it to Scott's place. It's not so much the penthouse itself, although it's nice, obviously. It's that he's there.

Tiff purses her lips, crossing her arms. "Moving in together. That's heavy shit, girl," she says as a smile breaks out.

"I mean . . . I know you'd be on your own but—"

Tiffany laughs, hugging me. "I *knew* this would happen!" Tiff raises her head to the sky, as if speaking to the heavens. "Why did I let this girl out? The first taste of dick and she's ready to abandon me." She brings her head back down, looking at me. "No way, girl. I'm just kidding. I'm *so* happy for you. If that's what makes you happy—if *he* makes you happy—go for it!"

"Are you sure?" I ask, and Tiffany laughs again.

"Hell yes! Don't you dare worry about me. You go get you some of that fine ass man of yours—morning, noon, and night, in every room of that penthouse. And tell me all about it and let me live vicariously through you a bit, 'kay?"

I slap her shoulder. "Well, maybe not all the dirty details, but I'll say that he's fucking amazing. His tongue . . . his cock . . ." I trail off, already mentally rehashing half a dozen different encounters. Scott has turned me into a totally horny dirty girl, always ready for him to take me again.

"Ugh, you lucky bitch. I'm so jelly! He got any brothers?" she asks laughingly.

"Yeah, but let's not go there. For damn sure. You driving tonight? Scott's picking me up later. I'm sleeping over because tomorrow is his birthday."

Tiff gawks at me. "Of course his birthday is fucking Halloween. That man is a devil in a suit, and I bet even better in his birthday suit."

I blush but don't tell Tiff my birthday breakfast in bed plans . . . especially not the part where Scott is my breakfast.

The drive to Stella's is filled with giggles and jokes and just an abundance of what makes Tiff and me besties. I'm gonna miss not seeing her every day, but I think I'm ready for this. No, not think. I *am* ready for this with Scott.

We get to Stella's and see a full parking lot, the pre-party, as Tiff called it, already in full effect. We sneak in the back to hit the break room for our two-minute last-prep rituals, trying to gear up for a wild, busy night. Stella pokes her head in, already flushed with exertion and hormones. "Hey, girls, hit the floor asap. It's a madhouse. Oh, and eighty-six onion rings tonight. Daryl hasn't made the delivery yet, for some reason, so Devin's doing double-time on fries because they're the new evening special."

Stella's greeting is one long drawl of flustered speech, and then she scoots off, back to the grind. "Well, guess we'd better hit it!" Tiff says with a steadying breath, bracing for the night. We walk out to the floor and she heads straight to a few tables to check in. I head to the bar to take over.

Carl is leaning against the bar, not bothering to move as I take over the station. I can see he hasn't done jack shit to set up for the busy night. Almost every fruit container is empty and there's a bar sink full of dirty glasses. I peek over at him, huffing my displeasure. The lazy fucker doesn't look drunk, but he definitely doesn't look sober. Surely, he's not drinking on the job? Stella would have his hide.

"What's up, Sweet Tits?" he asks, and I turn to face him fully, gawking. *Sweet Tits?* He's been an ass before, but never has he called me something like *that*. Maybe he has been hitting the bottle during his shift.

"I'm gonna pretend that didn't happen, and you're never going to say anything like that to me again," I growl, heading over to clock in. Carl doesn't seem to catch the message, just rolls his eyes and tosses his apron on the bar for me to clean up, just like everything else.

He grabs a bottle and a glass on his way out, sitting down at his preferred spot at the end of the bar. I shake my head, needing to let whatever shit Carl's up to tonight go because I've got a bar full of customers and Tiff's already waiting for an order.

I get to work, pouring beers and mixing drinks, running here and there, cutting up the garnishes Carl should've done, and generally being a completely badass bartender. Go me! Finally, I catch up and chug a cool glass of Coke to get a little sugar rush for the next crowd.

Hours later, I'm fucking beat, exhausted from the floor up. But Stella looks like hell. She's been the gracious owner all night, keeping an eye on the rowdiness and helping out where she can. But her usual top-notch bun of red hair is flopping off to one side, and she's not flushed but tomato-red. "Stella, you okay? Here, let me get you some water," I tell her, setting the cool liquid down in front of her.

She gulps down a healthy chug before exclaiming, "Holy shit. Tonight was insanely busy! But we did it. Great job, Maddie. Couldn't have done it without you, girl."

"No problem, Stella. You know I've got your back. Looks like the last few guys are heading out." I pause to yell out, "Thanks, fellas, come on back!" before turning back to Stella. "I'll get rolling on cleaning up, and we'll get out of here."

"Thanks, sweetie. I think I might have Tiff take me home real quick though, and then she can come back to help . . . if she doesn't mind. These old bones don't have any more left in them tonight. And tomorrow is Halloween. Luckily, we don't usually get too much of a crowd."

"I know I asked off, but if you need me to come in, I will. You know that," I say, crossing my fingers behind my back that she doesn't take me up on the offer, because if she does, I'll drop my plans and work for Stella. I always do.

"Nah. Of course not. Carl and me got the bar. Need to keep an eye on that boy anyway. Tiff and Devin are both coming in, and I've got a new girl shadowing Tiff so she'll be a spare set of hands. We'll be fine. Take your vacation day and then your usual weekend off after. Lord knows, you deserve it. Don't think you've ever had three days off in a row, girl."

She's right, and I feel a bubble of giddiness swirl up in my chest at the possibilities of three days alone with Scott.

Tiff walks by with a tray of glasses, and Stella calls out, "Honey, can you run me home real quick, please?"

Tiff nods. "Sure, but where's Carl?"

Stella shakes her head. "He's sleeping it off in my office. Seems he got a little too celebratory tonight. Again. He'll just sleep here, so you can lock him in when you leave, Maddie. Okay?"

I nod. "Sure thing. Hey, Tiff . . . just head on home after you take Stella. Devin should be about done in the kitchen, Carl's . . . well, Carl, and I'm off tomorrow night. I'll close up."

Tiff's face lights up. "Are you sure?" But she's already shooing Stella toward the door, so I know she's already agreeing with me.

Once they're gone, I put on some music and get to cleaning. If I'm gonna be gone tomorrow night, I want this place to be spic-and-span for Stella to start fresh. Tables, check. Dishes, check. Bar stocked, check.

I'm pushing the broom around the floor when I hear a voice over the music. "Islands in the stream. That is what we are." I giggle, turning to watch Devin's back-and-forth as he sings both Dolly's part and Kenny Rogers's part of the famous song. Getting his laugh, he dissolves into giggles too. "Girl, your musical taste leaves something to be desired. I'm gonna have to school you a bit on more recent musical genius . . . like EDM."

"No thanks, man. That stuff gives me a headache. *Boom-boom-boom.* And there are no words! Just the same beat on repeat." I mimic a loop with my hand.

"How dare you?" he asks, mockingly insulted. "Whatever, bish. I'm outtie . . . if you're good by yourself?"

I wave him off. "Yeah, yeah. I'm fine. Scott will be here soon. I'm just finishing up while I wait for him."

Devin heads out, and I hear him lock the back door behind him so I get back to the floors. I push the broom around some more, swaying and dancing and singing along as I sweep.

I'm lost in the music and the work until I suddenly sense a presence behind me. I jump, turning to see a red-eyed Carl hovering right behind me. "Jesus Christ, Carl! You scared the shit outta me!"

Carl's eyes get squinty, like he's seeing more than one of me and trying to focus on the middle one, hoping it's the real one. "You're a real bitch these days, you know that?" he sneers, pointing a thick finger at me.

Great, Carl is a mean drunk tonight. He's usually chill, maybe a bit depressing, but it must be the Devil's Night curse. I move away, putting some space between me and the stench of alcohol wafting from his pores. "I've always been a bitch, Carl. You just now noticed?"

He stumbles toward me, and out of reflex, I catch him, keeping him from plowing into the floor. "No. You didn't used to be a bitch. You were quiet, mousy. But now that you got some rich dick, you think you're better'n us."

I had been holding Carl up, supporting his much heavier weight with my own, but as he ramps up, the dynamic changes. He presses me against the wall by booth fifteen, his rank breath coating my face like mist. "Carl, you're drunk and need to go lie down. Now." I'm scared but keep my voice steely. This is Carl. He's my friend. Hell, he's almost family. And I have a moment of hope that he's going to listen to my bartender boss voice that brooks no argument.

He leans in, nuzzling into my neck, and I think he sniffs me before leaning back to look in my eyes. "I was gonna ask you out when you were ready, but you kept telling everyone you weren't dating so I waited. Res-resch-respecting what you wanted. But that asshole just comes in here, slamming cash and flashing dick, and you let him lead you out like a fucking puppy. Fuck that and fuck you, Maddie."

His quiet, lost little boy voice gets louder and louder, turning up my fear level with every decibel. I push against his chest, hoping he'll lose his footing, stumble, and let me get out of the cage he's created for me with his bigger frame. But he's drunk-strong, feeling no pain.

"Yeah, fuck you, Maddie." And with that declaration, Carl dives for my neck again.

I cry out, truly terrified now and pressing against him with everything I have, no longer holding back. "No, Carl. No. Leave me alone!"

There's a loud bang on the front door and Carl yells over his shoulder, "We're closed. Come back later." But whoever's knocking doesn't listen, thank goodness. With one more crashing sound, the door bursts open and Scott stands there. My knight in a custom-made suit. And this time, I'm so fucking glad to see him.

"What the fuck?" Scott yells, but he's already running across the room, charging at Carl. He lands a punch to Carl's gut as Carl swings wildly.

"You have fucking everything . . . why her?" Carl roars. Scott answers, but it's not with words. Instead, he lands one more wallop of a punch to Carl's jaw, knocking him out clean on the floor.

Scott turns to me instantly. "Are you okay? Oh, my God, Maddie. Did he hurt you?"

I shake my head, burying my face in his dress shirt. I've never been a damsel in distress before, and in fact, have argued that fact with the man holding me right now. But in this moment, I want to be the rescued princess because I'm done, stretched to my limit with shock and horror at what just almost happened. "I'm okay. Just please. I need to get out of here. Get me out of here."

Scott nods crisply. "Of course. Hang on." He walks over to Carl, and for a second, I think he's gonna punch him again, but instead, he rolls his unconscious body to his side, tilting his head so he won't choke if he pukes. *College Drinking 101 in action*, I think oddly. But when Scott wraps me back in his arms, puts me in his car, and drives me home, all of my thoughts blank. At some point, I think he gives me a bath because I feel warm water and smell lavender. But all I remember are cool sheets and Scott's warm body as the darkness takes me and I dream.

CHAPTER 24

SCOTT – AN HOUR BEFORE

I sit in my armchair, staring out over Bane, replaying today's meeting over and over . . . my dad's words, the look on his face, and then my semi-makeup with my brother and sister. We're not magically all golden and perfect siblings now, but our apologies are a start toward something better. And it's because of her. My Madison.

I watch a car drive by on the road below me, heading somewhere, and I wonder if it's too early to head to Stella's. She'd told me it'd be a busy night and she didn't need to be distracted by my sexiness taking up a paying spot at her bar, so I'd promised to work late and pick her up at closing time.

Eventually, I finish the single scotch I've been sipping on for the last half-hour and decide that I can always help Maddie clean up so we can get out sooner. Cleaning up the bar with her last time worked out pretty well . . . other than the tattoo freak-out. But since we're well past that, I'm sure she'd love the help. And I'd love to get her home and on my cock as soon as possible.

The drive over is smooth and seamless, but all that goes to shit in an instant when I arrive. The parking lot is empty and I realize they've left Maddie here to close alone again. We've talked about how unsafe that is even though the neighborhood isn't that bad, but Maddie just shrugged and told me that it was what it was. As if that made it okay.

I park and knock on the door, but there's no answer. I realize I can hear Dolly playing inside and a smile creeps across my face. That's my girl. I knock again, louder this time, and I hear a guy's voice, sounding loud and drunk. What the fuck? Who's here with Maddie?

I scoot over and peek through the blinds to the left of the door, and that's when I see them . . . Carl and Maddie. She's scrambling, trying to push him away from her, and he's pressing in tighter, pushing her against a booth wall. Motherfucker! I rear back and kick the door, likely busting the constantly malfunctioning lock, and burst into the bar.

It's a sea of red haze as I punch Carl repeatedly, although I distantly feel a few stings myself so he must've landed some too. At some point, I realize Maddie is shaking in my arms as I hold her tight, checking her over for any injuries. If I find a single scratch on her satin skin, I'm going to kill Carl. I know it in my bones. Luckily, she seems unharmed, just terrified. When she begs me to take her home, I can't help but give in even though every animal part in me wants to rip Carl limb from limb. Knowing if I do that, I can't take care of Maddie, I do the hardest thing I've ever done and leave him there on the floor to take Maddie home. She doesn't speak as I give her a bath, washing his stench and the residue of his touch from her skin and replacing it with mine. When I carry her to my bed, tucking her safely into the silk sheets we fucked on just yesterday, it finally settles the gnawing hole in my gut.

I watch her for a few minutes, or maybe it's hours. I don't know, but eventually, I realize there's something I need to do. Quietly, I tiptoe from the room and go back to the pile of Maddie's clothes in the bathroom. I dig around in her apron for her cellphone, punching in the code and knowing this conversation is not going to go well.

Ring. Ring. Ring.

"Maddie, honey? Are you okay?" Stella's voice is sleepy, and I almost feel bad for waking her, but then I remember the look on Maddie's face.

"Stella, it's Scott. Maddie's okay. Well, sort of. Look, something bad happened tonight at the bar."

"Oh, my God, what happened?" Stella sounds awake now, for damn sure.

"I went to pick Maddie up and Carl . . . he was coming on to her." I try to say it gently, knowing this is going to be hard to hear.

Stella groans. "Ugh, that boy. He was drunk as a skunk when I left, supposed to sleep it off in the office. I'll talk—"

"Stella," I interrupt, my tone hard enough that she quiets. "Stella, he had Maddie pushed up against the wall and was kissing her neck, and she was fighting him, screaming 'no', and begging him to stop. It was . . . bad." I pause when I hear her hushed 'no', but she resumes her quiet so I continue, figuring it's best to get the whole thing out at once.

"I had to break the door in, charge him to get him off her. We fought."

"Is he alive?" she asks, and honestly, I think she probably would've killed him herself if she'd been the one to walk in on that scene. It almost makes me wish she had.

"He was when I left. Unconscious, still drunk. Left him on his side so he wouldn't choke and set the door back as right as I could."

"Scott, if you hadn't . . ." Stella stutters and then dissolves into tears I can hear as she gulps and sniffs through the phone. "He's a good boy . . . lazy, sure, but this? I never would've thought he would do something like that. It's the alcohol. Not an excuse, of course, but he's not right. Been trying to talk to him, but he's not having it, won't take any advice from me."

I sigh. "Honestly, Stella, I don't give a single fuck about whatever problems Carl has or what you plan to do with his drunk ass. Madison is my only concern. And you put her at risk, leaving her there alone night after night, and this time, something happened. You left her there alone with an asshole too drunk to hear her 'no', and she's the one who paid the price. She hasn't even spoken since we left the bar, not through the ride home or a long bath or when I put her to bed. She's in shock." The blame I'm layering on her makes her tears ramp up, but I don't stop. "She loves you like a mother and would do anything for you, but this isn't right. She can't do this anymore. I won't allow it."

"What are you saying?" Stella asks, her voice wavering.

"Effective immediately, Madison's done working at your bar. Find someone else to run it."

"What?" Stella shrieks, but her voice is weak. "You can't just quit for her!"

"I just did. I'm going to take care of her now, like you should have and did for a while, and I appreciate that, but it's not working now. Don't call, don't text. All of you just leave her alone and let her heal, however long that takes. I don't know if she's going to wake up in the morning angry, sad, scared, or what . . . but I'll handle it. Just leave her alone for a while."

I don't wait for Stella to answer, knowing she'd never agree to that. As much as Maddie loves Stella, Stella loves Maddie back. She is partially at fault, but Maddie would forgive her readily because that's who she is. But I can't stand the thought of her going back to that place, being at risk that way. Not when she can stay here with me, safe and sweet and happy and . . . mine. I hang up the phone and press the button to turn it off. Once I'm sure it's a brick, I toss it in a drawer in the kitchen and head back to the bedroom.

I strip down carefully so as not to wake or spook her and slide into bed behind Madison. She snuffles in her sleep and turns over, curling into my side like a kitten. I run a soft finger along her skin, soothing her back to sleep and reassuring myself that she's okay. I hover on the edge of sleep all night, dozing but aware of her every breath, every movement.

❄

THE NEXT MORNING DAWNS CLEAR AND BRIGHT, at odds with the darkness clouding my mind. Maddie squirms against me before opening her eyes. "Mmm . . . good morning."

I'm already looking at her, have been for the last thirty minutes as she wiggled in her sleep and I tried to decipher if she was having a nightmare or just dreaming. So I see the moment she remembers what happened the night before. I see the light in her eyes dim and her shoulders scrunch up to her ears as she burrows deeper under the covers.

"Good morning. How you doing?" I ask gently, wanting to let her set the tone here.

Her eyebrows furrow together. "I'm okay, I think. I was freaked out last night for sure, but I'm okay. He was really drunk, and I'm sure he feels bad about the whole thing this morning."

It doesn't escape my attention that she doesn't say his name, just like she told me she avoided her ex's name for the longest time after that trauma. It's a sign she's not as okay as she's making out to be. I knew she'd try to downplay the whole thing. My sweet, forgiving girl, but she shouldn't have to forgive this.

So I take charge, leaving out a few key details. "I already called Stella and told her what happened."

Madison's jaw drops as her eyes widen. "What?"

"I wanted to make sure somebody checked on Carl first thing this morning because the bar door is busted. Stella said she'd handle Carl and that you were already scheduled for three days off, so take those plus however many more you want. All the time you need. I told her you'd call her later in the week to let you have time to process." She nods, so I tell her the last bit. "I turned your phone off. Stella will let everyone know what happened and that you're okay. It can just be us, and I can take care of you."

I hate lying to her, despise it to my core. But she needs time to heal and to see that this can be her life, here with me. No drunk assholes leering at her, no coworkers getting aggressively handsy, no late nights that wear her out to the point of exhaustion and put her at dangerous risk of God knows what. No, she can't go back there. I just need to show her how good it can be and she'll understand. She's got to.

Madison curls back into my side, her fingers tracing along my tattoo under her cheek. And God help me, I'm at peace with lying because I'll do anything to keep her by my side and protect her. Even if it's from herself.

CHAPTER 25

MADISON

Daily Horoscope, November 2nd
Libra - Still waters run deep . . . but a gentle disturbance to the surface can change the underlying sand foundation.

"Dude, give me that!" I say, reaching for the last nacho in the paper tray. But Scott doesn't give me the tray. Instead, he grabs the last remaining bastion of cheesy-beefy goodness, but he doesn't crunch into it for himself. No, he holds it up for me to eat it . . . from his fingers. I smile and grab his hand, holding it in place as I nibble the nacho and then lick the cheese from his fingers. His eyes zero on the display I'm putting on for him, watching as my tongue curls around his thumb and I suck it in to get every last bit of cheesy goodness and rile Scott up at the same time. Winning, indeed.

The last few days have been amazing. Surprisingly so, considering what happened at work a few nights ago. I still can't believe Carl was that drunk or that Scott had to rescue me . . . again. But he did and took it remarkably well. The next morning, I'd still been a bit of a mess and had completely forgotten my surprise birthday breakfast plans for him. But by late afternoon, we'd snuggled and talked about everything and nothing as I felt more like myself.

Granted, Scott hadn't been happy that I was willing to let bygones be bygones with Carl, semi-justifying his actions with the excuse of alcohol, but I know a sober Carl would be horrified that he'd scared me.

I'd felt like the bigger story was Scott making some inroads with his siblings. When he'd said that it was all because of me, I'd beamed even as I'd assured him that it was all his doing.

And just like that, the tone for my weekend off had been set. We've laughed and played, explored and experimented, and generally taken our mantra of 'new experiences' to heart.

Art museum exhibit about surrealism? Check, although neither of us knew what surrealism even was.

Picnic in the park while a band played folksy covers of rock hits? Check.

An amusement park with an inflatable obstacle course where Scott had beat my best time by four minutes? Check.

A romantic sunset sail around the lake's bay on a sailboat I'd thought was huge but the captain had assured me was a small personal watercraft? Check.

Restaurants? From fine dining to food trucks to a greasy spoon diner. Check, check, and check. Although the food truck Asian-fusion burrito was by far my favorite.

Shopping? Oh, yeah, that too. We'd left Stella's in such a hurry that I hadn't grabbed my overnight bag, and Scott had been adamant that we weren't going back there, nor was I going home because this weekend was ours and ours alone. So he'd bought me a few T-shirts and two pairs of jeans, at American Eagle, not the Armani place he'd wanted to take me to. He'd laughed when I told him that if I had on Armani jeans, I'd never be able to sit down for fear of getting them dirty. Then I'd laughed when he'd hopped up and stuck his ass in my face, letting me read the label on his own designer jeans . . . that he'd literally been sitting in the grass with.

So yeah, the last three days have been jam-packed with awesomeness. Through it all, Scott's been totally focused on me, and I've given him all of my attention. We left our phones at home, just enjoying life and taking it as it comes.

It feels good . . . freeing to just be with Scott, appreciating things both small and large about our experiences. About each other. Usually, my weekends off from work are spent hustling to catch up with shopping, cleaning, errands, and all the other things I put off while working, and maybe having a little fun with Tiff if it's in the budget. Or spending the days at the rescue, helping May.

The only niggling thought that bothers me is that we haven't had sex all weekend. My breakfast plans had been trashed because I'd been a bit sensitive still, but after that, Scott has kept me so busy that we've collapsed into bed in a tangle of arms and legs two nights in a row. He did touch me last night, gently rubbing my breasts and then my pussy until I had an explosive orgasm from the slow burn he'd built up in me. But I'm taking the reins back now, or at least starting the show, letting Scott know that I'm fine. Truly fine. And horny. So fucking needy.

I move to straddle his waist, sucking his thumb once again even though the nacho cheese is long gone. "Mmm . . ."

"What are you doing, Madison?" Scott asks, his voice gravelly, but I can tell he's holding back, unsure about this. He's been handling me with kid gloves all weekend, an uncertainty to his tone. I hate it. I'm not broken, not after Rich and not after the little scene with Carl. I want my Scott back . . . the bossy, dominant, growly man who takes me.

"Seducing you," I tell him, letting his see the lust in my eyes. "I need you, Scott. Fuck me. Please." I'm not ashamed of the hint of begging in my tone because if he wants me to beg, I'll fucking hit my knees. Might do some other dirty things while I'm there if that's what it takes to get my way.

Scott swallows thickly. "Are you sure? We can go slow, gentle."

His breath is erratic and I know he's holding back, controlling himself.

I grab his jaw, making sure he's staring me straight in the eye as I say this. "Don't you fucking dare. Fuck me like you mean it, Scott. Take me, ravish me . . . hard, rough, dirty. You won't hurt me. I know you won't. I trust you."

There's a flinch in the depths of his eyes, but it's gone so fast I think maybe I imagined it. But Scott does what I demand. He devours my mouth in a scorching kiss, the heat instantaneously creating an inferno. "Fuck, I've missed this," he growls under his breath. His hands are everywhere, kneading my breasts, my thighs, my ass.

Suddenly, he scoops me up from his lap and carries me upstairs to the bedroom like I weigh nothing, making me laugh, but his face is hard as he sets me down. He rips my T-shirt over my head and my jeans down, stripping me in seconds, before spinning me around. "Bend over."

I place my hands on the bed, presenting my bare pussy and ass to Scott as he stands behind me. I watch as he palms his cock through his jeans, grinning and swirling my hips to tempt him. My reward is the two smacks he lays on my ass, one on each cheek. I moan out his name, needy for more.

Scott drops to his knees, burying his face in my pussy from behind. His tongue traces up and down and makes me gasp.

Scott vibrates between my cheeks, tongue fucking me as he pushes on my back for me to bend over more. His finger begins to massage my asshole as he sucks and continues to tongue fuck my pussy. I'm shocked at first when I feel one and then two fingers slide in my ass, but it's amazing, his tongue and fingers stroking me at the same time. I moan, bending over more and offering myself as best I can to him. "Fuck . . . you really want my ass? It's yours."

Scott wiggles his fingers in reply, and my knees almost buckle it feels so good. The naughty pleasure just grows and grows as his fingers pump in and out of me and his tongue opens me up. I clutch at the sheets as the first tremors start in the back of my legs, rippling up higher as Scott slides his tongue over my clit and sends me over.

"Scott! Fuck!" I cry out as I start to come, his fingers curling inside me still, even as I clench around him. I gasp and moan, writhing against the bed until he steps back, wiping his lips and grinning.

Scott strips his clothes off, and I marvel at him the same way I do every time, incredulous that this god of a man wants me so fiercely. He climbs on the bed, leaning back against the headboard and waving me over. I take a mental snapshot of his wide shoulders, washboard abs, and of course, that thick cock at attention just for me.

I climb on, straddling his hips and sliding my wetness along his length, enjoying the moans I can pull from him.

Scott lifts his hands behind his head. "You want to be in charge this time?" His tone is teasing, sweet, and I appreciate the offer, but it's not what I want.

"Actually, I want you to fuck my ass, Scott. Claim me there like no one has before." My voice is steady, solid as steel, but he still asks if I'm sure. I nod, lining up over him.

He's completely still, holding my hips to help support me, letting me control the pace for now, but I can feel his excitement buzzing like an aura around him. "Fuck, Maddie. Even hearing you say it has me on the edge. I'm gonna take this ass, claim it as mine, fuck you so hard you see stars. Just let me in." He's gritting his teeth, his control beautiful. I want to tear it to shreds as he does the same to me.

For a second, I don't think I can do it. His cock feels so big that I doubt I can fit him past my tight hole, but I breathe deep, trusting in myself and in Scott. The pain's hot and burning for a moment, and then he slips in. I freeze, letting my body adjust as

Scott's fingers dig into my skin, holding me still. "Holy fuck, you're thick."

"Take your time. Breathe," he says, bending his head forward and taking my left nipple in his mouth. The feeling eases everything, distracting me as my ass relaxes, and I sink down, letting him invade my body more and more until I'm nestled in his lap, electricity arcing from my nipples to my ass. Scott moans, tugging on my nipple and making me gasp.

"God, I didn't expect it to feel so good." I groan as I start riding him, squeezing my ass, triggering Scott's answering groan. The feeling is different. I'm so full and tight. The head of his cock seems to be pressing against a new place inside me, building the energy at my core as my clit grinds against Scott's belly. "Mmm, you enjoying this?"

"Fucking love it," Scott groans, his hips rising to meet my falling ass. The soft slap makes me gasp in shock, but I love the intensity so I ride him faster, rising and falling harder onto his cock. Scott meets me thrust for thrust until I'm gasping, moaning as I tremble on the edge. "You want more?"

"Fuck . . . yes, give it to me," I groan. Scott holds me in place, buried deep in my ass as he moves us on the bed, slamming my back to the cool sheets as he looms over me. He lifts my legs to his shoulders, his eyes meeting mine. I know he's silently asking if I'm okay in the new position, and I bite my lip, squeezing his cock tight with my muscles in answer. He thrusts a few times, slowly in and out, getting us used to the new angle.

"Look at me, Madison," he commands, a hand on my jaw to keep my entire focus on him. "You're mine. I love you. I fucking love you."

With each word, he speeds up, his hips pounding against my ass and making me clench around him tighter and tighter, driving my tired body until he swells, his eyes locking with mine as he groans. I'm not sure if it's his movements or his words or both, but I fall over into a powerful orgasm, the waves wracking through my body as I cry out. "Oh, my God, Scott. I love you too."

He growls at my exclamation, pounding so deep there's a hint of pain, but it only adds to the pleasure. I want him inside me, everywhere, the way he's in my heart.

The first explosion of his cock is intense, and I scratch my hands down his arms so hard I may have drawn blood. But he doesn't care. All that matters is the love in our hearts. Scott pulses deep in my ass but then pulls out, still coming and squirting on my thighs and stomach, covering me with even more of his cum as he sits back on his heels, looking at me with surprise in his eyes.

"Damn, Maddie. That was . . ." He doesn't finish the sentence, just smiles that dimpled smile that drives me wild before leaning over to take my mouth in a kiss. His thoughts and feelings about what we just did, what we just said are in every swipe of his tongue against mine. And I tell him the same thing right back with my swirling tongue.

We're quiet as we shower, my shy, happy smile complementing his cocky swagger. And when we snuggle up on the couch, he covers us both over with a blanket, even though his warmth is all I need as he wraps me up in his arms.

Scott plays with my hair, twining it around his finger and then letting it twirl off. His voice is cautious as he says, "Maddie, that was intense, and it's okay if you . . . if you said things you didn't mean. I love you so fucking much. But it's okay if you're not there yet."

This man. He thinks I'm just throwing out love words casually, thinks he doesn't deserve them because he's never had them given to him, not once in his life. Which is a fucking sin. I turn, looking him in the eye. "I meant every word. I love you. Actually, I wanted to talk about my moving in again."

I can see the hope lighting his eyes, so I don't prolong the moment. "I'd love to."

I'd expected him to hoot and holler with joy, maybe do a little happy dance. But what he does is so much better. He pulls me even tighter against him, burying his face in my neck like he can't get close enough to me and whispers, "Thank you."

After a bit, Scott begins snoring softly behind me. Guess he's worn out from all our fun running around this weekend too. But I'm full of energy.

My future is bright, and there's nothing that can stop me.

My mind is swirling with thoughts about what could happen. Living with Scott . . . maybe one day transitioning from working for Stella? Not that I don't love it, I really do, but anything seems possible.

Not wanting to disturb him, I carefully get up, going to grab my phone from the kitchen drawer where he'd tossed his a few days ago.

As soon as I turn it on, my phone starts vibrating like a windup toy. Texts out the wazoo.

I smile at first, seeing Tiff's daily horoscope reports. But then . . .

Girl, you okay? I figure you're with Scott but haven't heard from you.

Stella's hired two new bartenders.

I gasp and scroll down.

OMG, where are you? Stella is falling apart!

Typing frantically, I text her back. *Spent the weekend with Scott and phone was off. What happened!?*

Call me. Now.

I peek over at the couch, seeing Scott sleeping peacefully, and press the button to call Tiff. She answers immediately.

"What the fuck, Maddie?" she all but yells in my ear.

Trying to keep my voice hushed, I whisper back. "What's going on?"

I can hear Tiff's inhale. "Honey, you'd better sit down. You ready for this?" I must make some noise of readiness, but I do it mindlessly, my brain already bracing for the worst based on the way Tiffany is acting.

"So remember how Daryl no-showed with the delivery? It was because he . . . he was . . . he was in a trucking accident on the other side of town. He didn't make it, Maddie. Daryl died."

I gasp as I collapse to the floor, pulling my knees to my chest as the pain shoots through my heart at the loss of such a good man. "Oh my God, that's awful. Stella must be beside herself," I say, the understatement of the century.

"Well, yeah, but to add insult to injury," she chokes out, not realizing the pain of the phrasing until the words pass her lips. With a gulp, she continues. "Yeah, and whatever happened with you and Carl the other night . . . he's been missing ever since."

"What? He was fine when we left. Well, unconscious and beat-up, but fine," I say, trying to make some sense out of the crazy things Tiff is telling me.

"I don't know. Stella called me in the middle of the night and asked me to pick her up early, said she wanted to give Carl a piece of her mind for fucking with you and making you quit, and she was a mess about Daryl when I picked her up, but we drove in anyway. But when we got to the bar, the door was wide open and Carl was gone."

"Wait . . . what? I didn't quit." Somehow, that tiny bit of information is what I grab onto in the midst of everything else.

"Uhm, well I guess Stella said Scott said you quit, but whatever. Point is, Stella is falling a-fucking-part. One son dead, one son missing, and the girl she loves like a daughter is ditching her."

"That's not . . . I'm on my way. Right now." I hang up with Tiffany and let my phone drop to the floor.

In shock, I stare at Scott, sleeping peacefully on the couch. He quit my job for me. Seriously? He quit my job, didn't tell me, and then spent the whole weekend with me like it was some fairy tale. All the while, lying to me. And those lies kept me from being there for Stella, who has always been there for me anytime I needed her. I let her down . . . because he thought he knew better than I did, deemed himself fit to make decisions for my life without even consulting me.

I'm furious. I'm afire with anger.

At Scott, at Carl, at Daryl, at Stella, and at the universe.

At myself. I knew better.

I go over to the couch, standing over him. He must feel my eyes because he stirs, looking up at me.

"What's wrong?" Scott says, his voice husky with sleep as he rubs his eyes.

"How could you?" I ask, wishing my voice sounded half as mad as I actually am. Instead, I sound more hurt than outraged.

But his eyes clear instantly, leaving no doubt that he knows exactly what I'm talking about. He stands up fast, the blanket falling to the floor. "Madison, I'm sorry. Look, I was so furious. You were in shock, and I didn't know if you were okay, and I just wanted to keep you safe. I hated that something like that happened. I called Stella. I was just so fucking filled with rage that you almost . . ." His words are a jumble, rolling off his tongue so fast he's stumbling over them.

"How dare you? You don't fucking own me, Scott. You don't get to decide that for me. Where I work, what I do, none of it. You don't get to decide that. I do. Me." My breath is heaving, the weight of his clipping my hard-earned wings rounding my shoulders.

"Yeah, I was freaked out and glad you were there that night, but you went behind my back, thinking it was okay to control my life like that, and then you hid it from me while we've been traipsing all over the city, having a grand old time."

"We have had a good weekend! That's what I wanted to show

you—what it could be like for us. Here, living together, spending our days and nights together. You and me together against the world. I talked to Stella in the heat of the moment and then didn't know how to back out of it, how to tell you," he admits, confusion clouding his voice, and I can see his brows furrowing together.

"You didn't tell me because that's what you really want. Did you think I was going to magically be okay with this because we had a good weekend? It was a lie. All I'll remember about those couple of days was that you looked me dead in the eye and decided that you could do whatever the fuck you wanted because you knew better than I did."

He collapses to the couch, his head in his hands. "Fuck. *Fuck*. Maddie, I'm so sorry. Tell me how to fix this because I don't know how."

"No, your little stunt has done enough damage. My family needs me. Stella is going nuts. Daryl was killed in an accident, and it seems Carl ran off after you beat the shit out of him. And she even thinks I abandoned her."

I see his shock when I tell him about Daryl and Carl, his jaw dropping and his eyes shooting wide-open in horror. But his face hardens as I rant.

"So no, I don't have time to fix your control-freak narcissistic tendencies, Scott. I'm going to take care of *my* family, the ones who take care of me. The difference is that they help me stand on my own."

I can't do this. I can't be here. Not a moment longer. I turn, heading toward the door, and then bend down to slip my shoes on. My necklace, Scott's necklace, swings forward as I bend over. It's a cold reminder of our differences, the ones I thought we could reconcile. The rich and the poor, the lost boy and the damaged butterfly, the cocky bastard and the sassy sweetheart.

With shaking fingers, I undo the clasp. It takes a steadying breath, but I set the jewelry on the table before looking at Scott.

"Madison, no. Please. We can figure this out. Let me take you to Stella's and . . ." He's right behind me, begging me to let this go. But it's one occurrence in a repetitive loop with him.

I shake my head, knowing if I speak, I'll break. I can feel the tears burning in my eyes already.

"Madison, I love you."

I open the door, but before I can walk out, Scott reaches out, grabbing my arm. I look down, overwhelmed with the sense of déjà vu . . . his hand, tan and large, wrapped around my pale, thin arm, just above my wrist. I flinch unintentionally, not able to stop the roll of my stomach. He must see my reaction because he lets go instantly, a look of horror on his face. "Fuck, Madison. I'm not him. It's not like that. *We're* not like that."

I look up, sadness pouring off me. "I know, Scott. You're nothing like Rich. I loved you."

Free of his grasp, I run out the door, banging down the steps even as I hear Scott yelling for my name from behind.

Let me go. Don't chase me, Scott. Please. Don't.

He doesn't.

As I hit the street below, the tears fall freely. All we shared, all I thought we were *going* to share . . . is over.

CHAPTER 26

MADISON

*S*tella's feels different when I come in, mostly because there are two new girls behind the bar. Behind *my* bar. Well, maybe it's not my bar anymore, I guess. I don't know, considering what Scott did.

One of them looks more or less lost, but the other might know what the hell she's doing. She's at least checking the recipe book when I walk in.

Ignoring them, I make my way to the back, heading straight to Stella's office. She's staring at her computer blankly, obviously not seeing what's in front of her and lost in her own mind. "Stella?"

She turns her head, but her eyes are dead, and she looks twenty years older than she was last week. "Maddie!" she exclaims, but her voice is weak, hoarse. Like she's been crying for days. Days that I haven't been here for her.

"Stella." My voice cracks, the tears coming hot and fast to wash down my face unrestrained.

Stella opens her arms, and I rush into them, dropping to the floor beside her chair as we hug each other tight. I can feel her shaking sobs echoing mine as we dissolve into messy, snotty, ugly grief at everything lost. My disappointment, my pain at

Scott's betrayal shrivels under the weight of Stella's pain. She has an aura of real loss . . . of her children, adults, but her babies nonetheless.

"Oh, my God, he's gone. I can't believe he's gone," she wails.

I'm not sure if she's talking about Daryl or Carl, or both of them, but it doesn't matter. The pain is palpable either way and my heart breaks for her. "I know, Stella. I'm so sorry."

Her voice catches and hitches as she fills me in. "He was north of town, you know where the state highway and the Interstate merge?" she says, and I nod. It's a badly designed onramp, and every couple of weeks, the news has another accident at Hang-man's Curve. "It was the other guy's fault, the State Patrol says. He hit the front end of Daryl's truck as Daryl was coming in."

"I'm sorry, Stella. I know Daryl was a good driver and a good son."

Stella half laughs, half sobs. "That he was. With a sense of humor that would have gotten his ass fired from anything other than being a trucker. That was my boy. So . . . sounds like you had another bad experience that night too. I don't know what to say, but I'm right sorry about that. I got the call about Daryl in the middle of the night shortly after Scott called. I tried to call you but . . . well, you know." She shrugs, as if any of this is easily explainable. "What are you doing here? Scott said—"

I put my head down in shame. "It doesn't matter what he said. I never quit, I never left, was just unreachable for the weekend. I'm so sorry I wasn't here for you, Stella. It's tearing me apart. After that shit with Carl, the thought of forgetting about work for a little while sounded like an amazing idea. Have you heard from Carl at all?"

She shakes her head. "No, my best guess is he's off on a bender. Selfish drunken fool. What he did to you, and then he's gone when I need him."

"Oh, Stella. I'm so sorry." I keep saying it over and over again, but I can't find any other words to express what I'm feeling to her. Deciding maybe it's not words I need, I hug her, and she squeezes me so tightly that I almost feel like I can't breathe, then she pulls back. "What was I thinking? I knew a man like that would come with a steep price. Even got a damn warning from beyond, but I ignored it, hoping like a fool for something to finally work out in my life."

Stella holds my chin gently. "You listen to me, child. Your life ain't that bad, and you've never thought it was. I get that you're having a pity party right now. Me too, and Lord knows, it's warranted with the shit storming down on us. But you know what we're gonna do?"

I look at her, the question in my eyes. She's a pillar of strength even as her world collapses, and I take power from her. If she can still be standing tall and proud, I can too. I wipe the trail of tears staining my cheeks, already feeling my resolve solidifying as she answers her own question. "We're gonna pull up our big girl panties and do the stuff that needs to be done. Together, as family. Because that's what we are, my precious girl."

Family. So much to that simple word. "Hey, I'm sorry about Carl too. I don't know where he went, but he was okay when we left."

Stella sighs and turns to look out the tiny window in her office. "I don't know either. I can't believe what he did to you. I have to think he was just wildly drunk, not that I'm excusing him in the least. But I can't focus on what he's doing or where he's at. I need to keep things running here and bury Daryl."

At her words, I can see the tears overtake her again. "What do you need me to do?"

Stella gestures vaguely out to the bar floor. "Help the new girls? Just keep it running for me, Maddie. Please help me keep it going. I'm gonna need this place to keep going."

I nod, knowing that I'll do anything for Stella, whatever she needs to ease the ache in her heart. Running the bar is definitely a weight I can take off her load. I grab a T-shirt off the shelf in the corner, the crisp new cotton feeling like a fresh start. I'm down, broken, and my heart's bleeding in tatters, but I've pulled myself up once before and I can do it again. This time is worse, so much worse, but I'm a survivor. Always have been and always will be.

I walk by the kitchen door, and when Devin gives me a sullen glare, I approach warily. "I'm so sorry, Dev." That's all he needs before he gathers me to him in a big hug, the smell of frying butter and spices filling me with comfort.

"Girl, we're okay. If you're back, you're gonna have some fancy footwork to do with that bestie bitch of yours. She's been going batshit crazy that you weren't responding to her. And she's been working doubles all weekend, so she's not only cranky and scared, but she's exhausted." I nod, thankful for the warning.

As I step out on the floor, I see Tiff across the room. Our eyes meet, and I can see her huffed sigh, but she comes over, so that's got to be a good sign.

She looks me up and down. "You don't look like you spent the past few days with the rich boy."

"I . . . I broke up with him when I found out what he did," I say quietly, looking down. "Tiff, I feel so terrible."

Tiffany takes a deep breath, then points to the break room. I follow her in even though we both know we can't afford to take a break right now.

It comes out in one long rush, with me barely pausing to take breaths. Tiffany's face slowly softens so that by the end of my long, rambling explanation, she's scowling again, but it looks different. "You never turned your phone on once?"

"Thursday night was rough. It was supposed to be a weekend of relaxing and forgetting work," I complain, fidgeting from side to side. "I even . . . God, this is embarrassing. I even told him I loved him!"

"Oh, honey . . . that fucking asshole," Tiffany says, her scowl deepening.

"That's exactly what he is. Fuck him. I should've known."

Tiffany gets up and gives me a silent hug. "I'm so sorry," she says. "The timing of this was just so awful. I'm sorry, Maddie."

"I just feel like an arrow has pierced my heart, and I'm keeping it from shattering to bits with sheer willpower," I admit.

"Not an arrow . . . a sting," Tiffany says with wide eyes. "Oh, shit, Maddie. The palm reader said you'd meet a scorpion, and he'd own your heart and then sting you. It's coming true. Fuck." Her voice ends with a breathy sound.

"And now I guess is the part where I suffer?" I say, remembering the rest of the prediction. The realization floats in the air between us.

Tiff recovers first, physically shaking off the hold the dire words hold over us. "Nope, not doing this right now. Right now, we are gonna get out there, work our asses off, and keep Stella's afloat while simultaneously preventing Stella herself from falling apart. She's gonna have to take a loan against the bar to pay for Daryl's funeral—did she tell you that?"

I bite my lip. I hate that she has to do that. I would've thought she'd be doing better financially with how things look in the bar.

We hit the floor, and I approach the bar, slipping behind it like I have a million times before. The place is a fucking madhouse, with a line of frustrated customers standing around the bar and the two new girls looking like deer in headlights.

"Come on, it's just a fucking whiskey sour!" someone yells, making one of the new girls wince. "It's not that fucking hard!"

"I'm just—" the girl says before starting to break down.

"Give it to me," I demand, pointing at her apron.

"What are you doing?" she asks but reaches for her apron strings. "You . . . you don't work here."

"I do now," I declare.

Fifteen seconds later, I've got my confiscated apron on, and I face the two girls, who are already looking at me like I'm in charge. I realize that . . .I am. "Okay, you." I point at the girl who'd been using the recipe book. "You're with me. All beer pulls are yours." She nods and scurries off to do as I bid. I turn to the other girl. "You . . . go help Tiffany. Whatever she needs, tables bussed, food delivered, drinks refilled."

She whispers, "Thank God." as she rushes off too. Okay, I can do this.

I turn to the bar, letting out an ear-splitting whistle. Patrons instantly look my way, most with hope for their much-needed drinks. "Okay, folks! Let's get these drinks a'flowing!"

There's a general cheer, even a few yells of "Maddie! Glad you're back!" It feels good, like I'm home. But there's a void in my heart, an empty spot where I thought my future lay . . . home with Scott. Not his actual house, although that too, but more that I thought *he* would be my home.

Luckily, the distraction of work and keeping busy serves me well, and I spend the next half hour catching up. Just as the bar starts to clear and normalcy returns, I glance over at Stella, who's finally made an appearance and is sitting quietly at the end of the bar in Carl's usual spot. She holds my gaze. We don't say anything, but I give her a small nod and she returns it.

Grief, loss, and pain swirl around us both like cloaks, and we burrow into it, not wanting the light even as we fight to stay close to its warmth.

CHAPTER 27

SCOTT

Daily Horoscope, November 3rd
Scorpio - Big changes and big decisions await you. Choices made today
will affect you for the rest of your life.

*M*ondays. The day of the week where everyone else is dragging ass, thinking about what they left behind at home and talking about what they did over the weekend.

Me? I saw Mondays as a chance to get ahead. I knew that if I hit the gas hard first thing Monday morning, I'd be four hours ahead of everyone else by the time they got done debating about whether the Patriots dynasty is over.

Now, though . . . now, I'm sitting at my desk halfway through the afternoon and not giving a solitary shit about work. All I can think about is Madison. It hasn't been twenty-four hours since she stormed out of my place, but I feel the loss acutely. I've tried to call and text her, but she hasn't responded.

I feel like such a fucking moron, a possessive fucker who wanted his shiny toy on his own terms. I knew it was wrong. It'd been eating at my core all weekend, but I'm decisive, a man of action. And I didn't know how to back out of it without causing even more problems, knowing it was going to set Madison off on another frenzy of push and pull. I'm a coward, something I never realized before, and I simply didn't want her to pull away from me. I wanted to drag her even closer, invade her the way she's done me.

As soon as she dropped the necklace, I realized how badly I'd fucked up. All I've done is analyze the number of ways I was wrong. Starting, of course, with the simple fact that I had no right to 'quit' her job for her. I mean, that's not the base issue . . . but what the fuck was I thinking? I deserve to lose Madison for that, if nothing else.

Because of me, she missed out on being there for Stella. Sure, she's probably with her now, but the damage is done. "Hell, maybe she was right. I just need to stay away," I mutter to myself as I sip at my third coffee of the day. "I might have been trying to make her life better, but all I did was make it worse."

I scold myself as I look around my office, guilt eating me that I even considered I might know better than she did about what her life should look like to be happy. She was right. I'm a selfish narcissist, more like my father than I care to recognize, and that's as horrifying as it is depressing. My actions may be different from his, but the foundational belief that I know best resonates off-key in my heart.

I finish my coffee and set it aside just as Robbie comes in, looking so excited he's virtually vibrating. "Dude, you've got to come to the meeting room."

"Why?" I ask, not wanting to do anything but sit behind my desk and wait for the hours to pass. Fuck it, nothing I do right now is good anyway, and the only thing saving me is my last name and the deal still being out there.

Robbie hooks a thumb urgently. "Teresa needs some numbers for upstairs. She said she needed them immediately. No one else knows them."

"Can it wait?"

Robbie shakes his head. "No can do, Boss Man. This has to be taken care of now."

I groan like an old man getting up from my chair, heaving myself to my feet. "This had better be good."

"Oh," Robbie says, giving me a little smirk as I walk by, "you're gonna love it. You'll see."

My suspicions are aroused, but Robbie says nothing else as I walk down the hall to the meeting room. I become even more suspicious when he stops at the door. "Open it," I half growl. "Or are you just being a dick?"

"Maybe. You open it," Robbie says, half smirking.

I grab the handle and throw the door open.

"Surprise!"

The cheer hits me in the face, and I stand there, somewhat stupefied, as the entire team starts cheering, popping champagne bottles and in general, making the entire room feel like a Super Bowl winner's locker room. I turn to Robbie, whose shit-eating grin now threatens to dislocate his jaw. "What the fuck is this?" I growl, the revelry not touching my darkness.

Robbie laughs, clapping me on the shoulder. "The deal, man! A little birdie from upstairs called me. It isn't official yet, but . . . we did it!"

"Wait . . . we did? Why am I the last to hear?" I ask, still stunned. I'm shocked. I thought for sure my dad would get his way. But somehow, somewhere along the way, all the hard work has paid off.

Robbie nods, pushing me into the crowded room. Everyone's congratulating me, and my shoulders are taking a pounding from everyone clapping me. "Thanks, Scott," Teresa says as she shakes my hand. "I won't forget that you gave me a chance to do something meaningful."

"You're . . . welcome. Thanks for your hard work," I reply, but inside, I don't feel like celebrating. I don't feel like eating a cupcake, even as everyone's 'toasting' by smashing chocolate and red velvet cupcakes together and chasing the sweetness down with gulps from their champagne flutes.

Even the thought of going upstairs when Dad makes the announcement official just so I can see the look of shock on his smug fucking face doesn't excite me. Who gives a fuck?

Robbie sees that something is wrong and comes over, handing me a glass of champagne. "Hey, man, you can unclench your asshole for a few hours. You did it. Nobody can take that away from you."

I nod and plaster a fake smile on my face as I go around. I don't even remember what I say when people come up to me, but when someone calls for a speech, I clear my throat. "I know everyone's expecting me to say that this great Scott Danger moment was brought to you by Scott Danger and represents the greatness that is Scott Danger," I start awkwardly, and it gets a few laughs.

"I didn't write that," Teresa snickers after having a few champagnes in quick succession. "Not enough Scott Dangers for you." She winks at me and then laughs out loud.

I smile at her but get serious. "But honestly, this is because of you guys. It was your hard work, busting your asses and putting your faith in me and my crazy ideas that brought us here, enjoying the fine gourmet fare of cupcakes and champagne as we embark on a new phase of Danger Enterprises. So don't congratulate me. Instead, look around and congratulate each other for a job well done and a reward well deserved. Please, let me be the first to say thank you. For everything."

The room's quiet for a moment before Robbie starts the serenade of applause. It feels genuine, not the polite business applause I've gotten used to, but the real clapping of people who honestly appreciate what I said. Robbie comes over, offering a handshake. Behind him, the door opens and Dad's secretary enters. "Mr. Danger? Your presence is requested in the board room."

I nod, adjusting my tie and looking at Robbie. "How do I look?"

"Lose the frosting by your lip," he says, smiling. "Go, man, go. And thanks for what you said."

I head upstairs, but I still feel so empty. This is what I've wanted, what I've worked for, what I've dreamed of, but right now . . . I don't care. And that is a punch to my gut as I stand outside the door, taking a last moment alone to school my features.

Entering the board room, I nod respectfully to the assembled men and woman before taking my usual seat.

Dad, sitting on his throne at the head of the table, stands up. "This morning, after much discussion and hard negotiating, the board made a majority vote decision that Danger Enterprises will be moving forward with the proposal Scott's team put forward."

There's muted applause, and the board members shake my hand. Liv looks genuinely happy for me as she gives me a kiss on the cheek. "Congratulations, Scott. You deserve it."

"Thank you," I echo for what feels like the thousandth time as Chase comes forward. "Chase."

"Good job, lit . . . Scott," he says, still a hint of a smirk on his face.

Chase offers me his hand, and we shake, and I'm surprised when he pulls me in for a hug, speaking quietly in my ear. "I think you were right. We can be better, do *more*. Danger Enterprises is lucky to have you. Me too."

Chase leaves with the rest of the board, and I blink, stunned. I think my relationship with my siblings just took a considerable turn for the better, even more so than our apologies a few days ago. But more than that, I'm astonished the board actually backed my play.

When it's just Dad and me, I see the pained look on his face as he steeples his fingers below his chin. "Well . . . it appears you were right."

I nod, and he slumps down in his chair, looking older all of a sudden. "The board went against me," Dad says, rubbing at his jowly cheeks. "They've never done that. I'm not sure how to take it. How to react. But this is still my company. You just got your way on this one deal." His gaze narrows on me, and I can see the evaluation . . . what I have that the board sees that he doesn't, if I manipulated my way into this win, and how he can circumvent me and take the reins as his own over this deal.

I look back at him, and I realize something. He's got nothing other than his reputation as a win-at-all-costs businessman, the façade of a strong, powerful man. The reality is very different. His children practically despise him, his wife left him, and his girlfriend is a pretty obvious gold digger. And to top it off, he backed the wrong horse. I still find it hard to feel sorry for him because he created this life of image and pride, not caring about the emotional consequence to anyone else. "You can say congratulations like everyone else."

Dad snorts and looks out the window, where the stars are gleaming in the evening sky. "You'll be wanting a better office now, elevation to a chief executive job. Guess you deserve it."

I nod. That is what I wanted. Before.

I thought it would finally make me worthy in my dad's eyes, but I can see that nothing will ever make that happen. It's not a flaw in me. It's one in him.

But I've worked so hard, we all have, to reach this point. I try my damnedest to focus on work. "Actually, the title . . . yes, that is warranted. The office space? We predict that we'll need a larger in-house team for support of AlphaSystems, so in lieu of an office on a higher floor, my team will take over the floor below mine when their lease is up." It's not a question. It's decisive and not up for debate.

But right now, all of it . . . the office, the promotion . . . it seems meaningless without Madison. She should be the one I'm sharing this with, holding her in my arms as we celebrate and knowing the world is at our fingertips. Instead, I'm sitting here feigning attention in the boardroom while Maddie is probably working her ass off and rightfully hating my guts.

I asked her once if she was happy at Stella's and she'd told me she was. I didn't believe her because I couldn't imagine it. But when she'd asked me if I was happy at work, I don't think I even knew what happiness actually felt like. But now I do. I was happy with her.

Sure, the old saying is, if you love someone, let them go. If they return, it was meant to be. But goddammit, I'm not leaving it up to fate. I'm going to fight for Madison, and if afterward, she still walks away . . . well, I'll accept it knowing I did everything I could. But right now, I need to apologize, see if there's any chance she can forgive me.

I turn and head out of the board room, not stopping when Dad calls after me. "Where the hell are you going?" He's pissed I'm walking out even though he's hardly saying a word, just staring off into the skyline mid-existential crisis, like it's my duty to hold his hand while he contemplates how this could've happened.

"There's something I need to do," I call over my shoulder. He thunders something about how there's nothing more important than this, but I ignore him. In fact, I ignore everyone as I head downstairs, going through the team area toward my office.

Robbie, who's had a few more glasses of champagne while I was upstairs, calls out. "Hey, Boss Man, where you off to?"

"Madison," I call, heading into my office and grabbing my keys off my desk. When I turn, Robbie's there, a look of glee on his face.

Robbie nods and steps aside. "Party on, dude. I'll take personal care of your share of the bubbly. Go celebrate with your girl."

I don't correct him. He doesn't know about the stupid stunt I pulled because I've been hiding in my office all day, sullen and pouting.

It's late when I get downstairs, and traffic's hell downtown. Unbeknownst to me, there's a fucking concert, and I crawl through bumper to bumper traffic. I'm almost tempted to just jump out and start running, but I finally get clear of the stadium.

Just when I think things will start to move, I see flashing lights and I growl, slamming my hand on the steering wheel. Honestly, a re-route? What the fuck is going on?

It's like something, everything is preventing me from getting to Madison. But fate can fuck off. I'm making my own, snapping my fingers and making her my bitch. Well, or pleading with her to please let me get to Maddie, to somehow make this all right again.

I need her. I love her.

My Madison.

CHAPTER 28

MADISON

Daily Horoscope, November 3rd
Libra – Echoes of the past threaten your future.

I RINSE THE DOG HAIR AND STENCH FROM MY HANDS in the big stainless-steel sink, watching the bubbles swirl down the drain, wishing they'd take my broken heart with them. I think an empty void, a wasteland where my heart used to be would be preferable to this deep aching.

Yeah, Marie. Thanks for the heads-up about the suffering. Spot on, bitch. I wish I'd listened, believed her. But even if I had, I still would've fallen for Scott. I still believe that. I couldn't have resisted his charms.

"Maddie, baby . . . really, just go home and get some rest. I can handle the dogs today," Aunt May prods me, handing me a handful of paper towels and flicking her head at me, telling me without words to shoo.

She'd been relentlessly loving all day, listening as I'd told her everything. She had even promised to take Stella a casserole first thing tomorrow morning, which I know will be appreciated.

"Are you sure? I know you had help all weekend," I start but can't finish the sentence. I breathe, steeling myself. "You had help while I was with Scott this weekend, but I'm scheduled to help today. I'm fine. Or fine enough." The implied 'see, I even said his name without crying' is silent but understood.

Aunt May scoffs. "Girl, you're about useless today . . . for good reason. Go home, take a nap, and get ready for your shift tonight. I have volunteers coming in later today, but Stella needs you at one hundred percent."

I nod, giving in because I know she's right. I toss the paper towels in the trash and grab my purse from the office as she watches me with worried eyes. Right before I leave, she calls out. "Hey, Maddie, you might be a sparrow again right now, but I've seen you fly. You'll be an eagle again."

Aunt May's Dolly-isms. Even now, they give me a smidge of comfort, a hint of a smile. It's a start, but before the spark of flame catches, it dies out, leaving me cold once again. "Thanks, Auntie. I'll be by tomorrow if I can."

I don't even pet Maple and Syrup as I walk out, a zombie unaware of the life surrounding her.

BY THAT NIGHT, I'VE FORCED MYSELF TO RALLY. NOT able to smile and be my usual self, but at least finding distraction in the busy work of running the bar.

My new helper, Dana, isn't half bad, and she keeps the beer flowing smooth and suds-free with a smile. She looks great too, her dark hair and smoky eyes giving her a sultry exotic look. Thank God she's eye candy for our tip jar tonight, because I'm definitely not holding up my end of the bargain there.

Tiff had done our last-minute tweaks for me, finally throwing a knotted bandana around my rat's nest of hair and forcing three thick layers of mascara on my lashes because I flat-out refused to put on makeup.

Funny to think that only a few weeks ago, I wouldn't have been seen without a full face. But Scott made me feel comfortable in my own skin and appreciated the flaws I hated, like my freckles and the little birthmark on my jawline. When he kissed and licked them, appreciated the beauty in them, I could finally see it too. And now, without him, I just don't give a fuck. Am I masked? Am I exposed? Not my concern. I'm just here to help Stella and serve drinks. Everything else is unimportant, trivial shit, easily dismissed.

Hustling along, setting out drink after drink, I get lost in the repetition. I still have moments where Scott takes over my mind . . . when a customer ordered a Snow Queen martini, I'd thought they were fucking with me at first and almost came over the bar. Or when a drunken college guy flirted with me, I had a flashing image of Scott white-knighting me again . . . and sometimes, I look up and down the bar feeling like I'm missing something to realize it's not a drink order. It's him.

I'm swirling a white rag though a pitcher, setting up for the next round, when I hear it.

"A whiskey shooter, Wild Turkey, with a half-finger of water."

I slowly turn, trying not to drop the pitcher, and it's *him*. The same shit-eating grin, with the dimple on the left side that I thought was so fucking sexy when we first met. Those same devious-looking, psycho-killer eyes that I thought were just naughty before I realized just how deep the crazy went. It's Rich, my ex-ex-boyfriend.

"What are you doing here?" I demand.

"Trying to get a drink, but the service here sucks," he says with a smile, like it's a private joke. My jaw drops at his gall.

I clack my mouth closed, disgusted with him.

"Please leave," I say with as much forceful strength as I can inject into my voice. I will not cower to him, not ever again.

"Why?" Rich asks, leaning on the bar and grinning more, his five o'clock shadow crinkling as he chews his ever-present bubblegum. "I haven't done anything to anybody."

I look for help, recognizing in one sweep of my eyes that my bar knife is way at the other end of the bar, Tiffany is in back, taking her break, and Stella looks like something that the cat dragged in after it got run over in the street. I'm on my own. But I can do this. He doesn't have a hold on me anymore. "What do you want?"

"A Wild Turkey, finger of water," he says again. I grab the cheap booze, pouring it for him and setting the tumbler in front of him. Rich takes it and sips his drink. "So . . . hear you been dating a big shot."

"That's none of your business," I reply automatically, not wanting to give him any ammunition. A beat later, I realize he said it not to get information but to let me know that he already knew. It sends a chill down my spine that he knows anything about my private life at all. "How'd you find out? Have you been following me?"

"Maybe," Rich says faux-casually. "A man has to have hobbies, after all."

My heart freezes, and I nearly turn to call 9-1-1, but the cops will just make him leave the bar. A stressful scene is the last thing Stella needs. And in some twisted way, I want to handle Rich on my own. Aunt May was right. I can fly like an eagle. I might be broken right now, but it's not because of a pussy like Rich. With him, I can handle myself. A tiny voice whispers in the back of my mind, *and if not, there's a roomful of people who might jump in to help if it gets ugly.*

I head down to the other end of the bar, where I get a couple of locals a microbrew. Tiffany comes out, and I give her a little look, and she glances and sees Rich, her eyes narrowing. "Should I get Stella?"

"No . . . but keep your eyes open and watch my back. I don't want Stella to be stressed out if she doesn't have to be," I whisper.

I go back to work, hoping Rich will leave, but after twenty minutes, he's still there, obnoxiously rapping his tumbler on the bar. "Another Wild Turkey!"

Sweat dots my forehead, but I head down the bar. "Rich, I don't think—"

Quick as a snake, his hand shoots out to grab my wrist. "You dumb bitch, you don't think. That's your problem. I want to talk."

"Let go of me!" I hiss, trying to keep my voice down. None of the other patrons notice anything, and I try to pull away, but Rich's grip is iron hard.

I look at his hand wrapped around my wrist, like he did so many times before. Sometimes gentler, sometimes more forceful, but that last night . . . it'd been different. He'd been testing me to see where my boundary was. He didn't think I'd push back. He was wrong then, and he's sure as fuck wrong now.

"We're *over* and I have nothing to say to you."

"Over?" Rich growls, pulling me closer to the bar. "You walked out on me. I never said it was over. I fucking own you," he snarls. "You wouldn't be shit without me. Who the fuck do you think you are?"

Fury fills my body, and before I even think about what I'm doing, my free hand swings out, slapping him across the face. In the moment of shock, both his and mine, I twist my wrist, jerking away. "Let me go!" I yell, stumbling back. The bottle of Wild Turkey tumbles and shatters on the floor like a bomb, freezing everything in the bar.

Rich laughs, shaking his head. "You stupid bitch. Just like you to—"

I don't let him start up with his gaslighting insults, interrupting him to yell, "Get out. Now!" as patrons stare with dropped jaws and wide eyes.

Every bit of anger I felt each time he hurt me, emotionally and physically, pours out of me in waves of hot resistance. He made me weak, drop by drop, bit by bit, so subtly I didn't even notice it at first. But I see it now, hear the countless manipulations he put me through echoing in my head. And they wash away in the tide of my strength. I am powerful. I am capable. And the people in my life, especially the men, need to fucking realize it.

Stella is suddenly next to me, the mama bear out of her hibernation and her hand trembling with rage as she grips Slugger, our steel-core baseball bat. "Get the fuck outta my bar!"

Rich looks unconcerned, brushing off his jacket. "I was just leaving anyway. See you around, sweetheart." The endearment that had once seemed loving sounds ominously sinister.

Rich retreats, and as the door closes, my shakes start. Tiffany rushes over to hug me while Stella strokes my back, and the patrons give us a little bit of space. "Are you okay?" Stella asks. "I didn't see him come in."

"I'll . . . I'll be fine," I whisper, staring at my hands until they stop shaking. "I was hoping I'd never see him again."

"You keep the bat near you under the bar, you hear?" Stella says. "Take that thing straight to his head if he comes back in here. If I see him, I'll do it myself."

I nod and set Slugger near my station, where I can get it quickly. I'm proud of the way I stood up for myself, so much different from the times before. But as the adrenaline wears off, my hands keep shaking. For the rest of the night, I try and concentrate, but by the time last call comes, I'm weak and shaky.

Tiffany notices, coming over after she shoos the last customer out. "You okay, hun?"

"I don't feel good," I admit. "Stomach feels like I had too many Devin burgers."

"I heard that!" Devin growls, but Tiffany ignores him.

"I don't blame you. After that fucker came in, I've had my head on a swivel all night. Here, you go on home and let me finish up with Stella. You've done that enough for us, and tonight, we can return the favor. You just get home, lock the door, and try to sleep. Text me when you get there, 'kay? We'll be fine here."

I know I should decline. But I feel off-kilter, and curling up in my bed and hiding away from everything sounds like a relief.

"Thank you," I mumble, exhaustion taking my voice. "I really do need to lie down."

Tiffany shrugs. "That's what friends are for."

I head to the back, slipping my sweatshirt on over my work tank top. It's getting cool at night, and it feels good to have the extra layers. Leaving, I stick my head in to say goodnight to Stella. "Hey, heading home. Tiff will close up, and I think Devin's gonna take you two home."

"Thank you, honey," Stella says. She somehow looks stronger, but still older. "And Madison, if that son of a bitch ever comes back in . . . you whack him first, ask questions later, got me?"

I nod, giving her a thumbs-up. Devin offers to walk me to my car, and though it seems silly, I play it smart and agree. The full moon's out, and it's already cool enough that a light mist is rising from the ground as we cross the parking lot. I keep looking around, but everything seems clear. I don't see anyone as I get in and lock the doors before cranking the engine. Devin waves, running back inside to finish up for the night. And I pull out, ready to collapse in bed and hit restart for tomorrow.

I'm barely halfway home, though, when I notice the car in my rearview mirror. Something about the shape of the lights niggles in the back of my mind. I change lanes . . . and the car does too. I slow down to let them pass . . . but they slow down too.

I speed up, but the other car closes the distance, and my heart freezes when I finally recognize the car. It's Rich. The black matte paint, a custom job that was his pride and joy.

I step on the gas harder, but I'm driving a twenty-year-old Toyota with wheezy valves and a worn automatic transmission that even right off the assembly line has an engine like two hamsters under the hood.

Meanwhile, Rich is driving a car with three hundred and seventy-five horsepower, a number he drilled into me. He must've bragged about it a thousand times. The wide tires grab the pavement and gobble up the distance between us, and as he gets close enough, I can see the grin on Rich's face.

Terror grips me as I whip around a curve, but he takes it easily, seconds later back on my bumper so close I think he's going to run me off the road. I lay on my horn, hoping to get him to back off or to get someone's attention, but it's late, and we're in an industrial part of town. Nobody's nearby.

I whip the car left and right, trying to shake Rich, but he's on my bumper like a magnet. As we pass a warehouse, he bumps me from behind. Not hard, just a tap, but enough to tell me he's not fucking around. He's upping the ante, ready to play a game I'm nowhere near prepared to handle against a psychopath.

I cry out and press the gas harder, but I was already almost to the floor, and my leg quakes with the force. I see another turn up ahead, and I swing right, hoping to make it to the gas station ahead, but it's still about a mile away, the light of the sign filling my vision like a beacon of hope.

The scream that comes out of my throat as Rich taps me again, sending my car careening out of control, is louder than the scream of the bodywork of the Toyota letting go. My rear tire gives out, and I feel the car start to flip as darkness overtakes me.

CHAPTER 29

SCOTT

*M*y phone's vibrating like crazy in the car seat beside me, but it's just Dad. Fuck him. I ignore it, letting him leave his messages to rant. He wouldn't understand and it'd just enrage him more if I answered and told him what I'm doing.

The drive to Stella's, which normally takes just over thirty minutes most nights, takes almost four hours, putting me more and more on edge with the need to see Maddie and apologize, plead, grovel, whatever it takes. It's just after midnight by the time I pull into the parking lot. I slam the car in park and all but run in. "Maddie!"

Tiffany, who's working a mop across the floor, looks up. "You." There's enough venom in her voice that I know Madison has told her everything.

"Where's Madison?" I ask, trying to choke down the panic rising in my throat. "I . . . I need to talk to her."

"She's had enough of creepy fucking exes tonight," Tiffany says, turning back to her mopping. "Get the fuck out of here."

"Tiffany, please. I love her. I need to at least apologize to her," I reply softly. Tiff doesn't even turn around, and my chin drops in

283

defeat as I run my fingers through my hair, searching my mind for something, anything I can say.

"You look like shit." Tiff says, and I look up to find her watching me curiously.

"She's everything," I say simply, but then try to explain the depth of my madness. "I had a huge victory at work today, a project I worked my ass off on for months, but when everyone was celebrating, I felt . . . empty. I don't even fucking care anymore. None of it matters without her. I just want Madison, not under my thumb but right beside me. My strong, beautiful Maddie who doesn't do a damn thing I expect and couldn't care less about my last name." My eyes roll up to the ceiling as I fight the tears threatening to spill. Dammit, I'm a fucking monster of a man in a business suit. I'm not gonna cry like a pansy bitch, but it's close, so close.

She studies me for a minute, weighing the truth of my words, which feels like the most severe judgment I've ever received. She's deciding whether I'm worthy of even begging for forgiveness from Madison herself. Finally, she sighs. "She just took off. Said she was heading home. Her ex came by tonight, rattled her pretty bad."

The fear jumps in my throat again, and I nod, turning and running out the door as I yell over my shoulder, "Thanks, Tiffany." I put every bit of horsepower I can coax from the engine to work as I lay a streak of rubber on the pavement, rocketing out of the parking lot to head toward Madison's apartment. The streets are eerily deserted now, and as I push my car faster, fear rises along with the bile in my gut. Something's wrong. I don't know how I know, but centuries of primal instincts embedded in our modern minds make me certain of it.

I take the most direct path, but when I pull up to her apartment, there's nobody there and I don't pass Madison's car the whole trip. Slamming my car in reverse, I drive back toward Stella's, trying to keep my eyes open along the dark roadways, looking for any sign of her or of her car. I roll the windows down, wanting my every sense to track her, needing desperately to find her and barely refraining from screaming my fear into the quiet of the night.

I'm near the warehouse district when I hear it, the throaty, rumbling growl of an old-school engine, revving like an angry demon. Stopping, I stick my head out the window, trying to determine where it's coming from, panic gripping me as something tells me that this is what I'm looking for.

But the buildings around me don't help. All they do is bounce the sound around the concrete and steel surfaces. Driving to the next intersection, I hear it again, followed by the sound of crunching metal.

I smash the gas pedal to the floor and turn. I see them in a block, the all-black old-school muscle car and the beat-up Toyota, looking almost miniscule as the black car closes in again. Madison tries to whip the car around a curve and the muscle car surges forward, hitting the back bumper.

"NO!" I yell as Madison loses control, a tire popping, and suddenly, she's airborne, flipping over as it goes off the road. My heart freezes, and I slam on my brakes, hoping that I'm not too late.

Madison

DARKNESS.

The pungent smell of gasoline.

I can smell something . . . burning? What the hell's burning? Wait . . . it's me. Something's hot, pressing against my leg. I struggle, but my belt's locked and I'm trapped.

As the burning gets hotter, I scream and flail, fighting desperately to release the belt and get free. Smoke starts to fill the cab, but then I feel hard, strong hands grab me by the shoulders, and I have a flash of relief that someone is helping me get out of the burning car. I hear the *snick* of a knife snapping open, and a chill races through me. I remember that sound.

Rich . . . he always carried a butterfly knife, and I remember that sound distinctly. He was proud of it, always eager to show it off.

I try to struggle, but the burning and the fact that I still can't see stops me from doing anything but getting in my own way. Rich clamps his hands tighter and yanks me out of the car.

The first clean breath of cool night air rushes into my lungs like a sweet gift. The next thought, though, is sheer terror as I look up and see Rich staring down at me, an evil grin on his face. "You've brought this on yourself, my Maddie." His voice is eerily calm, in stark contrast to the panic racing through my body. I've moved from one danger, being trapped in a burning car, to another, alone with Rich in the dark parking lot of an abandoned warehouse.

"Rich," I rasp, trying to crawl away, but my legs aren't responding right, dragging numbly behind me as my palms grind into the rough concrete. He grabs a handful of my hair, and I slap at his arms, yelling out, but he ignores me as he hauls me up. My legs barely hold weight, and I lean drunkenly against him in a fight to not crash back to the hard ground.

"You're mine," he says, dragging me toward his car. "Now get in."

"No," I argue, trying to claw at his hand. He ignores my fingernails and grabs my throat, cutting off my air.

Suddenly, I realize something. This time, it's not an ass slap that got a little too rough or a pinch that was a little too sharp. This isn't even like the last time, where he did real damage to my wrists from his punishing grip.

No. This time, it's not gonna be a little bruise to my body or my ego. This time, I'm going to die.

The thought grips me in a panic, granting a sudden burst of strength to fight back, fight for my life. I kick my feet, aiming for his legs, his groin, and push and pull on his hands, trying to loosen his hold. But my head is spinning from the lack of oxygen, and Rich is so much stronger than me.

The darkness closes in, my eyes locking on his victorious grin, full of ugly promises. My last thought is that I hope whatever he does, I won't feel it.

CHAPTER 30

SCOTT

*S*topping on a dime when going over a hundred miles an hour isn't an easy task, even for my car. But with a squeal of brakes, I force the stop and jump out, sprinting toward the smashed car as smoke starts to rise. My heart is in my throat. Madison!

It's dark, but in the small flame's light, I can see someone approaching the car. I don't know who the suited man is, but Tiffany's words echo in my mind, and I realize it must be Madison's ex, Rich.

I run harder, my shoes slipping on the cool pavement, and I wish I was wearing anything but dress shoes and slacks right now.

It seems like I'm running in slow-motion as the scene plays out in hyper-speed in front of me. I watch in horror as Rich reaches into the car and Madison cries out. He pulls her out of the car, and I have a flare of joy that she's alive and free, and fighting back like a she-devil even though she's in bad shape. Her left leg is smoking, she has a forehead gash that is dripping blood down her cheek, and her voice sounds rough and crackly from the smoke as she yells. The flames from the engine compartment of her wrecked car rise higher, reaching into the night at an odd angle because the car is almost completely flipped on its roof. She struggles, but he grabs her hard by the throat and drags her closer to that black car of his. I know with every fiber of my being that I have to stop him before he gets her in that car.

I dig deep for more speed but feel a punch to my gut as she sags in his hands. Rich catches her under the arm, but before he can take two steps, I'm there.

I don't give him any warning. He doesn't deserve one. I hit them both in a tackle, pulling Madison into my arms as I roll to the ground, cushioning her fall before getting back to my feet to defend her unconscious form.

"What the fuck!" Rich groans, holding his head as he rolls over and bounces to his feet. His eyes land on me, and his face transforms from confusion to utter rage. "You. Thought you could take her from me? No! She's mine."

Spittle flies from his mouth as he yells, all façade of decency washed from his mannerisms. He's a dog with a bone, a predator with its prey. But Madison is none of those things. Not to him. Not to me. Not to anyone.

"She isn't yours. She never was. And if you can't recognize that she's a strong fucking woman who stands on her own, that's your mistake," I growl, stepping forward.

A flash of silver appears in Rich's right hand, and I see him snap out a knife. He holds it in front of him, waving it back and forth, looking comfortable with the blade. "She is mine. I made her what she is and she needs me."

I've fought before. Chase and I have brawled on more than one occasion. But we've never used knives. And a cotton dress shirt doesn't exactly do a lot for protection.

"She doesn't need you. She doesn't need anyone. She's the strongest person I know."

In that simple truth about Madison, Rich's Achilles heel comes to me. He's arrogant but weak. He needs to dominate someone to feel powerful himself. The insight gives me an angle to manipulate. "That's why you gave her so much shit . . . to break down her defenses, thinking if you could tame her, you'd actually be worth something. But you couldn't do it. You know why?" I ask condescendingly.

He stalks around me, swinging the knife in wide arcs that get closer and closer. He doesn't answer, so I keep talking, watching intently for an opening. "Because you're weak. She doesn't need to be tamed. She is beautiful in her powerful independence, just as she should be." I see a flicker of recognition in his eyes and know he already knew that and just got off on squashing her spirit. I go in for the verbal kill. "The truth is . . . you went to battle with her, and she won, fair and square, because you're weaker than she is." He reacts just as I'd hoped he would, and I'm ready for his attack, but he's slow. My God, he's so slow. I see the knife coming from what seems like a mile away, and as he arcs toward my face with the steel, I catch the inside of his elbow with a chop and the knife clatters to the ground.

Rich punches back, and I take it on the left cheek, the pain blooming across my face and firing me up with a fresh shot of adrenaline. I hit him with a hard one-two to the ribs in return that makes him wheeze as his breath whooshes out in a gush. I shove him back, and he hits his car, bending backward over the hood as I grab him by the lapels of his jacket.

"Don't . . . ever . . . lay . . . a . . . hand . . . on her!" I grunt, accentuating each word with a bounce of the back of Rich's skull off the hood of his car. Rich gets his knee up between us and pushes me back, and I stumble as my shoes slip on the pavement and I lose a few inches of ground.

"She's mine!" Rich howls as he pushes off the hood to tackle me. We roll across the pavement, but unlike my teenage wrestling matches with Chase, there's absolutely no restraint. We volley punches, brawl for position, and I end up on top, my hands locked on his throat as I start bouncing his head again.

"She'll never be yours," I shout, letting go with one hand to cock my fist back. "And you'll never hurt her again."

I let my fist fly, and I hear a satisfying crunch as I connect with Rich's nose. His head sags, and I drop him to the pavement, unconscious and bleeding.

Once I know the threat is incapacitated, I scramble off him. He's unimportant right now.

Instead, I rush over to Madison, who still hasn't moved. "Maddie?" I ask her, shaking her shoulder lightly. Panic grips me again as she doesn't respond. "Madison? Madison!"

I check, and she's not breathing. Reaching into my pocket, I grab my keyring, thanking my pain in the ass of an insurance company for insisting on a 'panic button' for my car. One push, and I've got full 9-1-1 support rolling to my GPS location, letting me focus on Madison.

A coldness drops over me, a thin veneer that I've felt before whenever I've been in high-stress situations. It's what allows me to remember the CPR classes I took at work, letting me clear her airway and check for a heartbeat before giving her rescue breaths and starting compressions.

I'm still working as the police show up, three squad cars squealing to a stop with sirens and lights flashing.

"Sir . . . sir, we've got her," one of the cops says. "An ambulance is right behind us."

I collapse to my knees next to Madison, and the cop takes over as I exhaustedly beg him to save her. Another officer asks me questions, and I give a quick, disjointed accounting of Madison's history with Rich and what happened tonight. They write it all down, handcuffing Rich when the black car comes back as his and slipping the knife they find on the ground into a plastic bag.

"Sir . . . we'll need a complete statement downtown," the officer says as the ambulance is about to pull off. I nod and head toward the rig. "Sir!" he yells out behind me.

"I'm going to the hospital with Madison. Meet me there if you want, or I'll come downtown later," I reply, climbing in. The paramedics look at me, then at the cops, one of whom climbs in. It's a tight fit, but we're on the road. "How is she?"

"Heartbeat is steady and stable now. She's had some trauma to her throat from the strangulation. We've had to intubate her, but the fact that we could is a good sign," the paramedic says, cold but kind.

I grab her hand, watching worriedly as we fly down the road, praying we get to the hospital quickly enough.

CHAPTER 31

MADISON

Daily Horoscope, November 5th
Libra - There is the pain of suffering, the pain of loss, the pain of regret . . .
but there is also the joyful pain of healing to live another day.

Beep.

Beep.

Beep.

I know that sound. Hell, anyone who's grown up in the TV age has to know that sound. It's a heart monitor. Which means I'm in a hospital. Which means I'm alive.

The joy is instant, the confusion hot on its heels. What happened? I remember . . . something. Heat. Fear.

I hear a kind voice, calm and reassuring next to me, "Hey, you're okay. Take a gentle breath. Easy now."

I crack open my eyes to see a young woman, barely older than me, wearing blue scrubs. I do as she says, taking in a slow, deep breath and wincing at the pain as the cool air moves through my body.

"Good job. You're in the hospital but you're doing fine. Can you tell me how you're feeling?"

I take a moment, forcing my spinning mind to focus on a task and evaluate my body. "Well . . . mostly, it's my head. It's throbbing. And my leg hurts."

The nurse nods. "Well, you just relax. Let me grab the doc and we'll see if we can get you some pain meds."

She pokes her head out of the sliding doorway that looks sort of like an airlock. A second later, she reappears with a grey-haired man wearing a matching set of scrubs.

"Welcome back, Madison. I'm Dr. McDermott. The nurse says your head and leg are bothering you?"

I try to nod, but the movement is more difficult than it should be. My neck feels stiff, immobile.

Dr. McDermott stops me. "Oh, let's try not to move your neck for a couple more days. Everything's fine, swelling is going down now, but the muscles are going to be sore, and the internal structures still need a bit of healing time."

"More days?" I ask, catching the first part of his speech before losing track of what he's talking about.

"Oh, yes, you've been with us for two days now. Healing well," he reassures me.

"Two days?" I ask, surprised. "I've been here two days?"

"Three, actually. They had you in the ICU for the first twenty-four hours," the nurse says.

"What . . . what happened?" I murmur, not sure if I'm asking them or myself. I try to rack my brain, but it's all fuzzy and makes the throbbing worse.

Dr. McDermott answers me, thankfully, stopping my pain-inducing train of thought. "You were in an accident. You sustained a pretty nasty burn to your left leg," the doctor says, and I look down to see my entire left thigh wrapped in white gauze. "You're young, so it's too early to tell, but you could end up with a scar. More worrisome, though, was your head injury. You took a hard double-hit to the head. You'll likely have a headache for several more days, but you should be fine."

His words give focus to the confused images in my mind as I try to think. I remember driving, then the lights, and a bump. "Rich," I murmur, shivering. "He made me crash, attacked me. I fought back but he must have really fucked me up."

"You're lucky the damage isn't worse. It seems you had a guardian angel that night. He's been watching over you ever since too."

"Angel?" I ask, confused. "I don't . . . I don't even remember an accident. Just flashes."

"That's probably a good thing for now, but it'll likely come back to you."

I shiver, and the doctor pats my shoulder. "That's nothing to worry about right now. You need to relax and focus on getting better. By the way, someone's waiting for you outside. Would you like a visitor?"

"Aunt May?" I ask, and the doctor shakes his head as he goes for the door.

"Three nice ladies—May, Tiffany, and Stella—have been here around the clock, but they just stepped out," the doctor says. He opens the door and gestures to someone, then leaves. My heart skips a beat when Scott steps in.

"Madison, I—" Scott whispers, stepping forward before stopping. "They wouldn't let me see you except through a window." His voice cracks almost as much as mine has been, but his seems to be choked with emotion.

"What happened?" I ask.

Scott swallows. "He was chasing you, bumping you with his car, and I watched you flip. Your car skidded across the parking lot, and I died inside thinking there was no way you'd be okay after that. I ran for you, but Rich got there first, cutting you out of the burning car. As fucked up as it is, I'm glad he did or the burns would've been worse." His eyes track down to my leg, and I feel the anger in his gaze, even through the gauze.

"But then he started choking you, and I tackled him. We fought . . ." Scott tells me the story of how he punched a knife-wielding Rich, eventually knocking him out.

I can see the ghost of a shiner on his cheek. Rich must've gotten in a decent punch or two, but it sounds like Scott was my guardian angel like the doctor said. I don't know what would've happened if he hadn't been there. I don't remember all of what he's telling me, but I remember fighting like hell as long as I could. I also remember giving up and letting the darkness take me to avoid whatever Rich had planned. I'm glad Scott didn't give up on me.

"Why were you there?" Though I intend for my words to sound grateful, they sound accusatory.

Scott winces. "Be patient, please. I'm still so jumbled on all this, and it seems so long ago now. You left, and I was devastated, so angry with myself that I'd fucked up, and I didn't know what to do. Give you time? Chase after you? While I tried to figure it out, I went to work and got word . . . the board went with my proposal."

"Congratulations." I say, meaning it sincerely because I know it was his dream.

Scott nods automatically. "Thanks. But . . . I didn't care. It felt meaningless. Empty. What I wanted was you. So I left and went to Stella's, but traffic was . . . well, whatever. When I finally found you, it was just as Rich flipped your car." He stares off into space for a moment, and it's like I can see the scene replaying across his mind as he tenses and grimaces at the images only he can see.

"When we were fighting, Rich was such an asshole, still mouthing about how you needed him. I reminded him how you were strong, didn't need him or anyone else, and are so fucking beautiful in your independence. I meant it. Every word."

I interrupt him, already seeing the truth on his face as he speaks but fishing for him to spell it out. "Really?"

He grabs my hand, dropping to his knees beside the bed. "Fuck, Madison. I never meant to make you feel like I thought you were weak or like I was trying to take control of your life. I never should've done what I did. Flat out, I had no right. I'm sorry. So fucking sorry. I was just so scared, and I overreacted and wanted to protect you, but . . . I never meant to crush you. I want you to shine like the badass you are."

His words are jumbled, running over one another as he tries to express himself, but I hear the underlying honesty in them. The truth is that he didn't mean to hurt me and does think I'm strong and capable, even appreciates that about me. Under his gaze, I feel that way too, even if I am down for the moment.

I look into his eyes and realize another difference between Rich and Scott. Scott did what he did not to keep me under his thumb, but to free me in his own way.

He never pressured me to stay with him or to move in. He let me take time even when he was full-throttle committed to me. It was seriously presumptuous and fucked up, but we both come with some damage and baggage, and I can see this situation played right into both of our fears and insecurities. And no matter what, I know how I feel.

"I forgive you," I reply, squeezing his hand.

What else is there to say? I mean, the man saved my life, and the other shit that happened wasn't his fault.

Scott lets out a sigh of disbelief. "Thank you. Fuck, I know that forgiving me is one thing but being with me is another. But I love you, Madison. So fucking much."

"I love you too," I whisper.

Scott stands up to lean over the bed, planting a tender, sweet kiss to my lips. As we part, I lick my lips, tasting the stale coffee on his breath, and I know that he's been here, by my side, not in front of or behind me, the whole time. I'm already strong, whole all by myself, even with the dings and cracks in my spirit. But his presence makes me feel like a better version of me, like his love smooths over those fissures, both appreciating them and filling them with sparkly, glittery bits of love.

Damn, maybe those pain meds the nurse swooshes into my IV are kicking in.

In my mind, I can hear Dolly's sweet voice . . . *This ol' heart ain't gonna break your heart again.*

CHAPTER 32

SCOTT

Daily Horoscope, November 10th
Scorpio – *Dreams are nebulous things, ever changing as you do.*

"Are you sure you're going to be okay?" I ask, knowing it's the tenth time in as many minutes.

Madison rolls her eyes at me, the same response I've received the last five times. The first five, she was patient and understanding. Now, I have no doubt she's about to kick me out of my own bedroom.

"Fine, I get it. I'm just nervous to leave you," I admit. "You're sure you don't mind?"

Madison doesn't nod, knowing that it's still uncomfortable to do so, but she hums her agreement. "Mmmhmm. Just send in Marisol with breakfast when it's ready. I want to eat before Tiff gets here later."

Marisol was one of our first negotiations as a newly reconciled couple. The doctor had stated that Madison would need a dressing change to her bandaged leg twice per day once she came home, and she'd wanted a home health nurse to visit for the procedure. I'd laughingly vetoed that idea before backtracking to suggest—strongly suggest—that having a short-term nurse actually move in with us for the care made more sense. It'd taken some conversation, communication, and negotiation, but when Madison had met Marisol, instantly connecting over their love of music and dubbing themselves 'The M&Ms', I'd definitely been the winner. Well, and Madison won too, considering she got round-the-clock care in the comfort of my penthouse. It's still 'my' penthouse, not 'ours' as she asserts the living situation is short-term, but I'm hopeful we can negotiate that, too.

"You got it, baby." I pause, plopping carefully on the bed next to her. "You know, I wouldn't go if I didn't have to. The board scheduled the meeting when we thought you were still going to be in the hospital. I'd thought I could sneak away for a couple of hours while May or Tiff was visiting."

"It's fine. Go to the meeting and take care of some work while you're there. Disappearing for a week with no notice isn't exactly up to the Danger standard." She says it jokingly, but she's right. Dad has called and texted multiple times, but I've ignored them all after sending an email to the board stating I'd had a family emergency and wasn't to be disturbed. I'd directed them to Robbie, and he's been a great gatekeeper, holding the hounds at bay while keeping me informed of the news around the office in once-a-day catch-up sessions.

One of those sessions had been to schedule this mandatory meeting.

I nod. "I know. I've just realized that I don't want to be my father —nothing like him—and I'm afraid if things keep going the way they were, that's what I'll become. I want to love and be loved, not just feared or respected. I want the Danger name to mean community, not a one-man war for individual recognition."

Madison reaches up to run her fingers through my hair, and I lean into her touch, needing her. I've missed her body. She's nowhere near ready for me to ravage her, but she's not even cleared for gentle lovemaking yet. So her touches, little pets of her skin on mine, whether she's stroking me or I'm brushing along her satiny skin, are all we have right now. It's enough because she's enough, just as she is.

"So do that. You've talked about striking out on your own, making your own way. But you don't have to, Scott. Make the Danger name be exactly what you wish it could be. Make your own dream come true. God knows, you've got the drive to do it. So do."

I bask in her praise, letting her faith in me settle into my bones, into my heart and soul. With a big breath, I pack it away to take with me, hoping it will buoy me through the day as I walk into a meeting with an agenda that is yet to be disclosed.

"Thank you, Madison. I'll check in with Marisol throughout the day. I love you." I press a kiss to her mouth, groaning as she delights in pressing it deeper, teasing and tempting me and knowing I can't do a damn thing about it. "Not yet. Dr. McDermott said you'd need another week."

She huffs, the pout of her lips extra-adorable because Madison is decidedly not a pouty type of woman. She's a get-out-of-my-way, get-shit-done type. The surprise of seeing her disappointment at not getting my body eases some of my own urges. We're in this together, just like everything.

I stand, walking toward the door and adjusting my cock in my slacks where she can't see me. *No sense in giving her ammunition to tease me further*, I think with a smirk.

"Hey, Scott?" I look back and see the grin on her face, and I know I didn't hide anything and that she's well aware of where my hand just was. "Kick some ass, baby. And then come home and tell me all about it."

I wink and give her my full, wide smile, knowing it drives her wild. After a quick check-in with Marisol for the day's plans, I head to the office, choosing to take a Town Car for the day instead of driving myself because I need the time to compose myself.

I'm unsure what I'm walking into today. It could be as simple as the board wanting an update on Madison, my work plans, and the new partnership with AlphaSystems. It could be much more serious, like them dismissing me for my disappearing act. Or anywhere in between. I realize that I hope it's not the latter option, liking Madison's suggestion to make the Danger name into something I'm proud of. I can't do that if they let me go for abandoning them, but if they can't see that Madison is more important, then that's their loss.

Delores pops up from behind her desk as I enter my office. "Good morning, Mr. Danger." I nod, returning her greeting, and head to my desk. She follows, mere steps behind, and sets a steaming cup of green tea on my desk. "Thought you might like an early pick-me-up without the jitters of coffee, sir."

I love that she doesn't wait for a response, doesn't question my plans for the day or anything else. She just returns to her desk and gets back to work. Delores and I are a good team, and I have no doubt she's kept my office and agenda in tip-top shape in my absence, fixing things to the best of her abilities.

What she can't control, no matter how hard she's tried, is Robbie. He barges in the door, not bothering with knocking or letting Delores announce him. But I grin, giving him a big hug and patting him on the back.

"How's she doing, man?" he asks, the same thing he says every day when we talk. I appreciate that he's accepted Madison as a part of my life, because she's the most important part.

"Good. Hanging with Marisol today, and Tiff's coming over. What about here? Any gossip on the meeting agenda?" I ask, hoping for a nugget, no matter how small.

He shakes his head. "Nope, not a word. Which means it's coming from on-high. Anyone else would snitch, but not your dad or his PA. They're both as tight-lipped as a nun's pussy."

I laugh at his irreverence and rise to offer him a handshake. "Thanks, Robbie. I needed that. Wish me luck, I guess. If not, it's been a helluva ride . . . and you'd better get ready for an address change because if they kick me outta here, I'm taking your annoying ass with me."

"Pshaw, if they kick you out, I'm hauling ass behind you, flying fingers at the board's sourpusses." He grins and flips off the ceiling like the old guard upstairs can see.

It's time to face the music . . . or maybe just to hear an update, a stupidly wishful, innocent voice whispers. Yeah, doubt that.

I walk into the boardroom, expecting glares and curious stares, but what I get are concerned expressions of condolences and shock at what happened to Madison. Murmurs of 'so scary' and 'such a lovely young woman at the gala' reverberate around me. Okay, not so bad . . . maybe.

Then, my dad walks in and a hush falls over the room as the temperature drops by a degree or two. It's been over a week since I've seen him or talked to him, refusing all contact, and I know he's beyond pissed at me. But looking at him now, I can't muster up a single fuck. I've been to hell and back, as well as heaven and back, with Madison over the last week. Every pain and exam, every step of progress and bit of regression, every 'I love you' and reminder of how badly we almost lost each other. It's been *a lot*. And Dad's petty need for attention seems childish and useless.

He looks around the table, his eyes landing on me last. Intentionally, I'm sure. His version of a silent slight, but it doesn't even hit target with my newly-developed apathy regarding him. "Thank you all for coming today. It was so generous of you to take time out of your busy schedules to address some actual work at Danger Enterprises." Again, everyone in the room knows he's talking to me, and I can feel their eyes judging my reaction to his insult.

Finally, after his dramatic pause gets comically long, he continues. "I have led Danger Enterprises for almost forty years, through difficulties and celebrations, creating a name synony-mous with strength, calculated risk, and strategy. I take pride in knowing the great things I have created within these walls, this building, and of course, this city."

I control the urge to roll my eyes. As if he did all that alone. I've only been here for a short time, but there are men and women on this board and in the company who have served for many of those same near-forty years, right alongside my father, who have arguably done just as much, if not more, for the success of the Danger name than Robert Danger himself.

"And because of the empire I have created, it is with bitter sweetness that I admit the time for me to move on has come."

Wait. What? The whole room just got a shot of adrenaline, and the buzz is palpable as everyone waits for the words . . .

"I, Robert Danger, hereby give notice to the Board of Directors of Danger Enterprises of my intent to vacate the role of Chief Exec-utive Officer, pending board approval of my replacement. I will retain a voting position on the board, as afforded by my shares within the company."

The formality leaves his voice a bit, his tone slightly more casual, although still as upper-crust as can be. "It's been an amazing run, and I appreciate your support at every turn."

And there it is. The board went against him and this is his Hail Mary. He knows he's done for, their vote for my proposal a first step in a change of the game. And he's nothing if not a brilliant strategist, willing to jump in and create the new rules himself before anyone gets the chance to.

"As my last mission as CEO, I'd like to suggest my son, Chase Danger, as my replacement. He's diligent, ambitious, holds the Danger name in high regard, and will see that it is not sullied in any way, but will, rather, improve and grow our stronghold within Bane and beyond. If needed, we can adjourn to allow time for votes to be considered carefully."

Of course, he recommended Chase, but for once, it doesn't

phase me. The little boy inside me cries out, desperate for the approval he never received. But the man I have become recognizes that my father is simply not capable of giving that which he doesn't have . . . love. He's never known it and doesn't understand it . . . not even for his children.

I look to Olivia and Chase, both of whom seem just as surprised as I am. Chase even looks a bit pale, his eyes wide with uncertainty. But I'm not uncertain. He will be a great leader. He always has been. He's a different leader than I am, will take the company in different directions than I would. But he will keep the Danger name safe in his hands. Honestly, Olivia would do just as well. She's a shrewd negotiator, innovative and willing to take smart risks. It's a shame Dad never saw her strengths either. In the moment, I have a sense of peace . . . with my siblings, with the loss of my dream to be the CEO. Even with my dad, to some degree. He's just not that important in the new priority list I hold dear.

My dad seems to consider the matter closed, preparing to call for the adjournment of the meeting. But from the end of the table, a voice calls out. "I move that we accept Robert Danger's resignation as CEO of Danger Enterprises. I further move that we vote on a replacement CEO now."

It's Charlie's voice, the executive who originally backed my proposal.

Dad laughs a bit, telling everyone that there's no rush, but another voice sounds out. "I second the motion."

And like that, it's done. Dad's resignation is accepted into the record. And voting opens . . . now. I never foresaw the meeting going this way, that's for damn sure.

For a moment, I think Dad is going to let Chase give a speech outlining his vision for the company, and I wonder if he has something prepared. But Dad stands, taking the spotlight for himself.

"I think you all know where my strengths and weaknesses lie. And I'm proud to say that one of my greatest accomplishments is this man sitting to my right," he says, gesturing to Chase, who looks grossly uncomfortable with the public praise. "Please consider our past, present, and future. I have built something grand in Danger Enterprises and am blessed to see its progress under the new leadership of my son, Chase."

Instead of the sharp sting of rejection I usually feel, the bitterness is gone and I simply feel indifference. The competition between Chase and me is over, and I no longer feel angry toward his golden child status. Instead, I feel bad that although his treatment has been drastically different from mine, it has still given him baggage and damage.

Charlie gives a polite golf clap, indicating the speech is over, and Dad sits down, a pleased smile drifting across his face. "Okay, for a position such as this, the voting will be open. We'll begin with our exiting CEO and work down the hierarchy. Agreed?" At the nods around the table, the vote begins.

Dad, of course, states confidently, "Chase Danger for CEO of Danger Enterprises."

The next vote is for Chase as well.

But the third is for . . . me.

So's the fourth. And the fifth. And the sixth.

Dad is turning red at the head of the table, a vein popping above his eye as his heart races at the unexpected votes.

Chase and I eye each other, shock written clearly on our faces, but there's no ill will. It feels good.

It's already solidly in my favor, much to everyone's shock. But when it's Olivia's turn to vote, I'll admit that I'm interested to hear what she has to say. Her vote can't put me or Chase into the role, but I'm curious as to her take on the whole thing.

Her voice is calm, her speech sounding practiced even though I know she's talking off the cuff. "I have served this board and this company for several years. Beyond that, I have been a part of this family my whole life. My brothers are both skilled businessmen in their own rights, beyond whatever name they were born to, perhaps even in spite of that name." She gives Dad a hard look before scanning the group. "It is with delight that I would see either of my brothers as CEO. Therefore, I abstain from this vote." It's the perfect move. She chose both of us by choosing neither of us.

Charlie knocks on the table. "With voting being held by a strong majority, Scott Danger is the newly-elected Chief Executive Officer of Danger Enterprises." And just like that, I'm the CEO.

There's a cheer and a round of applause as I stand to accept the position. "Wow. Thank you all so very much for placing your faith and your trust in me. I promise I won't let you down. I will keep Danger Enterprises synonymous with progress and powerful strategies to take us into the next century. I have learned a lot recently, what it takes to be a good man . . . a good partner . . . a good leader. And I think that we each have, as my father said, strengths and weaknesses."

I look to my dad, who is obviously hanging on to his frayed control by a single thread.

"And I think that by working together, we can both mitigate and utilize these jagged pieces of our business puzzle to take us further, consider new ideas, and build something better than we've ever known." I see smiles and nods around the table, knowing I've got them on the hook. Hopefully, they're solidly secured there because I'm about to test their faith from the get-go.

"To that end, I would like to make my first official motion as CEO of Danger Enterprises."

There's a breath of anticipation in the room, everyone wondering where I'm going with this.

"I move that a panel of CEOs should control Danger Enterprises, with me focusing on our technology and long-term solutions division, my brother, Chase, serving as lead for our short- and mid-term capital investments, and that my sister, Olivia, be placed over diversified markets, where her interest in finding no-name brilliance can be fostered. By spreading out our resources, we can secure a stable present and a growing future for Danger Enterprises."

It's a bold move, brazen and potentially as stupid as can be, but I think it's brilliant in its simplicity. We are simply different people with different strengths, but each with a right to our namesake company. I glance at Chase, who looks hopeful, like I took his favorite game away and then promised to play it with him. Olivia smiles widely, a full cat who got the cream smile, with white teeth and everything, so I know she's delighted. We can do this, be this, siblings who run the family company together.

Dad guffaws loudly, slapping his hands on the table. "That's preposterous. See? This is why I wanted Chase. None of this crazy, pie-in-the-sky daydream shit. Business doesn't work this way. Never has and never will. It's not a flower field where everyone holds hands and sings *Kumbaya*, Scott."

I smirk, knowing that I do actually have an advantage here. I didn't just come up with this idea. It's been mulling in my mind while I sat at the hospital with Madison, a seed of a dream that my siblings and I could someday be better, closer than we have been.

"You're right, Dad. That's not how business has worked . . . in the past. And that's the point. It is how it can work in the future. If we can conceive of a way to create AI, to talk to thin air and have a package show up on our doorstep, for our cars to park and stop themselves without the driver's engagement, then surely, we can have three siblings work together. It is not unprecedented. There are plenty of other successful companies that have a panel of CEOs, and the hierarchy design works quite well for them. I think it would work even better for Danger

Enterprises because we are inherently invested in doing so. It's our name on the building."

Dad clacks his mouth shut, his eyes narrowing at me. Checkmate. The king is dead. And it's time to start a new game, one with our own rules.

The vote goes quickly this time, passing with only one holdout . . . my dad.

And with one more knock on the table, I become one of the CEOs of Danger Enterprises.

CHAPTER 33

MADISON

Daily Horoscope, November 10th
Libra – *Picture perfect is only surface deep. True beauty is in the flawed depths.*

I'VE BARELY FINISHED THE HEALTHY EGG-WHITE omelet Marisol brought to me as I sat on the couch when I hear the banging on the door. I have a flash of fear at the loud sound, but it's quickly abated when I hear Tiffany in the hallway. "Open up, bitch. The ice cream's melting!"

I laugh, and Marisol gives me a weird look. "Did she say ice cream? It's ten o'clock in the morning!"

I nod, a big grin on my face as Marisol opens the door and Tiff barges right in like she's owns the place. "Yes, ice cream, for the root beer floats. Now, important question . . . one or two scoops?"

Marisol looks to me, finally saying, "If you're okay, Maddie, I think I'll escape to my room for a bit, give you time to visit with your friend. Call me if you need anything, and do not get up without me—Mr. Danger's explicit instructions—and I don't want to upset him." She looks terrified of Scott and would probably shit herself if I told her that I got off on his telling me what to do just so I could do the exact opposite. Drives him and me crazy . . . and we like it like that, apparently.

But she escapes, and Tiff winks at me. "Now that that's handled . . . one or two?"

Knowing the right answer, I tell her, "Two." I watch with delight as she commandeers Scott's kitchen—I mean, our kitchen . . . still not used to that. A few minutes later, she brings me a foamy mess of ice creamy goodness, and I take a tiny sip and moan at the deliciousness.

"Damn, girl, you barely took a taste and are acting like it's damn-near orgasmic. You that thirsty?" Tiff wiggles her eyebrows at me, laughing at her own joke.

"Just taking it easy on the cold ice cream. I definitely do not want a brain freeze post-concussion," I say matter-of-factly. "Actually, yes, though . . . getting pretty desperate for the D, living with Scott and not able to do anything about it. He's always walking around shirtless and taking showers naked to torture me," I say overdramatically.

Tiff laughs. "Would you rather the man take a shower with his clothes on?"

"Maybe . . ." I say, then giggle softly, still careful with my voice and my head. I'm definitely feeling a bajillion times better than I was a week ago, but certain things still trigger a headache, like loud noises or flashing lights. So no TV and no crazy laugh fest like Tiff and I would usually do.

Instead, we're chill, curled up on the couch as we catch up.

"What's the latest on . . . Rich?" She pauses before she says his name, unsure of my reaction. But I'm fine now, moving beyond the fear and into the anger portion of my recovery, even if I do have occasional moments of panic. But Scott's always there to talk me through it, or I have mantras I tell myself over and over on a loop.

"Still in county jail," I tell her. "When the DA arraigned him, they denied bail, so he's sitting there until the trial, and by the time it's all over, Rich won't be getting out for a long time. They got the whole thing . . . car chase, hitting my car, the choking . . . from multiple angles on various security cameras. So there's no way he can deny it. They're mostly just arguing over a plea deal sentence because Scott is adamant that Rich gets the maximum sentence. I tend to agree."

It's a relief, one I never thought I'd get. Rich's manipulations and abuse were always so subtle, so sneaky, I never thought I'd see him actually punished for any of it. I hate that it had to get so bad for him to be caught, but I'm glad he's at least not free to do it to another woman.

Tiff nods. "I hope he rots there myself, but I'm glad to hear you feel the same way." She takes a long lick around the rim of her float, catching the drips of suds before they can run down the cups she brought with her to 'keep it real'. "So, how're things with Mr. Moneybags?"

I GRIN, LAUGHING AT THE NICKNAME BECAUSE SCOTT'S money is really the last thing I care about with him, but it's the flashy thing most folks see first. "Really good. Great, actually. He's been taking great care of me, and we've had some pretty deep conversations about the future and the past . . . mostly about how messed up we both are. We're making our edges a little more obvious to each other, as awkward as fuck as that is, so that we can keep from getting cut."

TIFF HAS A MOMENT OF WISDOM. "DADDY ISSUES, Mommy issues, trust issues, control issues, insecurity . . . you two are a veritable cornucopia of therapy waiting to happen." It's ugly when she says it like that, even though she's half-kidding, but she's not wrong.

315

WE ARE PRETTY FUCKED-UP PEOPLE, BUT AT LEAST WE can be fucked-up together and help wipe away the dirt, reveal the shine underneath the pain we've each had, maybe even heal some of the damage with love and a spit polish. It's not a pretty process. It's a bit two steps forward and one step backward, which Scott says is my favorite dance, while his only move is forward, full steam ahead. But it's our dance.

TRYING TO LIGHTEN THE MOOD, I TELL TIFF WITH A raised eyebrow, "Yeah, we've definitely agreed on no Mommy or Daddy kinky shit and that he can be a control freak all he wants while we're having sex because I like it then, but outside the bedroom, we're equal partners. Ones who say 'I love you' and give reassuring comments like a fucking Hallmark movie."

"Y'ALL ARE A HALLMARK MOVIE! EXCEPT FOR THE bossy bedroom stuff. That's more Skin-a-Max After Hours. Bow-chicka-bow-wow," she says with a little shimmy. "But he's the rich knight come to save the day of the poor barmaiden in distress."

"YEAH, DEFINITELY NOT," I TELL HER, KNOWING I'D told Scott that several times when we'd first started out and she's well aware of that fact. "I know we're annoying as fuck, but it's working for us. Especially while we're still learning better communication. Feels good."

TIFF LOOKS AROUND THE BIG ROOM, TAKING IN THE tall windows, the plush couch we're sitting on, and the bright kitchen before her eyes settle on my face, searching it just as closely. "Are you happy here? With him?"

I BITE MY LIP, NOT BECAUSE I'M UNSURE BUT BECAUSE

I know that if I yell my joy the way I want to, I'll surely scare Marisol and likely have a headache from the noise. Instead, I tell her the truth quietly. "So happy. I didn't know it could be like this, Tiff. It's beautiful and he's mine. And I'm his. And it's . . . us." Halfway through, I give up the battle against the tears and let them run down my face, feeling cleansed by the salty release of happiness.

"I'M REALLY HAPPY FOR YOU, MADDIE. IF ANYONE deserves a happily ever after, it's sure as fuck you. Just to clarify, you're living here forever now, right?" She says it casually, but it sounds like a loaded question.

"UH, YEAH," I HEDGE. "WHY?"

TIFF SMILES. "'CUZ I'M GETTING A NEW ROOMIE NOW that you're out. Devin needs a new place to crash. Guess his current roommates are getting a bit too bitchy for his taste, so he wants something a bit more chill. Plus, we can carpool."

IT FEELS A LITTLE LIKE SHE'S REPLACING ME, WHICH stings. But I know that's not the case. Tiff is my bestie through and through, and Devin is a great guy, so I'm glad they can help each other out with bills. "All right, he can have my room, but I get dibs on the left end of the couch anytime I come over."

TIFF SMIRKS AT ME. "DUH. OF COURSE. THAT'S *your* end."

"HOW IS STELLA DOING? I HATED THAT I WAS STILL IN the hospital when she had the funeral for Daryl." Stella had offered to hold off for my release, but I'd known she needed closure. It'll be an open wound for a long time, but at least the service gave her a chance to grieve and connect with family and Daryl's friends.

"She's doing as well as can be expected. She misses Daryl terribly, but she's a strong woman. Right now, she's in survival mode . . . *just keep swimming, just keep swimming.*" Tiff mimics the popular kids' movie line. "But we're keeping the bar running like a well-oiled machine. Still no word from Carl though. Stella's afraid he's dead somewhere too. He's an ass, but he's never disappeared before so she doesn't know what to think."

I nod, hoping Stella at least gets an answer because the not-knowing is soul-crushing. I know that Carl did scare me, and he was grossly inappropriate, but in the scope of everything else that's happened, it seems so much less of a big deal now. Of course, if he comes back, I'll probably feel quite differently about that, and I'll never risk being in a vulnerable position with him again. But that seems nebulous and full of 'what-ifs' . . . what if he shows up, what if he doesn't think he did anything wrong, what if I were alone with him again? I just can't think about it right now, and I vow to handle it better when and if Carl ever shows up.

Tiff and I hang out all day, vegging and talking and laughing until Marisol runs her off, saying, "Mr. Danger is on his way." Tiff had feigned fear and scurried out like a field mouse who'd seen the plow coming. But she'd left the supplies for a root beer float for Scott, so I know she approves of him.

Scott stalks into the living room when he gets home. There's an energy to his presence. I don't notice the void when he's gone, but when he returns, everything suddenly feels right, like a piece I didn't know was missing is returned to its rightful place.

He places a chaste kiss to my forehead and sits down on the couch next to me. He looks distracted, and I wonder about his meeting today. I'd been so busy with Tiff that I hadn't been concerned about his not calling, figuring he was busy playing catch-up since he's been out with me for a week. But his voice is gravelly. "Hey, baby, can we talk?"

Oh, shit. That's the beginning of the end, never a good question to hear. My heart races, and my voice is quiet. "Of course. What's up?"

His eyes are scanning the rug, his fingers fidgeting, and finally, he gets up, pacing across the room, back and forth in the sunset light coming in the windows behind him. It worries me. The back and forth is my part of the dance, and I wonder if it's my turn to be the full-throttle dance partner.

"So, the meeting today wasn't what I expected."

"Yeah?" I prompt.

"My dad resigned as CEO. It's effective immediately, although he keeps his voting position on the board." His voice is clinical, like he's reading statistics on a graph.

"Okay, so what does that mean? I feel like you're

spoon-feeding me something big, slow and easy so I don't freak out."

He grimaces. "Maybe. Dad backed Chase as his replacement, but the board . . . they voted me as CEO." His pacing stops as he eyes me, waiting for my reaction.

"Oh, my God, Scott! That's awesome! Congratulations! That's what you've always wanted." I'm genuinely thrilled for him. It's his dream come true. I hop up and grab him in a big hug. He melts into me for a moment, then holds me back a little, his hands still on my upper arms.

"There's more. I made my first move as CEO, and they agreed with me. Everyone but my dad voted to make all three of us joint-CEOs . . . me, Chase, and Olivia." His eyes look to mine, and now I see it. He's not mad, not cold or upset. He's in shock, stunned at the turn his day has taken.

I pull him to me, cupping his face in my hands, knowing what he needs. "I am so proud of you, Scott Danger. You are a good man with so many talents, but your biggest gift is your heart. You were literally given the thing you've wanted most in your whole life, the personification of your value, the symbol of success. And rather than flaunt it, revel in it, or in your own self, you shared it with the people you knew would appreciate it the same way you do. You are such a good man, and I love you so much."

The words click in his mind, but it's his heart that hears them, the relief and sheer joy transforming his face to a big smile. "We did it, Madison! Thanks to you, I've got my siblings and my company. And because of you, I have a better future than I could've dreamed. Thank you, baby. I love you so much!"

HE GOES TO SWOOP ME AROUND IN A CIRCLE BUT remembers the concussion protocol at the last moment and settles for picking me up to kiss me passionately. It's everything we need. Not quite a perfect fairy tale, but so much better than either of us had ever envisioned.

EPILOGUE

MADISON

Daily Horoscope, December 24th
Libra - All the stars line up for you. Enjoy the day, and remember that
while jumping in with both feet isn't always the wisest decision . . .
sometimes, it's the best decision you can make.

"So, last day before vacation. How does it feel?" I ask Scott as we get off the elevator and head to his office.

"Like I'm forgetting a million things to do and have a million more lined up after that," Scott says, rolling up the sleeves of his shirt. He's been working hard alongside his siblings for over a month now, and it's going surprisingly well. I think they're still tip-toeing around each other a bit, from what Scott tells me, but they're handling the diversified businesses they've invested in without issue.

Most amusing is the way Daddy Danger has taken to claiming the whole thing was his idea, a dramatic show of the strength the Danger name personifies. Scott had laughed and laughed the first time Robert said that, taking a bit of evil glee in correcting his father publicly in front of the board. No, they didn't forget, but Scott definitely doesn't feed into his father's ego.

We get in his office and shut the door. "All right, get what you need quickly and let's get out of here. You don't need a to-do list for a holiday vacation," I tease him. "Though I think it's kinda sexy when you go all Expert Planner on me. Say something dirty," I tease, curious what he'll say to play along.

"Mmm, how about . . . Let's check the weather, make sure it's not cold as balls in our destination city." I giggle at his faux-seductive tone and the way he emphasizes 'balls' intentionally. But the real tease is in what he said, because we are going on a holiday vacation, but he hasn't told me where we're going.

"Not even one clue?"

"No way. One hint, and then you guess and ruin the surprise. This is one of the things you're going to have to let me control." His face is the epitome of smug cockiness, and I should hate it. Instead, it turns me on and makes me want to be a brat back, just to irritate him into spilling the vacation details or into finally fucking me.

It's been a few weeks since I got clearance to resume all my usual activities from Dr. McDermott, and we have made love. Soft, sweet, tender, beautiful love making. And I'm *so* done with that, not forever but for now. Because what I really need is to get fucked. And what Scott needs is to fuck me. Rough and hard and dirty, without worrying about my concussion or my leg.

The thought of my leg reminds me of the nagging pain, and I settle gratefully into the chair behind Scott's desk, stretching out my leg and rubbing my thigh.

Scott looks at me worriedly. "You okay?"

"Achy, but not too bad," I admit, rubbing at the scar. After my bandage came off, it wasn't as bad as we'd feared, and while the rehabilitation has meant a lot of stiff mornings, the scar is mostly more itchy than painful these days.

"But I might need you to kiss it better?" I say, faux innocence in every word as I trace a fingertip from my knee up my inner thigh toward my pussy. I purposefully drag my skirt hem higher, careful over the large Band-Aid that's now all the burn requires.

Scott's eyes are already laser-focused on my finger, his lips parting, not panting yet, but definitely on board with my seduction. "What are you doing, Maddie? Your leg . . ."

"Is fine. So's my head. You know what's not okay, Scott?" I ask him.

He shakes his head. "No, what's wrong?" I can see that whatever I say, he'll want to fix it. Slay the dragon, solve the problem, make it all better for me. That's just who he is, and I'm getting used to it, recognizing it for the demonstration of love that it is. And even using it to my benefit, like now.

"My pussy. It's empty and needy and needs to get fucked. Hard, like you mean it. Think you can do that for me, Scott?"

His voice is tight, the warning as clear as the need. "Madison . . ."

I reassure him, wanting to put his mind at ease so he'll give in and give me what I want. "Doc says I'm fine, all good to go. So . . ."

I can see Scott's internal struggle, his desire to protect me warring with his raging desire to take me. His need to be inside me wins, thankfully. He lifts me to the desk, pushing my skirt up to my waist so that my ass presses against the cold wood. And then he takes my vacated seat in his office chair.

"Lean back and let me see this pretty pink pussy." He groans at the sight of my bare lips, already wet with need for him. "No panties, Maddie? Fuck, you're in so much trouble. Walking around with my pussy open to anyone passing by."

I smirk, knowing I'd done it on purpose in a premeditated seduction plan. Scott's not the only one who can make a plan and see it to fruition. But he wipes the smirk right off my face as he traces a finger through my folds, the sensation amplified by the ferocity of my need. "Fuck, Scott."

He chuckles darkly. "Oh, no, Maddie. You're not even close to getting fucked yet. Tell me, whose pussy is this?"

I don't hesitate, knowing what he wants to hear. "It's yours. Just yours. Always."

He dips his chin, his eyes locked on my center. "Mine," he growls and then claims me with his tongue. He swirls the tip over my clit, faster and faster, pressing harder against me to drive me wild. Finally, he's owning me, and it's exactly what I need.

He slips a finger inside me, giving my pussy something to squeeze as he slams inside me and then pulls out, doing it over and over again.

I'm on the edge of a rising tidal wave already, embarrassingly quick after the weeks of sweet softness. "That's it, Madison. Come on my face and I'll fuck you over my desk." His promise is enough to make me crash over, wanting this moment but wanting the next just as much.

I spasm, shudders crashing through my body in waves, one right on top of the last, keeping me drowning in the depths of pleasure. "Scott! Oh, fuck, yes!"

As I finish, Scott stands, yanking me from the desk to turn me around. He positions me with my left knee on the desk, checking to make sure that it's comfortable, not pulling on the healing skin or putting pressure on the bandage. But once he's satisfied I'm good, it's on.

The clink of his belt is the only warning I get before he slams into me balls-deep, immediately beginning to pound into me. Finally. This is what I've needed, what I've been missing, Scott unleashing the tether he holds on himself, all the while tightening the one he holds on me.

He's bossy, domineering, in charge of me right now. And I fucking love it. Later, I'll want him to ask my opinion on matters, big and small. Right now, I want him to take me, claim me any way he wants, and bask in his power.

"So damn tight, Maddie. Relax. Let me in, because I'm coming in either way. I've needed this pussy like this, raw and rough . . . and mine." He smacks my right ass cheek, carefully avoiding my left still, his awareness of my needs still firmly in check even as he loses it.

I cry out, encouraging his punishing thrusts, and he leans over me, laying open-mouthed kisses along my neck. He's reclaiming me there too, his attention like a salve healing the ugly memory of Rich's hands strangling me. The combination of rough and sweet does me in, and I'm swept away again.

My pussy's pulsing clenches trigger him too, and I revel as he shouts out my name while filling me with his essence. He gives one last thrust, jetting the last drops deep inside me before stilling.

Eventually, we dress and collapse back to his office chair, me sitting sideways in his lap to keep the pressure off my bandage and injury. Suddenly, there's a rapping knock on the door.

My eyes open wide and shoot to Scott. We'd thought we were alone. It's Christmas Eve, after all, and all the employees have the day off to spend with their families.

Scott shrugs and calls out, "Come in." Like my sitting in his lap moments after we fucked is perfectly normal for his office.

The door opens slowly to reveal Chase, a big shit-eating grin on his face. "Hey, guys, just wanted to check in but didn't want to interrupt."

I blush instantly and furiously, trying to move from Scott's lap. But he holds me in place, grinning and laughing. "Thanks for waiting, Brother. What's up?"

Chase shakes his head like he'd expected a bigger reaction, but that's all he's getting. Their teases are different now, more friendly brothers than competing rivals. I've heard them on the phone, and Chase has stopped by a few times to discuss Danger Enterprises business stuff when they couldn't coordinate times at the office, especially at first when Scott was helping me with my rehab as much as possible. And each time I hear them tease, I hold my breath, but they seem to be moving from the past and opening up to a future.

"Just wanted to confirm that we're on for Christmas morning at your place? You're sure?" Chase asks.

I don't let Scott answer. I do it for the both of us. "Chase, Christmas is for family, and you are ours. So you'll get your ass up, pick Olivia up, come over and open presents, and then we'll eat lunch. My Aunt May is making her famous loaded baked potatoes and banana pudding. You don't want to miss it."

I can see the relief on Chase's face, but he still looks for confirmation from Scott. I feel Scott's nod, and Chase looks pleased.

When Robert had mentioned in passing that he was planning to spend the holiday season in Aruba with his young blonde girlfriend, we'd honestly been pleased because that meant there was no reason to lie about not wanting to spend the holiday with him. He's a bit less obnoxious now that he's not CEO, but he drives the siblings crazy and there's not enough good blood between them to allow them to let it go. Instead, they all just flinch at his continued barbs, regress into old habits, and as for Scott, he needs extra reassurance of how much I love him for days after an encounter with his dad.

So I'm glad he bailed. We might actually have a happy holiday memory for the siblings without Daddy Dearest. Hallelujah!

Chase nods, then smiles, looking at me then at Scott. "You found a good woman, Scott. Madison . . . good luck."

THE NIGHT AIR IS COLD, BUT THAT'S OKAY AS SCOTT and I head into Stella's. I'm not working tonight. Stella said that I'm off the schedule for all of December and part of January until my leg's ready to work again. But tonight is the annual Christmas party at Stella's, and this year, it seems more important than ever.

"Merry Christmas," Stella greets us as we come in, dressed in what has to be one of the most glorious ugly Christmas sweaters ever. "It's good to see you looking so happy."

"It's good to see you smiling, Stella," I reply, giving her a hug. I look around the place, seeing the smiling faces all aglow with holiday spirit and feeling at home.

The party goes well, and things get even better when Carl shows up. Apparently, after he'd sobered up Halloween morning, he'd realized what he'd done to me and was horrified, much like I knew he would be. He'd taken off, ashamed and unable to face his actions and apologize. He'd started a bender that only got worse when he got word about Daryl's accident.

But somewhere in the mess, he'd truly hit rock bottom and decided he wanted a change. He'd returned to Bane sober after a month in rehab, proud of his thirty-day chip and wanting to apologize to everyone to make amends.

It was a tearful reunion, but Stella forgave her son for missing Daryl's funeral, and Carl promised he's going to be better. His apology to me was awkward because Scott had stared him down, virtually slicing him to ribbons with his eyes. But I forgave him, even if I won't be alone with him. It brings up too many triggers for me after everything. But he's understanding about that too, knowing it'll take time and being trustworthy to build up people's opinion of him once again. He's even got a new job, one that keeps him away from alcohol.

"To a Merry Christmas," Stella says, lifting a glass of ginger ale in deference to Carl. "While we will miss those who are not here, we're happy to have a new member to our extended family. Scott, you're a genuine pain in the ass . . . but we're glad to have you with us."

With cheers all around, it's time to really enjoy the Christmas party.

"So who wants to see how many Christmas cookies I can eat in ten minutes? Who's ready to film?"

"NO, TIFFANY!" several of us shout at the same time.

EPILOGUE

SCOTT

December 25th

Scorpio – The best gifts are not found under the tree.

he morning air is chilly, but it feels good to watch over the city with Madison from our apartment, making a new tradition as we blend her family and mine. "Thanks for this."

Maddie shrugs. "Chase and Liv were so surprised by my invitation for Christmas, and I'm kinda curious to see how they handle Aunt May. She's feisty."

I laugh. "You told me she was, but I don't know if I really understood until I saw her tackle a pissed-off Rottweiler with a rolled-up newspaper!"

There's a knock at the door, and I open it to see May, all decked out in holiday finery. Well, for her, that means her hair is down long and she has on a blouse with her jeans instead of a t-shirt. But I know she made an effort to make a positive impression, and that's good enough for me.

I greet her warmly, inviting her inside and taking her coat.

"May, it's good to see you again," I say, giving her a hug. "How're the puppies?"

"Sagging . . . oh, you mean the dogs," May jokes, making me laugh. I have laughed more over the past month than in the entire previous twenty-six years of my life, and it feels good. "They're doing great. I was able to make some last-minute placements. Seems some folks really do want to give a dog a home for the holidays."

"Good," I say. "Glad they got their Christmas wish and are home for Christmas morning."

"Are you two planning something?" Madison asks, and I shrug. "Scott Danger, don't you try that look with me. You had the same look on your face last night at Stella's, and I know you've got something on your damn mind."

"Maybe I do, maybe I don't," I tell her, laughing.

May takes off for the kitchen, taking over like it's hers even as she oohs and ahhs over things she takes delight in, like the fact that there are two ovens and a refrigerator large enough for her biggest cookie sheet. I've never noticed or cared, but I'm glad she's excited. May and Madison bustle this way and that, and I watch from my perch on the barstool, enjoying their easy camaraderie.

The doorbell rings again, and I go to open it, greeting Chase and Olivia. There are no hugs this time, but we're finally getting comfortable with one another.

"Merry Christmas, Chase, Olivia. Come on in. The bosses are in the kitchen, and I think our job is to stay out of their way." I guide them into the living room after tossing their coats on the entryway hooks.

From the corner of the kitchen, I hear Maddie's voice ring out, "I heard that!"

I grin, yelling back, "Am I wrong?"

May comes into the living room, wiping her hands on a towel.

"Hell, yes, you're wrong. Now, all three of you, get in here and wash up. I need someone to peel the potatoes, someone to set the table, and someone to knead the dough for biscuits. Decide amongst yourselves who does what. I hear y'all are good at that these days."

Yep, feisty. That's May. I grin at Chase and Olivia, who return the smile, all three of us following orders and filing into the kitchen to help. Apparently, none of us get to be the boss today.

The hustle and bustle in my kitchen increases as the five of us work alongside each other. I'd never considered that the sizeable space might seem small, but with all of us in the middle of food prep, it does feel full.

Once everything is prepped and the ham is locked away into the oven to bake, I take a chance on being the whiny kid ready for some Christmas fun. "Come on, let's open our presents."

It's the best Christmas morning ever as each gift is opened with as much noisy paper tearing and throwing of ribbons, bows, and other crap as possible. Food is cookies, of course, with a side of fudge and great coffee, and with each gift, my excitement grows.

"Oh, Aunt May, that's beautiful!" Madison exclaims when May models a leather jacket I got her. "You look like Jamie Lee Curtis in it!"

"Hell, I'm never taking it off then," May says. "Thank you, Scott."

I nod and open a present from May, a key. "What's this?"

"Key to the front door of the shelter," May says. "You deserve it for everything you've done for us."

I laugh at her practicality, knowing that this is a big gesture from her. "Thank you, May."

Olivia seems to like the cashmere shawl I bought her, and Chase grins like a loon at the pair of home plate baseball tickets I bought for him . . . and me.

Finally, it's time for Maddie's surprise.

I reach behind the quirky Charlie Brown tree Maddie had begged me to get, trying not to mess up her carefully arranged ornaments or messily tossed tinsel. Grabbing the large, flat box, I offer it to her.

"What is it? Can I shake it?" she asks, giddier than I've ever seen her. It's adorable, and I want to bottle the flush on her cheeks and make her whole body pink up that prettily for me.

"Don't shake it, just open it," I say, nerves sweeping through me.

Maddie looks into the box, pulling out the thin stack of papers. "What are these? I don't understand." Her eyes jump from the papers to me.

"These are the plans for the new and improved, expanded May's Animal Rescue. They start construction once the ground thaws." I point out little details on the paper. "Beyond the rescue areas, there's space for a sales side. Kenneling, training, that sort of stuff for families who adopt, or even those who get their pets elsewhere. There's office space for an in-house vet if you want. I'm guessing with the influx of animals you can help, there will likely need to be more daily hands on deck, especially some help overseeing everything. Interested?" I ask Madison.

"Do you have to ask? Hell, yes!" she exclaims. "But how?"

I grin. "Olivia helped me set it up through her division as a diversification of our charitable donations. Essentially, Danger Enterprises made a venture capital investment in you and May. Together, you can change so many animals' lives and make Bane a better place."

Maddie looks to Olivia, telling her 'thank you' before plopping into my lap and covering my face with kisses. "Thank you, Scott! Oh, my God, this is going to be amazing!"

"Well, I'm kind of hoping that you keep saying that," I say, setting her on the couch and getting down on one knee. "I have one more present."

I reach into the pocket of my jacket and take out a simple box, opening it and holding it out to Maddie. Before I can speak, she whispers, "Scott."

"Maddie, you fill my heart with love. You complete my soul. I want to make a life, make a family with you. Will you marry me?"

She looks back to May, who smiles but isn't surprised. "He asked Stella and me for our blessing last night."

I laugh and hold out my hand. "Madison Danger sounds . . . fabulous."

CHRISTMAS IS LOVELY, FULL OF JOYFUL CELEBRATION and surprises. But I have one last trick up my sleeve. Madison had encouraged me to spend the week between Christmas and New Year's at the office, knowing that all the time I've been away while helping her had set me behind.

But it's the holidays, and most of the office is a ghost town anyway. So I planned a little getaway for us, destination unknown . . . to Madison.

Knowing we have an early flight, I wake her while it's still dark. "Madison, rise and shine, porcupine," I sing-song.

She cracks one eye. "What the hell did you just say? And why so early?" My girl is a lot of things, but a morning person is not one of them.

I grin. "Huh, it just came out. I think I had a nanny when I was little who said that every morning." Madison's other eye opens, and she has a flash of sadness at a little version of me being woken up by a nanny every day. "As to why . . . it's because we're leaving. Surprise!"

LAUREN LANDISH

She pops up in bed. "We're leaving today? Where are we going? Will you tell me now?"

"Nope, have to wait and see, but you need to get a move on." I don't have to tell her twice. She's already thrown the covers back and made a beeline for the shower to get ready.

I head to the kitchen to start the coffee, knowing we're going to need it today. Grabbing the first cup, I stand by the window, watching the sun rise over Bane. My city, my family's city. I have a different approach than my father's prideful ownership. I'm ready to tackle the responsibility of making it the best it can be for the people, not for myself. It's a weight I gladly wear upon my shoulders, not a pedestal I stand atop.

From behind me, I hear a soft 'ahem' and turn to see my naked fiancé standing in the doorway. "I don't know what to wear. Shorts, pants, fancy, casual? You gotta help a girl out."

I look her up and down, knowing the clock is ticking on the flight but not able to resist. "Come here, Madison." She walks to me, beauty personified, from her wet mess of hair to her bare face, to her curvy body, even with the healing injuries and scars, external and internal. She is strength, perseverance, and independence. She is need, doubt, and fear. She is the sparrow and the eagle, all in one. She is mine.

I take her mouth in a kiss, dropping the empty coffee mug to the carpet softly. I kiss down her neck, laving her pink nipples with licks and kisses, knowing I could spend all day right here, but I'm hungry for more. And so is she.

Madison turns, facing us toward the window, and drops to her knees before me. She looks up at me, raw desire in her eyes. "One thing. After this, can you fuck me like before? Hard and fast by the window?"

My breath catches as she slips my pajama pants down and my cock springs up. "I can never say no to you."

"Yeah, you can," she teases, grasping my thick cock and licking her lips. "You just don't want to."

336

Before I can answer, she wraps her lips around my cock and sucks, taking me in deeply. I guide her up and down my gleaming shaft with a gentle hand in her hair, loving the way she can take me into her body. She sucks me with love and devotion.

Years, maybe even decades of this? Of loving sex with this wonderful woman? I can't wait for every day of it.

I moan as she bobs up and down and fondles my balls. Reaching back, she teases my taint with her soft fingers, but there's no need for more. I can't wait any longer. I lift her off, my eyes wide and my chest heaving. "To the window. Keep that up and I'm coming in your mouth."

"Who says that's not what I want?" she taunts, getting up and turning to the window.

She's glowing in the flaming morning light of the sun, and I take a mental snapshot, needing this moment in my memory bank for all eternity.

My cock slides against her pussy, and she moans, ready for more. But before I can enter her, she looks back at me. "Scott . . . what if I stop the pills?" Her voice is soft, the question belying the obvious truth that it's what she wants.

"You think we're ready?" I ask, pulling back and sliding my cock between her lips again. My head drags over her clit, and she gasps, nodding her head.

She puts her hands on the window, pushing back against me, trying to take me in.

"I want a family with you . . . as many babies as you want."

"Let's start with one," I say, a huge smile on my face. I pull back, adjusting my cock so that I'm pressed against her entrance, and I pause, teasing her with the tip, knowing she wants more, so much more . . . all of me, everything I can give her. I want that too.

I push in, and there's that fresh like the first time instant where she's so damn tight, but then she relaxes, letting me sink in deeper.

I pull back and thrust again, grunting as I fill her balls-deep. We go hard and fast, knowing that we're cutting the time short, but it's a good quickie, the sharp slap of my hips on Madison's ass sending a good shiver up her spine as my balls come forward to smack her clit.

"Fuck, your cock feels so good . . ." she groans, her fingers digging into the window as she pushes into me, fucking me back. But I keep her pressed to the glass, letting the city see that she is my woman.

"I love you," I growl in her ear as I speed up more, our bodies driving against the glass and thumping throughout the entire penthouse.

She squeezes me, trembling on the edge, and I groan as I let go, not able to withstand any more of the delicious onslaught. Needing her to get there, to come with me, I reach around her hip to thrum at her clit. We're both groaning, sobs tearing from our throats as I fill her and she spasms around me.

I plant a hand on the window next to hers, exhausted but kissing her neck. "My . . . I . . ."

"That was better than ever before," she whispers, covering my hand with hers. "I love you, too."

We disentangle, and I can't help but grin at the mess we made of the window. "It looks like a frosted outline of two people fucking on the thing. There are handprints and tit prints, and a nice steamy outline."

"Should we clean it before we go?" she asks, not at all embarrassed by the art we've created.

"Nope, gotta go . . . plane leaves in one hour. For Paris."

Madison's eyes are so wide they nearly bug out of her head, and her jaw drops wide open. "Really? Oh, my God, are you serious?"

I take the invite of her open mouth and cover her with a kiss before telling her, "Yes, for real. Now, let's go."

She's off and running toward the bedroom. My naked savior. I might have saved her from a few dangerous situations, but she's the one who's saved me . . . from myself. The biggest Danger there is.

EPILOGUE

MADISON

Daily Horoscope, January 12th
Libra – I dare you.

"ARE YOU SURE ABOUT THIS?" TIFF ASKS AGAIN. I think she's scared I'm going to go batshit crazy on her again or that something bad is going to happen.

"I am. I still don't believe, exactly. But you gotta admit, she was right," I tell her again.

"But was she really?" Tiff argues.

I quote the prediction that started this whole roller coaster . . . *"Your heart shall be his . . . then will come the sting. You will suffer . . . oh, girl, will you suffer . . . and then you shall burn.* That's literally what she said and actually what happened. Maybe I'll just tell her I only want the good stuff this time? Although that scary sounding prediction worked out pretty well in the end."

Tiff nods, but she's still not convinced.

This time, it's me opening the door to Marie Laveau's House of Voodoo and shoving Tiff inside.

This time, I expect the Jamaican-accented greeting.

This time, I sit down with an open mind and an open heart.

"Ah, the forgotten child who is no longer forgotten. She is found, she is freed," Marie says wisely, and I swear she has a twinkle in her eye that wasn't there last time.

"I wanted to apologize for how we left after the last reading you gave me. We were freaked out because it sounded so negative. Well, it was bad, in a lot of ways, but . . ." I stammer, trying to explain how I got here again.

"Understandable, child. So the prediction was true. You were stung by the scorpion after giving him your heart and have suffered greatly. I see fire in your recent past. Flames of pain, flames of rebirth." Marie's eyes trace along my skin, but she seems to see deeper, or maybe beyond me.

"Yes, I was literally burned when my car caught fire." I don't want to tell her too much about Rich. That's not what I care about. I'd like to know about my future with Scott, maybe how many mini-mes or mini-Scotts we'll have running around. Or if the rescue will be successful. Things that matter to my future.

But Marie laughs. "Child, my prediction speaks not of this accident. You burn still, bright and heated, with the flames of love. You will burn forever."

My jaw drops. She didn't mean the car fire? She meant my love for Scott will burn eternally. That's beautiful and something I already knew. "Thank you, Marie. I think that's what I needed."

Marie dips her head once, almost a bow before her chin jerks up once more. "The spirits, girl. They want me to tell you . . . *say forever you'll be mine.*"

Beside me, I can feel Tiff's confusion as she looks at me, her brows pulled in tight. But I understand. I don't know how Marie does it, how she knows, but I start to hum the old Dolly tune . . .

Forever I am yours, say forever you'll be mine.

ABOUT THE AUTHOR

Other books by Lauren:

Get Dirty Series (Interconnecting standalones):

Dirty Talk || Dirty Laundry || Dirty Deeds

Irresistible Bachelor Series (Interconnecting standalones):

Anaconda || Mr. Fiance || Heartstopper

Stud Muffin || Mr. Fixit || Matchmaker

Motorhead || Baby Daddy

Connect with Lauren Landish
www.laurenlandish.com
admin@laurenlandish.com

Made in the USA
San Bernardino, CA
29 July 2020